THE SCARLET THREAD

That night Clara put in a call to her father in New York.

The line was crackly. 'How's my little girl?' he kept asking.

She cried down the telephone.

'What's the matter, sweetheart? What's wrong? Aren't you happy? Come on tell Poppa.'

'I will,' she promised. 'Oh Poppa, I miss you and Momma. I've been so happy, but something's gone wrong. There's a woman. She's making a play for Steven. Poppa, what can I do?'

There was silence for a moment. She thought they had been cut off. Then her father's voice came back on the line.

'You leave this to me, *cara mia*. Just tell me the name of this dame and where she lives . . .'

THE SCARLET THREAD

Evelyn Anthony

THE SHERIDAN
BOOK COMPANY

This edition published in 1994 by
The Sheridan Book Company

First published in Great Britain
by Hutchinson 1989
Random House, 20 Vauxhall Bridge Road, London SW1V 2SA
Arrow edition 1990

Printed and bound in Great Britain by
Cox & Wyman Ltd, Reading, Berkshire

ISBN 1–85501–472–6

To my dear friends
Tony and Shirley
with my love

1

It was dark and cool inside the church. It smelt of incense and candle grease; there were statues of the Virgin with the Christ Child nestling in her arms, and saints in ecstasy. The images were painted and gilded, with crowns and paste jewels glimmering in the dim light. It was the last place in the world Angela had imagined when she pictured her wedding day.

She held on to his arm as they walked up a side aisle close to the altar. Marble and gilding surrounded a writhing Saviour on his cross.

He said, 'Sit down and wait here, sweetheart. I'll go find the priest.'

She sat on a rickety wooden chair. There were no pews.

There was a woman on her knees, polishing the floor.

They had driven up the steep hillside over the narrow rutted little tracks that led to the village. It clung to the hill as if it had grown out of the rock. They left the Jeep in the tiny piazza close to the church and he had taken her by the hand and walked up cobbled streets to show her the house where his grandfather had been born. It was poor and mean, with tiny windows and a low door that no full-grown man could have passed through without stooping. Geraniums bloomed blood red from little pots and cracks in the walls. Washing hung limply from an upper window.

It was blindingly hot, and the red Sicilian dust was in the air they breathed. 'His name was Stefano, too,' he told her. 'That's what we'll call our boy. Let's go back to the church.'

The woman had finished polishing the floor. She straightened up, rubbing the small of her back to ease an old ache. She turned and stared at Angela for a moment. Her face was sallow and wrinkled like an old map. There was no expression on it. She picked up the tin of polish and stuffed her rags into it, then painfully went down on one knee before the altar and crossed herself with her free hand. It was a strange pantomime to Angela Drummond. She wondered whether Steven had found the priest. The old woman went out and Angela heard the door close. She ought to pray, she thought suddenly. Even in this alien place with its sickly smells and guttering candles she should remember her upbringing and pray for God's blessing on her wedding day.

So different from what she had imagined. The church at home in Sussex where her mother helped with the flowers and her father dutifully read the lesson once a month. The vicar who had baptized her would marry her to some faceless young man, with a ribbon of brides-maids behind them and the pews full of friends and relatives in neat suits and flowery hats. There were no uniforms then, because this was imagined before the war broke out and all their lives were changed. Her brother wouldn't be an usher now, because he was dead, killed in a bombing raid over Germany in 1942. She'd done her nursing training and gone overseas; a lot of other young men had died. She didn't kneel; she closed her eyes and tried to make some kind of prayer from her thoughts. It wasn't easy. No formula came to mind. I love him; please let us be happy.

The priest was sitting down. He had a spreading bald patch on the top of his head. His cassock was dusty and stained. He looked up at the American captain and said slowly, 'Why do you come here? We're at peace now. We don't want you.'

'That's not why I've come,' was the answer. 'I've come for myself.'

'You've come to bring back the men of blood,' the priest said. He wore spectacles; he took them off to wipe on his sleeve. 'There's nothing for the Falconi here,' he said. 'Nothing.'

'You don't understand. You're not listening to me. Listen to me, Father.'

'The word comes even to Altofonte,' the priest said. 'The Americans are bringing you back to prey on us. To bleed us, like you have done for all the years till we drove you out. Altofonte is poor. You can't squeeze anything from us. You can't bleed a corpse. Tell your people that.'

'My grandparents and parents were born here,' Steven Falconi said quietly. 'I've come here to be married. You can't deny me that. That's all I want from you. Nothing else. I've brought my girl; she's waiting in the church.'

'No.' The priest got up and the rickety chair creaked with relief. 'I won't marry you. There's blood on your hands.'

'She is carrying my child,' Steven Falconi said. 'Out of honour I ask you to marry us.'

'No,' the priest answered. He opened the sacristy door into the church. He saw a girl in nurse's uniform sitting in the shadows. 'I won't pardon your sin. Take your woman and leave my church.'

Steven Falconi didn't move. 'If you marry us, Father, we will forget Altofonte. You'll be left in peace. I guarantee you won't be troubled. Ever.' He crossed to the door and closed it quietly. 'You'll never see or hear from us again.'

It was the tried and proven negotiating term. Do this favour and I promise a favour in return. Refuse me . . . There was never any choice then. The priest knew there was no choice now.

'You swear this?'

'On my family's honour,' was the answer, and he knew that oath was never broken. Like the oath of silence.

The priest sighed. 'God forgive you. And me.'

'I will wait outside for you,' Steven Falconi said. 'You've made a wise decision. You won't regret it.'

'I remember your grandfather,' the priest mumbled, not looking at him. 'I was only a boy, but I remember him. He was a murderer.'

'I'll wait five minutes, Father,' Steven Falconi said. He went out of the sacristy into the body of the church.

There was nothing to warn Angela Drummond that day when she went on duty. It seemed a day like all the others. The base hospital at Tremoli was set up after the Americans captured Palermo; Angela had joined it from Tripoli. Casualties were still coming in from fighting round Messina where the British were. American losses had been less light. The American boy she was tending had lost both legs when his tank hit a mine. He was unconscious and from experience Angela knew that he was going to die. He lay as bloodless and still as if he were already dead. She heard a voice say behind her as she bent over, checking the failing pulse, 'Nurse – is this Lieutenant Scipio?'

Angela straightened. 'Yes it is. I'm sorry, but you can't come in here. You'll have to go.'

He was tall and very dark, with an infantry captain's tabs on his battledress. 'We grew up together,' he said. 'I heard he was brought in. How bad is it?'

'Very bad,' Angela answered, her voice low. 'He's lost both legs. Please, Captain, you shouldn't have been let in.'

'I'll come back,' he said. He stood staring down at the dying boy. 'I'll come tomorrow. Take care of him.'

'We take care of them all. Now, please . . .'

He nodded and turned away. She could see he was moved. If they had grown up together . . . She bent closer to the bed. The name was on his chart. Alfred Scipio, Lieutenant, 5th Army, aged twenty-three.

What a waste, Angela thought, as she had thought so often at so many deathbeds. A waste, like her brother who was blown to oblivion over a blazing German city.

'Nurse Drummond!' The ward sister's voice was sharp. 'What are you supposed to be doing?'

'I'm sorry, Sister, I was just checking the patient's pulse. It's very weak.'

'It doesn't take five minutes, Nurse, and that's how long you've been dawdling. Over here, please. Help me change this dressing.'

She had forgotten the American infantry captain. At the end of a long day she was too tired to think of anything.

When he came the next day, as he had said he would, there was another man in Scipio's place. He had shrapnel wounds, second-degree burns to the chest and arms. He would recover.

The captain came into the ward and straight towards her. 'He's gone,' he said. 'Lieutenant Scipio's gone. Where is he?'

Angela had said the same thing many times before. 'He died last night,' she said. 'I'm so sorry.'

He looked over to the bed with the stranger in it and said, 'It's better for him. He wouldn't have wanted to live like that. Thank you, Nurse. Thank you for taking care of him.'

'I only wish I could have done more . . .' Suddenly she was so tired and saddened by the futile words. Her eyes filled with tears that overflowed. 'Poor boy,' she said, and turned away from him. 'Please go, I'll get into trouble if the ward sister comes in and finds you here.'

'When do you come off duty?'

She answered without thinking, wiping the tears away. 'Seven thirty.' It was unforgivable to give way and cry. She was an experienced nurse with the North African campaign behind her.

'I'll wait outside,' he said quietly. 'I'd like to thank you for taking care of my friend. My name is Steven Falconi.'

She didn't mean to let him persuade her to drive into Palermo to have dinner. He seemed to know exactly where to get good Sicilian food.

'Where did you and that poor boy grow up?' she asked. 'Where do you live in America?'

'New York City,' he answered. 'Scipio was two grades down from me in school, but his family knew my family. I graduated from college and joined the army. He'd already enlisted. His mother was crying to my mother for weeks. She didn't want him to go. Have some wine –it's good. Do you like the food?'

'Yes, it's the best I've eaten.'

'I'll tell them,' he said.

He spoke fluent Italian. The owner of the little café was never far away. It seemed to Angela that he was always watching Falconi. She hadn't meant to stay so late but they went on talking and the time passed. It was close to midnight when he drove her back.

'I'll come tomorrow,' he said. 'The same time?'

'I get off at three tomorrow,' Angela said. 'It's my rest day.'

'We could go into the country if you like,' he said.

They stood by the Jeep, not touching, but the air between them seemed almost to vibrate.

For something to say, she asked, 'What about petrol?'

'I can get enough,' he said. 'I'd like to show you this part of the island. It's very beautiful. Do you like mountains?'

'Depends,' Angela answered.

'We can take a drive,' he went on. 'I'll bring some food and a bottle of wine. Would you like that?'

'It sounds wonderful,' she answered. She held out her hand. He took it and came closer to her. 'Thank you for dinner,' she said.

'Thank you for coming. See you tomorrow.'

12

'Yes.' He still held on to her hand. 'Goodnight,' Angela said, and he let go. She glanced back as she turned the corner of the nurses' quarters and he was still standing there, watching her.

The back door had been left unlocked. Her friend and room mate, Christine, had left it open in case she got back late. Angela closed and locked it. She hoped Christine would be asleep. For some reason she didn't feel like answering questions about the evening.

But Christine was awake. She was a professional nurse, three years older than Angela. It was an odd friendship between opposites. She was extrovert, while Angela was shy; she made no secret of her liking for men and her enjoyment of sex, and it was a long time since she had cried over a death in the ward. She thought the younger girl was sweet-natured and needed someone to look out for her. It was time she had a boyfriend. She took life much too seriously.

'You must have had a good time,' she said. 'It's after twelve. What did you do?'

'We had dinner and we talked.' Angela undressed quickly.

'What's he like?' Christine persisted. 'Typical Yank? Make a pass at you?'

'No.' Angela smiled at her. 'We shook hands, believe it or not. It was rather old-fashioned.'

'But you enjoyed it,' her friend insisted. 'Seeing him again?'

'Tomorrow,' Angela answered. She got into bed and settled down.

'That's quick,' Christine remarked. 'What's his name?'

'Steven. Steven Falconi,' she murmured. 'We've got to be up at five thirty, and I'm dead tired. Now go to sleep. I'll tell you all about it tomorrow.'

'I'm seeing my new fellow tomorrow.' Christine said. She switched off the light. 'I'll ask if he knows him.'

She had met her latest boyfriend a month before. He was married, she told Angela, but all the nice ones were.

13

A lieutenant colonel, no less. Generous and good fun. There were nylon stockings in her drawer and supplies of chocolate and whisky for the asking.

His name was Walter McKie and he was some big wheel in the military administration in Palermo. Details like that didn't interest her. She was intent on squeezing what fun she could out of the war and one day, when it was all over, she might hook someone and settle down. But it was played strictly for laughs until then. Naturally, Christine was a very popular girl and never lacked admirers.

She wondered about this American with the Italian name. 'Old-fashioned' Angela called him. Christine tried to imagine any of the Americans she knew being described like that. She'd ask Walt tomorrow night, if she remembered. He might know something about Falconi. There was a distinctly star-struck look in Angela's eye when she came in. Christine had never seen it before and there had been several young officers in Tripoli who'd taken Angela out, and one who'd obviously fallen for her.

Tonight had been different. Angela lay awake in the darkness long after her friend had fallen asleep. It had been a strange evening. He'd talked a lot about Scipio and how he'd promised Scipio's mother to look out for him when they were overseas. He hadn't expected ever to see him once they embarked, but the promise was a comfort to the family.

'We're all very close,' he said, in answer to her question. 'We come from the same background. That's important to us.'

He had very black eyes; fine eyes, she thought, set well apart, and a striking face with a high-bridged nose. Not handsome exactly, but not a face you'd forget.

And a soft voice, with a measured way of speaking, as if American was a language he had taken pains to learn. She closed her eyes and felt the sense of sexual power

14

flow over her again. No man had made her feel like that before. There'd been a brief affair in Tripoli with a young Scot she had felt sorry for, but nothing to compare with this. It was almost frightening and she wished she could stop thinking about tomorrow and the trip into the mountains. It would be dawn soon and time to get up and begin the early round of the ward. She slept at last and seemed to be shaken out of sleep almost immediately. It was five thirty and the red Sicilian sun was creeping up over the edge of the horizon.

They couldn't drive beyond a certain point. Not even the Jeep could hold the twisting rutted track up the mountainside. So he found a place with some shade. He'd brought food and wine.

He was always watching her; whenever she looked at him, he was considering her with that deep stare.

She said, 'Why do you look at me like that?'

'You're beautiful,' he said. 'I like to look at you. Does it bother you?'

They were sitting in the shelter of a rock. She drained the last of her wine. 'Yes, it does. I feel as if I've got a dirty mark on my face. And I'm not a bit beautiful. You don't have to say that.'

'So what are you then? What do other men say to you? Give me that.' He took the empty cup and filled it.

'I don't want any more,' Angela said. 'It's too hot, I shall only go to sleep.'

'You haven't told me,' he reminded her. 'What do your other boyfriends tell you?'

'I haven't got any boyfriends,' she answered. 'You're the first person I've been out with since I left Tripoli. In the family they say I'm not bad-looking. That's about it.'

'So that's English understatement,' he said slowly. 'Tell me about your family, Angela. Where do you live? What kind of people are they?'

'Oh.' She stretched and sighed. 'It seems so far away. A million miles from this bloody war and all the misery.

15

My home's in the country, a village near Haywards Heath in Sussex. It's very gentle countryside, not dry and fierce like this. We haven't any mountains, only nice smooth rolling hills. It's green and cool and everyone complains if it rains and worries about their gardens if it doesn't. My father is a doctor; so was my grandfather. He lived and practised in the same house as Daddy. My mother was born in India, her father was in the Indian Army. We're very ordinary, Steven, nothing special about us.'

'Brothers and sisters?'

'I had a sister but she died when she was little, before I was born. I had one brother, Jack. He was killed in the RAF. We were very fond of each other. I was closer to him than to either of my parents.

'I'm sorry,' he said. 'Why did you choose nursing? Because of your father?'

'No, not really. Because of Jack being killed. I didn't want to go into the WAAF or the Wrens; I didn't want to be a wireless operator or a driver or anything connected with the fighting. I wanted to help, not hurt anyone else. Not very patriotic, am I?'

He watched her for a moment. 'It's a lousy war, but it'll be over some day soon. And then you'll go back to Haywards Heath and forget all about this.'

'What about you?' she said. 'Falconi's an Italian name. And you speak it fluently.'

'Sicilian,' he corrected. 'That's not the same thing. We're not Italians. We're many different races: Arabs, Moors, Greeks. Sicily was always being invaded. There's Italian in us too, but we're not the same people, not at all the same. My family came from a little village not so far from Palermo. In the hills. My grandfather moved to America. My father and mother followed him later. I was seven years old and I had to learn to speak English. We all speak Italian among ourselves. We keep the old traditions, go to the church, eat pasta. Have big families.' He looked down at her and smiled. 'Not like Haywards Heath,' he said.

16

'Do you feel American?' Angela asked him.

'I'm a citizen. My father took out papers. I went to an American school and an American college. I graduated; I played football for the college; I joined the army. I'm American. But maybe Sicilian too.'

They sat in silence for a while and the heat shimmered round them.

Angela said, 'I've changed my mind. I'll have some wine if there's any left.' It was heavy and it didn't help her thirst. She turned the cup and let the red stream out across the ground.

'Do you know what you're doing, Angelina?' he said beside her. 'That's a libation to the gods. We give something back of the good wine to the gods of Sicily so they won't ruin our harvest. Sicily has lots of gods, did you know that?'

She shook her head. The wine was soaking away into the ground like blood.

'It's a pagan country,' he went on. 'The Church tried to civilize us and drive out the gods that came with the Romans and the Greeks, but we kept them hidden. They're still here, all round us. Can't you feel them?'

She didn't answer. She let him take her and pull her close and begin to kiss her, slowly and then fiercely.

The ground was hard and the rock dust clung to them as they lay naked on the baking earth. Their passion swayed them to and fro out of the shadow of the rock and they came to their climax together in the molten glare of the sun.

As he dressed her in the shade he said softly in Italian, '*Io ti amo, amore mia*,' and held her close against him.

'Do you?' she asked him. 'You don't have to say it . . .'

'I love you,' he said in English. 'Say it to me in Italian.'

She stumbled over the words and he repeated them until she followed him: '*Io ti amo, amore mio*.'

It was the second time they were together and the first time they made love. She conceived immediately.

*

'What happens when he's posted?' Christine demanded. 'They're all going, as soon as the weather's right. Walt says it's going to be a bloodbath. He gets killed and you're left with an illegit! Angela, be sensible,' she begged. 'You can't go through with it. I'll help you.' She looked at her friend and said, 'You're only just over the six weeks. It'll be a day off with a bad period. No one'll know.'

Angela sat up. She had been violently sick in the sluice room and sent to her room to lie down. She felt dizzy, but the dreadful nausea had passed.

'I shouldn't have told you,' she said. 'I wish I hadn't said anything. Have you got a cigarette, Chrissie? I've run out.'

'Yes, here. Keep the packet. Thank God you *did* tell me. You can get away with throwing up once, but what are you going to say if it happens every morning? Don't you realize you'll be chucked out and sent home in disgrace?'

'He wants to marry me,' Angela answered. She lit the cigarette. It tasted bitter.

'He can't and he bloody well knows it,' Christine retorted. 'He'd never get permission. One mention about getting married and they're posted within forty-eight hours. I wish you'd let me talk to him. Listen, if he loves you, he won't let you go through with this.'

'You don't know him,' Angela said. 'I keep telling you, Steven isn't one of your "Yanks". He's different, he'd want the baby. I just haven't told him yet. I wasn't even sure for the first couple of weeks.'

'He's no different from any other man.' Christine turned away impatiently. 'Oh, I know – he loves you, he wants to marry you.' She hesitated and then said, 'I'm sorry, but I'm going to be cruel. You'll hate me for saying this, but I think it's all pie in the sky. He'll sail off with the invasion fleet and that'll be the last you'll ever hear of him. And you'll have buggered up your life for nothing.'

18

'I won't get rid of it,' Angela said slowly. 'You're not right, Christine, but even if you are, I won't kill my own child. So don't mention it again, will you? I'm seeing Steven tonight. I'll tell him.'

'You do that,' Christine said grimly. 'And if you change your mind, just let me know. But it's got to be soon. I'm not mucking around with anything at three months. Now I'd better get back to the ward. I'll say you're asleep.' She went out and closed the door hard. It was as near as she dared go to slamming it with frustration.

Angela stubbed out the cigarette. It wasn't a comfort any more. There was no sign of the change taking place in her body. Just the sudden revulsion from the stench in the sluice room and the acrid taste of tobacco in her mouth. Steven had rented a room above the café where they'd eaten that first night, and they spent every free moment together. For a moment she laid a hand on her stomach. She wasn't afraid of what was to come. Tough, practical Christine couldn't understand that total lack of fear. She thought it was irresponsible, unrealistic.

'For Christ's sake,' she'd insisted. 'It's not a *baby*, it's not much bigger than a pinhead!'

Angela hadn't even tried to explain to her that this was not the point. It was Steven's child. Conceived on the hillside, or the hard little bed in the room above the café. She didn't know and it didn't matter. All that mattered was the intensity of her love for him and of his love for her. She had no doubts about that love. He couldn't marry her, but that didn't matter either. They'd find a way to be together when the war was over. The invasion of mainland Italy was very close. She didn't believe he would be killed. She lay back and closed her eyes for a moment. She would tell him. She would choose the moment when they lay together in the aftermath of making love.

After a time she got up, put on her cap and apron and went back to the ward. The sister looked up briefly as she reported back for duty.

'You're sure you're better, Nurse? Good, there's plenty to do.' She watched Angela while pretending to read through some charts on her desk. She'd never been sick before and the ward was only half full now. The worst casualties had died or been sent to another hospital. If it was food poisoning, she wouldn't have recovered so quickly and come back on duty. Everyone knew about her affair with the American captain. He was always hanging round outside waiting for her. She was a good nurse and the sister hoped quite genuinely that she hadn't made a complete fool of herself. There'd be no mercy for her if she had.

He held himself above her; the single light bulb flared over their heads. His body glistened in the heat. Angela reached up and ran both hands from his shoulders to his belly and down to his thighs.

'I want you,' she said. 'I want you so much it hurts me . . .'

'*Cara bella, bella,*' he groaned and came down on her, and the love talk was silenced as her mouth reached up for him. Her cry was fierce and brought him to a turbulent climax that left him collapsed and emptied with his head cradled between her breasts.

Angela stroked his hair. It'll be a dark child, she thought, and smiled with happiness. His weight pressed on her and she said softly, 'You mustn't lie on me, darling.'

'Why not? I like to feel you next to me . . . You like it too.'

Angela ran one finger down the side of his face, tracing the line of his brow, to the prominent cheekbone, round the curve of his jaw. For a moment the tip of her finger teased his lips apart.

'It might hurt the baby,' she said.

'I'm going to marry you.' He had taken her out in the Jeep and driven down to the quayside where the sea breeze brought coolness.

It was dark and they held each other close. Christine, she thought. Christine, how very wrong you were.

'I'm going to find a way.'

'You can't,' she told him. 'After the war, we'll get married then.'

'And have my boy a bastard?' He cursed in Italian.

Angela had never seen him angry. She was calm and happy and reassured. She teased him. 'How do you know it's a boy?'

He frowned and said, 'Because I know it is. Boy or girl, it's my child. Our child. Don't make a joke, Angelina. We'll get married. I'll find a way even if I have to . . .' He stopped and eased her a little away from him. 'You want to marry me, don't you?'

'I don't care,' she said. 'I love you, that's what's important. I'm so happy about the baby, I don't see that anything else matters.'

He was silent for a moment. He *was* angry and she realized it suddenly.

'You don't understand,' he said. 'It matters to me that my child is a Falconi, born into my family. And that they accept you. They will, *cara mia*. They'll love you and be happy for us. But not if the child is born in dishonour.'

Dishonour! She said slowly, 'Steven, you sound like something out of the Middle Ages. We can't get married because you won't get permission. Everyone knows it's American policy to stop this sort of thing. There's nothing we can do about it except I have the baby and we get married and make it right as soon as we can.'

'It won't be right for us,' he answered. 'You don't realize, people will disrespect you. Listen to me, sweetheart. You're happy and not making any sense. Let me decide what to do and how to do it. You must be protected. You must have my name. I'll think, I'll find a way round. Now I'm taking you back. It's late.'

He walked her to the nurses' quarters, stopped and took her in his arms. She had been quiet all through the

21

drive back. He had upset her. He had been a fool, forgetting that she wouldn't understand.

'I love you,' he said and kissed her gently. 'I want this child and I want to be with you for the rest of my life. You're off on Friday afternoon?'

'Yes.' Angela held tight to him. She had been near tears on that drive back.

'I'll have arranged something by then,' he said.

They came out of the cool, dim little church into the blinding sunlight. For a moment they paused and he slipped his arm around her. The street was empty in the midday heat. No wedding party, no friends to greet them, not even a flower for her to carry. But his family would accept the marriage. Accept her and their child.

It had been a hurried ceremony, conducted swiftly in Italian. He had prompted Angela to answer in English. The priest was sullen; he refused to take Steven's offering. He didn't bless them or shake hands. He turned and hurried back into the sacristy, divesting himself of his stole as he went. But it was valid. It would be entered on the church register. Steven looked down at her with tenderness.

'Not much of a wedding for you, my darling,' he said softly. 'But I'll make it up to you.'

'It was a beautiful wedding,' she insisted. 'Don't be silly. He just wasn't very friendly, that's all. I suppose it was because I'm not a Catholic.'

He guided her down the street. The Jeep was parked near the tiny piazza. He turned and lifted her up and placed her in it.

'Your bridal car,' he said.

She laughed and held his hand. 'No white ribbons and confetti on the floor,' she agreed. 'But it's the happiest day of my life.'

'Wait till we get home to New York,' he promised as they drove. 'We'll have such a party. You shall have everything to make up for this. A reception, a dance; all your family from England. We know how to celebrate a marriage. It'll be the biggest party in New York City. I'll buy you a diamond, a proper ring. My father will give you pearls for a necklace. And we'll get presents from all our friends. Very good presents. Enough to set up a whole house. Our people know how important it is to be generous.'

'Steven,' she interrupted. 'It all sounds lovely, but I don't really mind. I'm married to you and that's what matters.'

'We'll have a honeymoon,' he went on. 'I'll take you anywhere you want to go. Florida, the West Indies . . . My uncle has a house in Palm Beach. We'll have one too.'

'If you go on like this, I'll start thinking you're rich,' she said.

He looked at her and smiled. 'We're not poor,' he answered. They were speeding along the road now towards Palermo. They passed a convoy of US Army trucks. The GIs whistled at her and she turned in her seat to wave to them.

'I wonder if making love will feel any different now we're married,' Angela said.

'It'll be better,' he promised.

They had a few hours together before she had to go back to the hospital. 'I'll make it better for you than ever,' he said. 'Stop waving at those *ragazzi*, my darling. You belong to me now.'

'That's a nice thing to call your own GIs,' she protested. 'It means ruffians, doesn't it?'

'From now on,' he answered, 'it means all other men.'

'He's given her a watch,' Christine announced. 'Solid gold. She showed me. Walt, she pretty well hinted they'd gone through some kind of marriage service. She's been sick most mornings. I've managed to cover for her, but Sister Hunt's got a beady eye on her. I just don't know how long she's going to get away with it.'

Walt McKie reached across the table and patted her

hand. He had grown very fond of Christine. They dated regularly and she didn't go out with anyone else. He had even begun to forget about his children. His wife was out of mind except when he got letters, usually complaining about the hardships of managing the house and the children on her own.

'Quit worrying about her,' he advised. 'This guy Falconi seems genuine. It sounds like he's just as crazy about her as she is about him. They'll work something out.'

Christine shook her head. 'You haven't met him; I have. I went into Palermo with Angela for a drink. I said something about the baby. He looked at me and I tell you, it was really scary.

' "You offered to help," he said. "Angelina told me. Do yourself a favour. Keep out of our business." She didn't hear it and I didn't say anything, but it gave me the creeps, the way he said it. There's something funny about him; she always said he wasn't a typical Yank, and she's too right. Walter, could you find out about him?'

He said in surprise, 'Find out what?'

'Whether he's married,' Christine suggested. 'That'd be in his records. He's odd, I mean it. He's scary.'

Walter McKie grinned at her. 'Maybe he's just not your type,' he said.

'You can say that again,' she retorted. 'I don't like Eyeties anyway.' She smiled at him. 'I like my men fair and chunky with nice blue eyes. Remind you of anyone?'

'Could do,' he answered. He really was very fond of her, no kidding, he thought suddenly, and wasn't at all alarmed. She'd love Cincinnati. He ordered them another drink and let his imagination run free. The pert little girl he'd married fifteen years ago was a very dim memory now. The dissatisfied, self-pitying woman she'd become was a memory he could do without.

'Will you see what you can dig up?' Christine asked him.

'Okay, if it'll make you happier. I've a friend at HQ

24

who'd have access to personnel records. But don't expect anything soon. We're going to be very busy in the next few days.'

'Oh God!' Christine exclaimed. 'You mean it's coming?'

'Any minute,' he replied. 'Everyone's on standby, waiting for the weather report.'

'Thank God you won't be going,' she said.

'You're not to say anything,' he enjoined. 'Not to your friend, Angela, or anyone. It's going to be a hell of a fight. It was tough enough here, but they'll defend mainland Italy every inch of the way. You'll be busy up at the hospital, I guess. That'll take your mind off things.'

'I suppose so.' She sipped her glass of wine. She didn't want to think about the invasion, or the casualties that would come pouring back. The war was bloody awful, and getting what enjoyment you could, while you could, was the only way to keep going. 'You will ask about Falconi, won't you? As soon as you can. He'll be shipped off too. Funny, Angela didn't say so. She didn't say he was on standby.'

'Maybe he didn't tell her. He'll be going. His division is scheduled to make up the second support force. Now let's forget it, shall we, Chris?'

'Let's,' she agreed. 'I'm hungry. How about eating?'

'Here or back at my hotel?'

'Here first, and back at the hotel for coffee,' Christine suggested. 'You know how much I like American coffee. Especially your brand.' She squeezed his knee under the table.

The 5th Army sailed for Salerno on 9 September 1943. Walter McKie was right when he said the fighting would be hard and bloody. The base hospital was crammed with the wounded. There was no free time for anyone in the aftermath of the landings. Angela worked until she fell exhausted into bed. But she was happy. Her fear that Steven would join his regiment in the assault was unfounded. By some miracle he had stayed behind in Sicily. He was needed by the military administration as liaison officer with the civilian authorities on the southern part of the island. They snatched brief meetings in the hospital grounds on odd days. He was anxious about her. She looked thin and pale and often burst into floods of tears when some of the wounded died.

'Why don't you give it up?' he asked her. 'Apply for a discharge. They'll send you home when they know you're pregnant. You could injure yourself working like this. You could lose the baby.'

They were walking hand in hand under the trees in the grounds. He stopped and took her in his arms.

'I could get you sent back to the States,' he said. 'I have friends who could fix it. My family would take care of you.'

She raised her head and stared at him. 'Steven, that's impossible! Nobody could arrange that.'

'I could try,' he insisted. '*Cara*, listen. Sometime I'll have to go to Italy. They'll want me over there.'

'You said you wouldn't,' she protested.

'Not to Salerno,' he said. 'To Naples, when it's cleared of the Krauts. Same sort of job I've been doing here. I want you out of Sicily before I go. Will you do it? For me, for the baby?'

'I can't,' she answered. 'I can't leave while this is going on. I can't just walk out on the wounded and think of myself. I'll stay on at the hospital till I can't go on any longer. Don't ask me to do anything else.'

'Let me see what I can do anyway,' he insisted. 'I won't commit you to going. Let me see if it would be possible.'

'So long as this hospital is taking casualties, I'm staying, Steven. Nothing will happen to me, or the baby. Now I have to get back. Kiss me and try to understand. I have a duty too. It's here.'

He walked back with her and she turned and waved as she hurried through the entrance. He didn't understand. He loved her too much to care about principles. Someone

26

else would come in her place. She should think of herself and their child first, and do what he wanted. There would be a way to make her change her mind. He had been taught that there was always a way.

The city of Naples and the surrounding countryside were under Allied control. Italy had surrendered, but the Germans in Italy were fighting, and fighting hard.

Steven Falconi arrived at the Military HQ in Palermo with four other men in US uniform. He was the only commissioned officer. They were shown into the private office of a colonel wearing the flashes of US Intelligence. He got up from his desk and shook hands with them one by one.

'Captain Falconi. Sergeant Brassano, Sergeant Rumoranzo, Corporal Cappelli, Private Luciano. You guys know each other, I expect?'

Steven Falconi answered. 'Our families are acquainted.'

'Sit down, won't you?' The colonel was courteous, even friendly. He offered cigarettes and produced a bottle of whisky. They accepted a drink and a smoke and watched him and each other with the dark wariness he had grown used to among such men. 'I guess we have achieved what we set out to do in Sicily,' he said. 'With your family backgrounds, you, Captain Falconi, Brassano and Capelli, have provided a very necessary liaison with the civilian authorities here in Sicily. But Southern Italy is going to be a much more important and difficult area for us to control. Rumoranzo and Luciano have Neapolitan connections and there are a number of US Army personnel with Calabrian relatives and influence already over there. You will each be assigned certain sections of the civilian administration to approach and explain our point of view. We want you to get their cooperation. And just as important, find out who might be unreliable, who could be working for the Fascists.'

'We understand,' Steven Falconi said. 'I guess we can bring the people concerned into line.'

27

The others nodded. The one named Rumoranzo spoke in a heavily accented English, with the ugly twang of New York's East Side running through it.

'We said we'd deliver. Don't worry about it, Colonel. These guys know us. They'll go along with us and that means they go along with you.' He glanced at Falconi, and his expression showed a brief glower of dislike. Fuckin' officer, just because his fuckin' family had ideas about themselves. College and all that shit. He looked away. He felt like spitting the saliva gathered in his mouth, but decided not to. The colonel was not one of them, but he had a hard reputation.

The colonel stood up. Falconi did so at once and the others followed.

'Gentlemen, the US Government will be very grateful for the help you're giving us. Now if you go along to Major Thompson's office, he'll fill you in on the details. Goodbye and good luck.'

He shook hands with them and opened the door. When it was closed he went back and poured himself a drink. Rumoranzo had been released from San Quentin jail, his sentence for extortion and violent assault commuted in return for his special service in the US Army in the Italian campaign. The silent Luciano was a murderer, reprieved from the electric chair for the same reason. Cappelli was a known mobster and killer without convictions, but with a fraud case pending. Brassano was buying out a close relative and Falconi had bargained his education and intelligence against a tax demand that would have kept the Falconis in litigation with the Internal Revenue for the next ten years at a cost of a million dollars or more.

They were the scum of the earth, in the colonel's opionion, but they were needed, if the Allies were going to govern Sicily and Italy and rout out any Fascist underground resistance. He swallowed his drink and consoled himself with the belief that they would all end up the same way when the war was won and they

28

returned home. This was only a respite for men convicted, or suspected, of some of the worst crimes
committed anywhere in the world. He was on the
telephone when his colleague, Major Thompson, came
in. He said, 'Sit down, Jim,' in an aside and went on
talking.

Finally he hung up. 'Goddamned transport; there's no
military aircraft available. We'll have to send them over
on a supply ship. Any problems?'

'No problems,' Major Thompson said.

'Help yourself.' The colonel pointed to the bottle of
scotch.

They were friends, who had worked together in
civilian life and joined up together. Both were FBI
veterans.

'What a bunch of shit,' Thompson remarked. 'You
know the one that really sticks in my craw?'

'Falconi?' the colonel suggested.

'Yeah, Falconi. The college education, the nice
manners. He even speaks good Italian. That's the kind of
mobster we *don't* want back home. Cappelli and the rest
of 'em know what they are. Falconi stayed on and put in a
request.'

'What kind of request?' the colonel asked sharply.

'Not the usual. He didn't want concessions for some
son-of-a-bitch relative over here or any of that crap. He
wanted a passage back to the States for some dame he's
got pregnant.'

'You're kidding! She's Sicilian?'

'No. She's English and she's a nurse at the hospital in
Tremoli.'

'For Christ's sake – what did you say?'

'I said it couldn't be done. He didn't like that. He
wouldn't take no. He just said he had a lot of work to do
for us and he felt we should do him this favour. You
know the score, Bill. It sounded just like they talk back
home. You owe me. That kind of crap.'

'So?' The colonel leant forward. An English nurse. A

29

Sicilian girl he could have understood, but not this. They never married outside their own people. He wanted to send her home to America. To his family. The colonel scowled. It was an outrageous request and the sheer nerve of it made him boil.

'I said I'd see about it. I said I'd let him know, but it didn't look promising. I talked about the complications, the passage home, the immigration, illegal entry, you know the sort of stuff. He didn't give a goddamn. He just sat there and said, "You can fix it for me, Major. You can fix it." Afterwards it clicked. Some colonel in the Legal Department was asking personnel questions about Falconi. He told the guy there was a nurse involved and he wanted to find out if this son of a bitch was on the level. Personnel stalled and came to me. I said, "Tell him the guy's okay. No wife, no criminal record." What do I do, Bill? It can't be fixed and he knows it. But if we say no, he'll find some way to shit on us. They always do.'

'Get hold of this colonel. What's his name?'

'McKie,' Thompson said. 'He's a lawyer, comes from Cincinnati. I made a few inquiries about him when this stuff came up about Falconi. He's shacked up with another nurse up there. She's buddy–buddy with Falconi's girl. I guess that's why he was asking questions.'

'Let's give him a few answers, Jim,' was the reply. 'If this nurse is any kind of a decent human being, she'll solve the problem for us when she knows what her boyfriend really is.'

'Sit down, Miss Drummond. Cigarette?'

'No thank you.'

It was a small office in the Municipal Building in the centre of Palermo. The Stars and Stripes hung from the flagpost over the entrance; the mayor and his officials had been moved out to make room for the American occupying forces. Walter McKie had driven her into the city. Major Thompson took a Lucky Strike from the packet and lit it. Pretty girl, he thought. Blonde and blue eyes; just the type these bastards went for . . . she looked strained and apprehensive.

It had taken a lot of persuading to get her there. Even so she didn't know why she was asked to come and see him. Just that it concerned Captain Falconi. McKie was no fool; he hadn't even hinted that there was anything wrong. Thompson didn't feel sorry for her. She was lucky, only she didn't know it yet.

She said suddenly, 'Major, has anything happened to Steven?'

He'd sailed for the mainland three days before. There was an ache in her breast as if the parting had been a physical blow.

'No,' he answered. 'He landed and he's busy right now, I guess. Miss Drummond, you're close friends, I understand?'

She flushed. 'Yes. We are. Major, what is this all about? What have my private affairs got to do with you?'

'Before he embarked, Captain Falconi asked me to arrange a passage to America for you,' he said.

He had very cold, dead eyes and he made her feel antagonistic, as if he were some kind of enemy.

'He did mention that,' she admitted. 'I told him I couldn't leave my post at the hospital.'

'It would be strictly illegal,' Thompson went on. 'A forged passport, for example, official instruction to all kinds of people to look the other way. He knew all this, of course, but he still tried to pressure me. So I thought before I went any further, I'd better talk to you.'

She thought Steven was being accused and she didn't hesitate. 'I'm having a baby,' she said. 'That's why he asked; he's worried about leaving me alone. If anything happened to him, he wanted me to be where his family could look after us.'

She had guts, Thompson decided. She wasn't going to let Falconi take any blame.

'How much do you know about Steven Falconi, Miss

Drummond? How much has he told you about this family of his?'

'I don't understand you,' she said. 'Walter, what is this all about? Why did you persuade me to come here? I think I'd like to go.'

McKie laid a hand on her arm. 'Listen to him, Angela. Don't walk out now.'

'Miss Drummond.' Thompson stubbed out his cigarette and stared at her. 'Have you heard of the Mafia?'

'Mafia? I don't think so.'

McKie's hand was still on her arm.

'You've heard of gangsters in America? Seen movies about them?' Major Thompson had such a flat ugly voice, deliberately toneless.

'Major,' she began, but he interrupted her.

'Your friend Falconi was born in Sicily. They came from Altofonte.'

For a moment she saw the pink-washed houses on the hillside and the church where they had married.

'I know,' she said. 'I know they came from Sicily.'

'A lot of people came to the States from here. And from Italy. They brought the Mafia with them. Murder, extortion, prostitution – every dirty vice and racket in the book. That's what they brought to America. And that's what Steven Falconi is – a hoodlum. And that's why he's over here. I'd like to show you something, Miss Drummond. Read it.' He got up and handed a dossier to her. He was surprisingly small and thickset without the shield of the desk.

Angela looked up at him. 'What is this?'

'Falconi's criminal record,' he said. 'You'll see there are no convictions. We could never make anything stick. The Falconis are big-time racketeers on the East Side. They're into everything. Betting, vice. They've moved into the unions. You don't pay your dues, you don't work. You talk back and you get beaten up the first time and murdered the second.'

The blue-covered dossier was open in her lap. His

photograph was in the top right-hand corner. Full face, profile. It was hard to recognize him at first because his expression was flat and dead. But it was Steven.

'Take your time,' she heard Thompson say.

Intimidation with threats. No case brought for lack of evidence. Family connections. The typescript blurred as she read, then pitilessly came back into focus.

Grandfather: Stefano Falconi. Emigrated to US 1928 to escape conviction for three murders. Convicted for bootlegging, served jail sentence, released, re-arrested on charges relating to unsolved murder of rival 'family' boss. Released for lack of evidence. Founded the Falconi 'family' on the East Side. Died in hospital after assassination attack 1933.

Father: Luca Falconi. Mafia debt collector Palermo. Suspected of two murders, not arrested because of lack of evidence. Intimidation of witnesses in a related case. Emigrated to US 1925. Naturalized 1931. Head of the Falconi East Side family since 1933. No US criminal convictions but indictments on charges of attempted murder, attempts to pervert the course of justice by bribery of witnesses in corruption charges against members of the Teamsters' Union; currently under investigation by the Internal Revenue.

'Angela, are you okay?' she heard Walter McKie say and she was seeing the room, the major lighting yet another cigarette, the blue dossier open at the last page on her knee.

'I don't believe this.' She said it again. 'It isn't true. I don't believe it.'

'It is true,' McKie said. 'He's a mobster. That's his police record.'

Grandfather, father and son. My family. He talked about them so often and she had a picture of them in her mind. Like other Italian families, a tribe of uncles and aunts and cousins. We speak Italian together, go to the church, eat pasta, have big families . . . His words were mocking her as she looked first at Walter McKie and then at Thompson, impassive behind his desk, blowing smoke into rings while he waited.

'He's in the army,' she managed to say. 'He couldn't be in the army . . .'

'He's got no criminal conviction,' Thompson answered. 'Not that it matters in the case of guys like him. We've let murderers out of jail to come back here. Don't ask me why, Miss Drummond, because I'm not proud of it. We need them, that's all I can tell you. You never asked Falconi what he was doing here in Sicily?'

She just shook her head.

'What did he tell you? Administration?'

'Yes, something like that.'

'Yeah, well, you could call it that. You see, people round here know that name. They're scared of guys like Falconi. It makes them cooperate with us. So now he's in Naples. You still want to go to the States, Miss Drummond? You want your kid brought up with the Falconis?'

Angela closed the dossier. She didn't want to see the photograph of him again. Dead eyed, full face, profile. Gangsters. You've seen them in movies, haven't you? Murder, extortion . . . every dirty vice in the book. The mean little house in the narrow street where Stefano Falconi was born. He had murdered three men, that indictment said.

She stood up; she drew away from Walter McKie as he tried to take her arm. She walked over and placed the dossier on the desk.

'I don't believe my Steven is the man in this,' she said. 'I know him and he couldn't do these things. But I can't argue with the rest of it. I'd like to go now, Major, if there's nothing else.'

'Would you like a scotch?' he offered. 'You look as if you could use one.'

'No thank you. I'd just like to go.'

He opened the door for her. 'No passage to the States?'

'No,' she said. She didn't shake hands with him. 'We got married, you know. In the church in Altofonte.'

34

Thompson nodded slowly. 'I wondered about that. Murder's OK, but they won't accept a bastard child. You've had a lucky escape, believe me.'

She walked past him through the door without answering. McKie didn't try to catch up with her till they were out in the street.

'You want to go back to the hospital right away?'

'Yes. I told Sister I wouldn't be away more than an hour.'

She turned back her sleeve and the elegant gold watch gleamed in the sunshine.

'He gave me this,' she said slowly. She slipped her hand into the neck of her uniform and drew out a chain with a gold ring on the end of it. 'And this. They came from the same jeweller's. I passed there one day and the place was boarded up. They've never been open for business. How did he get the ring and the watch?'

McKie didn't like the look of her. He said, 'What the hell does it matter? I'm sorry, Angela. I'm sorry you had to find out. Can Chris and me do anything to help?'

'I don't think so,' she said quietly. 'From now on I've got to help myself. Do you think I'll stop loving him?'

'Sure.' He turned the Jeep into the short drive up to the hospital forecourt. 'Sure you will. What worries both of us is the baby. How are you going to manage?'

'I'll be all right,' she said. She stepped down and looked up at him. 'I'll have some part of him in my life. That's something. Goodbye, Walter.'

'I'll be seeing you,' he called out.

She nodded and quickened her pace as she came to the entrance.

Sister Hunt checked her watch. She noticed that Nurse Drummond was a terrible colour and bit back the rebuke for being a few minutes late.

'Sister,' Angela said. 'When I come off duty, I'd like an appointment to see Matron.'

Sister Hunt had been hoping she would go of her own accord.

'Very well. I'll ask when she can see you, Nurse. Over there, bed number eight. He had a transfusion an hour ago. Pulse and respiration to be monitored.'

'Oh, Angela! I'm going to miss you. But you're doing the right thing.'

'I'll miss you too.' For a moment they embraced and she saw Christine was close to tears. She was close to them herself. She hadn't cried, even when the matron spoke of the disgrace she had brought on the nursing service and on her family. She had been calm, almost detached throughout the interview. At the end the older woman took a little pity on her.

'You're very young,' she announced. 'But you have your life ahead of you. You must think about adoption. I'm sure your parents will advise you that's the best course.'

For a moment Angela paused. 'If they do,' she said. 'I shan't take any notice of them. Goodbye, Matron. And thank you. I'd like to go on with my duties till the last moment, if I may.'

'You may.' The tone was freezing. 'But only because we're so short of trained nurses.' Then the door closed on her.

'You promise you'll keep in touch,' Christine said. 'You'll write and let me know how you are, and what you have, won't you?'

'I promise.' Angela hugged her once more. 'And give my love to Walter, won't you? Say I'm sorry I didn't see him to say goodbye.'

'I'll tell him.' Christine was grateful. 'He had to do it. He couldn't let you walk into that, once he knew. You've been very good about it, Angie. It means a lot to me, I'm fond of him.'

'I know you are and he's fond of you. It's been such fun working together and you've been a real friend to me through all this. The last couple of weeks have been sheer hell . . .'

'They're a lot of cows,' Christine declared. The senior staff had borne down on Angela for the least infraction. She had let the side down and only Sister Hunt, renowned for her fierce adherence to the rules, had gone out of her way to be kind. 'They can stuff themselves now. You'll be back home before you know it. And a nice sea voyage'll do you good. I wish I could have seen you off.'

'Don't worry. I've got transport. I'd better go. I'll write and you write back. Here, take this. It's a present.' She thrust the little box into Christine's uniform pocket. 'It'll stop you being late,' she called out and started quickly down the stairs.

Christine opened it. Inside was the gold watch Steven Falconi had given Angela.

The hospital ship docked at Southampton. Angela had worked her passage among the wounded being repatriated from the Italian campaign. There had been no time to think and little time to feel. Feeling would come later, when the reality of what she had done sank in. She hadn't written to Steven although letters had arrived from Naples. She didn't open them. She didn't trust herself. Later, when she was safe in England and the last link between them broken, she might read what he had said.

Southampton in late October was grey and chill in the early morning. A thin rain fell as they docked. Those able to had climbed on deck to cheer at the first sight of home. Leaning along the railing, beside the young airman she had helped to climb up, Angela's heart was as sad as the morning. There was no one to meet her. They had only just had her letter. A letter explaining that she was coming home and would ring when she arrived. She couldn't hurt them by taking the coward's way and writing what had to be told to them face to face.

'Oh Gawd,' the boy beside her kept repeating. 'Oh Gawd. It's so good to be home. Aren't you glad, Nurse? Aren't you bloody glad?'

'Not as bloody glad as you,' she said and managed to smile at him. 'Are you being met?'

'Mum and Dad,' he announced. 'They're down there somewhere. Can't bloody well see anything in this mist.'

There was a cheer when they actually docked and then the gangway rattled up and the first trickle of men on stretchers and in wheelchairs was helped off the ship. The rain had stopped by the time Angela had gone down and gathered her bag of belongings. There was no sun, and in spite of her cloak she shivered in the cold. There were long queues at every public telephone. Someone, seeing her waiting, called her and gave up their place. She didn't know how forlorn and tired she looked.

Her mother's voice sounded crackly and far away. She had only a little English change to feed the coin box.

'Darling, Angela darling. Where are you?'

'I'm at Southampton. I'll catch a train home. No, no, I'm fine. How are you? How's Daddy? I don't know. It depends when I can get a train. No, don't keep anything hot for me, God knows when I'll get there. Yes, longing to see you both too. I'm running out of money. Bye, Mum darling.'

She pushed the box door open and an eager serviceman thrust into her. 'Sorry, must phone the wife . . .' For a brief moment he looked after her. He wondered what on earth she had to cry about.

'How do you mean there's no line? I know there's a goddamned line!'

The army telephonist went red. She took off her headphones and stood up. Officer or no officer, she wasn't going to be talked to like that. And by a Yank. 'I'm sorry, Sir, but I've told you. There is no line to that number on the island. I'm closing the switchboard.'

He moved a little nearer to her. He looked dangerous, as if he might do something violent. 'It's the military hospital at Tremoli,' he said. 'So don't give me that crap about no number. Try again.'

He reached into his pocket and pulled out a wad of money. 'How much will it take? Twenty US dollars?'

The military hospital. Hadn't he heard? She thought: I'd better be careful. I'd like to give him one in the eye, but I'd better not chance it.

'Just wait a minute, please. I'll get someone.' She hurried out of the office to find her sergeant. She wasn't going to give that nasty customer any bad news.

He had been busy for the last fortnight, meeting groups of partisans in the wild Calabrian countryside, cut off from all communication with Naples. There was no letter from Angela waiting for him and he had sent off three in succession through army channels before he went up country.

No letter, no message from her, nothing. There were no civilian lines of communication open, so he had naturally gone to the military telephone service. It was ten o'clock at night and the offices were closed. Only the sullen English ATS girl was on duty. He shouldn't have lost his temper with her. He should have kept calm.

'Evening, Captain. Can I help you?'

There was a hostile look in the man's eye. She'd gone in and complained, of course. He wouldn't get much cooperation from the sergeant either.

He said, 'I've got to get through to this number. It's very important. Your operator said there was no line. Telephone communication was established over a week ago with Sicily. So I know there's a line. Will you try it for me?'

The sergeant said flatly, 'The military hospital at Tremoli doesn't have a line, Sir. It was bombed to the ground this morning.'

It was a freak, they told him. A German Heinkel, off course and limping away from the beachhead at Salerno, jettisoned its load over Sicily and the hospital was hit. The plane crashed shortly afterwards in the mountains. It was called an atrocity, though the most likely explanation was that the pilot didn't even see the Red Cross

39

markings on the roof of the building. The way the Heinkel dived into the mountainside, he was probably wounded or dying at the controls.

Steven was put on board a reconnaissance plane. When they landed, a Jeep and driver were waiting for him. No casualty lists were available yet. Nurses and patients were still being brought out of the debris. Some had been identified, others were crushed beyond recognition. A temporary morgue had been set up while the rescue work was going on. The driver told him all about it as they approached the devastated site.

There was still a huge pall of dust hanging in the air. All the buildings had been destroyed and fire had broken out in the rubble, adding a new dimension of horror. He could smell burning. Water had turned the ground into areas of squelching mud. There was debris everywhere. He picked his way through it, looking for someone, anyone, who could tell him if Angela Drummond had been rescued.

'Eighty per cent killed,' the driver told him, 'probably more when they get the last lot of bodies out. Lousy bastards, bombing a hospital.'

There was a casualty list of sorts, one of the NCOs in charge of digging people out shouted across to him. Down at the warehouse off the Via Pressoli. They were taking the dead down there for identification.

It was a meat storage unit and they had kept the temperature cold. He went in and the chill and the smell of death nearly turned his stomach. A medical orderly gave him a typewritten list.

'It's chaos,' he admitted. 'Half of the bodies will never be identified. Nurses, patients, Italians cleaning out the wards. Christ, Captain, it's been worse than any combat I've been in.'

Her name was not on the list. He heard the orderly say, 'We've got personal effects over here. Do you want to take a look?'

There were stains on the gold watch. Bloodstains, and

40

the face was shattered. Steven Falconi picked it out of the box. The orderly looked at him.

'You recognize it?'

There was no answer. The man turned away, leaving the captain alone. Better to let him cry it out.

2

The damp mists of early morning had lifted. By afternoon it was a beautiful autumn day. Angela had forgotten the brilliant reds and golds that glowed in the sunshine. The air was clean and cool, with the fresh smell of rain lately fallen; she had breathed desert dust for so long she had forgotten that too.

It all looked so familiar and yet so strange. She got a lift from the station and walked the last half mile to the village near Haywards Heath. Her childhood and young life rose up to greet her; there was the little school she and Jack had gone to before they went away to what her father called their 'proper schools'. The green with the war memorial in the centre, some faded flowers at the base. She wondered when they would put her brother's name there. In memory of those who gave their lives for King and Country in the Great War, 1914–1918.

'Their names liveth for evermore'. She knew the words by heart. Other names, another war, 1939 till when?

The house was close to the green. There was the old eighteenth-century brick wall, with the iron gate and the slope of the red-tiled roof above it. The gate squeaked, as it had always done. Her father's polished brass plate shone in the last of the evening sunshine. Dr Hugh Drummond, MRCP,LRCP,B.Ch. Inside the front garden there was a wooden notice staked firmly in the grass. Surgery, it said in black letters, and an arrow, pointing to the side of the house. Would he understand?

She rang on the doorbell. It jangled inside the hall. The

bell had been there during her grandfather's time. The surgery door had an electric buzzer. She lifted her bag and waited.

Then she heard the quick footsteps. She could imagine her mother hurrying to the door. She would understand, surely. The flash of imagination became reality. The door was opened and Mother was there with her arms wide, with Father in the background. There was joy on their faces, a warm welcome home for their surviving child.

'We're disgraced, you realize that? Absolutely disgraced,' Hugh Drummond said.

Her mother was crying. Her father, holding his dead pipe like a weapon pointed at her, kept moving in small circles round the room. She had been home for twenty-four hours before the chance came to tell them. She had been tempted to say nothing at first. Their eagerness to look after her made it more difficult. Jack's death had aged them. Her mother's grief had turned inward, gnawing at her energy and enthusiasm for life. She was grey-haired even before her daughter sailed overseas.

Angela had slept late, exhausted by the long journey. The tiny child was making its own demands upon her. Her father had a morning surgery. He joined them for lunch, as he had always done. There were no concessions to shortages and rationing. The dining room table was polished and laid, and the daily help, who'd been there since Angela was a toddler, did the washing up afterwards.

'My goodness, you've put on weight, Angela. That dress is quite tight. I suppose it was all that rich Italian food.'

The dress wouldn't do up properly. None of her skirts fitted comfortably either.

'Mummy. Daddy,' Angela said. 'I've got something to tell you. It's not the food, I'm afraid. I'm going to have a baby.'

43

Her mother was pouring tea. There was no coffee to be had. She stopped, the pot suspended, and slowly a red flush crept up her face.

Her father spoke first. 'I hope that's a joke. Even if it is in bad taste.'

'No.' Angela tried to keep her voice steady. 'I wouldn't joke about a thing like that. I'm pregnant. That's why I've been sent home.' She looked at their stricken faces and was saying, 'I'm so sorry. So sorry to burden you with this,' when her mother burst into tears and her father lost his temper.

'Disgraced,' he repeated. 'Thrown out of the Red Cross and sent home. I can't believe it. Angela, how could you have done such a thing?' He didn't wait for an answer or an explanation. 'Didn't you think how we'd feel? What about your mother? Hasn't she gone through enough after Jack's death, without you letting us down?'

'Don't. Hush, don't,' her mother pleaded. 'It's no good going on like this. Calm down, darling. Don't upset yourself.' Then to her daughter, 'He's not been at all well lately. He shouldn't get worked up.'

'I don't want to upset either of you,' Angela said. 'I didn't know you hadn't been well, Daddy. I shouldn't have said anything. I wish to God I hadn't. I wish I hadn't come home at all.'

She got up and stumbled out of the room because she had started to cry. There was no key in her bedroom door. She wanted to lock them out, to weep her disappointment and hurt away without either of them having second thoughts and coming up to talk to her.

She put her hands on her stomach and clenched them defensively. 'Poor little thing. Nobody wants you. I won't stay. I won't have you born here if they feel like that . . .'

And of course her mother came and knocked after a little while and sat on the bed and tried to make amends.

'Daddy didn't mean that. He was just upset. We've talked it over and, of course, we'll do what we can for you. You must understand, my dear, it's quite a shock for us.'

'I know it is.' Angela felt so weary. She looked at her mother for a moment and said the unthinkable. 'Weren't you in love, Mummy? Can't you remember how you felt?'

'Of course I was,' she protested. 'But I would never have done anything till I was married.'

'I am married,' Angela said. She got up and started aimlessly combing her hair.

'What do you mean? You never said anything about being married!'

'It won't count here,' she said. 'But he wanted it. He minded a lot about the baby. So he got a priest in Sicily to marry us. He's American. He wanted me to go to the States to his family.'

Her mother said in a hesitant way, 'Why didn't you?'

'I had a good reason,' Angela said. 'I didn't want to bring up the baby in that environment.'

'Bring it up? You mean you're going to keep it?'

Angela put down the comb. She set it straight in line with her old silver hairbrushes and the little glass jars with silver lids.

'Don't tell me you'd want your grandchild to be adopted.'

'It might be the best thing for you,' was the answer. 'But there's no need to talk about that now. Come downstairs; your father's very upset, Angela. It's become so dreadful and we were so excited to have you home.'

'All right, Mother. You go on and I'll tidy myself up and come down. Just ask him not to shout at me, will you?'

'He won't,' her mother promised. 'He'll be calm. We've got to work out what we're going to say to people.'

'That's not a marriage,' Hugh Drummond muttered. 'Some mumbo-jumbo, without a certificate or any legal proof. He just made a fool of you, Angela.'

45

There was no use trying to explain Steven's attitude. She remembered Major Thompson's contemptuous remark: 'Murder's OK, but they won't accept a bastard child.' What would her father make of that?

'I've been thinking,' Angela said. 'I shouldn't have come home and just landed you with this. You're right, Daddy. It was bad enough losing Jack. I've got a little money; I can go to London and get a job and have the baby there. It'd be best, wouldn't it?'

'No, it would not!' he retorted. 'Don't be silly, Angela. Of course you'll stay here, it's your home. You can have the child in the cottage hospital. So don't even think of doing anything else, please.'

He was not a man given to displays of affection. Even the ritual kiss goodnight was dropped before she became adolescent. But he showed his irritation easily enough. He lost his temper with his children, but he found it impossible to demonstrate his love. They were supposed to take it for granted, but Angela never did. She couldn't see the remorse behind the sharp reproof. His reaction had been cruel and he was ashamed of himself.

Joy Drummond understood him. She said to her daughter, 'Angela dear, your father and I love you and we want to help you. We were just shocked and upset. You weren't very tactful, you know.'

'It wasn't very easy for me,' Angela answered slowly. 'I could have written, I could have told you on the phone. I thought that'd be cheating and I owed it to you not to do that. Anyway, as you said, Mummy, we've got to have a story ready. What do you want me to say? I got married in Sicily and my husband was killed at Salerno? People round here won't question that.'

'You're determined to keep the child?'

'Yes. Absolutely determined.'

'You may change your mind,' her father suggested. 'I've known it happen.'

'It won't happen to me.'

'What name will you take?' her mother asked. 'What was *his* name?'

'It doesn't matter. I don't want the baby to have an Italian name.'

'You said he was American,' Joy Drummond protested.

'Italian American,' Angela explained. 'I'll think of an English surname.'

It was hard for them and she must make allowances. Their lives had run on in the same sedate routine for over thirty years. Trivia was their safeguard against sorrow. The loss of the daughter who died in babyhood, the death of their only son. And now, to them, the disgrace of an illegitimate grandchild.

Her mother said, 'My grandmother was a Peters; that's a nice name. What do you think, Hugh?'

'Too short,' he said. 'Like Smith or Brown. It's up to Angela anyway. It's surgery in half an hour. I could do with a cup of tea.'

'I'll make it,' Angela offered.

'No, no, you sit down. I won't be a minute. Mrs P. made some biscuits.'

Her mother hurried out. There was a long silence. Her father lit his pipe and puffed at it aggressively. Angela put a small log on the fire and poked it into a blaze.

'I want you to know one thing,' she said. 'I was really in love with him. I still am.'

'After the way he treated you? After leaving you in this predicament?'

'He didn't. I left him. I told Mummy. He wanted me to go to America and wait for him with his family. I said no. I got myself sent home and I shall never see or hear of him again. But it wasn't anything cheap and I'm not ashamed of it. I just hope you won't be either.'

'Shame doesn't come into it,' he said. 'Damned tobacco's so wretched these days, can't get my pipe to draw properly. Why did you leave him, if he wanted to do the decent thing? I don't understand you.'

I can't tell you, Angela decided. I can't risk you turning against the baby if you know about Steven. You couldn't come to terms with it, any more than I could.

'There was a very good reason, but that's all I can say. I've got to make a new life for myself and the baby and try to put it all behind me. But it's not going to be easy.'

'It certainly isn't,' he agreed. 'Especially if you meet someone and want to get married. But that's all a long way off. I think it'd be better if my partner, Jim Hulbert, looks after you and does the delivery. He's a good chap and knows his stuff. I was never that keen on obstetrics. He'll look after you. You'd better have a check-up in a couple of days and get things on course. Ah!' He got up as his wife came back into the room. 'Joy, give me that tray – it's quite heavy.'

Joy Drummond managed one of her bright smiles. 'Angela, tea and a biscuit? Better make it two now.' Her eyes were red-rimmed as if she had been crying.

'Thanks, Mummy. One biscuit'll do.'

Her father went off to the surgery and she helped to prepare their dinner.

'You'll need a ration card and extra orange juice and cod liver oil for the baby,' her mother chatted on. 'It's awfully good the way mothers are looked after these days. Mrs P.'s daughter is having a baby and she was saying only the other day that she's better fed and healthier than Mrs P. ever was.'

It was odd, unreal. Angela peeled potatoes and felt as if she were watching a play, with someone who looked like her among the cast. The daily, Mrs P., and her daughter, the free orange juice and vitamins provided by a thoughtful Government. The child of a Mafia gangster nestling in her womb. The memory of the burning sun of Sicily on their naked bodies the first time they made love. 'If you marry,' her father had said, seeing the practical problems. There would never be another man after Steven Falconi. She came up to her mother and put an arm round her.

'Thank you,' she said quietly. 'And thanks to Daddy, too.'

'That's all right,' Joy murmered. 'I'm sorry we took it badly to start off. I do hope you'll forget about it. Now will you make the gravy or shall I?'

'Oh, dear,' Joy Drummond said. 'Whatever's the matter? You look as white as a sheet.'

The letter from Walter McKie came with the early post. Angela opened it at breakfast with her mother – tea, and toast with a thin scrape of butter and some of the precious jam ration.

'Angela, are you all right?'

Angela covered her face with her hands. For a moment she felt everything round her fade, as if she was going to faint with the shock. Her mother got up and came round to her.

'What is it? What's happened.'

'My best friend is dead.' Angela held on to the flimsy airmail letter. 'The hospital was bombed, just after I left. She was killed, Mum. They were nearly all killed. Oh, Chrissie, Chrissie . . .' she wept.

'You mustn't do this,' Joy admonished her. 'You mustn't get upset like this. It's bad for the baby.'

'I can't believe it. I can't believe it happened. I wrote to tell her about the trip home and ask how things were. This is from her boyfriend. It was a freak, he says. A German bomber unloaded and then crashed into the mountains.'

'What a terrible thing.'

'The place was full of wounded,' she went on. 'Nobody had a chance. Mum, I think I'm going to be sick.'

Afterwards, when she lay on her bed, she read the letter again. Steven Falconi had come back to Sicily to search for her. He had left, believing she was among the dead. Thompson had arranged a return flight to Naples for him the same day. He hadn't told Steven any different, so she had nothing to worry about. Christine was dead. And the last glimmer of hope had died with her.

Walter had put it into words. Steven wouldn't be trying to trace her now.

The boy was born on 18 May. It was a short labour and the midwife delivered him. There was no need to call Jim Hulbert. Her parents hurried over. Her mother brought flowers from the garden.

'Eight pounds,' Hugh Drummond remarked. 'He's a big chap.'

'He's very dark,' Joy Drummond announced. 'Lots of black hair.'

'Italians *are* dark.' Angela's father had a snap of irritation in his voice.

'Not all of them,' she protested. 'Some are quite fair. Think of the Old Masters, they painted blonde people. How are you feeling, Angela? It wasn't too bad, was it? He's a dear little boy, isn't he?'

'I'm fine,' Angela said. 'Just tired, Mum. That's all. It was quite quick for a first baby. He is lovely, isn't he?'

'Yes,' her mother agreed. She touched the top of his head with her finger. Poor little thing. No father. People round about said what a tragedy for Angela, losing her husband like that, and wasn't she brave. But Joy wasn't sure how many really believed it. She had called herself Lawrence after a distant Drummond connection. The child would be registered under that name. The birth certificate would show he was illegitimate, but there was nothing they could do about that. It could be kept locked away.

'Come on, Joy. We mustn't tire her. We'll be off now, Angela, and you go to sleep. I'll tell the nurse to come and take the baby. Nice little chap. Big, too,' he repeated.

'We'll pop back at tea time,' her mother promised. 'Or I will anyway, if your father's busy.' She bent and kissed Angela's cheek.

She was alone then, in the little sunny room, with the flowers from their garden arranged in a vase on the windowsill. A beautiful sunny day, 18 May 1944. She looked down at the child in the crook of her arm. Steven's son. He would never see him or know him.

The nurse came in and said, 'Mrs Lawrence. Tears? Now, now, not after such an easy time and that beautiful boy at the end of it. Here, let me take him. You go to sleep and I'll bring him back at tea time.'

Nineteen days later the invasion of Europe began. The Germans were in retreat and the end of the war was in sight when the child was christened in the village church. He was called Charles Steven Hugh. There was a party held at the house afterwards. It was a very nice party and the Drummonds enjoyed it. They were especially pleased that Jim Hulbert was paying so much attention to Angela. He was a good man, too old for war service, but steady as a rock. They didn't put it into words, but their hope was mutual. It would solve everything if something came of it between them.

On 18 May 1950 Steven Falconi got married. It was his little son Charlie's sixth birthday. Three thousand miles from the children's tea party in England, Steven drove his new wife away on their honeymoon and called out another woman's name as he took her virginity.

They had married in Palm Beach. First a full nuptial Mass in the Church of Santa Margarita and then a huge reception at his uncle's house. She was a beautiful bride: dark haired with brilliant black eyes and a voluptuous look about her. Clara Fabrizzi, the only daughter of Aldo Fabrizzi, who controlled the garment district in the East Side and had just acquired a string of hotels on the Florida coast. A marriage of dynasties, the Fabrizzi uniting with the Falconi. Both families were pleased; other alliances would follow as a result. She was an heiress and a rich prize, even for a man as important as Steven Falconi. They looked good together, leading off the dancing that

51

evening. He was tall and some kind of war hero, only no one knew exactly what he had done to get his Distinguished Service Cross. Apart from what he had done for the families in Sicily and around Naples. Business was re-established and, even after such a short time, money was filling the coffers and finding its way across the Atlantic via Switzerland.

Her dress had cost a fortune and there was another fortune in diamonds round her neck. She was twenty-one, her virginity guaranteed by her family to the Falconis, and she was passionately in love with the man they wanted her to marry. The men exchanged crude jokes about the wedding night, and the women, some of them well past their first blush, wondered what it would be like to have Falconi take you to bed. None of them could claim to know, because he hadn't looked at any of his own women since he came back from the war.

There was music and dancing and a lot of men got drunk, while others slipped away and talked business in little groups. The weather was hot, sunny as in the Old Country, and the ocean lapped blue at the edge of the private beach. Special caterers had come in from New York with the best Italian dishes and the finest Italian wines and French champagne. Two rooms in the mansion itself were given up to displaying the wedding presents. The ice-blue Cadillac with bulletproof glass and armour plating surrounding the chassis was Aldo Fabrizzi's wedding present to his son-in-law. It waited outside for them, festooned in white ribbons.

The fathers stood together, watching their children circling the open-air dance floor, leading off with the band playing 'The Wedding Waltz'. Fabrizzi was small and stocky; in his youth he had been a boxer and he still walked with the light spring of a man used to moving in the ring.

'They look good,' he said to Luca Falconi. 'Your boy and my little girl. They'll have fine-looking children.'

Luca Falconi nodded. He was pleased. Happy about

the whole arrangement, happier still because his son had found a suitable wife and would settle down at last. The war had been bad for Steven in many ways. He was a stranger when he came home to them. They were proud of his medal, but angry that he risked himself to get it. What was the need to transfer to an infantry unit and get into the worst of the fighting round Rome itself? Still, he had come back to them and taken up his responsibilities. A very good organizer and a real money man. He owed the first to the army and the second to his college education.

'He'll be a good husband,' Luca assured Fabrizzi. 'He doesn't run around with women. He doesn't gamble. You know my son – no vices.'

'No vices,' Aldo Fabrizzi agreed. 'Except he likes to work all the time. But my Clara will teach him how to play. He's going to be a lucky man.'

'Talking of luck, and talking of gambling,' Falconi said. 'How about us opening a new casino in Nevada?'

'Musso runs the gambling there, you know that.' Fabrizzi had a habit of pulling at his lower lip when he was thinking about business.

'Together,' Luca suggested, 'we are bigger than Musso. Why the fuck should he have all the cake? Think about it. He's not so young and that son of his is eyeballed on dope. He wouldn't give us trouble.'

Fabrizzi nodded. 'I'll think about it. We'll talk to-morrow, maybe. I better dance with my wife.'

Falconi took some champagne. Fabrizzi had a passion for big-breasted blondes. His little plump wife had only managed to give him the one daughter. If she knew about the women, she never said anything.

Pity he hadn't had a chance to try Steven out on the idea. Gambling was very big money and getting bigger. It was time to give Tony Musso a push and see what happened. He might just take a fall.

'I'm so happy,' Clara whispered to Steven as they circled.

'You love me, don't you, Steven?' She had beautiful eyes and they were limpid with her love for him.

'You know I do,' he answered, and drew her closer to him. She was everything a man could want. There was passion in her. It had smouldered during their courtship. It was Steven who drew back. They'd have children.

He'd bought a magnificent brownstone house on East 52nd with a breathtaking view over the Hudson River. His father was building them a holiday house at Palm Beach as his wedding present. And together the two families would enlarge their business interests.

Clara was an educated girl – that was important to him. He couldn't have married a girl with no interest beyond her home and the bambinos. Clara liked going to concerts and the theatre. She had an eye for modern art, which he couldn't understand, but if she wanted pictures, that was okay by him. He desired her. No man could help but want her, and he pressed her closer still until the waltz became one of Sinatra's popular romantic songs. There'd been women in his life since he came back after the war. They were professionals. They didn't expect anything more than a cheque or a mink coat. Nothing had filled the void in his life, not even the devotion to business that occupied every moment of his days. The empty space was there inside him. He had tried to get himself killed because the pain of losing Angela and his child was driving him mad. He sought relief in killing those who had killed his love, and had been decorated for it. He told no one what had happened when he came home. He could still dream of that dreadful dust-filled wasteland, with the smell of burning corpses in the air, and wake up sweating at the memory.

He held his new bride tight against him and believed that love for her would grow and fill that emptiness.

They had rented a house at Boca Raton for the first part of their honeymoon. The staff were hand picked. They were Falconi's people and the house was guarded day and night. There were enemies along that coast. Later they would fly off to Europe where the bodyguards weren't necessary. Clara had grown up with armed men watching her father and dogging her wherever she went. It was part of the lifestyle of a Mafia chief's family. It even made her feel important when she was a child.

They had dinner on the terrace, with the moon rising like a silver medal in the sky and the sound of the waves whispering against the shore. Steven raised his glass to her.

'*Carissima*. How hungry are you?'

'I'm hungry for you,' she said. 'And I've no shame about it. I don't want food, my darling. I want you to take me.'

He didn't need to undress her, to teach her anything. She stripped off her clothes and stood white and naked before him. In the blaze of passion that engulfed him, it became another woman in his arms, another voice that cried out under him, and the name escaped him without his knowledge. 'Angelina.' The silk-sheeted bed felt like the dusty earth of Sicily and the sun of long ago burned his back.

'Angelina.' She lay frozen beside him. He stroked her breasts and murmured to her in Italian, but she couldn't move or answer. It had been painful, but she rejoiced when he hurt her because it fused them together. It was a fierce and primitive satisfaction, as much emotional as sexual, when he spent himself inside her. And then she heard another name, repeated twice, at the moment of fulfilment.

'Angelina.' Steven was asleep, one arm anchoring her to the bed. She lifted it and slid away. The salt taste of tears was in her mouth. She was naked and cold, with sweat drying on her body and a soreness from the ruptured hymen. There was a little blood, as proof of her womanhood. She should have been so proud of that. She pulled the unworn nightdress over her head and got back into bed. Unhappiness welled up in her, until she rolled away to the very edge and sobbed into the pillow.

When he woke in the morning and drew her towards him to make love again, she stiffened and drew back.

'I hurt you, *carissima*,' he whispered. 'Forgive me. It'll be better for you this time. Come here to me.'

He tried to take the rigid body in his arms, to soothe and stroke her into a response. She turned her pale face up to him. There were great dark circles under her eyes.

'Tell me about Angelina,' she said. 'You called her name last night. Tell me about her.'

I owe it to her, Steven convinced himself. I've hurt and humiliated her and I've got to put it right between us. She's my wife now. I'll make her understand.

He took her out on to the terrace in the early morning sunshine and held her hand while he spoke of what had happened in Sicily seven years ago. Clara listened, watching his face, judging every intonation in his voice. She saw the pain in his eyes as he relived the nightmare of the devastated hospital. When he spoke of finding the watch with her bloodstains dried on it, he looked away.

'You married her,' Clara said. 'You married her in the church.'

'She was pregnant with my child,' he repeated. 'What else could I do?'

'Nobody told my father about this,' she said. 'That wasn't very honourable.'

'Nobody knew,' Steven protested. 'You are the only person in the world I've told about it. They're dead and it's over. I love you, Clara. I don't know how it happened last night, but you've got to forget it.'

'You didn't have to marry her.' She spoke quite coldly now. 'She wasn't Sicilian. How did you know the child was yours? How many other men did she fuck besides you?'

The crudity astonished him. He felt a sudden flare of anger. 'Don't ever use that kind of word again, Clara. And don't talk about her that way. I've told you, she's dead and you don't need to be jealous. Now get changed and we'll go for a swim.'

'What did she look like?'

He felt the anger come again at her persistence. He wanted to hurt her for what she'd said about Angela and the child. 'Not like you. Blonde and blue-eyed. Very pretty.'

He saw her flinch. I love her, he said to himself, but she's got to learn not to go too far with me. 'I said we'd swim.' He turned to go inside. 'I've told you to get changed.'

Women didn't disobey their menfolk. If it wasn't a father it was a brother and then a husband. She got up and followed him inside. They went down to the beach side by side. He didn't hold her hand or say anything. He dived in ahead of her.

She thought: I don't have to be jealous. She's dead, she and her child. But I heard her name cried out instead of mine and I saw the look on his face when he talked about her. If she was alive, I could go to my father and he'd know what to do. But she's dead, and I can't touch her. And I love him so much I'll have to submit . . .

She came up to the house after him and into the bedroom and threw herself on the bed. She undid the bikini top and lay there with her loins covered and her breasts swelling as she looked up at him.

'I'm your wife, Steven, and I love you so much I could die. Forgive me.'

He made love very kindly and gently, trying to gain her forgiveness, but she turned like an animal and clawed and bit, as if her ferocity could bind him to her and drive out the dead. And she said, gasping in his arms, 'You'll forget her. I'll make you forget her . . . I'll eat you alive till you can't think of anyone else.'

Desire drained away from him. 'Behave yourself,' he commanded her and she shrank back, wounded. 'That's not what I want from you. I pay for that, Clara. I don't want it from my wife.'

She spat a vile Sicilian insult at him and he slapped her across the face. Two of the men patrolling the outside of the house heard their voices raised, looked at each other and shrugged. They were in shirtsleeves and slacks, shoulder holsters unfastened to give instant access to their guns if anyone approached. They heard the new Donna Falconi shrieking hysterically at her husband and one of them sucked up his saliva and spat.

'I'd take my belt to that one if I was him. She needs the shit beating out of her.'

His companion grinned. 'You ever seen the Don lose his temper? Holy Jesus, he'll kill the little bitch. Come on, let's leave 'em to it. You take the south side of the house, I'll go round the east. Giorgio's keeping his eyes open out back.'

They sailed to Europe on the *Queen Elizabeth*. They were reconciled because they had to be. There was too much at stake beyond their personal happiness and they accepted this in their different ways.

Steven argued with himself that Clara was still very young and her parents had spoiled her rotten. But she loved him and he knew he must come to terms with her jealousy. It would pass in time as she matured and her self-confidence grew. He had asked too much of her too quickly. He chided himself for having underestimated the fiery Sicilian temperament.

When she cried and begged him to love her, he came very close to tenderness as well as sexual desire. They'd be happy, he insisted. They had to be because the families were now bound by a far-reaching business alliance.

Clara suffered. It was a new experience and she was driven mad by the pain of loving her husband and not possessing him entirely. Her life had been protected, cushioned against the least disappointment or frustration. She was helpless in this situation, at the mercy of her emotions and an unbridled temper. Suspicion tortured her, so that she watched him constantly. She tried to please him and was never sure she had succeeded. She was beautiful, and the admiring looks of men aboard the liner told her that she could have any man she chose. But the ghost of a dead woman mocked her in Steven's arms. And the ghost of a dead child. That at least she could send quickly to its grave. She knelt by her bed at night and prayed to the Virgin and the Saints to make her pregnant.

She knew her father was delighted with the marriage. In saner moments she realized that he would dismiss a wartime love affair with a shrug and wonder what she was complaining about. He wouldn't be pleased if there was trouble. He expected a good marriage, grand-children to gladden his old age and all the benefits of a treaty with Luca Falconi. She would have to win Steven, and the way to do it was to give him a son as quickly as she could.

They were very happy in Paris and miserable in Monte Carlo. The splendour of the great French city enchanted Clara. She visited every art gallery and, to please her, Steven bought several expensive modern paintings for their new home. She wandered through the Louvre, pointing out this work or that, trying to fire his interest.

'I wanted to study art,' she said. 'Poppa wouldn't let me. I really wanted to be an artist.'

'You can take it up now,' he suggested. 'There'll be plenty of free time. Why don't you?'

'I don't mean that sort of artist,' Clara protested. 'It's not like cookery classes or flower arrangements. It's your life, if you're serious about it. You have to live for painting, Steven. Maybe I wouldn't have been any good.'

He could imagine Aldo Fabrizzi's reaction to such an ambition for his only daughter.

'I don't think starving in a garret is your kind of life, sweetheart,' he said gently. 'You were made for better things.'

They shopped in Paris. Clara fell in love with Dior's

59

designs and they suited her. She was beautiful and Steven felt proud to see heads turning when they entered a restaurant. And Clara shopped for him. There were lavish presents of ties and shirts from Charvet and a magnificent platinum watch. She stood beside him, watching his reaction, demanding over and over if he liked this or that. She was a child at heart, he thought: extravagant, impulsive, demanding, but it was all part of being in love. No half measures were possible. The extremes of her nature were a surprise to him. The Sicilian courtship, albeit American style, had left them little time to get to know each other in any depth: when they managed to be alone, every moment had been taken up in hungry sexual exploration – and just as quickly stopped before it went too far.

Underneath the facade of culture and education there lurked a primitive Sicilian woman, single-minded in her love, black-hearted in her hatred. And clever. She had a brain and its keenness surprised him. He thought of that thwarted ambition to be an artist. The more he understood her, the less he dismissed it, as he had done in the Louvre. She could have lived a life of dedication, of obsession, if she wanted something badly enough. Only her capacity for self-discipline was in doubt. But she was still the adoring bride, willing to be guided, erotically submissive to whatever he asked.

They were very happy together in Paris; so happy she begged to stay an extra week. The week lengthened into a fortnight.

She said to him one day as they walked arm in arm up the Faubourg St Honoré, 'You love it here as much as I do, *caro*, don't you?'

'I guess I do,' Steven agreed.

'Then why don't we buy an apartment here?' she said triumphantly. 'I could use part of Poppa's settlement. We could come in the spring maybe, when you weren't too busy. Why don't we, Steven?'

He stopped, taken by surprise. Her eyes were bright with excitement.

'I've even asked around,' she admitted. 'There's a lovely apartment for sale in the Rue Constantine. Couldn't we see it?'

Steven hesitated. This was a honeymoon. Time taken off from the important things in life. Their home was in the States. A place in Florida was realistic. An apartment halfway across the world was not. She saw the refusal coming and the brightness changed to a sullen, tearful look, full of reproach.

'Clara, sweetheart, it's a crazy idea. We'd never spend any time in it. How could we? We're going to have a place in Palm Beach. We'll have kids – we won't want to leave them behind.'

Kids. She bit her lip. That very morning, she'd known she wasn't pregnant. The idea of a romantic rendezvous in Paris was some kind of compensation for that disappointment. Every year, she had imagined, they could slip away and have a secret honeymoon in the place where they had started to be really happy.

'We could just look at it,' she said. 'What's the harm? We're not doing anything else this afternoon.'

'If you look at it, you'll like it,' he answered. 'And we'll have an argument.'

'If we don't like it,' she countered, 'there won't be an argument. Steven, darling, it was just a silly idea, I guess, but it sounded like fun. I was going to surprise you. See it this afternoon and buy it for us. Maybe I should have done.'

'Maybe you shouldn't,' he countered. 'I don't like that kind of a surprise, sweetheart. If you're bored, we'll go see the place. But not to buy or rent or anything. It's just wasting everybody's time, but if that's what you want, okay, we'll do it.'

It was a mistake to have indulged her and as soon as the concierge let them in, Steven knew it. One magnificent reception room over thirty feet in length with a fine Louis

XVI marble fireplace and a brilliant Beauvais tapestry running the length of one wall. It was possible to buy it with the apartment, the agent explained, because it was too big for the owner's new house. Long windows opened on to a tiny balcony. Clara stepped out on to it. She didn't look at Steven; her instincts warned her not to pressure him. The elegance and beauty of that marvellous room must have their own effect.

The dining room was long and narrow, the walls covered in crimson silk. The parquet flooring made their footsteps echo. The bedroom was small, without a view and painted a cold French grey. The bathroom, by their standards back home, was primitive. It could be changed, modernized. The bedroom, which was such a disappointment, only needed clever colouring and a handsome bed. Ideas chased through her mind but stopped on her tongue. He wouldn't agree. She knew he wouldn't. He would see all the practical disadvantages and simply say no. It was her money, but he would still feel he had the husband's right to dictate how she spent it. She walked back through the rich dining room and into the great salon and there was a tight little set to her full mouth.

She said sweetly, looking up at him, 'I know we can't have it, *caro* but isn't it lovely?'

'It's one hell of a room,' he said, looking round once more. 'It's got everything. If we didn't live three thousand miles away. Thank you,' he said to the agent, who understood that this was not going to be a sale. 'You won't have trouble selling this.'

She slipped her hand through his arm as they walked out on to the street. For a moment she turned and looked back at the building. The facade was white stone, built in the handsome classical style of the Second Empire when Napoleon's nephew, the last emperor, had remodelled Paris to his grand design.

'Well, never mind,' she said. 'It was fun seeing it.'

He was surprised that she gave in so easily and grateful

because she continued to be sweet-tempered for the rest of the day. It was not usually like that when she didn't get her way.

It all went wrong in Monte Carlo when the scene was set for a romantic climax to the honeymoon before they flew back to New York via London.

They had a suite booked in the Hotel de Paris, overlooking the harbour. Big flower arrangements and champagne cooling on the side awaited them with the manager's compliments. The weather was perfect; the sea sparkled like a big blue diamond and the yachts rode in arrogant splendour at their moorings. There was a gala night at the casino to which they had been invited, thanks to a friend with influence who owed the Fabrizzis a favour. He had secured the coveted entrée to the social event of the season.

Clara was exquisitely dressed in a cream silk Dior evening dress. It flattered her pale skin and the long, silky black hair that swung down to her shoulders. She wore her father's present round her neck and Luca Falconi's diamonds in her ears. She entered the casino on the arm of her tall husband and registered the looks of admiration. There was a flush of happiness and pride in her cheeks, partly due to the secret she was keeping from Steven. The Paris apartment was hers. She had concluded the deal before they flew down to Nice.

The manager and his assistant saw that entry. They were men of impeccable manners, suave appearance, sharp eyes and cash-register memories.

'That's the one,' the assistant murmured.

For a moment the manager's automatic smile came loose. 'How did they get in here, Pierre?'

He whispered a local name. 'He wanted an invitation for a friend's daughter and her husband. On honeymoon, he said. He vouched for them personally. I said, pass the names through to my secretary and she'll see they get an invitation.'

'If His Highness gets to hear of this, you're fired,' the manager muttered, bowing his head in greeting at a distinguished gambling client. 'The Mob's never set foot in here till tonight. I want him watched. I want someone on his tail when he's eating or gambling or taking a piss. He's come here for something. I want to know who he talks to, who seems to know him. And see that name's struck off the list.'

'Falconi?' the assistant said under his breath. 'I've already done that.'

'I mean the bastard that got him in here,' the manager said, moving forward to kiss an English duchess's hand.

There was a performance by a troupe from the Ballet Russe which nearly sent Steven to sleep, after a magnificent seven-course dinner enhanced by the finest wines and vintage champagne. And afterwards the guests were free to gamble and that was when he came to life. Every detail of the doyen of casinos was already filed away for future reference. The rich decor, the air of exclusivity, the impeccable dress and bearing of every member of the staff, all in full evening dress.

The gala was graced by the Prince himself and a large party. Clara stared with open curiosity and for a moment the Prince stared back, trying to place this new beauty. Steven was not beguiled by princes, but he was beguiled by the source from which so much royal revenue was drawn. The air smelt of money: cigar smoke and expensive scent, out-of-season flowers that bloomed from every stately vase in every available space, and the indefinable odour of human excitement as the tables began to fill up.

He passed through the roulette salon. Every kind of gambling was in progress, from simple blackjack to the heavy silence of the baccarat room where fortunes were lost and a few made. Class! The word screamed at him. That was the keynote of the whole place. Discreet, opulent, challenging the clientele to prove they had the money and the nerve to play there.

It was the greatest contrast to the casinos in Nevada. They were noisy, garish, staffed by hoods in tight tuxedos with the holsters bulging under their arms. Whores draping themselves round the bars and gambling tables, on a percentage if they got the customer to drink and bet more than he meant to, before he was taken upstairs to be fleeced.

Even the biggest and smartest casino run by the Musso family in Las Vegas itself was second rate compared to this. All they had in common was the croupiers, who had the same feral look in the eye, the same slick movements and doubtless the invisible button near the knee to alter the draw of the cards or the balance of the wheel.

Class, he said to himself. Here they had made losing money into a privilege. He moved a little closer to the baccarat table. A blonde woman wearing enough rubies and diamonds to pay off the National Debt was playing with demonic concentration. She wasn't beautiful because the mask of greed distorted her face. She was winning, the counters piling up at her elbow. After each hand, she pushed a handful into the slit in the table for the croupier.

'*Merci, Altesse,*' he said each time, and made a little bow.

Someone close to Steven murmured to him in English. 'You wouldn't think the Germans lost the war to look at that, would you?'

'She's German?' Steven said.

The man was in his middle thirties, with a beaky English face and a slight drawl. 'Princess Beatrix von Arentz,' he answered. He had been told to follow the American and, in his view, the best way to watch someone in a place like this was to talk to them. It wasn't the conventional method, but then he'd never done anything conventional in his life. Except gamble away his own inheritance.

'Stinking rich husband,' he volunteered. 'Amazing how they pull themselves up by the boot straps, isn't it? I think he made it out of scrap.' He had a rather high-pitched laugh which he muffled by his hand. 'Plenty of that around in Hunland after the war. She's crazy. She comes here every night and never moves from that table till they close. She's the princess, by the way. God knows what sewer the husband crawled out of. He usually goes home by now and leaves her to it.'

'She's winning,' Steven remarked. 'She's winning an awful lot of money.'

'Not as much as she's lost,' the Englishman remarked. 'Casinos are like bookmakers, don't you think? They always end up with a profit. Do you play?'

'No,' Steven answered.

'The beautiful lady?'

Clara was close beside him, motionless and silent. The Englishman said, 'I'm Ralph Maxton. I do the PR here.'

'My wife,' Steven responded. 'She doesn't play either. I'm Steven Falconi, glad to know you.'

There was a sudden burst of applause. The princess had won on a huge wager. Now she looked beautiful in a lean, Nordic way, all bone structure and pale blue eyes. She gave a brilliant smile.

Clara said to him in Italian, 'Take me home.'

He looked round in surprise. 'Why? You said you were enjoying it. What's the matter?'

She said in a furious whisper, 'You've been staring at that blonde for long enough. I'm going.'

He said to the Englishman, 'Excuse me,' and followed after her. She moved very quickly, pushing her way to the cloakroom.

He was waiting when she came out with her wrap. 'Just a minute, Clara. Just wait a minute. You've had your fun, but I'm not ready to go yet. This is business, you understand?'

'What do you want to do, try and pick her up after I've gone?'

Their voices were low, but it was obvious they were having a row. Steven saw one of the staff moving

66

towards them with a determined expression that said more clearly than any words: We don't allow unpleasantness here.

'Okay,' he said. 'We go back to the hotel. And by Christ Almighty, Clara, you're going to get this straightened out!'

She wasn't afraid of him. He was livid with anger and any other woman would have backed away. But Clara didn't. She tore off her necklace and then the earrings and threw them wildly across the room.

'You stood there staring at that bitch,' she shouted. 'Looking at her, looking at her tits. I saw you! Blonde, like that other whore!'

He didn't slap her. He didn't trust himself. He looked at the screaming fury a few feet away from him, accusing him of an imagined lust.

The happy days and passionate nights spent in Paris had vanished like a daydream. The bitter, violent row at the start of their honeymoon in Boca Raton was not a single incident. He'd seen the faces of their bodyguards and known they'd heard that ugly quarrel. He'd struck her then because she'd lashed his dead wife and child with her jealous tongue and cursed him like a washerwoman. If he touched her now as she called him a liar and ranted about betrayal, he might lose his temper. He dared not do that. He was so angry and disgusted that it wouldn't be safe. He turned and walked out of the bedroom door, slamming it on her.

She followed, dragging it open. 'Where are you going?' she demanded. 'Back to the casino? Back to find her?'

He calmed himself. He unclenched his hands and made his voice quite even.

'I'm not your father. You've got us muddled up. I'm going out and I'll see you when I come back. If I come back.'

He heard something smash as he walked down the

67

passage to the lift. He went to the bar and ordered himself a drink. 'Bourbon on the rocks,' he said. 'You have Camels here?'

The barman said smoothly, 'We have all brands, Monsieur.'

'Two packs,' Steven said.

'Very good, Monsieur. I'll bring them to your table.'

The bar was quite full. He wasn't interested in the people. He needed to sit somewhere alone and put down that drink as fast as possible. What the hell am I going to do with her, he asked himself. The bourbon lit a fire in his stomach, but it didn't help him find an answer. He had thought he was in love with her; he wasn't. The second bourbon induced a mood of bitter honesty.

He had blinded himself with sexual desire and the advantages of combining forces with the Fabrizzi family. He'd married the girl for the right reasons, except that they were wrong for both of them.

And with her female instinct she divined the truth. No matter how he indulged her, or made love to her, she didn't hold his heart. A life of hell yawned at their feet unless something could be done. He hated her brand of violent temper; in a few years she would be a shrew. He hated the jealousy that exploded into insults and accusations without listening to a word of explanation. It was like living with two people – the charming, lively companion and passionate bedmate changed into a spitting fury, foul-mouthed as any slut. There was a simple remedy available, and he knew his own father and his younger brother would recommend it. Teach her a lesson once and for good. If it laid her up for a few days, so much the better. A man has to be the master. Her father would understand that. He wouldn't let it happen more than once, but he would see the need and look the other way.

But I can't do it. Steven Falconi tipped down the last of the bourbon. If I'd been left to be my father's son, without the years at college in America; if I'd never

68

known Angela, I might have used my fists on my wife. But I can't. He didn't mean to think of Angela. She came into his mind and materialized as if she were flesh and blood. The third drink was having its effect.

He could see her so clearly; hear the distinctive English voice, see the shy smile. He had fallen in love with her as he would never fall in love with Clara. But she was Clara's best protection from her own culture. He couldn't hurt Clara, because he had known Angela. The irony of it made him smile for a moment. How she would burn if she knew that. She'd rather suffer his violence than be indebted to the dead woman he had loved.

'Excuse me, do you have a light?'

He glanced up at the woman standing by his table. Jesus, he thought, they have them in here too. She was very attractive, elegantly dressed. He didn't stand up. He flashed his lighter for her and she bent down to the flame.

'Thank you,' she said. 'I must have lost mine. Are you staying here?'

'Yes. Would you like a drink with me?' He was appraising her openly. Good figure, nice breasts, expensive scent. He thought of Clara and the revenge appealed to him.

'Thank you. I'm very bored. I hate being alone. I'd like a glass of champagne.'

She would order that, of course. She spoke very good English and he liked the French accent. He wondered what the price tag would be.

'I'm staying here too,' she volunteered. 'I come for a month every summer. It's such a comfortable hotel.'

She smiled at the waiter who came to take the order. He seemed deferential.

'Good evening, Madame.'

'Good evening, Jacques.'

'Champagne for the lady.' The formula slipped out before Steven could stop himself. 'And a bourbon on the rocks for me.' He could screw as well when he was drunk as sober.

She said, 'My name is Pauline Duvalier. When my husband was alive we spent longer here. He liked to gamble. It bores me.'

'Like being alone?' he asked her.

She extinguished the cigarette half smoked. He noticed a square-cut emerald on her left hand. A very big price tag, by the looks of that.

'You haven't told me your name,' she reminded him.

She had calculating eyes, but there was humour in them. He wondered what she found amusing.

'Steven Falconi.'

'That could be Monacan,' she remarked. 'There's a lot of Italian blood in the people here.'

'How's the champagne?' he asked. He swallowed hard on the bourbon. He was feeling like it. Anger was a form of arousal and he was very angry with everything. Most of all with fate and himself.

'It's nice. Are you alone here?'

They didn't usually ask that. What the hell business was it of hers anyway?

'No. My wife's upstairs. You're an attractive lady, you know that?'

'I should hope so,' she said and she laughed. 'You're an attractive man. Very attractive. I've been watching you getting drunk and thought: What a pity. What a waste. Would you like to come up to my suite? I don't want any more champagne and I think you've had enough to drink.'

He got up from the table. He was quite steady. 'Suite?'

'Suite,' she repeated. 'I have the same one every year. Perhaps I should make something a little clearer to you. I am inviting you because I want to. If I see a man I want, I don't wait for him to ask me. Shall we go?'

'Sure, why not?' he said and followed her to the lift.

It was a better suite than his. Inside the door she turned to him and smiled.

'I'm not a *poule de luxe*,' she mocked him gently. 'You

70

don't have to pay me, except in kind, Monsieur Falconi. I like to be undressed. Shall we go through to the bedroom?'

She woke him before five o'clock. 'In half an hour the hotel cleaners come on duty. If you go now you won't meet anyone.'

He sat up, stretching wearily. It had been a long night, and she had tested him to the limit of his stamina. She smiled down at him in a friendly way. She wore a silk dressing gown and was smoking one of his Camel cigarettes.

'I enjoyed myself,' she said. 'I hope you did too.'

He got out of bed and took the cigarette from her, drawing on it deeply. The taste of her was in his mouth and on the end of the cigarette.

'How often do you do this?' he asked.

'Not too often,' she answered. 'When I see a man I like. Your clothes are over there on the sofa. How long are you staying here?'

'Another four days.'

'We could meet again,' she suggested. 'Perhaps you'll have another row with your wife.'

'How the hell did you know that?' he demanded.

She shrugged. 'A woman alone has to be careful. I asked about you before I introduced myself. There's only one reason a man on his honeymoon sits by himself and gets drunk. What are you going to say to her?'

Steven finished dressing. 'That's my business.'

She shrugged again. 'Of course. I shouldn't have asked. You know my suite number. If I don't hear from you, I wish you bon voyage and perhaps one day if you come back to Monte Carlo . . .' She opened the door for him and held out her hand. 'Goodbye, Monsieur Falconi.'

They hadn't once used each other's first name.

'Goodbye, Madame Duvalier.'

They shook hands. She closed the door immediately

and, throwing the dressing gown on the floor, slipped back into bed and fell asleep.

Clara heard him come in. The long hours of that night had passed without the mercy of sleep for her. The broken shards of china lay on the floor where she had thrown it. They splintered as he walked on them. She couldn't weep any more, or rouse herself to anger.

I'm broken, she said to herself. He's broken me. If he comes back I'll kiss his feet, I'll tear my hair and grovel if he'll only come back and forgive me . . .

She ran to him, tripping over her nightdress in her eagerness. She threw her arms round him and her tears welled up again and poured down her face as she clung. She smelt the other woman's scent upon him and gave a cry of anguish.

'Where have you been? All night long I've waited.'

The scent was in her nostrils. She almost gagged on it. Joy. The most expensive scent in the world.

'Sit down, Clara,' he said. 'Stop crying and working yourself up. I want you to listen to me. Listen very carefully.' He held her away from him, forcing her to sit on the bed.

'You went with another woman,' she forced herself to say. 'I can tell.'

'You're right, I did. And every time you do what you did last night, I shall find myself someone else. Maybe for one night, maybe for longer. I never looked at any blonde in the casino. My mind was on business. Family business, Clara. I was calculating how much she must have lost that they were letting her win so much. My father and yours think it's a business we should get into. 'All you could think of was that I wanted to screw her. So you threw a big scene and we had to leave before I was ready. You screamed at me like some whore off the street. So I'm telling you. You want me faithful, you want me to be a good husband? Then you never do that again. You never speak of my wife, Angela. I said my wife. Close your mouth, Clara. Don't say anything.'

'Why don't you hit me?' she demanded. 'You're killing me instead.'

'Because it wouldn't stop you,' he answered. 'I know you by now. You wouldn't care so much as you'll care about this. There's a woman in the hotel. I can see her any time I want. It's up to you. Now I'm going to take a shower. Think about it. And clear up that mess on the carpet before the breakfast gets here.'

She was sitting up in bed when he came back. She'd brushed her hair and rubbed a little colour into her lips. She'd collected the broken china and cut herself, so there was a handkerchief with a little stain on it wound round her hand and tied at the wrist. She held out her arms. 'I've been punished enough. Forgive me.'

He made himself embrace her. He pitied her and hated himself, but his heart was cold and his spirit weary. He wondered if the pendulum would swing upward again.

She closed her eyes and stayed quiet. A woman in the hotel, he'd said. Not a whore. Whores don't use Joy, it's too expensive. She'd find her. She made herself that promise as she leaned her head against him and they seemed to be at peace.

She did her best to make amends. At her suggestion they returned to the casino that night, and the German princess was at the baccarat table, gambling with increasing recklessness. She was losing.

'Hello.' It was Ralph Maxton again. Word had come through to the manager's office that Falconi was back. He bought them champagne and tried his charm on the new bride. She was extremely beautiful, if you liked the type. He saw the single-minded concentration on her husband, and thought it must be rather a bore to be adored to that extent. Falconi was easy to talk to. He asked a few questions, which Maxton parried, and finally went to another table where the stakes were lower and politely lost a sum of money. It was a gesture and, in spite of himself, Maxton applauded it. He had style, this

Italian gangster. Unlike the ones he'd met in Nevada while he was ruining himself. He was surprised when Mrs Falconi suddenly spoke to him. Falconi was still at the table, taking the shoe this time.

'Are you married, Mr Maxton?'

He laughed. 'Oh Lord no. Not in this job. No wife would put up with it.'

'But a lot of women come here on their own,' she remarked. 'They like gambling, I suppose.'

'Yes, they do. Women get the bug as badly as men. Some of them are widows or divorced. They come and play roulette and enjoy some company.'

'And I suppose they pick up men?' The question was posed with an innocent stare that didn't deceive him for a minute.

'Not in this casino, Mrs Falconi.'

She shrugged and turned away from him. She couldn't stop thinking about the woman in the hotel, the woman who wore Joy.

She wondered how long Steven would stay. She wished this irritating Englishman would go away and pester someone else. She wanted to be alone with Steven, to reassure herself that all was well between them. Tomorrow I'll go to the head porter, she thought. I wonder how much money it will take.

The head porter couldn't help her. He pretended not to see the roll of notes she took out of her handbag. It was more than his job was worth to take the slightest risk. He made as much in a day's tips as the lady was offering.

'I'm so sorry, I can't help you, Madame,' he said. 'Perhaps the reception desk could assist you.'

The reception declined to look at the register and tell her which of the clients was a single lady. Clara was pressed for time. She had dressed hurriedly and come on ahead of Steven to make her inquiries. Back home, she'd have got what she wanted, but not here. She swore under her breath. He'd picked her up – in the cocktail bar most likely. The smell of bourbon was as strong as that hated

74

scent when he came back in the morning. She went to the bar. There were several couples having a drink before lunch. And two women alone. One she didn't even look at. She was grey-haired, absorbed in a novel. The other one? Clara stared at her and some primeval instinct guessed that she need look no further. She passed close by. The woman was sipping a Campari. The scent of Joy stung in Clara's nostrils. She moved back to the bar itself. She was amazed at her own cunning as she leaned over towards the young barman.

'Isn't that lady a famous actress?' she whispered. 'My husband said he met her last night.'

'No, Madame.' The boy shook his head. 'That's Madame Duvalier. She's a regular guest here. Comes every year. Maybe she said that to play a joke on Monsieur Falconi?'

'Maybe.' Clara gave a savage smile. She turned and looked once more. Much older, sophisticated, very chic. She went outside to find Steven.

They chartered a boat and sailed round the coast. There was a picnic and a lot of wine. She felt sleepy and sensuous in the heat and wanted him to make love in the cabin. It seemed better to her than ever. She felt she had reached him again and that surely, please Virgin Mother and all the Saints, she would conceive this time . . .

Afterwards they dived off the boat and swam in a sea as clear and cold as sapphires.

'What are you thinking about, *caro*?' she asked as they dried in the sun on the foredeck. She reached out to take his hand, but he didn't notice. Hers lay outstretched towards him, until slowly the fingers curled up.

'Business,' he answered, his eyes closing against the glare of the sun. 'I think we should look into casinos back home.'

'That's Musso's territory,' she said dully.

'There's room,' Steven answered. He wasn't used to discussing things like this with a woman and he changed the subject. Only men talked about business. 'I'm going for another swim,' he said and dived off without waiting for her.

That night Clara put in a call to her father in New York.

The line was crackly. 'How's my little girl?' he kept asking.

She cried down the telephone. 'What's the matter, sweetheart? What's wrong? Aren't you happy? Come on, tell Poppa.'

'I will,' she promised. 'Oh Poppa, I miss you and Momma. I've been so happy, but something's gone wrong. There's a woman. She's making a play for Steven. Poppa, what can I do?'

There was silence for a moment. She thought they had been cut off. Then her father's voice came back on the line.

'You leave this to me, *cara mia*. Just tell me the name of this dame and where she lives.'

Clara did so. She said, 'Thank you, Poppa. Thank you,' and cried again. Then she hung up.

They flew to London first. It was a typical English summer, chilly and overcast. Clara was cold and bored. Even the art galleries and museums were dull by comparison with the glories of Paris. She hadn't mentioned the apartment in Paris to Steven. There'd be a right time and place, but it hadn't come. She went to the Italian church in Clerkenwell on a private pilgrimage and prayed for a child.

'Don't worry about it,' he told her. 'It'll happen. In God's good time, as my mother would say.'

'It's not what she'll say to me,' Clara protested. 'I want a honeymoon baby. They're always lucky children.'

She nestled into his side and murmured, 'I'll be glad to go home. I want to move into our own house.'

Steven said, yes, he would like that too, and went on thinking of the Musso family and their stranglehold on the gambling in Nevada. The honeymoon was over. It was time for Clara to become a wife and hopefully a mother very soon. And for him to get back to business and the man's world.

He had been watching Pauline Duvalier for three days. First in the hotel bar, then the restaurant; now her luggage was coming down and her car waited at the entrance. He had never even met her eye and she didn't notice him because he was middle-aged and bald. She drove herself in a prewar Lagonda. He envied her the car, but he followed it easily enough up the winding route of the Moyenne Corniche carved out of the face of the mountain, way above the coast. He saw her turn into the gates of a villa.

Big expensive place; must have wonderful views. It was to look like a robbery. He drove past and then managed to turn higher up and came down again. He eased the car just inside the gates. There were tall pine trees providing shade and privacy. He couldn't see the house once he was under them, and that meant he couldn't be seen. Living up there it had to be a daylight job. The gates would be closed at night and a car's headlights would be seen for miles. He got out and slipped his hand into his trouser pocket. He was stocky and powerful, underneath a layer of fat. He was past his best by fifteen years, but still a strong man. He was good with women and the elderly.

There'd be servants about the place. His watch said eleven thirty. Not time for lunch yet. He crept on the soles of his feet, keeping in the shadows, under the trees.

It was a big villa indeed, with a large open terrace and doors leading into the rooms. He was close against the wall when he saw her. She came out on to the terrace. She was smoking a cigarette and she'd changed into slacks and a shirt. Robbery with violence. She stood there for some minutes. Thinking of something, frowning.

In the old days he had collected from the brothel-keepers in Marseilles. When he was young, they gave him a choice of the girls along with the protection money. Then he moved to Nice after a bit of trouble when one of his victims died after a beating. The man was a greedy ponce who didn't want to pay up. There was plenty of work in Nice. Shopkeepers, restaurants, brothels – they all paid dues and he was one of the debt collectors. He had a wife and three children. They lived in an apartment on the seafront. He was well paid. He did odd evenings at the casino as a bouncer.

The woman still didn't move. Then just when he thought he might have to come up behind her on the terrace, which he didn't fancy, she swung round and went inside. He pulled the stocking over his head. He carried no weapon. He followed her. She didn't see him or hear him. He rabbit punched her and she fell without a sound. He locked the door and heaved her up from the floor and threw her on to the bed. She didn't feel anything because she never recovered consciousness. When he had finished he turned out the drawers, threw a few things on the floor and put a gold necklace, two rings and a gold lighter in his pocket. He slipped out and got back to his car. He was sitting in front of some traffic lights in Beaulieu when Pauline Duvalier's maid came to call her for lunch.

The doctors at the American Hospital in Nice told reporters that they doubted the unfortunate woman would survive her injuries. Every bone in her face had been smashed and she was certain to lose the sight of her left eye. It made headlines in the national press.

3

'It's very sweet of you, Jim,' Angela said gently. 'But I don't want to get married again.'

They were sitting by the fire and he had taken her hand and asked her to think it over for the third time in the past year.

'You don't have to hurry about it,' he said. 'You've got the boy's future to think of and he really needs a father. I'm very fond of him and he's fond of me. All I want is to make you happy, Angela.'

He was the soul of kindness and honesty. By now her father had retired with a bad heart and Jim Hulbert had taken over the practice with a younger partner, who was married and had a baby. He wasn't a bloodless man either, in spite of the difference in their ages. Most women could have been very happy with him.

Myself, Angela thought, I could have settled down here and been a good doctor's wife, spent my life in the village where I was born, and raised my children as I was raised. If I hadn't met Steven Falconi. If he didn't look at me out of my son's eyes.

'I know, Jim,' she said. 'But it's no use pretending I'll change my mind, I won't. I know all the arguments against it, but I know I can bring up Charlie myself. In fact, I asked you over tonight because I've got something to tell you.'

He looked downcast. It hurt her to refuse him, to dash his hopes. But it would be less than honest to stay on and let those hopes survive.

'You're leaving here,' he said.

'Yes, I am. How did you know?'

'Your mother mentioned something.'

Mrs Drummond had been her tactless self, too anxious to mince words. 'You'd better do something, Jim, before she goes off and gets this job she's so set on. Go and ask her again, won't you? Make her change her mind.' The parents wanted the marriage. It secured the practice, gave Angela a home and a husband they liked and trusted. And most of all provided a stable background for the boy.

They loved Charlie in their own way, but his foreign looks distressed them. 'There's not a drop of Drummond blood in him,' Angela's father used to complain to his wife and then add guiltily, 'but he's a fine little chap all the same.'

Angela said, 'I've applied for a job with a firm in London. They want a personnel officer. It sounds interesting and the money's not too bad. I went for an interview and they've accepted me. My nursing training helped.'

He thought: Not only that. Don't you realize what an attractive, intelligent woman you are? He said: 'What about Charlie?'

'He's eight,' she said. 'It's time he went away to school. The village school has been fine up till now, but he's got to be properly educated. My father's taken out a policy right through his public school. He's been awfully generous. So, in two weeks I'm moving to London.'

He said nothing for a moment. He smoked a pipe and took it out to fill it and tamp down the tobacco. Lighting and drawing it took some time.

'All right, my dear,' he said. 'Maybe you know what's best. I love you and I always will. If you change your mind and get fed up with London, I'll be here. We've had some very happy times together. Kiss me goodbye, will you?'

'Of course I will,' she said. 'I don't know what I would have done without you, Jim. You've been a darling to both of us. Thank you for everything.' She went into his arms and he kissed her.

'Good luck anyway,' he said. 'I'll be off now. We could have dinner together before you go.'

'I'd love to,' Angela said.

When he had gone, she poked at the fire and poured herself a glass of wine before she went to bed. It was sad, but also a relief. She didn't want to marry him or anyone else. She had to change her life, break away from her son before he became too dependent upon her, and hope that sometime she would find personal happiness. The idea of a job appealed to her more and more, as her son grew older and needed her supervision less.

I've got a lot of energy, she decided. And it's eating away inside me instead of being put to something useful. I'm bored, too, if I'm honest. I'm not ready for a life bounded by the village and its activities. If I had a man I loved, if it was possible with Jim, yes, but not otherwise. I'm going to see what the outside world has to offer before it's too late.

She got up, set the guard in front of the fire and locked up. Her parents were long ago in bed. She opened the door of her son's bedroom and looked inside. He was asleep, sprawled in the manner of small boys, halfway across the bed, with the pillow crumpled under him. Gently, Angela pulled it away and settled him properly.

He murmured and she bent down and kissed him. For a moment his arms locked round her neck.

'Mum?' It was a sleepy whisper.

'Yes, darling. Go to sleep. Goodnight.'

'Night.' He drifted away immediately.

For a moment she watched him, half lit from the open door.

I wonder where your father is, she thought. I wonder what he'd think of you. He's probably forgotten all about us. Men don't mourn. Only fools of women like me do that.

She closed the door firmly and went to her own room.

*

81

She found a flat in Chelsea. It was a top-floor walk-up, meanly furnished, but it was the most she could afford. Charlie was left behind with his grandparents and she went home to him every weekend. After the summer he started at his preparatory day school. Angela tried not to think about that separation. The first month, she almost gave up and went home.

She worked for a big firm of medical suppliers in Wigmore Street. The job was interesting. She liked people and was popular. But London was cold and unwelcoming to a lonely newcomer. Her neighbours in the converted house muttered good morning, and hurried past. Every evening she came back to the empty flat and in desperation began going to the local cinema alone, or taking long walks on the Embankment.

The weekends were overshadowed by the journey back on Sunday evening and the wrench of leaving Charlie behind. He had his father's deep, black eyes and they filled with tears when she kissed him goodbye. Joy Drummond didn't make it any easier.

'You've grown thin!' she declared, examining Angela on her second visit home. 'And you look so tired. I bet you're not eating properly!'

'Mother, I'm fine. I have a very good lunch and I cook for myself in the evenings.'

Joy ignored her signal to stop and went on relentlessly. 'Cook for yourself? Good Lord, haven't you made any friends? Don't tell me you sit there night after night on your own!' She sighed and said, 'I don't know why you want to do this, dear. I really don't. We all miss you, especially Charlie, don't you darling? Why on earth don't you drop the idea and come home?'

Angela kept her temper. Her mother meant well, that was the trouble. She thought: I can't get angry and tell her to please shut up, but any minute she's going to have Charlie in tears.

She said in a too-loud voice, 'I love my job and I'm

very happy. Now Charlie and I are going for a walk before lunch. Come on, darling.'

Joy Drummond looked after them and sighed again. She had a habit of talking out loud when she was alone. 'What a fool of a girl,' she said. 'Turning down someone like Jim who's so fond of her . . . going off to London to live by herself. Don't tell me she likes it. She looks perfectly miserable.'

She was still expressing every thought aloud when she went inside to see if her husband wanted anything. He was leading a very quiet life since his heart attack. He had mellowed. He missed his daughter and worried about her, but, unlike his wife, he never put his feelings into more than a very few words.

'Angela home?' he asked.

'Yes. She's gone off for a walk with Charlie. It's a lovely morning. Do her good after that awful London air. I can't breathe when I go up there.'

'You haven't been to London for three years,' he remarked.

'I couldn't breathe then,' she retorted. 'I wish she'd be sensible. She's so obstinate, that's the trouble.'

'Takes after me,' Hugh Drummond suggested. 'I think she's done the right thing. If she's not going to marry Jim, she's got to make a new life for herself. We won't last for ever. Leave her alone, Joy. Let her work it out for herself.'

'Oh, I will, I will. I was just talking, that's all. It'll be worse when Charlie goes away to school.'

'It'll be better,' her husband countered. 'Now, what's for lunch?'

It had been a long and busy day. Angela was tired. A niggling headache was just beginning. It was almost time to go home. Home had never seemed less appealing in terms of the impersonal flat and a long solitary evening ahead. She told herself not to be childish and stacked her papers ready for filing. An early night wouldn't do her any harm. The trouble was, there were so many early nights. The door to her office opened. She looked up. It was a girl called Judy from the accounts department. They'd had coffee together once or twice during the morning. She was popular and breezy. There was a jauntiness about her that suddenly brought Christine to mind.

'You finished, Angela?'

'Yes, nearly. I've just got to put this lot away.'

'We're going round the corner to the pub, why don't you come along?'

Angela hesitated. They were all younger than she was.

'Come on,' Judy urged. 'There's a crowd of us going,'

'I'd love to,' Angela said. 'I won't be a minute.'

She didn't even notice that her headache had gone. The pub round the corner from Wigmore Street was smoky, full of noise and people. The atmosphere was cheery. She had a gin and tonic and found herself saying how difficult it was to make friends in London.

Judy, sinking her second gin and orange, agreed heartily.

'Oh, you can drop dead in London and nobody'll even notice. I come from a small town on the south coast and I nearly died for the first few months up here. But you've got to get out and help yourself. That's what I found. No good waiting for the neighbours to knock on your door 'cos they won't. Knock on theirs first and say: "Hey, here I am, come in and have a drink or something." That's what you have to do.'

Angela was enjoying herself. People drifted in and out and most seemed to know each other. She discovered that it was a regular rendezvous for a lot of the younger staff in the office.

'We call ourselves the PPCs,' one young man told her, balancing a pint of beer in one hand and waving a cigarette about with the other. He was pleasantly tight, and so, Angela realized, was she.

'PPC? What's that?'

'Professional pub crawlers! We crawl from this pub to the next pub till we can't crawl any further.'

She thought it was the funniest thing she'd heard in years.

It was a great meeting place, that pub. There was an easy comradeship about pub life in London that she would never have found in the country. Friendships were struck up and continued beyond the confines of what was known as the Medic's Arms. Nobody even knew its proper name. There were no barriers of class and age. Harley Street specialists stood elbow to elbow with antique dealers and shop assistants, and Angela's tipsy friend who worked in the surgical appliances department. She was asked out to dinner, to the theatre. She took Judy's advice and gave drinks parties in her tiny flat.

An earnest young radiographer with a practice in Welbeck Street started taking her out regularly. Once he knew she was a doctor's daughter, he began to think of marriage.

There were other, less happy memories of those early years in London. Charlie, coming back from his first half term at boarding school and saying, 'Mum, can I have a picture of you and Dad? The other boys have pictures.'

And the sad lie she told him. 'You can have one of me, darling. But I haven't any pictures of your father. He was killed so soon, you see.'

Her mother dying unexpectedly from cancer. So quickly and with such little warning that she couldn't believe it had happened. Her father looking very old indeed after the funeral, refusing to let her give up her job and look after him.

'Don't be a damn fool, Angela. Things are going well for you. You're happy up there. I've had a good innings and I'm all right. Old Mrs P. can look after me and you pop down when you can. I'll miss your mother, though.' He had devastated Angela by bursting into tears.

Happy memories, sad memories, and always the joy of her son to enrich what was good and compensate for what was not. He was thirteen and just going to public school. Very tall, better-looking than his father, with something of the Drummonds in him after all. He had become the light of his grandfather's life. There were photographs of Charlie playing in the school First Eleven, Charlie in the rugger team as a winger, even disguised in fencing mask and suit posing with another little boy for the school magazine.

Seeing her father at every sports day, prize-giving and school concert, Angela thought: What a lot he's given to Charlie. And what a lot Charlie's given to him. My son has the father he needed and Dad's got a son to make up for the one he lost in the war.

The Wigmore Street job had led to better things. She was a personal assistant to the medical director of a large private health insurance company. She had taken a secretarial course and gained a diploma.

She heard about the vacancy from a friend. She had a lot of friends by now. If she spent an evening alone it was from choice. The attic flat in Chelsea was replaced by a smart service flat in Sloane Avenue, with a restaurant and maid service. Total privacy for a woman living alone if she wanted it. And sometimes she did. She'd had many men friends, but only two lovers in the five years since she came to London. She was not in love with either of them. There was no commitment beyond a mutual attraction and compatibility. When marriage was mentioned, Angela was firm. She wasn't interested. Charlie didn't need a stepfather, just as he started adolescence. It sounded reasonable. The truth wouldn't be believed. She faced that truth in the loneliest hour of the night, when the clock by her bedside showed four in the morning and she knew sleep wouldn't come. It didn't happen often. But when it did, she admitted that her love for Steven Falconi had not died. It would one day; it must. But not yet. Perhaps never, because her son was his living reminder.

Money was not a problem. Her salary was generous

and surprisingly her mother had left her everything. It wasn't riches, but it provided an income and a little capital when she needed it. 'To my beloved Daughter, Angela Frances Lawrence,' the will said.

Hugh Drummond's explanation was typically down to earth. 'Of course she left everything to you. I don't need anything. I'm quite all right. We talked about it and she said you were the one who'd benefit most. And the boy, of course. Quite right.'

She wore her mother's engagement ring, the little sapphire with two diamonds on either side, and the Sicilian wedding ring she'd worn round her neck at the Tremoli hospital. Falconi's ring. She was Falconi's wife so long as she wore that ring. And Charlie had a dead hero for a father.

Her son was fifteen when she decided to change her job and take him away for a holiday. Her relationship with her boss had reached a difficult phase. It wasn't a working one any longer. She didn't want to start an affair with him and the only solution was to leave. It was the end of August and they were together at Haywards Heath in the old house, with her father and a decrepit Mrs P. going through the same routine of forty years.

'When do you start your new job?' he asked her.

They were sitting out in the garden. It was hot that year and the doctor didn't like the sun. He sheltered under a big coloured garden umbrella that hadn't been used often enough to fade. Charlie was lying on his back, holding a book in the air.

'End of September. Charlie, you can't read like that. Why don't you sit on a seat?'

'Don't nag, Mum,' was the response. 'I like reading lying down. Don't I, Grandpa?'

'Used to like it myself,' Hugh Drummond agreed. 'Pity you had to leave your old firm,' he said to Angela. 'Though I suppose it's a good thing to move on.'

'I think so,' she answered. She wouldn't have dreamed of telling him the real reason. 'It'll be interesting and I'll travel. That's what really appealed to me, even if it is less money.'

'Never thought you'd be a businesswoman,' her father said.

'I'm not,' she insisted. 'I just smooth the edges for the businessman. I'm a good organizer, I enjoy it.'

The job was a complete break from her last position. Secretary and personal assistant to the head of a small but dynamic advertising firm. And no personal problems likely there. The man she would be working for was not interested in women. He lived with his partner. He had the flair, and the older man the money. Angela thought they were both cultivated, pleasant and amusing. 'Working for us,' as the younger told her, 'won't be easy, Mrs Lawrence, but I promise you it will be fun.'

She looked down at her son, still obstinately reading with the book high above his head, and smiled. He was going through a lanky stage, outgrowing himself. His first round of serious exams was approaching next term.

She said suddenly, 'Charlie, I've been thinking. I could do with a holiday. Somewhere abroad. What do you think? Shall we go away somewhere?'

He rolled over and sat up, bright with expectation. 'What a super idea! Where shall we go?'

'How about France – lots of sunshine.' Seeing his face she said, 'Wouldn't you like that? We could take a friend so you wouldn't be bored.'

'Oh, I wouldn't be bored, Mum. I'll go to France if you want to. I went off to Belgium to stay with Leo last year and you stayed at home.'

'That's not the point,' Angela said. 'Look, darling, it's a holiday for both of us. Now I asked you – where would you like to go? Come on, *you* say.'

He hesitated for a moment. 'Well, I'd really like to go to America. I know it'd cost too much money, but Jordan went there when his sister got married. They went to New York and he said it was the most *super* place. He never stopped going on about it. I suppose we couldn't go there, could we? Just for a week?'

'New York,' she heard her father say. 'What on earth do you want to go there for? All those frightful bloody skyscraper things? What's wrong with France? You'd get lots of swimming and tennis.'

'It's the skyscrapers I want to see,' his grandson insisted. 'The Empire State, the Rockefeller Building. Jordan climbed right up into the Statue of Liberty's head!'

'Charlie, darling,' Angela said. 'Would you really like to go there?'

'Oh, Mum, could we? You mean it? A week'd be fine, if we could manage it.'

'I think we could afford more than a week,' she told him. 'On one condition.'

'Anything,' he promised. 'You just name it!'

'You don't read your French translation upside down from now on. And when we get back, you work really hard for good results.'

'Don't you worry. I'll get distinctions in every subject! New York. I can't believe it. Wait till I ring up Jordan and tell him!'

'Not on my phone you don't!' Hugh Drummond called after Charlie as he rushed into the house. 'They jabber on for hours, these young people. No idea of the cost. Can you afford this, Angela? I can help out a bit if need be. Always thought America was damned expensive. He was jumping up and down, wasn't he? Very excited.'

'Yes, he was,' Angela agreed. 'Don't worry, Dad. I've got some extra money. Mum's dividends have been very good lately. Charlie deserves a real treat. He's had such good reports right the way through. He'll love it. We'll go.'

She went up to London to see her new boss before going away. The office was in Holborn, three floors of an old house, with a clean decor inside, modern artwork and a nice office for her. David Wickham was her boss. He showed her round the building and then took her upstairs.

'If you want anything changed, Mrs Lawrence, just say so. I'm a great believer in the effect of environment on one's work. A lousy wallpaper would put *me* off, so why shouldn't it affect someone else?'

'I wouldn't change anything,' Angela answered. 'It's all so smart. Not like the first place I worked.'

He laughed. 'The Truss Shop – I can imagine! I hope you're going to take a vacation before you start. I warned you, we'll work you into the ground.' He affected slight Americanisms like 'vacation'.

'I'm going to New York with my son,' she told him. 'Just for ten days.'

'How exciting! Is it your first visit? You'll love it. It's the most dynamic place on earth. I feel completely revitalized the minute I get there. Where are you staying?'

Angela mentioned a modest little hotel on the West Side. Wickham summed up the situation instantly. She was a nice attractive person, and she would fit in well. He knew the background. War widow, one son, making it on her own.

'That's a crap heap,' he said. 'You can't stay there. Why don't you let me fix up something for you? No cost either. I've got a whole mass of friends over there. Leave it with me. I'll call you in a few days.' He said 'call' instead of telephone.

'I couldn't,' she protested. 'I haven't even started working for you yet, Mr Wickham.'

'Let's make it Angela and David,' he countered. 'And don't worry. I'll have my pound of flesh – in fact you could look up a couple of clients for me while you're there. That'd make you feel better!'

'Yes, it would,' she said. 'Much better.'

'I'll be in touch,' he promised. They shook hands. He had shrewd eyes but they were kind.

90

'Thank you,' she said. 'Thank you so much. My son is so excited about going.'

'You'll have a great time,' he said.

They flew on the Stratocruiser. Charlie's enthusiasm was such a reward. The much admired Jordan from school had only sailed over on a boring old liner. Flying on this super plane was just so grand. It was a long flight and they both slept after a time. They landed early in the morning at Idlewild and the crisp, bright New York air was like champagne. The trite old cliché came to mind, but the adrenalin began to flow as they drove into Manhattan. Angela found herself as impressed as the excited boy beside her. The famous skyline was more beautiful than any photograph. The sun shone, sparkling on the river. The trees in Central Park were changing colour. Suddenly the world was full of energy and magic. She put her arm round her son's shoulder and hugged him.

'It's wonderful, isn't it, darling? We're going to have a tremendous time.'

Thanks to David Wickham they'd been lent a small apartment on East 70th Street. Two bedrooms, a living room and two bathrooms. And the luxury of television. Wickham had provided them with a list of restaurants that were good but not expensive and some suggestions for sightseeing. The two clients she was to contact had offices on Park Avenue. She could call them after a few days.

Charlie loved everything. He loved American food, American soft drinks, hamburgers and ice-cream parlours. They went to the Frick Museum and he even enthused about that to please Angela; the Statue of Liberty by boat, up into the dizzy height of the great head, with the panorama of the Hudson River spread out below them. They walked in Central Park and took a ride in a horse-drawn carriage. They strolled down Broadway at night, marvelling at the lights, and went into a cinema to see the very latest hit movie. They ate Italian and Chinese and the days sped into each other until one morning Angela realized that it was time she paid David Wickham back for all his kindness.

The first client gave her an appointment in his office at eleven o'clock and then invited her out to dinner. He was a very important manufacturer of luxury leather goods, with stores in seven major cities right across the States. He was also nice and, in true American style, eager to show her the best restaurant in the city. She accepted and left Charlie in the apartment for the evening with a supply of Coke and hamburgers and the television.

'I've got a headache,' Clara Falconi stated. 'I've had a headache for three days. Not that you give a damn, of course.'

Steven didn't even turn around. He knew all about Clara's headaches. He'd said to her once, driven beyond patience by her complaints about her health, his family, their life together, 'You've got the headache, but I've got you. And Jesus, that's some headache, I can tell you!'

It led to one of their worst rows. He stayed away for a week while she calmed down and went to see yet another specialist. There were no children after nine years, and no explanation either. She didn't conceive and Steven broke every male taboo by going for tests himself although he knew they were a farce. He'd already got one woman pregnant. The tests showed a high fertility rate. At least it gave him a respite from Clara. She was always accusing Angela of deceiving him. More than anything, he wanted to stop her taunting him with that.

She dismissed the idea of adoption with scorn. He didn't press it. He didn't want someone else's child.

'Ever since Sunday,' Clara said, 'I've had this god-damned pain in my head. You know I hate those lunches with your father and mother and your brother and his bitch of a wife sneering at me. They push those children up my nose every chance they get! I won't go again. I've made up my mind.'

92

He turned and said, 'My father likes to have the family for Sundays. And when he asks us, Clara, we go. Like we go to your family. I don't hear you griping about that.'

'They understand,' she retorted. 'They're *my* family. Don't you think Poppa's disappointed? Don't you think he'd like grandchildren?'

'After nine years, he's forgotten.' Steven was brutal. Aldo Fabrizzi was no friend to him. Clara had seen to that. He went to the Fabrizzi house for their family gatherings, and Clara was not going to disrespect his parents.

'Well, I'm not coming tonight,' she countered. 'My head's bursting. You can entertain your congressman on your own.'

'Okay.' He didn't argue. It irritated him because the congressman was bringing his wife. He was a valuable contact. They were having trouble with a Federal investigation into gambling, and he needed the congressman's news and views. They were talking of an open hearing for a Senate committee. That had really alarmed Steven. It had taken five years of pressure to remove the old warrior Musso from his position of monopoly. His son had died of a heroin overdose. Fabrizzi had arranged for someone to give him a lethal fix.

But Musso gathered his men and held fast. He wanted no partners and he loosed a little well-aimed violence at the Falconi and Fabrizzi families himself. Some minor characters had died.

The Falconis and Fabrizzis were so well guarded that it was impossible to target them. They bought up property as close to the Musso casinos as they could. He was constantly surveyed by enemies and several times fires broke out in the gambling halls. People began to drift away. Musso's take was dropping. He was old, his son was dead. He had a mild heart attack. Suddenly the fight was over. There was a meeting at which Steven was present and the truce was made. The deal cut Musso in for a good percentage of his own profits and the control passed directly to the Falconis with the Fabrizzis as equal financial partners. Steven was given the management of that side of the business. And he had built it up steadily over the last four years into a huge investment, branching out into hotels and restaurants and resorts, with the gambling as the lure. It was Steven's idea too to entice Hollywood stars down to entertain the clients. A veil of respectability was drawn over the uglier side of the organization. It became a kind of showbiz spectacle.

And he had remembered that impression gained in Monte Carlo. Class was all important to attract the big-time spenders. The smoky rooms full of housewives risking their few dollars on a crooked wheel were balanced by the plush salons and tuxedoed attendants paying court to the super-rich.

Steven was a big man: respected, admired and feared; when he talked, even the older men listened. He had proved himself. He had the brains. There were plenty of men around to supply brawn when it was needed. Luca Falconi was right to be proud of his eldest son. Proud of the younger boy, Piero, with his clutch of handsome children. He wasn't clever like Steven, but he was tough and he made his father think of the old days, when a man had to think fast and act faster to stay alive. But they were the old days. It was just like any other business now.

Steven finished dressing. Clara watched him bitterly. She wondered whether he would call up some other woman and take her along. There were always other women. Like her empty womb, her jealousy obsessed her.

No, she decided. The congressman was a family man. He took bribes from the Families, but he was careful of his reputation. Steven wouldn't take out one of his whores instead of his wife. She hoped it embarrassed him. She hoped one day she could reach close enough to hurt him as he had hurt her. He picked up his wallet, buttoned his jacket and went to the door.

'Steven.' Her voice commanded his attention. 'Don't wake me when you come in.'

94

'Take a sleeping pill,' he said and went out.

He had a driver and a bodyguard who would sit in the front seat, keeping watch. The car was plated and the windows bulletproof.

'Les A,' he told them as his bodyguard ushered him into the back seat. He leaned back, searching for a cigarette.

She wouldn't come with him. Okay, she wanted to be persuaded, cajoled. She wanted to do her duty as a wife and make out it was some kind of favour. To hell with her. He said it to himself, lighting the cigarette, seeing the traffic weaving in and out. There'd been a murder attempt on him eighteen months ago. Driving along like this, slowed up by the traffic. A car pulled up alongside at a traffic intersection and the next thing the window slid down and a gun was pointing at him. The glass shattered but held. His driver didn't take a chance. He shot the lights and sped to safety. Nobody knew who was responsible. He and Clara were going through a particularly bad time in their marriage when it happened. They lived a life of hell together and there couldn't be a divorce. Not while Aldo Fabrizzi was alive. When he died, Steven would file against her outside New York City and she could do her goddamnedest after that. His father hated her; all the Falconis hated her now. Not just because she was childless, but for the bile on her tongue and the arrogant way she behaved.

He dismissed her from his mind. He had business on hand. Maybe a pleasant evening. He liked the food at Les A. His taste had changed over the years and the mammoth Italian meals his relatives and compatriots enjoyed didn't appeal to him so much. Clara wouldn't eat more than a mouthful of pasta. She said it ruined her figure. She was very conscious of her looks. She spent lavishly on clothes and furs and treatments. She was beautiful as a mature woman. He couldn't bear to sleep with her anymore.

He met the congressman in the bar. He behaved

gallantly towards the congressman's blonde wife, kissing her hand. She thought he was very attractive. Dangerous too. She liked that. They ordered rye whiskey and she chose a brandy sour. Steven had been making small talk, apologizing for Clara's absence, when he happened to look straight at the door and saw Angela walk in ahead of an older man. The lights were flattering, not too bright, the atmosphere a little hazy with tobacco. But he saw her. She even hesitated for a few seconds, so that he had time to stare at her and make sure he wasn't going crazy.

'Mr Falconi?' the congressman's wife inquired. He didn't answer. He didn't hear her speak. He sat and stared at a dead woman who had come to life and was smiling, walking towards a table not twenty yards away.

'Mr Falconi, do you have a light? I've left my lighter at home.'

It was the second time she'd asked. He felt for the gold Dunhill and clicked it for her.

'I'm sorry,' he managed to say. 'I've just seen an old friend. Excuse me.'

He didn't go up to her. He went to the barman. 'There's a man and a woman over there. Do you know them?'

'I know him. Mr Forrest. He comes here often. I don't know the lady.'

'Are they booked for dinner?'

'I guess so. He asked for the menu.'

'What the hell's he doing?' the congressman murmured to his wife.

'I don't know. I don't see any old friend at the bar. He's talking to the barman.'

'They're funny guys,' her husband said. 'I'm sorry, honey, I'm going to have to talk a few things over with him. It won't take long. I thought his wife would've been here.'

'That's okay.' She smiled at him. 'I don't mind. Just so long as you throw me a word now and then.'

Steven leaned closer. He had money visible in his hand. A number of folded dollar bills.

'Get Luis,' he said to the barman. 'Tell him to call the lady to the phone when they're at dinner. And give me the nod before he does it. You got that clear.'

'No phone to the table?' the man inquired.

'No. Out in the booth.'

'You know her name? Who's calling her?'

'Try Drummond,' Steven said. 'Don't say who's calling. There's fifty here. Twenty for you, the rest for Luis. No mistakes.'

'No mistakes, Mr Falconi.'

He went back to his guests and said, 'Shall we go to the table? We can order upstairs.'

As they went out he glanced behind him. She was sitting with her back to him. He could see the shining blonde hair and the set of her neck on her shoulders. It wasn't an illusion. It couldn't be. Everyone has a double somewhere in the world. He'd heard that said and not believed it. He didn't believe it now. He wasn't mistaken. Even with her back to him he knew her. He went through the motions of ordering dinner, studying the wine list, while he watched and waited for her to come into the restaurant. He had to see her once more. In a clear light, making allowances for sixteen years.

She was different, of course. The girl of twenty was in her thirties now; older and sophisticated. A black dress, very simple; the same sun-coloured hair he used to thread through his fingers. The same look in the eyes. And the slight smile he had imagined on her lips so often at the height of his frantic grieving.

A furious anger engulfed him. He had to keep his hands out of sight because they shook with the force of it. She wasn't dead. She'd cheated him. She'd gone and left him believing she was dead and their unborn baby destroyed by a bomb that killed someone else. He hoped he was making sense; the congressman was talking about the Federal investigation.

'You know what it is when these sons of bitches get their teeth into a thing like this. However straight your operation is, they're going to start screaming corruption and racketeering.'

'I know.' He heard his own voice answering and was surprised how normal it sounded. 'That's why it's so important for us to know what line they're going to take, so we have a chance to put our case. We'll have the best legal advice, but we don't want to get caught up in an investigation, be subpoenaed. My father's not so young and he's got a weak heart.' The lie tripped off his tongue while anger twisted his insides into knots.

It was her. He couldn't be mistaken. He recognized every movement, every gesture. 'Try Drummond,' he'd said. It was the last chance to prove that the woman wasn't Angela. If she were some incredible look-alike she wouldn't respond to the name. The message would be meaningless.

The head waiter, Luis, moved towards him and gave Steven a slight nod. He watched as Luis went to the table and murmured to the blonde woman. The congressman stopped in the middle of a sentence. Falconi was paying no attention. He was staring at a couple across the restaurant. The woman was on her feet, her partner rising only to be waved back. Steven saw the anxious expression on her face as she hurried out. He had wept tears for her, believing her dead. She was alive and he had been betrayed.

He said to the congressman, 'Excuse me. I'll be right back,' and he was following her out to the telephone booth on the lower floor. He was just behind her as she pulled the door open. She had lifted the receiver when he thrust in with her, pulling the door closed, sealing them inside. The booths were soundproof. If she screamed, no one would hear her. It was light enough to see her face, for her to see him. He crushed her against the wall and caught her arm, locking it behind her. The telephone receiver swung on its cord, knocking against them.

She said, 'Steven. Steven.'

He didn't hear his name, only the voice he knew so well. He leaned on her, hard, hurting her, and whispered, 'Angelina?' He felt her body forced against him and he knew that too. 'Angelina,' he said again. 'Where have you been all these years?'

'Steven? It's you, Steven?'

'It's me,' he told her.

'Let go my arm,' she said and her voice trembled. 'You're hurting me.'

'We're walking out of here,' he said. 'We're going somewhere we can talk about old times. I have a gun. You try and get away from me and I'll kill you. You understand me, Angelina?'

'You don't need to threaten me,' she said. 'I understand. I'll come with you.'

He smiled down at her. 'Sure you will,' he said. He drew her out of the booth, gripping her by the elbow so tightly that his fingers sank into the soft skin. 'Downstairs,' he told her. 'We get your coat. You send a message to the boyfriend and you make it sound good.'

He forced her down the stairs and paused at the reception desk. 'Send a message to Congressman Fuller,' he said to the hat-check girl. 'Say I've been called away suddenly.' He dug into his pocket and scattered change. 'And the lady's leaving too. Aren't you, honey?'

'Yes,' Angela said. She spoke to the girl. 'I'm with Mr Forrest. Tell him my boy's not feeling well and I've had to go home.'

'You have a coat?' the girl asked her.

'It's a cape. It's over there . . . my ticket . . .'

'Never mind the ticket,' Steven interrupted. He took the cape and threw it over his arm. He called to the doorman. 'Call up my car, will you, Stanley?'

He was holding Angela so tightly she couldn't have pulled away. He hurried her out on to the pavement and thrust her into the back of the car as it pulled up, his bodyguard shielding him before he slammed the door and jumped into the front. It moved off at speed. He leaned forward and spoke to the driver.

'The apartment,' he said and then closed the glass partition.

Angela said, 'Where are we going?' He wasn't holding her now. She had drawn away from him into the corner. There was a red mark on her arm that would turn into a bruise.

'To a place I take my whores,' he answered. 'The honest ones, I pay them. What sort of a whore runs out on her husband – never sends a word, not a letter, nothing? Tell me, what sort of a *woman* does that?'

She saw the hatred in his face and turned away. 'My God,' she said. 'What's happened to you?'

'Go ahead and pray,' he mocked her. 'You'll need to, Angelina.'

'I'm not afraid of you,' she said. 'So you needn't threaten me.'

When the car stopped he told the driver in Italian to wait and then he turned to Angela. 'We're going up to my apartment. There's a man behind us. So don't try anything.'

She didn't answer. She walked into the lobby and into the lift. On the fourth floor they got out and Steven's bodyguard unlocked the front door and went ahead of them.

'Okay, Don Stefano,' he announced and stood aside for them.

'In here,' Steven directed.

She found herself in a large duplex, with sprawling white sofas and mirrored glass. She saw herself and him reflected everywhere she looked. He faced her, rocking slightly on the balls of his feet. His hands were clenched into fists.

Suddenly he reached out, caught her left hand. 'You married again? You married some other bastard? What happened to my child?'

'I'm not married,' she said. 'That's my mother's ring and the wedding ring you gave me.'

'You got rid of my child?' he asked her and his voice was very quiet. 'You went home and you got rid of it?'

She looked at him and suddenly he saw contempt and an anger to match his own. 'If you think that, you can go to hell. I had your son, Steven.'

He said slowly, 'Now tell me why you ran out on me.'

'Because I found out what you were. I didn't want my child brought up to be like you. And how right I was! You're vicious and cruel, Steven. I couldn't see it then, but I can see it now. You threatened to kill me and I believe you meant it. You're everything they said you were!'

'Who said?' he demanded. He took a step towards her. 'Who said? What are you talking about?'

She turned away from him. 'They sent for me,' she said. 'Major Thompson, and another man. They showed me a dossier. They told me what you were really doing in Sicily. I'd never even heard of the Mafia, but I didn't need to. It was all there. Your family, the people you wanted me to go and live with – murder, crime, every vice in the book. That's just how he described you. I tried to deny it. I tried to defend you. But it wasn't any use. I couldn't live with you. I couldn't have my child brought up with people like you. So I got myself dismissed and I went home.'

'Why?' he questioned. 'Why did they tell you?'

'You asked for a passage for me,' she reminded him. 'At the end of it they asked me if I still wanted to go.'

'And you said no,' he countered. 'So they got themselves off the hook. By showing you all that crap.'

'Wasn't it true?' she challenged him. 'Isn't it true now?'

He didn't answer. He sat down heavily, staring up at her.

'I got back to Sicily when I heard about the hospital. I searched for you. I was going crazy. They were still digging bodies out. Nobody knew who or how many

101

were still buried there. I was trying to find you. I saw the watch I gave you, all smashed up. Blood on it. They said it was found on one of the bodies.'

'I gave it to Christine,' she said. 'She was killed.'

He didn't seem to hear. 'I thought you were dead,' he went on. 'You and the baby. I tell you, I went crazy. You talk about what I did in Sicily? I'll tell you what I did after I got back to Naples. I went into a regular unit. I wanted to fight. I wanted to kill the bastards that killed you.'

There was silence then. The mirrored images were still. At last he spoke to her.

'Will you have a drink? You look like you could use one.'

'No, I'd like to leave.'

'Of course. Sure. Would you mind if I had a scotch? It won't take long.' He poured himself a drink. His hand was shaking. He had behaved like a savage. Threatening her, using his strength to hurt her. 'You're vicious and cruel.' Those were her words and they were no less than he deserved. He came over to her and held out the glass. 'Take a little,' he said. 'We used to share our wine, remember?'

'It was a long time ago,' Angela answered. 'Things have changed.'

'You haven't,' he said. 'I knew you as soon as you came in that door. For sixteen years I thought you were dead, Angela, and then you walked into that bar and I thought I'd gone crazy. Do you have any idea what it felt like to see you alive and know I'd screwed up my whole life?'

She took the glass from him. She sipped the whisky.

'It must have been a shock. It was a shock for me too. But it's sixteen years. You've made your life, Steven, I've made mine. And I really want to go now.'

He said, 'Can you forgive me? Can you forgive me for treating you like I did? Can you try and understand a little?'

'There's nothing to forgive,' Angela told him. She

handed him the glass and for a second their fingers touched. 'I shouldn't have said those things to you. You frightened me, Steven.'

'I know,' he said. 'I know. I wish I could make it up to you. Sixteen years. It's a long time. Won't you give me a few minutes?'

He's suffered, she thought suddenly. It's in his face and his eyes. He's not been happy. 'All right,' she said.

'And you'll forgive me? You'll try to forget how I acted?'

'I'll try,' she promised. 'If you'll forgive me for hurting you all those years ago.'

'Tell me about the boy.'

'He's fifteen now. He's at school in England. He's doing very well.'

'What did you tell him?'

'I said you were killed just after we got married. I changed my name to Lawrence and said I was a widow.'

'You could have found someone,' he forced himself to say. 'You didn't have to go it alone.'

'I didn't want anyone,' she answered. 'I had my parents. We lived with them till he was eight. I didn't want to marry again, although there was a man who asked me. But I didn't love him.'

'I guess it wasn't easy, bringing up the boy without a father.'

'He made it easy. He was a lovely little boy and he's growing up into a fine young man. I'm very proud of him, Steven. I think you would be too.'

There was no anger, no menace left in him.

She said, 'I'd better be going now.'

He came over and held out his hand to help her up. She hesitated and then took it.

'Do you have to go?' he asked her.

'Yes. It's getting late.'

'Will I ever get to see my son?' He was still holding her hand.

'You must be married,' she said. 'You must have other children.'

'I'm married,' he agreed. 'We have no children. We never will have. It's a marriage made in hell. Angela. Don't leave me. Please don't leave me.'

'I've got to,' she answered. It was like a madness, feeling him closing in on her, the appeal in his voice and eyes. 'If you want to see him,' she said. 'He's here. I brought him with me. He'll still be up.'

She drew back from him. Another moment and something might have happened that must never happen between them now.

He draped the cape over her shoulders. 'What does he look like?'

'You,' she answered. 'You'll see for yourself.'

In the lift he said to her, 'Why didn't you wait for me? Why didn't you trust me, Angela? I'd have changed my life.'

'Would you, Steven? Honestly?'

'I guess not,' he admitted. 'I'd have just talked you out of leaving. Jesus, I could have sent money, helped you out.'

'Without coming to find us and bringing us back?'

'The first thing I'd have done,' he said. 'How well you got to know me, even in such a little time.'

He handed her into the car. She gave the address of the apartment. Suspicion flared in him for a moment. 'How come you're not in a hotel? Who owns this place?'

'A client of the company I'm going to work for,' she explained. 'It's very small, but it's much nicer for Steven. And it's saved me a lot of money.'

Satisfied, he relaxed. He told the driver to wait. Angela opened the front door. It's two floors up,' she said and went ahead of him.

On the first landing he stopped her. 'Who do you say I am?'

'Mr Falconi, who gave me a lift home from the dinner.'

At the apartment door she pressed the buzzer. It opened and Charlie stood there. 'Hello, Mum. You're back early. Have a nice time?'

They were inside and Steven Falconi could see his son clearly. Tall, dark, open faced. A Falconi through and through from the black hair to the olive skin and the deep black eyes.

He heard Angela say, 'We did finish early. This is my son, Charlie. Mr Falconi kindly gave me a lift home.'

The boy held out his hand. 'How do you do, Sir.'

He shook it. 'Glad to know you, Charlie.'

He had a strong, confident grip. It's like looking in the mirror, Steven thought. Doesn't he see it too?

'Do stay and have a drink, won't you?' Angela invited. For a moment their eyes met over the boy's head.

'I'd like that,' he answered.

'Scotch? Or I have some wine if you'd rather.'

'Scotch,' he answered. 'Water and ice. Thank you.'

'I'll get it,' Angela said and went out, leaving him alone with his son. He found it difficult to speak.

Young Charlie said politely, 'Do you live in New York, Sir?'

'Part of the time. Mostly I'm in Florida.'

'New York's such an exciting place,' the boy enthused. 'I've had such a super time. What's Florida like?'

'Very different. It's hot and sunny. There's good deep-sea fishing, and water-skiing.'

'Sounds terrific. I'd love to go there one day.'

'Maybe you will,' Steven said. 'You're in school in England?'

'Yes. I go to Highfields. It's a super school. I've got my first lot of exams next term.' He pulled a wry face. 'I've promised Mum I'll do well.'

'I guess you will,' his father said. She'd brought up a fine boy, he thought. The quaint English manners, calling him Sir. His young nephews were spoiled and truculent.

Angela's son said suddenly, 'Actually I'm half

American. My father was in the American Army. He was killed fighting in Italy. Just after Mum married him. Maybe that's why I like New York so much.'

'Maybe,' Steven Falconi agreed. 'I'm sorry about your father.'

'Mum told me all about him. He was jolly brave. Rotten luck for her though.'

'Here *is* your mother,' Steven said and got up. He took the whisky from Angela. 'I've been hearing about Charlie's school,' he said.

'And I've been telling him about my father,' the boy interrupted. 'Where was the place he was killed, Mum?'

'Salerno,' Angela answered. She didn't look near Steven Falconi. 'A lot of Americans were killed in that battle.'

She thought: Anyone who saw them together would know there was a blood relationship. They're so alike it's uncanny.

She said to her son, 'Darling, I have some business to talk over with Mr Falconi. Would you pop off to bed now?'

'Okay, Mum. Goodnight, Sir.'

They shook hands again. Steven watched him pat his mother affectionately on the shoulder. He was too grown-up to kiss her in front of a stranger. The door closed on him and they were alone.

'You've done well, Angelina,' he said slowly. 'He's a great boy.'

'I'm glad you think so.'

'I want to do something for him. For both of you.'

She shook her head. 'Not money, Steven. We don't need it. I've got a good job and my mother left me some capital. Charlie's school is paid for right through till he leaves. My father did that. It's good of you and I'll always be grateful, but we don't need anything.'

'Because of where it's come from? Is that it?'

'I didn't want to say so. I don't want to hurt you.'

'You're not hurting me. You could be hurting the boy.

106

What's he going to do when he leaves school? What about college – he's intelligent – who's going to pay for that?'

'I will, if necessary,' she answered.

He got up and paced up and down the small room. 'I can settle money on him,' he said. 'You can't stop me.'

'No, I can't. You can make him rich, Steven, and ruin his life. He'd ask questions. He'd find out that I'd lied to him; he'd find out what you did to make that money.'

'You deny him to me,' he accused her. 'He's my only son. And I married you, Angela. You're my wife, remember?'

'You have a wife,' she said. 'I'm sorry if you're not happy, but I shouldn't have brought you here. I shouldn't have let you meet him.' She got up and went to the door.

He came close to her and said, 'You feel nothing for me?'

'I love my son,' she answered. 'I've made a life for him and he's happy. I can't let myself feel anything for you, Steven, because of what it would do to him. Now please. Please go.'

She opened the door and stood aside.

'I don't believe you,' Steven Falconi said quietly. He reached out and put a heavy hand on her shoulder.

She said quickly, 'No, Steven, don't . . .'

'I won't, not with our son in there asleep. I'll go now, Angela, but I'll be back.'

She went to the boy's bedroom and opened the door. He was asleep. She remembered suddenly doing the same thing the night she refused Jim Hulbert and prepared to leave for London and a new start. She had done the right thing then, instead of taking the soft option. She must do the right thing now. For her son, not for herself.

'You feel nothing for me?' His question haunted her that long night without sleep and she dared not face the answer. Fear, anger, pity . . . a whisper of desire inside her when he touched her. Were those the sum of her feelings? Or was her love still there, a bar to other men, a weapon turned against herself? We have to get away, she repeated, we have to, before he comes again. And he will. I know him. I saw it in his eyes. He won't let Charlie go. He won't let me go. And God knows whether I'd be strong enough next time. I'm strong now.

'Mum, why do we have to go early?'

'Charlie, I've already told you. I spoke to David Wickham and he wants me to start next week. I'm sorry, but we've got to go back. I know you're enjoying it, but it can't be helped.'

'But when did you speak to him?' he questioned. 'You didn't say anything about it last night.'

'I didn't have time. Now stop arguing, will you please? I'll make it up to you another time. You don't think I want to go home, do you?'

He saw her blinking away tears. He said to himself something very scatological about Mr David Wickham which would have surprised Angela, and went in to put his clothes into the cases.

She phoned through and got tickets on the afternoon flight to London. They cost a lot more than the originals, but there were no cheap seats. She telephoned the second client Wickham had asked her to see, and made the same excuse as she had done to Forrest, who had to be telephoned too. Her son was ill and she was flying him home. Mr Forrest, who was extremely annoyed at being left in the middle of dinner, wasn't sympathetic.

She thought: He'll put in a bad word for me with the agency, and then shrugged it off. It couldn't be helped. She wished there'd been an earlier flight.

'I'll be back,' Steven had said. As she packed and tidied up the apartment, she dreaded hearing the bell, finding him standing there, forbidding her to go. But the hours passed and nothing happened.

'I'll go down to the deli and get something for us to eat,' she said.

'I'll go,' her son offered.

'No, you stay here. I'll get some hamburgers. And don't answer the telephone.'

'Why not?' he asked.

'Because I say so!'

She hurried out and he grimaced. He'd never seen her in such a bad mood and so close to crying as well. He said something even nastier about Mr Wickham and settled down in sullen mood to watch the wonderful American television for the last time. When the bell buzzed he pressed the catch release and opened the apartment door.

'Hello,' Steven Falconi said. 'Is your mother at home?'

'Er, no. She's gone down to get some lunch. Down to the deli. We're going back to England, worse luck!'

'Mind if I come in and wait?'

'No, no, please come in. I'll turn the set off.'

'Don't mind me,' Steven said. 'Go ahead and watch.'

'I'll get that,' he said as the buzzer went again. He opened the door to Angela and said, 'Let me take that,' and lifted the package out of her arms. He turned to the boy. 'If you were to take a short walk, Charlie, I might be able to persuade your mother to stay on in New York and finish your vacation. Would you do that?'

'No,' Angela started to say, but the boy bounded up in excitement.

'Could you? Oh, that'd be super. See you later, Mum,' and with a quick grin at Steven he dashed out of the flat.

Falconi glanced at the packed suitcases and said, 'I guessed right. I guessed you'd fly out today. I know you pretty well too. Before you start giving me an argument, will you listen to me first?'

'You won't stop me leaving,' she protested. 'You can't stop me.'

'I know that,' he admitted. 'Oh, I thought about it, Angela. I thought about taking you and my son to Florida and keeping you there till you'd changed your mind. But it wouldn't work with you. Don't look at me like that. Sometimes I think like a Sicilian, that's all. It wasn't serious. This is America. You're not allowed to kidnap your wife and son. Will you sit down a minute? I won't make a big speech, I promise you.'

'All right, if you promise to go before he comes back.'

'I promise,' he said. 'If you say so. But let's get this straight first.'

'Get what straight?'

'This,' he said and took her in his arms. She didn't resist. He was much too strong. She tried to hold out mentally. He murmured to her in Italian, kissing her mouth, her eyes, down to her throat. Just as on the Sicilian hillside all those years ago. The same words, and the same rush of passionate feeling. He let her go and said softly, '*Cara mia*, remember? I love you. I said it then and I say it now. You can't lie to me now, can you? You feel it too.'

'I feel it,' she said desperately. 'But it's no good. You can take me to bed, but it won't change my mind. It'll just make it harder for both of us.'

'If there was no boy, would you say that?'

'No,' Angela admitted. 'No, I wouldn't. I still love you, Steven. I don't know if I could shut my eyes to what you are, but I could try. But not with him. Never.'

'Tears,' he said, touching her cheek with his fingertip. 'You know, the first time I saw you, you were crying. Because that kid, Scipio, had died. It's time I made you happy, Angelina. Come stay close to me while I tell you something. In my family I'm the figures man. I add up all the sums and shape the policy decisions. It won't make any difference to you, but I don't carry a gun. That was a crazy lie the other night. I've been doing some calculating for myself. I have money, respect, my father's proud of me. I'm Don Stefano to a whole lot of people. I'm a big man. I've got bodyguards who'd die for me, a hundred guys who'd do whatever I told them. I'll be the boss when my father dies. I have no home life, no happiness,

110

no children. I go to whores for comfort. If I give it all up, will you come away with me and we'll start a new life? You and me and the boy?'

'You couldn't,' she said. 'You couldn't do it.'

'I can do it. I will do it. If you promise me we'll be together, I'll go into business for myself. Legitimate business. Nothing to do with the Families. I've thought it through. We'll leave the States. We'll live in Europe. I have to talk to my father first, but he loves me. When he knows about Charlie, he'll help. I have a younger brother. He can take over. I swear this to you, Angela. On my honour. You know what that means to a Sicilian?'

'I know,' she said. 'If you swear like that, I know you mean it.'

'Will you swear too?' he asked her. 'Swear we'll be together?'

She laid her hand against his cheek. It was an old gesture of tenderness between them.

'If you will do that for us, then I swear.'

'We'll be happy,' he promised. 'I'll never give my son reason to be ashamed of me. And one day, maybe he can learn the truth. Maybe he'll be proud of a live father in the end.' He took her hand and held it. 'You'll stay in New York till I've made arrangements? It'll take a little time.'

'I'll stay,' she promised. 'But what about my job?'

'No job,' he countered. 'That's all over. I take care of you from now on.'

She said, 'What about your wife?'

'She's not my wife. The marriage is null. She has no rights over me. I can walk out tomorrow. Kiss me, Angelina.'

Later, sitting close, his arms around her, a shadow came over her happiness. 'What about her family? Isn't she part of it too?'

'Sure she is – her father's boss of the Fabrizzis. That won't matter. It'll be fixed between her people and mine.

111

At a price, but it'll be fixed. Forget about it. There's the buzzer, my darling. He's back.'

Angela paused by the door. 'What do we tell him?'

'The truth,' he answered. 'You're staying on because I've made you a better offer. Hi there, Charlie, had a good walk?'

'Yes, thank you.' He glanced quickly at Falconi. There was a sympathy between them already. 'Was it long enough? Are we staying?'

'I managed to persuade her. You're not going back home just yet. And I'm taking us all out this evening to celebrate.'

There's a new woman, Clara said to herself. She was in the Elizabeth Arden beauty parlour, having a facial. She looked at the reflection in the glass. The mask covering her face had set hard; only her eyes stared back at her, circled in white like a clown's. She didn't need the expensive treatments. Her skin was soft and smooth as cream. A girl was squatting beside her, manicuring her nails.

A new woman, the inner dialogue insisted. He's out most nights . . . It's not just screwing. I know him, the bastard. It's different with this one. He's happy. He was singing this morning. I heard him. She rounded furiously on the manicurist. 'Mind what you're at – that hurt!'

'I'm sorry, Madame. Can you hold your hand still, please?'

Other men desired her, Clara knew. Men who detected that she was a woman in her own right, not just one of the soft little breeding cows they had chosen for themselves. But she didn't want any of them. She wanted the husband who slept with her only in hopes of conceiving a child. Since the last specialist report, he hadn't come near her. Not for months. He didn't care about that any more. She had abased herself, pleaded, offered herself without shame, but the next morning he was as far from her as ever. As least he suffered. That

112

helped her. Now he was singing the old songs under his breath, not even seeing her, brushing her aside when she demanded his attention.

I can't stand it, she went on, mouthing to the mummy image in the glass. I've got to find out. I can do something about it then.

The beautician appeared behind her. 'I guess we're ready now, Mrs Falconi. Gloria, have you finished Mrs Falconi's manicure?'

'I've just painted on the Quick Dry,' the girl answered. She glanced up at her client. Clara spread her hands, examining the newly painted nails. Steven's big diamond solitaire flashed on her finger under the light. The hands were white, pampered, with scarlet claws as if they had been dipped in fresh blood.

I got rid of the first one, the silent voice exulted. The one in Monte Carlo. And that bitch Lita Montini stopped sniffing round him after Poppa had a word with her father. He sent her back home to her cousins in Linsano for a whole year. I'll find this one, whoever she is.

'Gloria's done a good job,' the beautician smiled. 'But you've got beautiful hands, Mrs Falconi. Now shall we steam off that cleansing mask?'

An hour later Clara stepped out of the handsome building on Fifth Avenue. The doorman, uniformed in the distinctive Arden livery, summoned her car. She was going to a charity lunch at the Waldorf.

As soon as she got home, she would call the firm of private detectives who had worked for her before. They had reported on Steven whenever she felt threatened. Nobody knew about this, not even her father. He wouldn't have approved. He liked such things to stay within the family. Clara didn't want him to see the list of professional women who tripped in and out of the duplex on the East Side. She kept that humiliation to herself. She had come to terms with the whores; they were paid and they never lasted long. She didn't fear them and she was able to control her jealousy. Women outside that

category were a different matter. Apart from Lita
Montini, who had dared flaunt herself in Steven's
direction, there were no other rivals on an equal footing.
But from the night ten days ago when he went to dinner
at Les A without her, she reminded herself, that was
when she noticed the change in him. The agency
detectives could start from there.

'I'm going to see my father tomorrow,' Steven said. 'My
brother will be there too.'

'They'll try to persuade you,' Angela said. 'They'll try
to talk you out of it.'

'Sure they will,' he agreed. He reached across the table
and held her hand. 'But my mind's made up. When they
know that, when I explain everything, they'll come
around to the idea. I know them. They love me. My
mother will help; she hates Clara. Don't worry sweetheart, it'll all work out.'

'I do worry,' she said. 'I worry about you, I worry
about Charlie. It's all happened to us so quickly . . .
Sometimes I'm quite scared.'

'I know you are,' he said. 'I feel it. But you mustn't be.
I know what I'm doing. I know what I want, and that's
you and my boy, and nothing is going to stop me.
Shouldn't we be getting back?'

Angela had to smile. 'Darling, he's not a baby. He's
quite all right in the flat for one evening. He's had such a
wonderful time. He never stops talking about you.'

'We get along,' he answered. 'I never knew it could be
this much fun. Having a proper family.'

They'd gone to the theatre to see the latest Broadway
musical; taken trips in the steamers that plied up and down
the Hudson River; gone shopping at Macy's, where Angela
had to stop him buying the excited Charlie everything he
admired in the sports department. They drove out of town
to eat; he never took them to the Italian part of the city,
although his son wanted to go there. His friend, Jordan,
had discovered pizzas and raved about them.

Steven and Angela found times to be alone together. Tonight he had chosen a charming restaurant on East 56th Street. It was small, intimate and expensive. He never suggested they use the duplex apartment. They made love in the little rented flat while their son was at the cinema or wandering through the Frick. And Steven made plans. Plans for their new life together while Angela listened and forced herself to believe it would really happen.

She didn't doubt him; he meant to do exactly what he said. To break with his family, his background and his old life and start afresh far away from it all. She loved him for that single-mindedness as much as she loved the total commitment of their sexual desire for each other. And the gentler side that followed it, the tenderness to her and the over-protective attitude towards his son. As they lay together in the brief times they were alone, he promised her, as he had done after their wedding in Altofonte, that he would make up for it all. For the long years of coping on her own, of money shortages and holidays spent working so that young Charlie could have a trip now and then.

Angela let him paint the extravagant pictures because she knew how much pleasure it gave him. A fine house, lots of help, France appealed to him, wouldn't she like to live in France, in the South – sunshine and lots of things for the boy to do when he came home on holiday – a honeymoon, to make up for the one they never had?

'So many things I want to give you, my darling,' he would whisper to her. 'To spoil you and reward you for making me so happy. I'm going to make a pet of you. You're going to have everything you've ever wanted.' And he didn't listen when she protested that she only wanted to live happily with him.

'After I've talked to my father,' he said, 'we could have a weekend together. Maybe go down to Washington, the three of us. I could show Charlie the Capitol, the White House . . . it's a great city. We'd have a wonderful time. Shall we do that, Angelina? Would you like that?'

115

'I'd love it,' she said.

'Then it's fixed,' he announced. He turned her hand upside down and pressed the palm against his mouth. 'I ever tell you how much I love you?'

'Once or twice,' she teased him.

'You'll never leave me, will you?'

'I couldn't,' she said. 'You know that.'

'I know,' he said. 'I just need you to say it, before tomorrow. Now I'll get the check and we'll drive home. I want to see Charlie before he goes to bed. We can tell him about Washington.'

Luca Falconi still lived on the West Side. The house was a three-storey building with a garden surrounded on three sides by a high wall. Luca and his wife had brought up their sons there; they were attached to the house and the neighbourhood. It was easy to make secure with the wall round three sides of it and there were Falconi people in the houses opposite and on either side.

During the trial of strength with the Musso family Piero had persuaded his mother to move their living quarters to the back of the house for safety. The windows on the ground floor front were protected by grilles, and bulletproofed. The garden was a pleasant shady place with a table and chairs and umbrellas to keep off the hot summer sun so they could all eat outside. The Sunday lunches Clara hated so much were often held in the garden during the fine weather.

Luca liked being out of doors. He liked the security of his high wall and the peace of his garden. He did a lot of business out there instead of in the stuffy rooms inside the house. His wife, Anna, was like a magpie, always buying things they didn't need: tables and stuffed chairs and oil paintings of the Old Country. He used to joke about it. 'There's a whole industry turning out genuine fakes of views from Palermo just for you,' he liked to say. She missed Sicily even after so many years, and she spoke poor English. One reason why he'd sent Steven for a good education – he didn't want him growing up like the sons of other families, ignorant boys who knew how to use their fists but nothing else. His son had brains.

Piero didn't go to college. He had enough trouble getting through school. Not much brain there, but a good heart. A loyal son with a lot of his grandfather in him. Luca Falconi was content with his wife and his sons and his grandchildren. If he had a worm in his belly it was that barren bitch Steven had married. He blamed himself for that. It was a bad marriage; no children, no comfort for his son. Good for business; he acknowledged that. He reminded his wife when she complained about her daughter-in-law, but he only did it to stop her tongue. He was in full agreement with her in his heart.

They were together, his sons Steven and Piero, sitting out in the warm autumn weather. Anna had brought a big flask of chianti, and some olives and salami for the men to pick at. They spoke in dialect, as their fathers had done before them.

'My son,' Luca said to Steven. 'My son, what you tell me isn't possible. I'm not awake. I'm dreaming a bad dream!'

'It's no dream, Poppa,' was the answer.

'A fuckin' nightmare,' Piero muttered in English. He shook his head as he'd done several times before.

'A wife and a son,' Luca repeated. 'And you kept this secret from us? From me, from your Momma – all these years and you never spoke of it to us?'

'Forgive me,' Steven said humbly. 'It wasn't a secret. It was a grief. I kept it to myself. Such a grief. I wanted to get killed after it happened. I couldn't talk to anyone.'

His father nodded. He remembered only too well his crazy son getting a decoration in the war, risking himself. He'd been angry with him, but proud too. He had the medal and the citation in a big frame in his sitting room. Now he understood the reason.

'You had no right,' his father rebuked him. 'You should have told us. We could have helped you.'

117

'I know,' Steven admitted. He would never argue with his father over a family matter. He respected him too much. 'I was wrong. But I come to you now. You call it a bad dream; Poppa, to me it's like a miracle. After all these years I find my wife and I find my son. He's a Falconi – he's you and grandfather and me, all in one. And clever too. He works at school. His mother has brought him up to be a proper man, with pride in himself.' He knew how much this description would please his father. He said, 'I'm happy for the first time. For the first time in sixteen years I'm a happy man. I want them with me.'

Luca dismissed it instantly. 'It's not possible in New York. It's not possible in Florida. We all know what Clara is. She'd go to that old fart-hole, Aldo, and start screaming. Your boy wouldn't be safe. Nor would his mother. It's not possible,' he repeated.

'You could set them up some place else,' Piero suggested. He was in full sympathy with his brother. He had loved and admired Steven all through his life. He had a happy marriage himself and he doted on his sons and baby daughter. 'We've got a big country, for Christ's sake. You could put them in a fine house and visit with them. Once, maybe twice a week. It could be business. Clara won't know any difference.'

Steven poured more wine into his father's glass. Piero shook his head; he scooped up a fistful of olives and dropped them into his mouth. He spat the stones out with force and accuracy. His children loved watching him do it. 'Poppa's planting olive trees,' the eldest would say and they all laughed. His children were very spoiled. His wife was not allowed to hit them.

Steven said carefully, 'It's not enough. That's why I've come to talk to you. To ask my family to help me. I'd like Momma to be here too. Can I call her?'

'I'll call her,' his father said. He had a wary look that Steven knew well. He was expecting to hear something that he wouldn't like. 'Anna! Anna! Come on out here!'

Steven's mother came quickly. She looked at her sons

in surprise. This was supposed to be man's talk. Business. Women had no place in it except to serve the men.

Her husband said, 'Sit down, Anna. Stefano has some news for you. He wants to tell you something.'

Steven got up and pulled one of the chairs out for her. He bent down and kissed her on the cheek. She smelled of his childhood. Warm, spicy smells of herbs and cooking and the violet scent which she loved.

'It's all right, Momma,' he said. 'It's good news. Don't worry.'

He didn't get the chance to explain anything because suddenly his father spoke up and said it all in an angry voice which forbade her to be sympathetic.

'He married an English girl in the war. He married her in our church in Altofonte, so it's a valid marriage. She was carrying a child. He did the honourable thing. I would have supported him and taken her into the family. But he thought she was killed and the child with her, so he said nothing. He came home to us all and said nothing!'

Steven's mother had given a little cry of anguish. He quelled it impatiently. 'But it wasn't so. The girl was not killed after all. She is alive, with a son, and Steven has found her, here in this city. Not two weeks ago. That's what he has already told me. Now he has some more to say that he wants you to hear. So, tell us, Stefano. Why is Piero's suggestion not enough?'

Piero hastened to help out his mother. It flustered her when her husband was angry. She had never got over her awe of him.

'I said he could make a home for them over here, but not in New York or Florida where the Families have interests. Someone would find out. Clara would call a vendetta on them. That's what I suggested, Momma.' He glanced across at Steven. 'But he says no. He says it's not enough.'

'I want to be with them as my wife and son,' Steven

119

said. He didn't look directly at his father. 'As Poppa said, it was a true marriage. I married Clara in good faith, but it's not a marriage.'

'No,' his mother agreed in a low voice. 'You're right. Thank God there were no children!'

'I am going to leave Clara and live with Angela and my son as a proper family. I lost them once because of what happened in the war. I can't lose them again. I've come to ask for your blessing on what I'm going to do. You and Poppa and Piero, my brother.'

'What are you telling me?' his father interrupted. 'What are you really saying, Stefano? You can't throw Clara out and bring in another wife and child, without the Fabrizzi declaring open war. Piero is right. It would be a vendetta, down to the last of us and the last of them. Aldo Fabrizzi could never forgive such dishonour to his daughter. So what are you really saying, my son? You're not so clever that I don't see through you!'

Steven said, 'You know better than I do, Poppa. I can't live with my family anywhere in this country. I have to leave the States. I have to leave the Family. I'll tell Clara I'm leaving and going to live abroad. If you disown me as your son, then there will be no vendetta. My wife, Angela, and my son, Charlie, will be safe because no one will know they exist. There won't be a war between you and the Fabrizzis. If I am dead to you, to my own people, then Aldo Fabrizzi will accept that.'

He saw tears spill on to his mother's cheeks. She wiped them away with her apron, as her forebears had done in times of grief.

'You want to leave us,' his father accused. 'You want to be dead to us? No wife, no son can mean that much to any man! No. No, Stefano, I won't give any blessing to such a thing. If you do it, you go with my curse!'

'Don't say that,' Steven asked him. 'Don't break my heart, Poppa. Don't threaten me. You have Piero. He can run things for you as well as I can now. He has boys to follow on.'

'Leave the Family?' his father went on, disregarding him. 'Leave the Falconis and our old traditions? Our old ways? Live like a stranger among strangers, because of this woman and this boy? Ah, I won't curse you, my son, because you're out of your head! You've gone mad! But I curse them instead!' He got up, knocking his chair over, and stormed into the house. His voice was raised, shouting in rage.

Steven's mother said, 'He won't change his mind. I know him. He won't change. You can't do this, you can't break *his* heart for him. He needs you, *caro*, he's getting old.'

'He's strong like a lion,' Steven answered. 'And you know it, Momma. He could run the Falconi without Piero or me, if he had to! Don't cry any more. Go in to him. He always needs you when he's upset. Calm him down. I'll talk to him again when he's calm.'

She got up and went inside.

Piero lit a cigarette. He offered one to Steven.

'Ma's right,' Piero said after a pause. 'He won't give permission. He won't risk a fight with Aldo Fabrizzi and if you leave that bitch there'll be trouble for all of us. I've been thinking, Steven . . .' He inhaled and blew out noisily into the warm air. He was a very physical man, who ate and drank loudly and moved roughly, knocking into things if they were in his way. He had a naturally violent temperament. 'I've been thinking. There's a guy in Westchester. He runs a business. He has drivers who do contracts now and again. Not piece men; they specialize in cars. They'll guarantee to run anything off a fuckin' road and finish it off with fire. How about that for solving the problem? No Clara, no problem. I can arrange it.'

He tipped up the chianti bottle. It was empty. He looked inquiringly at Steven, his head a little on one side. 'How about it?'

'No! No, Piero!' Steven laid a hand on his brother's shoulder and pressed hard for emphasis. 'No,' he

121

repeated. 'You hear me? I mean it. You don't even *think* like that, you understand?'

'Okay. No need to break my neck. I just thought of it, that's all. If you say no, that's it. It's more than she'd give you. Remember that time someone took a shot at you at the intersection? I wondered about that bitch as soon as I heard.'

'Nobody touches Clara,' Steven repeated. 'We've never put contracts on our women. Just stop and think where that would end, for Christ's sake.'

Our women. Piero couldn't argue with that. But not women in general. The Syndicate murdered as many women to order as men. The wives and daughters of the Families were safe. But not Women with a capital W.

'Okay,' he said. 'Forget it. Pa's stopped shouting. Ma's getting to him. I'll go get another bottle. I'm thirsty. You?'

Steven said, 'Yes.' For something to say. He's my brother and we've loved each other since we were children. We're not alike and we've nothing in common outside of the family and the business. But we're fond all the same. I've got to remember that and not remember that he offered to have his sister-in-law murdered. He went into the house, brushing past Piero as he came out with more chianti. There was silence inside. He went to his father's sitting room and knocked on the door. His mother came out, closing it behind her. She stood with her back to it. Her voice was very low.

'He won't see you,' she said. 'He says to go away and think about it. Come back when you've seen sense.'

'I won't see sense, Momma.'

'Oh merciful Madonna – what are we to do? Listen to him, Stefano. He loves you. You're his pride, you know that! Think about it. For my sake.'

'I never lied to you, did I?' he asked her. 'No. Well I won't lie now. He won't change his mind. I won't change mine. I'll come again, Momma, just to say goodbye. And goodbye to you too. I love you.' He held her against him and comforted her, as so often she had done to him when he was a child. 'One day I'll bring my son to see you,' he whispered. 'I promise you. Now go inside and give my father my respects and say I'll come again in a few days. No more than that, eh?'

'No more,' she promised. 'And I'll go on trying, *caro*. I'll go on pleading with him.'

'Stop Piero finishing the bottle out there,' he told her gently. 'You don't want him going home drunk. You know how mad it makes Lucia.'

He let himself out of the front door. His car waited. As always he was ushered quickly into the back and driven off. He looked back to the old house where he had grown up, and then resolutely turned away.

He thought suddenly: When this is done, I'll be able to walk to places like other men. It had never occurred to him before. But it didn't ease the pain of that parting with his father. Only time would do that.

They flew to Washington the next morning. The boy sat between them and over his head they smiled at each other. He was full of enthusiasm, plying Steven with questions. Steven had bought a book on the history of the capital and pointed out the chapters he should read.

They were booked into a small hotel in Georgetown; expensive and exclusive. Angela couldn't stop him heaping every luxury upon them. He had booked himself into the Astoria in the city centre as a precaution. The congressman he had invited to Les A was not his only contact in Washington.

Over dinner that night, Angela turned to them both. 'Why don't you two go sightseeing? I'd love to do some shopping tomorrow morning. We could meet for lunch.'

Steven understood. She wanted him to be alone with his son, to draw them closer together. The pretence that he was offering her a job couldn't go on once they left America.

123

'Well, if that's all right with you, Sir?' He turned eagerly to Steven.

'I guess so. We'll start with the Capitol and the Lincoln Memorial. If your mother would like, we can all see the White House in the afternoon.'

'I'd love that,' Angela said.

Charlie went up ahead of them. He jumped at the chance to watch television in his room. They sat in the lounge and drank coffee and under the table Steven held her hand.

'Was it true about the shopping?'

'Well, partly true. I thought it would be nice for you to go off together.'

'You won't let me buy you anything? Some new dresses, a coat for the winter?'

'A mink coat?' she teased him. 'No thank you, darling. Where would I get the money? Charlie's not that naïve. We've got to do everything right till the time comes. You know, I wish it was tomorrow! I wish we could get on a plane and fly straight home, the three of us. How long will it take, Steven?'

'Aren't you happy?' he asked. 'Is it so hard to stay with me?'

'I'm uneasy,' she confessed. 'I keep thinking, it's all so wonderful, being with you, seeing you and our son getting to know each other and at the back of my mind there's this feeling that it won't last, that something will happen to stop it.'

'I shouldn't have told you about my father,' he admitted. 'That's what's made you worry. You mustn't, Angela. You've got to trust me. I can hurry things up from now on. Another week – is that too long?'

'I'm sorry,' she said. 'Of course it isn't. But I'll have to talk to David Wickham. He must have time to look for someone else. I wish you'd let me take the job till we get settled.'

'No job,' he insisted. 'I take care of you and my son. You don't work. When we leave, you go home, put

124

Charlie into school and then join me wherever. You'll have plenty to do, sweetheart, don't worry about that. It's late. Can I come up with you?'

He was playing with her hand, stroking the fingers and the wrist, moving the rings erotically to and fro.

'If you promise to go on doing that,' she murmured, and got up.

Piero's wife Lucia was playing with the baby when the telephone rang. Her husband was lounging on the sofa with his feet up, reading the sports page.

'Answer it, honey,' he mumbled.

She balanced the baby on her hip and went to pick up the receiver. She called out to him. 'It's for you!'

'Shit,' he exclaimed. 'Who is it?'

'He didn't say. Just says he wants to speak with you.'

'Okay, okay. I'm coming,' Piero grumbled. He threw the papers on the floor, heaved himself up and took the telephone from her. He bent and smacked a kiss on the baby's check. She chuckled. 'Yeah,' he said into the phone. 'It's Piero.'

'This is Luigi from Les A. I've been trying to reach Don Stefano, but he's out of town.'

Piero came alert. He waved Lucia and the baby away. 'So?'

Luigi's voice was low. 'Some guy's been asking questions about him,' he said. 'He slipped the girl on the desk a twenty and she told me.'

'What sort of guy? What the fuck was he asking?'

'Who was with him when he came to dinner here. One specific date; I remember your brother *was* here that night. This guy kept asking about a woman. He's an agency legman. I thought Don Stefano ought to know.'

'Yeah,' Piero said slowly. 'Yeah, thanks. Did your girl tell him anything? Did she take the twenty?'

'Sure she did. Said she'd seen your brother, but there was no woman with him. So the guy goes to Eddie at the bar and tries the same line. Eddie takes a twenty and a

125

phone number. He gives the number to me. I guess you want it.'

'I want it,' Piero answered. He wrote the number down and stuffed the scrap of paper back in his pocket. 'Thanks, Luigi. We owe you. I'll tell my brother.' He hung up and stood chewing the pencil for a moment. A private detective asking about Steven and a woman. Only one person would pay for that. He took out the paper and dialled the number.

'Taylor Investigators,' a woman's voice said in a bored tone.

Piero slammed the phone down. He swore under his breath, a long fierce Sicilian obscenity. A woman. Clara was spying on Steven to find out about a woman. It didn't take much to figure out who that woman would turn out to be. Steven had called her Angela. Piero thought on his feet and when he thought, he didn't waste time before he acted. Steven was out of town. If he was being followed and he was with the woman and his son, then Clara would be told.

He shouted out to Lucia, 'Put the kids to bed, will you? Stay out of the way till I call, honey.'

She came close to him. 'What is it? Trouble?'

'Trouble for Steven,' he said. 'I got to deal with it. Move your sweet ass, sweetheart.'

She made a provocative face at him and jerked her hips. 'I'm moving it,' she said. 'You just take care, that's all.'

It was all organized within an hour. Piero's trusted henchmen were summoned to the house and given their instructions. Half a dozen men got their telephone orders. Three to take care of the agency itself and the others allocated to the legman on the Falconi assignment.

Piero shouted for his wife when they had gone. He slapped her on the bottom. 'You been keeping it warm for me?' he demanded. 'The kids asleep?'

She smiled at him. He was a big, active man and sex was always an excitement between them. 'They're asleep,' she said. 'You want to go to bed?'

'What the fuck's wrong with the floor?' he demanded and heaved her up against him.

They were eating much later when the first of the calls came in. Piero answered, swallowing down his food.

'Okay, okay,' he said, nodding, wiping his hand across his mouth. Vigorous lovemaking always made him hungry. 'You tell Gino from me, he's done well. Tell his boys too. Sure . . . yeah.'

Lucia didn't question him. She filled his glass with chianti and dished out more lasagne. More calls came. The guy who had been asking questions at Les A wouldn't be asking any more. He'd gone through a sixth-storey window. All the way down. The agency staff had been worked over before the offices were smashed with pickaxes and hammers till they looked like a toothpick factory. The records were piled up in the middle and set alight. The dossier on Steven Falconi would be delivered to Piero that night.

He said again, 'You done well. Good, good,' and sat up after Lucia had gone to bed, waiting for the dossier. He flipped through it quickly. He hated reading; it made him impatient. The terms. Written reports to the client. Client. He cursed out loud. Clara Falconi. As he suspected, she was spying on her husband. He concentrated. Les A. No information there but during the week subject tailed to an apartment on East 70th. Occupants a Mrs Lawrence and her son. Subject seen with them at the theatre, in restaurants, on a boat trip round Manhattan Island. Piero had begun to sweat. He looked at the last date. Two days before. The reports to Clara were scheduled weekly. This was the first. They had intercepted it just in time.

Piero threw the folder down. There'd be another tail on Steven, wherever he was. But no agency for the tail to report back to . . . any professional would get that kind of message. He'd just fade away and count himself lucky. But Clara would pass the job to someone else. A dead man, a case of arson and a few people with the shit beaten out of them wouldn't worry Clara.

'He's nuts,' Piero lamented aloud, thinking of his brother; wishing he dared go against him and break the unwritten Family rule. It would have been simple. A perfect solution. He hated Clara so much he'd have run her off the road himself and enjoyed every moment of it. He imagined the car turning over and over and ending in a ball of orange flame . . . But Steven said no, and he had never disobeyed Steven in his life.

He wasn't greedy for more power, or ambitious to be the Don when his father died. He had everything he wanted. The idea of full responsibility didn't appeal to him. He preferred to take orders from the top. He coped with situations like the agency easily enough. Administration at Steven's level would worry him. Dealing with senators, that kind of crap. He put the idea out of his mind. His father was there, the rock on which the Falconi family rested. He didn't have to think so far ahead. Just far enough to warn Steven. In the morning. He'd call first thing. After he'd seen the newspapers. He'd given them some headline, he grinned to himself. Like the old days when he was a kid. And he was confident. Nobody would identify his men, nobody would talk. No one testified against the Families and stayed alive. The police would recognize the Falconi signature too, but there was nothing they could prove. And there were officers on the Family payroll who wouldn't pursue the incident too closely.

He locked the dossier away and went up to join Lucia. On his way up he looked in on his sleeping sons, and opened the nursery door a crack to make sure baby Catarina was all right.

'It was a great trip,' Charlie said to his mother. He'd picked up words like 'great' from his father; he said 'okay', trying hard to sound American, she noticed. 'He's so nice, isn't he, Mum? Paying for everything like that – he must be jolly rich!'

128

He glanced at her, uncertain how to say what was uppermost in his mind since that weekend. 'What sort of job are you going to do for him? Is he in the same sort of business as Mr Wickham?'

'No, darling. He's got a lot of interests in a lot of businesses. He wants me as a liaison between them – a super personnel job, I think you'd call it. Lots of travelling.' She decided to cross one bridge then and there. 'In fact we might have to live in France. It's not certain, but it is a possibility.'

He frowned. 'Mum, I wouldn't have to leave school, would I? I mean I'd hate that.'

'Oh, of course not – I wouldn't hear of anything like that! You'd just come over for holidays. It's not definite, Charlie, but it *is* likely. You wouldn't mind, would you?'

'No,' he said after a pause. 'Not if it's good for you. Wouldn't we live at home at all? What about Grandpa?'

'We'd spend time in both places,' Angela assured him. 'You could have your friends to stay in the summer – we'd be in the South, so he said.'

He brightened immediately. 'Gosh, that'd be super. Great!' Then he said, 'Do you like him, Mum? I think he's a bit keen on you.'

'Yes, I like him very much. He may like me, I don't really know.'

'Mum,' he announced in triumph. 'You're going red!'

She aimed a playful slap at him which he dodged. He went off whistling to spend some of his pocket money in the drugstore on the corner two blocks away. He loved going there and had made friends with one or two American teenagers who thought his clothes and accent were the cutest thing.

Angela hurried into the bedroom. He was quite right, she realized, seeing herself in the glass. She had blushed a guilty scarlet.

She was meeting Steven for lunch downtown. He had called her that morning as usual.

'I want you to meet me,' he had said. 'Don't bring

Charlie. There's a little place called the Garden, over on Forty-third. Take a cab, my darling, and be there by twelve thirty. I've got something for you. No, I can't tell you what it is. I have to go now. Twelve thirty, the Garden, Forty-third Street. I love you, *cara mia.*' Then he had hung up.

The air was turning cooler. She had bought a ridiculous hat with a brightly coloured feather during that Washington trip when she felt particularly happy. She decided to wear it for him for lunch that day. He had a surprise for her. It must be a present. She couldn't go on refusing him. She felt excited, a little guilty. A cruising Yellow Cab picked her up on the corner. The driver noted the address. He was a talkative man and he loved English passengers because they were too polite to tell him to shut up.

'How long you been here, lady?'

'Nearly three weeks,' she answered.

'You like our city?'

'I love it. I've had a wonderful time.'

'It's a great place. If it wasn't for the crime. Jesus, you seen the morning papers?' He didn't wait for her answer. 'Right across the page. Some guy working for a detective agency gets thrown out of a window six floors up and they take the agency apart. Three people in the hospital, half the building burnt out!'

'How terrible,' Angela said, not really interested. 'Who did it?'

'Mafia,' he retorted, making a face in the driving mirror. 'Three guys worked that place over and nobody even gives a description! Nobody seen anything, nobody heard anything. Jesus,' he said again. 'You don't finger those guys. It's Mafia for sure. I guess that agency was on to something. So they wipe it out! It makes me ashamed, you know that, lady? It makes me ashamed what people like you think of this city when a thing like that can happen. And what do the cops do about it? I'll tell you. Nothing! And for why – because half of them are on the payroll, that's why.'

130

Angela wasn't listening. Mafia. A man thrown to his death; people terrorized and beaten, too frightened to describe the brutes who had done it; a building almost destroyed by fire. 'I make the policy decisions . . . I don't carry a gun . . .' She held fast to that, insisting that it removed him from the violence, the taint of murder even at a distance. His promise – she held faster still to that because without it there was no possible choice but the one she had made before. He's giving it up. He's breaking with his past, with his own people. We're going away where none of this can touch us.

'Lady.' The driver had pulled up and was reaching to open the door for her. 'That is it. The Garden. That'll be two bucks fifty.'

Angela didn't know what she gave him. She left him with a five-dollar bill in his hand and hurried under the little green awning into the restaurant. Steven was waiting for her, sitting at a table facing the door. He took her coat and was guiding her to the banquette seat beside him. He looked strained and taut.

'That hat,' he said. 'I've never seen you in a hat before.'

'I bought it last weekend,' she said. 'Steven, what's the matter? What's wrong?'

He made a signal and the waitress hurried over. 'Two martinis,' he said briefly and then turned to Angela. 'Nothing's wrong, sweetheart. I like the hat. It suits you. How's Charlie?'

'He's fine. He's having lunch at the drugstore. There *is* something the matter. Please tell me.'

'You have to go back,' he said, speaking low. 'I've got tickets for the flight this evening.'

She sat staring at him. 'Go tonight? But why? You said a week.'

'Something's come up,' he explained. 'I want you and my son to leave by tonight. It's all fixed. I've got the tickets right here.'

'And I'm not to be told why?' she countered. 'That's not good enough. I wanted to take up my job and wait

131

for you. You said no. Now, suddenly it's all changed. You've got to tell me why.'

The menus were placed in front of them. The waitress began her set speech about the recommended dish.

'Not now,' Steven interrupted. 'Not right now.'

She went away with a sullen look.

Angela said, 'I'm not going unless you tell me.'

'I've been followed,' he said. 'My wife hired a detective. He was checking on me. It's not safe for you and Charlie anymore.'

Angela said, 'Does she know about us?'

'Not yet. But she will. So you understand now, my darling. You must leave tonight.'

He was surprised when she said, 'Could I have another martini?' and finished her drink at the same time.

'What would happen to Charlie and me if she did find out? You said there wouldn't be any danger. You said it could be fixed at a price. You're not telling me the truth, are you?'

'Don't say that,' he countered. 'I thought it would be like I said. I didn't know she suspected anything. One of the people they tried to question tipped off my brother. He warned me this morning.'

The waitress took the order. She didn't mention the menu again.

'Aren't they still following you?' Angela asked him. The martini was so cold it burned her throat.

'No,' Steven said. 'My brother fixed it. But she'll hire someone else. Believe me, Angelina. I wouldn't send you and my boy away unless I knew I had to. Don't look at me like that. It's going to kill me to let you go without me.'

'The agency,' she managed to say. 'The one burned down, where the man was killed – the cab driver said it was the Mafia. Steven, if you lie to me now, I'll know it. I'll walk out of here and never see you again. Was that anything to do with this?'

It was a long time before he answered. He didn't

132

pretend; he considered and made up his mind. 'I won't lie to you,' he said at last. 'If I lie now, it'll be the start of more lies. You won't trust me; I won't trust myself. If you leave me because I tell you the truth, then it wasn't going to work for us anyway. It was the same agency my wife used. I told you, my brother got the tip-off. He didn't consult me, because he didn't know where I was. I'd have stopped him. I've stopped him before. I'd have found another way. But he couldn't take the chance. He did what he felt had to be done to save your life and Charlie's. He bought me the time to get you away before Clara could go to her father. It could have been a matter of days. Piero knew that. He knows the way these things work. She gets to know about you and all it takes is a telephone call. So he gave the order. Here are the tickets, Angela. I can't drive you to the airport. I can't see you again after you leave here in case there's another tail on me. I can't even say goodbye to my son.' He said, 'Give me your hand, won't you? Don't turn away from me.'

Their hands met and gripped. There were tears in his eyes.

'You wanted the truth,' he said. 'You said something would happen. You said it just about the time it did. I'll come to England. Will you be there for me?'

Angela reached up and took off the hat. The bright feather brushed against him. 'I bought it because I was so happy,' she said. 'I loved the silly feather. I don't think I could eat anything, do you mind?'

He shook his head. 'You want me to get the check?'

'I was thinking,' she went on. 'While you were telling me about it, I was thinking. I knew already, as soon as I asked. I've always known what loving you was going to mean. So why am I shocked, Steven? Why haven't I faced it before?'

'Because you couldn't,' he said. 'You told me. You couldn't face it for the boy.'

'I couldn't face it for myself either.' She stared ahead of her, as if looking into the future. 'I can run away from

133

you a second time. I know you won't try to stop me now. We've been too close for that. I can go back to my job and my old life and tell Charlie the job has fallen through. He'll be disappointed; he said this morning, "I think he's a bit keen on you, Mum." He was teasing me, laughing about it. He'll forget about you. He hasn't learned to love you yet. But I have. I love you, Steven, and if you love me, you'll get on the plane tonight and come with us. If you do that, we have a chance. If you stay here, we'll never see each other again. Next time, it won't be your brother who does something like that. It'll be you. Now get the check and I'll find a cab outside. Give me the tickets.'

He stood up. He handed her the envelope. 'And I got this for you,' he said. It was a Tiffany box. Angela opened it. An emerald glowed on its cushion of white velvet. She closed it and put it into his hand.

'Give it to me tonight,' she said. 'On the plane.'

She didn't say goodbye or look back. She left him standing there.

4

'He won't see you,' Steven's mother repeated. 'He doesn't sleep, he doesn't eat – his heart is breaking, Stefano, but you know his pride!'

'I know it, Momma,' he answered. 'But there's no time for it now.'

He put her aside gently and went to his father's room. She watched him apprehensively, mouthing a silent prayer. She had wept when he came and told her. He was her favourite, her lovely son who'd made them all so proud. Steven didn't knock; he opened the door and walked in. His father was sitting in a chair. He looked up and started to his feet. Steven noticed how tired he looked.

Luca said, 'You come in here without knocking? Where's your respect?'

'Poppa,' he answered. 'I'm a man, not a boy. I have respect for you, you know that. But I have love for my father and I can't go without seeing you to say goodbye. Momma tried to stop me, so don't blame her.'

'You haven't changed your mind?' his father demanded. 'You're turning your back on your own people?'

'Not on my people,' Steven countered. 'Not on you or Momma or Piero. But on what Piero did last night. He's told you about it?'

'He told me. He did right.'

'He did it for me,' Steven said. 'But it's been done for business other times. That's why I'm leaving. There's no place for our kind of business in the life I want. I'm turning my back on that, not on you. Can't you understand? Can't you even try?'

'No,' Luca Falconi exploded. 'No, I don't understand! I give you a good education, send you to college, try to make something better than a hood out of you and this is my reward! You get fancy all of a sudden.' He struck his fist against the table. 'I should have treated you and Piero the same,' he said. 'I made a difference between you. I was wrong. Piero is a good boy. I thank God for Piero now.'

'I did my share,' Steven reminded him, becoming angry himself. 'I served my time like Piero. I helped make a racket into a multi-million-dollar business, bigger than you ever dreamed. So don't reproach me, Poppa. I don't owe you or the family anything more. But I promise you this. If you ever need me, if things get tough here and you want me, I'll come back. I swear it. I'm leaving tonight. I'll see Clara before I go. I'll make it easy for you with the Fabrizzi.'

He walked towards his father. He was a head taller. For a moment Luca glared at his son, daring him to defy him and come close. But Steven refused to be stared down. The next moment Luca was locked in an embrace that he wasn't strong enough to break. He heard Steven say, 'Goodbye, Poppa. Remember, If you ever need me.' And then his arms came up and held his son for a moment. He didn't speak. He didn't trust himself. Steven understood, and left him.

He called Piero. The car drove him uptown to the office block they owned with the half a dozen companies controlling various enterprises. His own office was on the top floor. It was big and luxurious as befitted his status. He went up in the elevator, opened the door to his private office with a special key. His secretary was outside at her desk as usual.

She smiled and said, 'Good morning, Mr Falconi.'

So far as she was concerned, it was legitimate business,

a trading corporation that paid big salaries and bonuses. Steven went through his desk drawers. He had a file of private papers, a list of his stock holdings, government bonds, property interests. A fortune of over two million dollars. Some quick to liquidate, others needing time. He called his brokers, gave some brief instructions and then hung up before they could argue. The rest could be left to Piero to realize and transfer. He trusted Piero to do what was best for him and to keep the details secret. He put some personal documents, including his will, into the shredder, then called down to his brother to say he was on his way.

'You're crazy,' Piero kept saying. 'You're selling at the wrong time. You're losing good money, for Christ's sake! What's Pa going to say? Why the fuck do you have to go *tonight*! I fixed the agency, Clara got nothing on you or the kid and his mother. Oh yeah. Yeah, she'll get herself another gumshoe, but so long as you've gotten them out, what can she do?'

'Nothing,' Steven answered. 'I'm not doing this because of Clara. I'm going now, Piero, before my life gets screwed up all over again. Wish me luck, won't you?'

'Ah, for Christ's sake,' Piero protested. 'You know I do. You know. If it's what you want – it's okay by me. Don't worry about the assets. I'll take the best advice and get the best for them.'

'I'll tell you where to send the money,' Steven said. 'I don't know where I'll be just yet. I'll square it with Clara, I told Poppa I'd make it easy for him. And you've got to go along, Piero. So far as you and the family are concerned, I'm yellow shit. You understand that?'

'I guess so.' His brother sounded uncertain. 'It won't be easy. But you're goddamned right. We can't have a war.'

'No war,' Steven agreed. 'But if Poppa or you ever need me, you just send word. I'll be back. Say goodbye to Lucia for me. Kiss the kids.'

Piero hugged him, fighting back a surge of emotion. He could best express it by cursing at the fate that separated them. He was so unhappy that he wanted to go and hit somebody.

No war. No war with the Fabrizzi. So his father said, and his brother. He'd said it himself. But now he wouldn't have minded. He lit a cigarette; he struck the match so hard it broke. He picked up the burning end, not feeling the pain as the little flame licked his fingers. Peace needn't be for ever.

'Is it the new job?'

Angela said, 'Yes, darling. But we have had a lot more time here than we expected, haven't we?'

'Yes, we have, Mum.'

He'd been very good about it, puzzled by the dramatic change of plan, but he hadn't grumbled. He helped her pack and together they tidied the little apartment. He stacked the cases in the hall and looked round wistfully. 'I'll never forget this place,' he said. 'It's been the best holiday ever. Is he coming to see us off?'

'Who?' Angela asked, knowing exactly who he meant.

'Your boyfriend,' he grinned. 'Sorry, Mum, only a joke.'

She didn't answer. She went into the bedroom and shut the door, saying, 'I must see that I haven't left anything behind. I'm always doing it.'

The bed where they had made love, talked of their plans for a new life: the small oasis of privacy. If she closed her eyes she could imagine him there with her, the feel of him close against her, the sound of his voice saying he loved her. I've asked the impossible. He won't come. I know he won't. She opened the door and shut it hard behind her, as if she were closing it on something tangible. On memories, on the exultation of their passion for each other, on the fantasy that they could extend it into the framework of an ordinary life. He won't come, the silent voice insisted. You know it.

'Charlie, darling, we should be going soon. The traffic gets so snarled up at this time of the evening. Ring for a Yellow Cab, will you?'

'Yes, Mum. Okay.'

She saw his bright face and forced herself to smile, thinking: You mustn't know, whatever happens. You mustn't know what we've both missed.

It was a long, slow journey to the airport, inching through traffic, while everywhere the lights sprang up and New York lifted the veil on its evening face. The cab driver didn't talk. Not like the one this morning, who had helped to wreck her happiness. She sat looking out of the window and seeing nothing but a blur.

'Maria, where's Mrs Falconi?'

The maid shrugged. 'I don't know. She gone for lunch. She no say when she come back.'

Maria was a widow. Her husband had been one of Don Luca's humbler 'soldiers' killed during the battle with Musso. Her reward was a free house and a well-paid job with the Don's eldest son. It kept her safe in the Family. The Family always looked after its own.

Steven went through to the big drawing room. Clara had gone overboard with some fag decorator five years ago and the place was cluttered with checks and stripes and tables thick with trivia which sent Maria crazy trying to dust. It wasn't the kind of room where he could put his feet up or spill ash on the specially woven carpet. It wasn't a home.

He poured himself a scotch and wondered where she was. Lunch was taking a long time. Lunch followed by her endless shopping bouts. His watch showed five o'clock. Angela's flight left Kennedy at eight. He had to pack an overnight bag, get there and check in. His ticket would be waiting.

He settled down to wait, stilling his impatience. She'd be home soon. She thought he'd spent the weekend in

Florida. That had been his only explanation as he hurried out of the apartment.

He'd made arrangements with the speed and efficiency of his business training. He'd taken the decision and acted upon it. Making the decision had been the hardest part.

To leave his family at such short notice; to wind up his life in a few hours and set off into a world he didn't know. A stranger's world, without the protection and support of his own kind. He was not a coward. He had faced death in the war, and death as part of his life as a Falconi. It was a risk inherent in his birth. It didn't trouble him. But after Angela left him at lunchtime, courage had been needed. The courage to cut loose from it all and make a new life with her and his son. He didn't hurry that choice. He stayed on in the little restaurant, ordered food he didn't eat and thought about the future. He thought of the look on her face, the despair and the confusion when she said to him, 'I've always known what loving you was going to mean. So why am I shocked?' Business, he called it. It covered a broad spectrum. It made murder and extortion sound respectable. He went through the books and added up the millions. He sat in on the meetings where the policies were formulated. He didn't carry a gun. Not since he came back from the war. He didn't have to. There were men with guns all round him, men sitting outside guarding the restaurant. They did the killing. Piero's men had responded to a personal call with clubs and hammers. They'd tossed a human being from a sixth-floor window to smash like an egg on the street below.

So it was done to protect him. To protect Angela and his son. Piero would do the same to protect a business interest. As his father would – as he had done in the past. And Angela had known. For all her innocence of his way of life, she had seen through to the fundamental truth. 'Next time it won't be your brother . . . it'll be you.'

And suddenly the choice was clear. Not easy, but clear beyond doubt. Who could be sure, Steven asked himself,

140

that without Angela's ultimatum he mightn't have been persuaded to some compromise . . . to keep some thread of attachment to his old allegiance. If he left that night, the thread would be cut for ever. Only his pledge remained, and nothing would stop him honouring that pledge if ever he was called upon. 'If you need me, I'll come back.' To his father, to his brother.

It left him with his honour. The waitress, anxious to clear the table and get rid of him, saw him smile slightly. How strong the Sicilian blood was still – as strong as in his son, with his dark hair and the Falconi eyes. One day he would take Charlie to Sicily. The choice was made with the thought. He had paid, slipped into his car and told the driver to go straight to his father's house.

Lost in his thoughts, he didn't hear Clara open the door. He looked up suddenly and saw her standing there, a ribbon-tied box on one arm.

'You're back,' she stated. She dropped the box on a sofa, slipped out of her mink stole. 'So how was Florida?'

'Hot and sticky,' Steven answered. 'You ought to know by now.'

She sat down facing him and crossed her legs. He could feel the tension coming from her. The detective agency, of course. She couldn't say anything, but she knew. 'Isn't it early for you?'

'Early for what?'

'To start drinking?'

He looked hard at her over the glass. He drained the whisky. 'I need it,' he said. 'So will you.'

She responded instinctively, as Piero's wife, Lucia, had done. She sat upright and said, 'There's trouble? What's up?'

'Trouble for me,' he told her. He saw a flash of satisfaction light her face and then vanish. 'What would you say, Clara, if I told you I was quitting?'

'Quitting? You mean quitting me? Leaving me?' She jumped to her feet then.

'Quitting you, quitting the Family.' He said it calmly. 'I've dealt myself out. And I've been dealt out. Finito Benito.'

She said, 'You're crazy. I don't believe you. You can't quit the Family and you can't leave me! You're drunk!' She turned away impatiently. 'I should have known better. Go sober up. Mario and Nina are coming round for dinner. Take a shower, do something!'

'Wait a minute,' he said. He stood up. She saw at once that her accusation wasn't true. 'I saw my father today. I told him what I've told you. I want out. I said it. He didn't believe me either. Not for quite a while, Clara. He said I was crazy too.'

She was rooted, listening to him. Her pale face was as white as the blouse knotted at her throat.

'But I'm not crazy. I don't want to go on in the business. I don't want to live with you. I don't want to do anything I've been doing since I got back from the war.'

She interrupted him with a furious cry. 'The war's been over since 1945! What the hell are you talking about?'

'You and my father,' he said. 'Saying the same words. He cursed me, Clara, do you know that?'

'I can believe it,' she said. 'So would any father when a son talked to him like that!' Then, with an effort she forced herself to be calm. She said, 'Sit down, Steven. I'll get you a scotch. You're not drunk. I shouldn't have said that.'

'Get yourself one,' he countered. 'I have to pack.'

She turned on him, frantic as she saw he meant it. She barred his way to the door. 'Pack? You're not going anywhere. You're not going to walk out on me, on all of us! Why? Why, Steven?' She caught his arm, her long nails sinking through the cloth, seeking his skin.

He wrenched away from her. 'Because I hate myself,' he said. 'I hate what I am, Clara. That's what I told my father. I want clean hands. I want a new life. That's when he cursed me. He called my mother, my brother, Piero,

142

and he cursed me in front of them. They didn't say a word. They didn't defend me, they just stood and agreed with him.'

'I'll curse you too,' she shouted.

He pushed her aside. She followed him into their bedroom. He was putting clothes into a bag. She was blind with tears. She came and caught hold of him and, in spite of what the years had brought her, her love for him came rushing back for the last time.

'Take me with you,' she begged. 'I don't care. They can throw me out too. I'll go with you, Steven.' She held on to him, weeping. She tore at her blouse, ripping the silk over her breasts in her anguish. 'If I'd had a child this wouldn't have happened,' she lamented. 'We'd have been happy. Oh, Mother of Jesus, why did you do this to me?' She rocked to and fro, and he took time to sit beside her and try to ease her pain. His heart was empty, but he could still feel pity at that moment.

'No child would have made any difference,' he said. 'This is something in me, Clara. It's been there always. Ever since the war. It changed me. It changed a lot of people. I have to go away and work it out for myself.'

He left her and closed the bag, snapping it shut. She looked at him, the beautiful make-up streaked from her tears.

'They won't let you go,' she said. 'Your father and my father. You know what it means when they curse you and cast you out? You know what happens in the Old Country? It's no different here.'

'I'll take my chance,' Steven said quietly. 'If they come, they come. Go home to your mother, Clara. She'll take care of you for tonight. My father will have spoken to your father by now.'

He went out and closed the bedroom door behind him. He left the house quickly. He had dismissed his car and bodyguard. They thought he was staying home for the evening. Outside he set off down the street to find a taxi cab.

*

143

'He's left his clothes,' Clara said. She had stopped crying.

Aldo Fabrizzi put his arm round her shoulders. 'So you see, it was just a fight he had with that old slob Luca. He'll be back, you'll see.'

'No.' She shook her head, refusing his comfort. 'He meant it, Poppa. He's gone. I told you, he's gone for ever. He's quit the Family; he's quit me.'

Her mother tried to help. 'An overnight bag means overnight. Maybe a day or two. Men get notions sometimes. He'll work it out.'

Clara ignored her. She meant well, but she was stupid. Clara couldn't tolerate her stupidity at that moment. She needed her father's shrewdness.

'Why hasn't Luca called you? He's cursed his own son and thrown him out. He has to tell you; he has to make it known to everyone.'

'He hasn't called,' her father stated. 'That's a good sign. Now Clara, sweetheart, calm yourself, eh? Go wash up and we'll have something to eat. You stay with us tonight. Momma's right; men get notions, they act like they're crazy, but then – they see sense. Luisa, how about some dinner?'

His wife hurried away to organize the kitchen. She did the cooking because Aldo liked her food and refused to have a cook in the house. His wife had fuck all else to do, he thought bitterly, with no kids or grandchildren to take up her time. He looked tenderly at his daughter. He hated to see her desolate like this. He couldn't bear it if she cried, when she was a little girl. It was worse now that she was a woman. How he hated that son of a bitch – he'd never made Clara happy. Given her no children – no joy in the last few years. But she loved him. To Aldo that was his only safeguard. If she was right and he had quarrelled with his father and walked out, then a joint sentence would be passed on him. Clara would be free to find another, better man. He went out to the kitchen to talk it over with his wife.

'My daughter comes home saying she's been deserted

144

and what do I do about it? Nothing! What kind of a father am I, eh? I wait for that arsehole Falconi to give me the news that his goddamn son has fucked up, while she sits crying . . .' He glared around him, as if Steven or his father were in view.

His wife said, 'You think it's right, Aldo? You think he's really left her?'

'I don't know,' he muttered. 'I was talking for *her* out there, not because I believe it myself, for Christ's sake. I'm going to call Luca. I'm going to tell him we have Clara here and I want to know what kind of crap we've been given!' He strode to the kitchen phone where Clara couldn't hear him.

The telephone was answered by Piero. He didn't wait for Aldo to explode but said, overriding him, 'We have a family crisis. A crisis for your family, too. My brother . . .' He managed to pause for emphasis, and his own emotion made it sound very real. 'My brother has broken our father's heart. My father can't talk to you, no. He's upset. He can't talk to anyone. You say Clara is with you? Yeah, I'm sure. My father wants a Family conference. Tomorrow. He says will you come to the house. No women. Just us, the Family. He says can you say nothing to anyone till tomorrow. Okay . . . Yeah . . . Believe me, for what he's done I could cut his balls off . . . Tomorrow, early.' He forced himself to say, 'Give love to Clara from Lucia and the kids,' and then hung up.

Aldo Fabrizzi put the telephone back. His wife looked up at him. 'It's true,' he said. 'He's screwed up on them too. We don't tell Clara tonight. Let her eat something and get some sleep. I see them tomorrow and I'll know what to do. I'm going to twist their balls for this, Luisa. No son of a bitch shames Aldo Fabrizzi's daughter!'

He stopped himself slamming the kitchen door. He wiped the rage off his face and went back to Clara. 'We'll eat soon,' he said soothingly. 'Let's take some wine together first, eh? And you smile for your Poppa, will you?' He reached over and patted her hand. It felt cold.

'I'll try,' she promised. 'Maybe you're right. Maybe he just blew his top and he'll come back when he's cooled off.'

'Maybe,' her father agreed. 'Now you drink this; put some colour back in the cheeks. And don't worry. Leave everything to me.'

The flight was called. Angela got up and walked with Charlie beside her. She had searched the departure lounge, watching the doors until the very last minute. With the broadcast announcement, her last stirring of hope died. They filed through and on to the aircraft. They were settled in their seats, hand luggage stowed away.

Charlie saw his mother's white face and said, 'Don't worry, Mum. You're not scared of flying, are you?' She hadn't minded on the trip out. In fact she'd been as excited about it as he was. He dug into his pocket. 'Here you are, have a candy. I bought some specially. They're jolly good. And by the way . . .'

'Yes,' she said, willing herself to smile at him.

'It's been the most super holiday,' he said. 'Thanks for everything.'

'I'm so glad, darling,' Angela said. The candy bar was soft and sticky in its wrapper. 'I'll keep it for later,' she told him.

She opened the book she'd bought for the journey and tried to make sense of the first page. It could have been Chinese. There were tears stinging her eyes, blurring the print. She mustn't let her son see. She was reminded of another journey, so many years ago, crossing on the hospital ship with her unborn child and the agony of parting in her heart. It was no less this time. She felt her son tugging at her sleeve.

'Mum! Mum, look! There's Mr Falconi. Gosh, he's on our plane!'

He was astonished by his mother's behaviour. The book fell on the floor and she was out of her seat, twisting

146

round to look as Steven came down the aisle towards her. And then pushing past Charlie, not even waiting till he got up to make room. And there was Mr Falconi, blocking the aisle for the latecomers behind him, saying to his mother, as he held both her hands:

'I thought I was going to miss it.' And his mother smiling and out of breath, as if something wonderful had happened. Like winning the football pools and coming into a fortune.

'I thought . . . I thought you'd missed it too.'

Then he was ushered away up to the front by the stewardess. Charlie bent down and picked up the book. His mother had trodden on it in her haste. Her high heel had scored right across the sickly looking heroine on the front cover.

'I don't want that, darling,' she said.

She was flushed and laughing at him and he said, 'Mum, did you know he was going to be on the same plane?'

'No, no, I didn't. But I was praying he would be!' And she linked her arm through his and squeezed it hard. 'I'll tell you all about it,' she said. 'I promise.'

The light came on instructing passengers to fasten their seat belts. The engines gained power, filling the cabin with a roar of thrusting energy as the plane began to taxi forward.

In a few minutes they were airborne, and the panorama of New York sparkled and glittered below them. Charlie leaned across to stare out of the cabin window.

He said to Angela as he sat back and the steep climb began, 'You're keen on him too, aren't you, Mum?'

'Yes, darling, I am. Is that all right with you?'

'It's great,' he said and grinned at her. 'I like him a lot. If you don't want that candy bar, can I have it?'

Piero turned from the window, letting the lace curtain drift back into place. 'They're here,' he said to his father.

'How many?'

'Aldo and that Kike lawyer of his. Two of his people besides the driver.'

'Let them in,' Luca Falconi said. He went to his favourite chair and sat down. The garden wasn't an appropriate place for this meeting. He was in mourning for a lost son. The gloomy sitting room was just right. There was chianti on the table. A big silver box of cigars. He looked like a man who had suffered a heavy blow. He looked like a man who grieved. All this was true. He must also look like a man who hated his own son, who had banished him from his life and forbidden his name to be spoken. Aldo Fabrizzi was not easily fooled. He had brought his lawyer to talk terms for Clara. Luca got up heavily, as if he had grown suddenly older, and shook hands with Fabrizzi.

'You know Joe Hyman? I brought him along to speak for my daughter.' Fabrizzi's eyes were like arrow slits in a stone wall.

'Come in; take some wine. Piero, you pour, will you? Mr Hyman, you'll have a glass?'

'Thank you, but I don't drink alcohol this early.'

'It's not alcohol,' Luca said sharply. 'It's wine.' He turned away. He hated Jews. He hated Poles and the Irish too. He looked at Aldo Fabrizzi and said, 'We have trouble, my friend.' He spoke in the dialect. He wondered if Hyman understood. Probably, since he worked for Fabrizzi, he would know Italian. But not the dialect.

'You have trouble and so does my daughter,' Fabrizzi agreed. 'Is he sick in his head?'

'I don't know,' Luca answered. 'Better if he was. There are doctors, clinics for that kind of trouble.'

'Then why?' The question came out like spilled gravel. 'Why has he left Clara and betrayed his family? Betrayed you and me, both.'

It was Piero who answered. They had rehearsed the scene together and he came in on cue. 'Because he's a yellow shit! Because ever since someone took a shot at him last year, he's been peeing in his pants.'

148

He stopped as his father held up his hand. 'You speak when I tell you, Piero. You have a big mouth. He's still your brother.'

'He's no brother of mine,' Piero insisted. 'And no son of yours, either!'

He gulped down a glass of wine and glared at Aldo and the Jewish lawyer. He had a reputation for violence; everyone knew he would get into a fight even now, just like he used to. He was believed, he could see that. He sat down. He'd played his part for the moment.

Luca said, 'Maybe Piero is right. He talked about enemies. He said to me here in this room, "I've had enough of the business. I want out. I've had enough of the Family." I reminded him. I told him what he owed to me, to our traditions. To Clara. "What kind of a life will you give her?" I asked him, and he stands there and says, "I'm going alone." I ordered him, Aldo. I pleaded, I begged. I never thought I'd live to see such disrespect from my own son. I gave him everything. You know how much I loved him. He was my eldest boy. I did everything for him. And he spits in my face and says he doesn't want it. He doesn't want what I've made for him.'

Aldo said nothing for a time. Then he shifted in his seat and said simply, 'I feel for you, my friend. But you have a good boy left. Me, I have only Clara, and her heart is breaking. It's a dishonour, you know that.'

'I know it,' Luca agreed. 'Those were my last words before I cursed him as his father. "You've dishonoured both families," that's what I said. "You're a coward and a traitor. You've no balls and you're not my son." A tear glinted in his eye and he let it drop on to his cheek. 'Ask what you want, Aldo. I'll pay the price of his dishonour to you and to Clara.'

'Where has he gone?'

They had been waiting for that question. 'He wouldn't say,' Piero interrupted. 'He wouldn't tell Poppa. He knows what's coming to him. There ain't no pisshole where he can hide after this!'

149

Aldo said quietly, 'You're looking for him?'

'The word has been passed,' Luca Falconi said. 'He'll be found. I think he's gone south. But we'll hear. It'll take time, that's all. When we find him, I'll do what has to be done.'

'You'll need a good man,' Aldo said. He glanced at his lawyer. 'He may have no balls now, but he had them plenty in the war. We take care of him together, Luca. That way, our interests are safe. And Clara holds her head up again. You talked about a price.'

'It's only what's due to her.' Luca nodded. 'And to you. I will provide for Clara.'

Aldo signified his satisfaction. He grunted and nodded. 'You're a man of honour,' he said. 'But first we have to talk about the business. Who's taking over from *him*?' He wouldn't lower himself to mention Steven by name.

'Piero,' Luca answered. 'And there's a cousin in Florida who's a good man with figures. They'll take care of everything together. I'm sending for the cousin. You will meet him; I know you'll think he's a good choice. Tino Spoletto, my uncle's sister's grandson. He's done good work in Florida.'

'When does he get here?' Aldo asked. He had never heard of the Spolettos before now. An idea was being born as he spoke. A very small unformed idea, but growing. If the Falconis were bringing in relatives that distant, then they weren't as strong on the administrative side as they made out. And Piero was a muscle man. Twenty years ago he'd have been running the protection rackets from the street. He'd never have seen the inside of that plush office on the West Side.

Luca was answering. 'Two weeks. He has to move his wife and family; find a place to live.'

He signalled to Piero, who refilled their glasses. The lawyer accepted a cigar. Nobody lit it for him.

Piero said in dialect, 'With my father's permission I'd like to ask something.'

'Ask,' Luca commanded.

Piero bunched his fists and squared his shoulders. He summoned hatred. He thought of Clara and the Fabrizzi who were forcing him to denounce and revile his brother.

'I want to be the one who puts out the contract. I want to do it and come to you, Don Aldo, and my father, and say, "It's done. I've wiped out the dishonour to my family."'

Luca didn't hesitate. 'I give permission, my son. I give the responsibility to you.'

'I said we should do it together,' Aldo Fabrizzi interposed. 'It must be a joint contract.'

Luca paused. It was going as he had expected. He was proud of Piero. Piero was doing very well.

'Give Piero three months,' he said slowly.

'A month,' Aldo amended, knowing it was nearly impossible to track down the miscreant in such a short time.

'A month,' Falconi father and son agreed together. 'We guarantee it.'

They had caught him and he accepted it. 'One month, thirty days. After that we join you in the contract.'

'Agreed,' Luca Falconi said.

'Maybe,' Aldo suggested, as if it were of little consequence to the main issue, 'You and me and Joe here should talk about some money for Clara?'

'The fucking house and half a million dollars!'

'We couldn't offer less,' Luca calmed his son. 'You know that. You don't think I want to give them anything? You think I like giving money to that barren bitch?'

'It won't buy them off,' Piero responded. 'No matter what you give them, they'll want Steven's head on a fucking plate!' He got up and banged his hand flat on the table so the empty glasses jumped. 'How're we going to do it, Poppa? How're we going to fool them?'

151

The old man looked up at him. He looked sad and tired and it grieved Piero to see his grief.

'I should be strong,' Luca muttered. 'He's betrayed us all. I shouldn't protect him. I should be strong.'

'You love him,' Piero said. 'I love him too. This isn't Sicily, Poppa. I've got Lucia and the kids to come home to; he had nothing. You're being a strong man. I believe that.'

'I can't forgive him,' Luca said. 'I can't forgive what he's done.'

'You don't have to,' his son said. 'But that's between us. Our family. We're not making a blood sacrifice for the Fabrizzi. So I ask you again: How do we fool them?'

'We give them someone else,' Luca Falconi said. 'Before the month is up. You said you would fix it.'

Piero nodded. 'I'll fix it. Now, Poppa, I'm going to call Momma. You look tired, you know that? And I'm going to tell her not to worry. She's been out there crying since those bastards came in here. And I'll call Lucia. You and Momma come over to our house for dinner tonight. See the kids before they go to bed. It'll cheer Momma up. And you too, maybe.'

'You're a good son,' was what Luca said as Piero went out. A good son with a brave heart, but it's going to take us all we've got to keep Aldo Fabrizzi from cutting our throats now that your brother's gone.

Clara rounded on her father. 'I don't want him dead! I don't want that, you hear me? I want him back!'

Aldo pitied her. He hated to see her crying and tearing herself to pieces, but she couldn't move him. He said, as his people had done for centuries before him, 'It's a matter of honour, Clara.' There was no appeal from that sentence. She should know this; for all the education and the fancy ways she'd adopted, she was a Sicilian and she knew as well as he did what had to be done. She couldn't move him. He said, 'I'm sorry, my little girl, but that's the way it is. If the Falconis don't find him in thirty days, then we find him. Now dry your eyes; go help your mother.'

Clara glared at him. As if she were a child. Stop weeping over the broken toy, *carissima*, go help your mother in the kitchen.

'No!' she shouted at him. 'I'm going home. I'm getting out of here.' She brushed her mother aside when she tried to reason with her, and Aldo stayed silent reading a newspaper while the women argued. She'd go, but she'd be back. Luisa didn't know how to handle her; she'd never been any good with Clara. He heard the front door slam. His wife came back into the sitting room. She sat down.

'She's crazy,' she said. 'I don't understand her. I don't understand how she could want a man who's done this to her.'

'It doesn't matter what she wants,' her husband said. He lowered the newspaper for a moment. 'I've spoiled her, that's the truth of it. Whatever she wanted, I said yes. But not now. She'll learn to live with it.'

Clara let herself into the house. The box with her new hats was still on the table in the sitting room, the ribbons tied. His empty glass was by the sofa. The emptiness, the silence made her want to turn and run out into the street again. She walked into the bedroom. How long since he had come there to make love . . . too long to bear remembering. Her frantic pleading mocked her. 'Take me with you . . . they can throw me out too.' But he had rejected her. Not cruelly, but with kindness. The kindness of finality. She couldn't cry anymore.

Maybe her father was right. Maybe the old solution to misery and betrayal was the only way. In the old days, the women kissed the wounds of their dead and cried out for vendetta. That cry was answered until the last member of the offending family had been killed.

Perhaps when Steven was dead, she might begin to live her life, to be free of the jealousy that tortured her, free of the desire that had brought her grovelling to him in the past. She kicked off her shoes and lay on the bed. How many nights she had laid there, waiting for him to come in, imagining the woman he was with.

Her eyes closed, she was near falling asleep from exhaustion. Then they opened suddenly and she sat up. There had been a woman. The agency hadn't found her because someone had murdered the investigator and bust the business. Steven had done it. Someone had alerted him that he was being watched. So the order was given and that was the end of the agency. And then he walks out. He walks out on his whole life, just like that.

She reached for the telephone. 'Poppa?'

'I'm eating, Clara.' He was angry with her.

She said, 'Poppa, forgive me. I was wrong. I'm sorry.'

'It's forgotten,' he said. 'You want to come home?'

'No. I'll stay here tonight. But I want to tell you something. When they find Steven, I don't think he'll be alone. I just want you to know that.'

She rang off before he could ask for explanations.

'Are you happy?' Angela asked him.

'You know I am.' He looked down at her. 'I miss the boy. He didn't want to go.'

'I know he didn't, but you mustn't spoil him, darling. He adores you, that's the trouble. But he had to go home and get ready for school. I'll have to go too.'

They were booked into the Savoy. For the first five days they had toured London together, showing Steven the city as he had shown them New York. They were so happy, the three of them, that Angela didn't know how she insisted upon their son going back to Haywards Heath. Or how she was going to follow him, leaving Steven behind.

'What am I going to do without you?' he persisted. 'Why can't I come and meet your father, take Charlie back to his school with you? You can't hide me, Angelina.'

'I don't want to hide you,' she protested. 'But as soon

154

as anyone sees the two of you together, they're going to know! Darling, try to be patient. Give me a little time to think of something. I can't just turn up with you and say to my father, "This is my husband. He wasn't killed after all. I told you a pack of lies." And what's Charlie going to say?'

'All right.' He turned away from her. 'All right, I won't argue. But I'm not staying here for long. I want my son and I want you. That's why I'm here.'

'I know,' she pleaded. 'I know, darling, but it's not so simple . . .'

'It wasn't simple for me either,' he said. 'I've got so close to my boy I feel I've known him all his life. We've done everything together, just like a family. Charlie accepted that. He's accepted me like a father. So you're going to have to square it, Angela. Because I won't wait around. Now I'm going out for a while.'

She called out, 'Steven, darling, please.'

But he didn't listen. He left the suite without saying when he would be back. He was angry and he was hurt.

She cried a little because she couldn't bear to be at odds with him. He'd been so generous, so loving. She sat by the window and looked out over the view across the Embankment to the Thames. It was dusk and the lights were springing up along the opposite bank, with a thin mist rising from the river. He'd given up everything to be with her and with his son. And she was hesitating, thinking of petty things like local gossip and facing her father with an old lie that didn't matter anymore. Charlie would accept whatever they told him. She had seen him and his father grow so close in such a little time. The bond between them was instinctive.

When he came back she was waiting for him. He looked at her. He didn't smile.

'Where have you been?' she asked. 'I was worried.'

'I took a walk.'

'We'll be late for the theatre,' Angela said.

'I'll shower and change.'

'Steven.' She came and put her arms round him. 'You're right. I've been selfish and stupid. I'm so very sorry, darling. I telephoned my father while you were out. I said I'd be home tomorrow and I was bringing someone with me. Someone very special. I told him to tell Charlie.'

'You mean it?' He raised her face to look at him. 'You really want it like that? I didn't mean to pressure you.'

She managed to laugh at him. 'Oh, yes you did,' she said. 'I've been sitting here feeling perfectly bloody for the past three hours. Are you happier now?'

'I'm happy,' he said and began to kiss her.

'The theatre,' she murmured. 'We'll be late.'

'To hell with it,' he said. 'We've got better things to do.'

'Well,' Doctor Drummond said. He'd said it three times. 'Well, I don't know what to say.'

He looked at his daughter and back to the man sitting beside her, holding her hand protectively. It was so confusing, such a shock, he couldn't quite take it in. My husband, she'd said. Charlie's real father. No, he wasn't killed. I told you a lie. And then the American breaking in, defending her.

'It wasn't her fault. She was right to do what she did. I wanted her to live in the States, bring up the child with my family. I scared her off. I asked too much of her. Now, I want to make it up.'

'I still don't understand it,' the old man said. 'It's all so extraordinary . . . quite extraordinary! Of course as soon as Angela said she was bringing someone home, I thought there was something in the wind, but I never expected this.'

'Not even when you saw him and Charlie together?' Angela asked.

Her father looked surprised. 'No. Why should I?' He saw them exchange looks and didn't understand why.

'They're very alike,' his daughter pointed out.

He considered for a moment. 'I suppose so. They're dark, you could say that. But I still don't see why you said he was dead.' He returned to the lie that seemed so unnecessary and so vexing. 'What a silly, irresponsible thing to do.'

Angela answered, 'I *was* silly and irresponsible, Daddy.'

'Didn't you mind?' he demanded of Steven.

'I don't mind now,' he said. 'It was like a miracle when we found each other in New York.'

'Must have been,' Hugh Drummond agreed. He cleared his throat and groped for his pipe, not knowing what to say next. They seemed happy enough. Fine-looking man, no wonder she hadn't wanted poor old Jim. He must have seemed like a stick-in-the-mud after this fellow.

'Does Charlie know?' he said suddenly. 'It's going to be quite a shock for him, you must realize that. What's he going to think of you, Angela?'

'We're not saying anything yet,' Steven answered. 'He's going back to school. It's a busy time for him. He's got his grades to think about. There'll be time enough. But we wanted you to know the situation.'

'I think that's very wise,' he said. 'If I was him, I wouldn't be pleased to find out I'd been told a lot of lies.' He gave his daughter an accusing look. He was thinking of his grandson. What they did with their own lives was their business. But he wouldn't have countenanced them upsetting the boy. 'God knows what your mother would have made of it all,' he announced, and, having stuffed his pipe, began to puff hard as he held the match to the bowl. Angela was wearing a big green stone on her left hand. He didn't know what it was. He wasn't much on gem stones and the thing was too large to be anything he recognized.

'How are you going to live?' he asked Steven that night, while Charlie helped his mother wash up the dinner plates. 'Do you have a job over here?'

'Not yet,' Steven answered. 'But there's no need to worry. I've got assets.'

'Depends,' Hugh Drummond muttered. 'Most shares bring in a pittance these days. As for government stocks . . . biggest damn swindle, if you ask me. We all bought them to be patriotic.'

Steven was glad Angela wasn't there. He understood the old man's need to ask questions, but he had a need of his own to answer them. She would have been embarrassed.

'I'm worth over a million dollars in stocks and bonds and I have property in the States worth more,' he said.

'Good God!' Angela's father stared at him. 'Good God. Have you really?'

'Really,' Steven echoed him. 'So like I said, you don't need to worry. I can take care of them.'

'I should think so,' was the answer. 'Nice to know anyway. I've left this house and whatever I've got to my grandson. Angela's got a bit from her mother, but I wanted Charlie to have something behind him. He won't need it now, I suppose.'

'He'll need it,' Steven answered. 'He'll be proud to have it because it came from you. He talked a lot about you.'

'Did he?' The old man smiled with pleasure. 'Did he, indeed? I think the world of him. He's a fine chap in every way. Straight as a die. And clever too. He'll do well, make no mistake.'

At the door of her single room Angela held out her arms to him. 'This is a nuisance, I know,' she said. 'But it can't be helped. It's only till Charlie goes back to school.'

He held her close. 'I can wait,' he whispered. 'So long as it's not too long. It wasn't as bad as you thought, was it?'

'No. I'd imagined all kinds of reaction from my father. He can be very difficult. He's mellowed a lot and all he cares about is Charlie. But he was good about it and you were wonderful with him. Thank you, darling.'

158

'I'm used to old people,' he said. 'We're brought up to respect them. It's important to us. Did you see our boy's face when we said we were both taking him back to school?'

'Yes,' Angela nodded. 'He was thrilled. When shall we tell him?'

'Tomorrow,' Steven said. 'I'll tell him. But I guess he knows already.'

'I'm going down to get some groceries for your mother,' Steven announced. 'How about coming along?' And as they walked from the house to the High Street, Steven said, 'There's something we want to tell you.'

The boy looked up at him. 'About you and Mum?'

'We're going to get married, Charlie. Will you be happy about it?'

'Gosh, I'll be thrilled skinny!' There was no flicker of doubt, no hesitation. His smile was a delighted grin. 'I thought you might when you turned up on the plane. It's super news. Just super!'

'I want to make your mother very happy,' Steven Falconi said. 'And I want to be a father to you, Charlie, if you'll let me.'

For a moment his son looked shy. There was a little colour in his cheeks that was close to a blush.

'It's felt a bit like that already,' he said. 'I hope you don't mind.'

'I don't mind,' Steven said. 'It's what I want most of all.'

If they hadn't been walking along a damp English village street with shopping bags in their hands, he'd have taken his son in his arms and embraced him.

The drove back to London from the school at Highfields. Steven had been introduced to everyone: 'This is Mr Falconi. He's going to be my stepfather.' The headmaster congratulated them and asked them in for a glass of sherry. It was the strangest world to Steven. A little world, with a set code of conduct that was so alien he might have been among Martians. He sipped the bad sherry and answered the predictable questions about how he liked England and where did he come from in the United States. Only they called it America, with shortened vowels. He felt as if he was just as alien to them. He hoped the education was good and that the school was the best available. There were a lot of things he didn't know about. Things he might want to change. He escaped from the headmaster's sitting room as soon as he could make an excuse. He found it stifling.

But Charlie was doing well. He was a credit to this odd, rigid system. The formality, the distance between the pupils and the staff that was so evident, had produced his son. He mustn't forget that. He must give himself time to adjust.

In the car on the way back, Angela said, 'I know you thought they were stuffy, darling. But they run that school very well. And he's so happy there. You could see that.'

'Sure he is,' he said. 'It's all so different from back home, that's all.'

He squeezed her hand and smiled. He didn't say anything, but he had already made up his mind that he didn't want to live in England. When they arrived at the Savoy there was a message for him. Nobody except Piero knew where to find him. He checked the time. His brother would be home by now. It wouldn't be safe to make contact through the office. While Angela bathed and changed to go to the Grill for dinner, he put the call through.

Lucia answered. She said, 'Wait, I'll get him.' She was a good girl. Not even in front of her own children would she call him by his name.

Piero came on the line. 'It's okay,' he said. 'Lucia's taken the kids upstairs. How are you?'

'I'm fine,' Steven said. 'Just fine. How's Poppa and Momma? How are things?'

'Okay, no problems. They came, had a meeting, we worked out the details. We paid your wife off.'

'Don't call her that,' Steven protested. 'Clara. How much?'

'Too fuckin' much,' Piero said. 'Half a million smackers and the house. You should've let me fix her when I offered. Now listen. Aldo wants your arse. No surprise, eh? We say we'll give it to him. So you got something you can send me? Clara gave you a wedding ring, didn't she?'

It was still on his finger, on the right hand.

'Yes,' he said. 'it's engraved with the date. My initial and hers.'

'Send it,' Piero said. 'Right away. You going to be at this number for a while?'

'A month, maybe more. What are you going to do, Piero? What's my father going to do?'

'Give Fabrizzi something to bury,' he answered. 'With your ring on it. The way I'll fix it, he won't exactly recognize him. Stay low and take good care, eh? How's the kid? He okay?'

For a moment Steven had a mental picture of the sitting room with hard little chairs, the walls covered with rows of boys posing for team photographs. Cricket. Football. The taste of the sweet, cheap sherry.

'He's fine,' he said. 'We just left him in school. Kiss Momma, will you? Say to Poppa – well, you know what to say.'

'Send me that goddamned ring,' Piero said and hung up.

Angela came into the room. She wore the same slim black dress he had seen that night at Les A. Her hair was loose and shining in the way he liked it.

'I'm ready, darling. How was your brother? Nothing wrong, is there?'

He came and took her hands. 'No. No, everything's okay. You're beautiful, Angelina. Let's go to dinner. I've got plans I want to talk over with you.'

They flew to Monte Carlo before Christmas. The weather in London was cold and miserable, with days of drizzling rain. As they stepped out of the plane, there were blue skies and a pleasant warmth in the air. A hired car waited for them. He took Angela's arm and hurried her across the road and into it. Then he checked himself. There was no need to move quickly, to seek shelter. All that was in the past. But old habits die hard. He still felt uncomfortable sitting in the middle of a public place without a wall at his back.

He had bought her a mink coat which she carried over her arm. She didn't need it in the mild mid-winter of the Côte d'Azur.

'It's so beautiful,' she said, gazing out of the car window at the bright sea below them, the land falling away from the curve of the Moyenne Corniche. Palm trees and handsome villas, charming little fishing villages, clinging to the edge of the ports. 'Darling, I'd no idea it was like this. I thought it would be dry and dusty. Like Sicily.'

'I thought you liked Sicily,' he said.

'I liked you, not the place,' she corrected. 'This is green and pretty.'

'It's a soft country for soft people,' Steven told her. 'Too much money. Too much of everything. Sicilians are hard because they've had to be.'

'You're not hard,' she said gently. 'That's what I love about you.'

'Not with you,' he said.

'Not with Charlie either,' she said. 'You'll spoil him to death, if I let you.'

'They wouldn't let him come,' he said. 'For one weekend. It's no big deal, but they wouldn't let him.'

'Of course they wouldn't.' Angela shook her head. 'He's only just gone back. How could they let him fly out here when everyone else was getting down to the term's work? Be reasonable, darling. I told you it was impossible but you would ring up and ask.'

'I hate that mean-mouthed son of a bitch,' Steven said. 'Back home, they'd have let the boy go for a weekend with his parents. Don't let's talk about it, sweetheart. You're used to being pushed around by creeps like that. I'm not. I hope you like the place we're staying. It's not fancy, but it's comfortable. We can drive into Monte Carlo inside of twenty minutes.'

'Are we going to the casino?'

He looked out of the car window. They were descending on to the coast road now. The signposts said Villefranche. They were very near.

'No,' he said. 'Not the casino. I've been there. Someone would remember me. These guys have photographic memories. They never forget a face or a name.'

Angela said, 'How can you trust this man, Maxton?'

'He's no friend to the Families,' Steven answered. 'They busted him for everything he'd got in Nevada. That's why the casino down here employed him. They've always kept our people out. We'll talk – if he doesn't like my proposition, I'll think of something else.'

'You could have started up in London,' she reminded him. They had argued about that, but Steven was adamant. Too many links with the States. That could come later. He couldn't explain that he was waiting to hear from Piero that, in their parlance, the goods had been delivered to Fabrizzi.

She was thinking of Charlie at school in England while they lived in France. It had sounded so easy when she spoke about it to him in New York. Easy for him too. All he seemed to mind was the prospect of leaving school and going with them. But there were holidays and half terms and the important things in a boy's life like sports days and prize-giving.

She closed her mind to the doubts. She had to think of Steven Falconi first – of his need for identity and purpose, and above all for his safety. That was the most difficult because they were so far away from everything connected with his past. Thousands of miles.

Villefranche enchanted her. It was like a toy fishing port with little boats laid up in the harbour, a few restaurants still open for local patronage. The season was long over, and apart from themselves the little hotel was empty. It was more of a guest house, with everything done by the *patron* and his wife. Steven had persuaded them to open specially with a tariff that was plainly a bribe.

They had dinner on the quay: good fish, rough wine from the nearby vineyards. She gathered the scraps and gave them to the starving cats that roamed outside. The other customers thought she must be American or English to waste good food on animals.

'It's basic,' Steven apologized, 'but it's not for long. Just till I talk with Maxton. Then I've got a surprise for you, darling.'

'I wish you wouldn't be so silly,' Angela said. 'I love it here. You forget, I'm not used to luxury and smart hotels. This is my idea of heaven, just the two of us and this dear little place . . . What sort of surprise? I don't trust you, Steven.'

'You're right,' he laughed at her. 'But I think you'll be pleased. I hope so. I love to see you looking happy.'

'I'm very happy.' She reached out and held his hand. 'I love you so much. And it changes all the time. I'm so glad you got rid of that wedding ring. I hated you wearing it.'

'Why didn't you say? I hated it too. What do you want for a wedding present, Angelina?'

'Darling,' she chided him. He was always buying her presents. The mink coat had been chosen without her and brought back to the Savoy as one of his many 'surprises'.

'I've got an engagement ring, my coat, all the clothes you've bought me. I don't want anything except that marriage certificate that makes it legal for Charlie. If it wasn't for him and Daddy, I wouldn't care a damn. I'm married already.'

'It'll be great having him here,' Steven said. 'And your father. He's quite a character.'

'He likes you,' she said. 'It's funny. He was always so offhand with me and my brother when we were children. When I see him doting on Charlie and spoiling him, I can't believe it's the same person. It'll be strange, won't it, getting married in a registry office?'

'It's only for the piece of paper,' he agreed. 'But we'll make it special. You'll see.'

The next day she left him behind and drove across to Monte Carlo. The man called Ralph Maxton was coming to see him at the hotel. Without realizing it, Angela had accepted the Mafia principle that women had no part in business.

Monte Carlo. She'd seen old movies centring on the casino with Hollywood heroes breaking the bank. She'd read about the gala evenings and the celebrities. Lady Docker had become a national figure to the British, starved of glamour by the war and the mean years of austerity after it. Millionaires were rare and enviable creatures; their wives, festooned with diamonds and draped in mink, were even more so. Monte Carlo was the dream setting for a fantasy world, presided over by a prince who had married a beautiful American film star.

It was beautiful; more beautiful than Angela had imagined with its backdrop of blue, cloud-wreathed mountains and the sugar-candy palace perched on a rock overlooking the sea.

She parked the car and walked. There were huge yachts, ocean-going by their size and tonnage, moored in the harbour, their pennants flapping in a stiff little breeze. The shops were opulent, discreet; the great names in French haute couture, the jewellers of world renown – Van Cleef and Arpels, Bueche Girod, Cartier – she passed the glittering windows, pausing now and then to admire without wanting to possess. She passed the splendid wedding-cake façade of the casino itself and was amazed to see that its doors were open and people hurrying inside. Middle-aged Frenchwomen, most of them housewives with shopping baskets on their arms, slipping in for a morning session in the Petit Salon, where the stakes were a few francs. And men too – ordinary, even poorly dressed. Driven by the same demon that possessed the rich who would come later. Greed and hope.

She had read somewhere that, for some unfortunates, it was the thrill of losing that impelled them. She wished Steven had chosen another business. Something that wasn't tainted by human weakness and venality. Impulse made her turn into a very large and expensive-looking hotel. There were no street cafés open where she was and the harbour was a long walk down. She was tired and rather cold. It was a very handsome hotel and a polite receptionist directed her to the cocktail bar. It was empty; she almost turned back. Then the barman smiled at her.

'Madame?'

She said, 'Would it be possible to order some coffee?'

'Coffee is served in the lounge, Madame,' he said.

'Thank you.' She didn't know where the lounge was. She felt conspicuous and silly for having come in. Then there was a movement and she saw that she wasn't alone after all. Another woman was sitting at a table in a corner, playing patience. She had grey hair under the soft overhead light. Angela sat down. The barman came to her table.

She said, 'Gin and tonic,' because it was the first thing she could think of. He brought it with a dish of olives and cheese straws. The bill was tucked underneath. The drink was iced and made her shiver. She drank half of it and decided to go. She put a five-franc note in the bill and got up. She didn't want to wait for change. As she left the table, the woman packed away her playing cards and turned round to signal the barman. Angela saw her fully in the light and just managed not to catch her breath. It was a travesty of a face: the left eye covered by an eye patch; the nose spread; a deep indentation where the right cheekbone should have been. Obviously she had suffered

166

a terrible accident, and been repaired by plastic surgery.

Her good eye was dark and large, with a penetrating stare that raked Angela from head to foot. She raised her hand and snapped her fingers imperiously. Diamonds flashed as she did so. The barman hurried over. He carried a bumper full of champagne. Angela kept her head down, avoiding the poor woman. How terrible if people stared.

It was really quite sharp outside. She should have brought her coat. She walked very briskly down to where the car was parked and drove back faster than she meant to. Maxton would have gone by now. She wanted to get back to the warmth and cosiness of their hotel, to find Steven waiting for her. She couldn't get the woman's broken face out of her mind.

'Why did you leave?' Steven asked.

Ralph Maxton was little changed. The nose was more prominent, the hair slightly thinner at the temples, but otherwise he was the same.

'We had a disagreement,' he said. 'The management and I agreed to part.'

'What sort of disagreement?'

He smiled. After all these years, how extraordinary to get a call from the gangster, Falconi, asking him to meet. And how extraordinarily fortuitous, considering his circumstances. He looked into that hard face and decided not to waste time telling lies.

'I started gambling,' he said. 'I hadn't turned a card or touched a chip in ten years and then one day I gave a friend some money and told him to play the wheel for me. We got away with it a few times, and then they called me in and said I was sacked. I'd broken the sacred house rule. After ten years I was out. No compensation, nothing.'

'Did you make money?' Steven asked.

Maxton gave the short, high-pitched laugh that Steven remembered. 'Good Lord, no. I always lost. It wasn't

167

that. It was the principle. I saw their point, but I thought they might have been a little more generous than they were. I'd given them good service.'

'I'm sure. So how long has it been?'

'A year.' He reached into his pocket and took out a packet of Gitanes. Matches followed. He inhaled, and sighed with pleasure.

The cheapest cigarettes, no lighter. A long year, as Steven judged. As if Maxton read his mind he said, 'I couldn't get work anywhere else, of course. The word gets passed round. I was blacked. So I did this and that and hung around. I've got used to living here and I've made some good friends. But . . .' He spread his hands in resignation. 'Even their largesse started to run out. Not that I blame them. So I was naturally intrigued to get your call.'

He talked a lot, Steven noted, but it was a good cover. He was shrewd and intelligent. He wouldn't have lasted ten years with the casino if he hadn't been valuable to them. But for the one weakness.

Steven decided to take the initiative. 'I took a chance. I remembered meeting you when I came to Monte Carlo. You were doing PR, you said. I made a few inquiries before I called.'

'The answers weren't *too* bad, I hope?'

'They told me what I needed to know about you. You were available. So I decided to talk to you about a proposition.'

Ralph Maxton stubbed out his cigarette. The movement showed that the edge of his shirtsleeve was frayed.

'Mr Falconi,' he said, 'before you tell me about this – er – proposition, there's something I must make clear to you. I inherited quite a sum of money when I was twenty-one. I also enjoyed gambling. I enjoyed it so much that it was becoming an embarrassment to my family. They suggested I went to America. My mother had connections in Boston and there was some mutter about banking and business. I didn't pay much attention to work, but I thought America would be fun. I had a pal I'd teamed up with in New York. Canadian, such a nice chap. We ended in Las Vegas. He got in so deep, I even went to the gentlemen concerned and actually pleaded with them to let him off. It wasn't a lot of money, actually, just a couple of thousand dollars. They were Italian American gentlemen like you, Mr Falconi. I'd dropped twenty thousand English pounds at their grubby little tables, but they wouldn't even listen. My Canadian friend went down to the beach one night and walked into the sea.' He produced the cigarettes again. 'Sorry, I'm being long-winded. But I don't and won't touch the Mafia. I thought I'd better explain my reasons.'

'You've explained them very well.'

'Can I finish my cigarette, or shall I go now, Mr Falconi?'

'You can suit yourself, Mr Maxton. After I've made one thing clear to you. I am not part of the Families any-more. You can take my word or not, but it's all you're going to get. And drop the Falconi. I won't be using that name here. All you need to know is what kind of a job I'm offering and how much it pays. And to keep your mouth shut, Mr Maxton.'

'Oh, I know how to do that. Shall we discuss the proposition then? As they say, I'm all ears.'

'I want to open a casino on the coast here. I want to finance it and run it, but I need a front man and I need someone who can engage the right staff and get it organized. You may, or may not, be the man I'm looking for. But I had to start somewhere.'

Somewhere you weren't known, Maxton decided. Not Nice, where the casino is established. Monte Carlo wouldn't let you through the front door. So you scrape the bottom of the barrel and come up with me.

'It sounds extremely interesting. Not particularly easy, though. Between the Principality, Nice and Cannes, they've got the big-time gambling tied up along the coast. With one exception.' He paused. The slightly mocking pose was cast off abruptly.

'Antibes is a possibility. It's near Juan les Pins – there are fine hotels, lots of rich clients. Grand villas, but no casino. The girls and boys go into Cannes which isn't that far away, or they come here. You might think about Antibes. Are you planning to build? That's millions, I warn you. And the French will make life hellish. They hate foreigners coming in.'

'I'd thought of buying,' Steven said. 'If I could find suitable premises.'

'Needs to be pretty big,' Maxton remarked. 'And central. That cuts out the old-fashioned Edwardian monstrosities inland. You've got to site it where it can be seen every day. Have you looked yourself?'

'Not yet. As it turns out, I'm going on to Cannes from here with my wife. Day after tomorrow.'

'Good opportunity. Give my regards to the charming lady.'

'It's not the same one. You can give them to her yourself if you come over to Cannes and help me check out what's available.'

'I'd be delighted. Does that mean I'm hired?'

'It means you're retained,' Steven said. 'Five hundred dollars to start. If we find something, we'll talk terms then. I pay in advance.'

'I am glad to hear it. My friends'll be even gladder. I can pay some of them back. What do I call you, if not Falconi?'

'Steven,' he answered. 'It's my name. After you've paid your friends back, get some new clothes. We'll be at the Carlton. Call me there.' He stood up.

Maxton didn't hurry. His attitude was cool. He was broke, but he showed neither gratitude nor respect. Steven had never met this type before. He supposed it was peculiar to the English. He didn't like it. But he needed the man. To start with. He held out his hand. It was their custom to confirm a deal by clasping hands.

170

Maxton looked surprised for a moment. When he did shake hands, his grip was firm.

Steven said, 'I'll make out the cheque. Or would cash be easier?'

'Cash would be *much* easier. Thank you so much.' He let himself out. 'See you in Cannes,' he said.

The smell of the strong, cheap tobacco was acrid. Steven opened the window to clear it away. He wondered suddenly whether he would ever see Maxton again. A gambler, a sponger; he'd sunk low in the last year. Only that curious arrogance was untouched by his vicissitudes – one of them hunger. His shabby suit hung on him like a sack. He might take the money and disappear. But Steven knew he wouldn't. Whatever he was, or had become, Ralph Maxton was a man who kept his word.

Steven had booked the best suite in the Carlton at Cannes as a surprise for Angela. There was no casino at Antibes. If he could find a building, get a foothold . . . Maxton knew people. Knowing the right sort of people had been his job in Monaco. He must get some decent clothes . . . Steven's mind was racing ahead, seeing possibilities, excitement rising as it used to do when he was planning an expansion of the family interests. He thought of his father and his mother and his brother. He suffered a pang of homesickness, of loneliness for them all that made him groan aloud. They had stood back to back with him when he asked. Never mind his father's anger. That was only just. They had been loyal to him. He only wished he could repay them. One day, maybe. If this project took off and was a great success. They'd have reason to be proud of him again. To forgive his rejection of the only way of life they knew. To understand that there were other ways to gain respect and maintain honour.

When Angela came back he took her in his arms and made love as if they had come together after a long separation. And in the evening they sat in their favourite

171

restaurant overlooking the sea. He told her briefly about Ralph Maxton.

'You'll see him in a day or two. I'm not saying any more, or it'll spoil my surprise. But it looks good, my darling. Everything's going right for us. We're going to have a wonderful life together. You and me and Charlie.' He leant across and kissed her. Outside the window, the hungry cats were waiting patiently.

'This is my wife, Angela,' Steven said. 'Ralph Maxton.'

'How do you do?' He shook Angela's hand and gave a tiny bow. He had a photographic memory for faces and names. He recalled the first Mrs Falconi and registered his amazement at her successor. An English lady: very pretty, poised but rather shy. She gave him a charming smile.

'Have a seat,' Falconi said. 'You'll have a drink, Ralph?'

'Thank you. That would be welcome.'

They had come up to the first-floor suite overlooking the Croisette. 'Come and meet my wife' was the invitation. He had imagined another sultry Italian, or perhaps some bottled blonde who'd hooked Falconi. He recognized Angela's type as soon as she walked into the sitting room. What the hell, he said to himself while they were introduced, was she doing with someone like Falconi?

'We've had a busy morning,' Steven announced. 'But I think we've found what we want, haven't we?'

'I think so,' Maxton agreed. 'Provided we can get the owner to sell it.'

Angela smiled up at her husband. There was no doubt about her feelings for him. 'That's wonderful news. But you mean it isn't on the market?'

'No,' Steven answered. 'But it's empty. Ralph heard about it. We went through the agents and looked at some properties, but they weren't suitable. Not big enough. Or too far out from the centre. This would be ideal if we can get it.'

She said to Maxton, 'How did you hear of it?'

He was quite an ugly man, but after a few minutes one didn't notice that. He had a most engaging manner. He gave her his full attention.

'Through friends, Mrs Falconi. You know I've lived and worked in Monte Carlo for some years and the Riviera's rather like a village. Everyone knows everyone else's business. This building belonged to a Russian aristocrat before the First War. He used to spend the winters here and he had a French mistress at the time. It was designed on a very grand scale; more like a palace than a villa. When the Revolution came, the count got the chop and the lady went on living there till she died. Then it was sold to a rich manufacturer who used to let it, and during the war the Germans requisitioned it. They didn't know quite what to do with it, but it was used as office and storage space. Very little damage was done as a result. A speculator bought it after the war. It was said he meant to sell it as a hotel, but nothing came of it. Too expensive to convert and run, is my guess.'

'It must be enormous,' Angela said.

'It is,' Steven said. She could see that he liked it and was excited. 'Too big for anyone to live in, but it would be just right for us. And wait till you see the site!'

'Directly overlooking the sea,' Maxton explained. 'With about four acres of grounds. They're in a bad state, but they could be landscaped and made rather beautiful. The main coast road runs a hundred yards away from the entrance.'

'It's ideal,' Steven insisted. 'It's perfect.'

'When can I see it?' Angela asked.

'Any time you like, Mrs Falconi,' Maxton said. 'I managed to get hold of a key.'

He hadn't fooled Steven. They had gone to the agencies and looked at everything unsuitable just to whet his appetite, and then Ralph brought him to the great crumbling palace by the sea and produced a key out of his pocket.

'A friend of mine knows the owner,' he explained with a slight smile.

'Let's see inside,' was all Steven had said.

Double commission. Real commission to the 'friend' whoever he or she might be, and hidden commission to Maxton if he brought off the sale. It didn't matter. He'd let Maxton know he knew when the time came. What was important was the potential of the place. They'd picked their way through the jungle of overgrown garden and into the vast, damp-smelling house, shuttered against vandalism. Steven didn't waste time. He didn't bother going up the stairs to the first floor, he only had to look at the sweep of them to imagine what an entrance they would make for the Salons Privés where the rich would go to lose their money.

He said to Ralph Maxton, 'I guess this is what I want. Let's go back to the hotel. My wife's expecting us.'

Angela turned to Steven. 'Darling, can we go after lunch?'

'Of course. That suit you, Ralph?'

Maxton had nowhere else to go, he was sure of that. 'Suits me perfectly,' Ralph agreed. 'What time shall I come back?'

Her response was generous. He liked her even more on account of it. 'Why don't you stay to lunch? Then we can all go together.'

'Good idea,' Steven added. His hesitation would have escaped anyone less acute than Maxton. For a moment he was tempted. But it wouldn't be wise. He stood up.

'You are kind,' he said to Angela. 'but I've arranged to meet someone. If I came back at say, three o'clock, would that be all right?'

'Fine,' Steven said. 'We'll see you at three.'

Angela got up too. 'I'm sorry you can't stay. Next time, you must.'

He gave his little bow and left them. He went down in the gilded elevator and out into the bright, crisp sunshine. Marvellous climate, even in November. He had a

174

new suit, a decent shirt and an overcoat. He felt for the key in his pocket and rubbed it between thumb and forefinger like a talisman.

'Good old Great-Uncle Oleg,' he murmured. 'What a laugh you'd have out of this.' Then he made his way inward off the Croisette to a small café where he ordered himself a cheap lunch. Falconi would buy the house. Maxton knew the type. When they made up their minds, there was no second thought. He was used to making big decisions with a lot of money involved. Used to getting what he wanted. Maxton drank very little; alcohol was not his weakness. You couldn't gamble unless you had a clear head. For ten years he'd kept clean, but he still didn't drink more than a glass or two of wine. Champagne with the clients when they were winning. When they lost, he paid for it, and encouraged them back to the tables to try their luck again. What a shitty way to live. What a wonderful way to die, at the end of it all. During that lean and hungry year, he had thought about dying. Nobody would have given a damn if he'd followed his poor friend of long ago into the sea and let it take him to its peaceful depths. He had considered the idea, even tossed a coin in his despair – and been relieved to see the toss in favour of living.

His friends had been so good to him; two women had helped support him and they had been the first to get some of his five hundred dollars back. One said she loved him and he believed her. But he didn't love her. He had never loved anyone because he hated himself.

This was a second chance. He was superstitious, as all gamblers are; he thought of fate as an entity, usually malignant, sometimes capriciously kind. Fate had brought him and Steven Falconi together in the casino all those years ago, binding them with an invisible thread. Fate had pulled on that thread at the last moment to save him. He would work for Falconi. Build up a new casino, take his place among the rich and wasteful people of this world. Great-Uncle Oleg, roistering with his French whore, would smile on him from the shadows. It was family legend that he had opened his trousers and pissed at the Bolshevik firing squad.

By three o'clock he was sitting in the front of Falconi's big hired Cadillac and they were driving to the Palais Poliakof. The first thing Falconi had said was they must change the name. Maxton agreed. He would think of some way to resist it later.

'Well,' Steven asked her. 'What do you think, sweetheart? Do you like it?'

He wanted her to enthuse; he wanted her to share his vision, to see the plaster freshly gilded, the rotten floors replaced and carpeted, the wrecked chandeliers sparkling and restored to their old glory. He held her hand and asked her to support him, and she did. Not because she could share his vision of the future, but because she loved him too much to cast a doubt. To Angela it was a huge, decrepit structure that would cost millions to put right.

But she held tightly to his hand and said, 'You'll make it wonderful.'

'And you'll help me?' he demanded. 'You'll go every step of the way with me, Angelina? I'll need you. I'll need you to take care of the decorating, the interiors – and the grounds – we'll make the grounds a feature. There's a terrace right on to the sea. I'm going to rebuild that, have it lit at night.'

Maxton had opened the shutters. They had walked up the great staircase and opened double doors on to a series of huge reception rooms with superb plasterwork ceilings and majestic marble fireplaces. The chill sunshine streamed in through cracked window glass and he stood with Angela beside him, visualizing how it would look.

Ralph Maxton had withdrawn, leaving them alone. He could see that she was bewildered, even overwhelmed, and admired her for concealing it. It wasn't her world. He knew what kind of world she had lived in. He could see it. A nice country house, a village, respectable,

176

professional father, Women's Institute mother. His own family owned villages like that in England. His mother had been president of this institute and that local charity until she died.

He had flown back for her funeral in the grim Derbyshire church where they were all buried, and hurried back to Monte Carlo the next morning. No one had been pleased to see him or sorry to see him go. He was an outcast. The epithet 'black sheep' had actually been used by an ancient relative still using the vernacular of sixty years ago. His father had been too occupied with his own grief to make any effort with a son who had caused his mother so much shame and anguish. Ralph felt they would all have preferred him not to have come at all. He fled back to his place of exile, where the sun shone and he was accepted by his peers.

No, this wouldn't be easy for Angela Falconi to encompass. This was dross and tinsel, in spite of its grandeur. No real values for her in Steven Falconi's dream. He went back downstairs to wait for them. He wondered what had happened to that other woman, with her obsessive passion for her husband. She'd stood beside him like a panther on guard over its kill. It was an unpleasant thought and it disturbed him. He mustn't be morbid. Or sentimental.

When they came down the stairs and into the entrance hall, he walked up to them smiling and said, 'Impressive, isn't it? Did you think so, Mrs Falconi?'

'Oh, yes. It's certainly impressive. My husband wants me to have it decorated. I'm going to need a lot of help.'

'We've been jumping the gun,' Steven interposed. 'It's not bought yet. It's not even priced. Come on darling, we'll go home. Ralph, we'll take you back and the car can drop you off at the hotel. It's up to you now to get the details. We mustn't run ahead of the deal before it's made.'

He whispered to Angela as they went outside and

177

Maxton locked up, 'I don't want him to think I'll buy at any crazy price. I'll get it, but at my figure.'

'But he's working for you, isn't he?' she asked.

'He's working for himself. And the owner, and then for me. Don't worry; I know these guys. They take a cut out of everything. That's okay, so long as it's not too big. Now, my darling, when we get back why don't we call Charlie? Tell him all about it?'

'Yes, of course we can,' she said. The school didn't encourage parents to telephone unless there was an emergency, but she didn't want to explain this to Steven. 'But I don't think it'll mean much to him,' she said. 'He's no idea what a casino even looks like.'

'He will,' he insisted. 'He'll get the idea when I've talked to him. It'll be his place one day.'

5

He was a humble man, a man of no importance in the Family hierarchy. But he'd had his hand in the till. There was no excuse because he was doing well enough out of his delicatessen, and the amount he paid in dues was the same for everyone with his profit margin. But he'd been greedy and dishonest, salting away part of his takings. And he'd been found out.

Piero Falconi liked to keep tabs on everything that happened, no matter how trivial. The conviction and punishment of a humble man who had turned thief was part of his responsibility. He decided to look at the condemned man. He'd been called from his shop and held in a warehouse. His wife was told he'd been sent out of town on Family business. She didn't protest. She hoped he wouldn't be away long because she had to manage the shop on her own. He didn't see Piero. He didn't see anyone because he was blindfolded. He had stood trial in that warehouse and argued with tears and pleading for his life. He told lies, hoping to be believed. He wasn't. He didn't know what his sentence would be.

Piero looked at him. The man was slumped in a chair, abandoned to fear and despair. About the right age; different build, losing his hair, but he'd do. Piero gave a slight nod towards the two guards. One of them moved quickly and without a sound up behind his victim, and slipped the noose of a garotte over his head. At last the man fell forward to the floor. It was not a quick death.

Piero said. 'Load him up and get him out of here. Take

him to Freddiano's place. He'll set it up like an accident.'
He walked out.

Freddiano was a truck driver. He had the body rolled
up in packing paper in the bottom of his truck with a load
of cases piled on top of it. He drove through the night and
the following day, stopping to eat at motels and snatch
sleep in his cab. He arrived in a small town on the south-
eastern seaboard when it was just getting dark. He was
tired and hungry. He stopped at a petrol station with a
small café attached. While he was inside eating, the
owner's two sons removed the body and loaded it into
the boot of a second-hand Ford. In that and a pick-up
they drove out of town and parked on an isolated road.
There wasn't a house in sight and no car had passed while
they waited. They took the dead man out of the boot. He
wasn't stiff to handle anymore. They put him behind the
wheel of the Ford. The older of the two sons of the garage
proprietor noticed something.

He said, 'Jesus!'

His brother looked where he was looking. The corpse
had lost a finger on its right hand. They poured petrol
over the front seats, drenching the figure slumped over
the wheel. They laid a trickle of petrol away from the
parked car; the engine was left running. They lit a twist of
paper and tossed it on to the oily snake creeping across
the road. Then both men took off at full speed for the
safety of the pick-up. They dropped flat behind it. There
was a roar, a bright sunburst of flame and then an
explosion as the Ford's tank went up. When they stood
up to look there was nothing left but a red and orange ball
surrounded by a river of flames.

When they got back to the garage, the truck driver was
drinking coffee and reading the sports page of the
newspaper. He paid the bill and left. Nobody said
anything.

The local police poked around among the blackened
ruins of the car and found what was left of the dead man.
The local newspaper carried a report of the accident and

180

the coroner issued a certificate of accidental death. The victim was identified by his brother on the evidence of a finger missing. The name was given as S. A. Falconi, a resident of New York State. It didn't mean anything to the people of Little Hills.

Three days after the inquest, a copy of the newspaper report and the death certificate, wrapped round a small cigar box, were delivered to Aldo Fabrizzi by special messenger. He read the paper, studied the certificate and, last of all, opened the little box. Inside was the real proof from the Falconis that the debt of honour had been paid.

He filed the death certificate. He was a practical man. Clara would need it when she remarried some day. He kept the wedding ring and threw the rest away. He looked at the ring and was satisfied. Clara had bought it herself, ordered the inscription. He had been irritated because she insisted on buying it at Tiffany's instead of using the local jeweller. The initials, the date, were as he had seen them. He indulged in a quiet moment of satisfaction. Vengeance was sweet indeed. Then he went to find Clara.

He hadn't expected her to react as she did. She looked at the ring and heard him say, 'He's paid for what he did to you. You can be proud again.'

And then she collapsed. She fell at his feet, screaming in hysteria. It shocked and terrified him. For a few moments he thought she had gone out of her mind. They got a doctor who sedated her and ordered a nurse to stay with her. His wife, Luisa, raved and accused him of driving their daughter mad with grief.

At first Aldo was distraught. He had relied upon her healthy hatred to sustain her. Instead he realized the intensity of her love. But he was tough, even with the child he loved. She would calm down. She would accept in her heart what she had agreed to in her head. He waited and after a few days he went in to see her. She looked ill, with deep black pits under her eyes.

He took her hand and held it. '*Cara mia*, it's time you got up. You have to live your life and start again.'

'Tell me something, Poppa?'

'Yes, *carissima*?'

'Was he alone?'

'Yes. He was alone. There was no one with him.'

She turned her head away. He squeezed her hand. He felt a response.

'I thought there was a woman.'

Aldo and his wife had thought so too, after their long discussions. He said. 'It seems there wasn't. But it doesn't matter. What's done is done. He shamed you and me and his own family. He's paid the price. But you're the one I'm thinking of – you should be glad, Clara. You should be glad you're free and justice has been done.' He spoke tenderly yet firmly to her in the Italian they always used when they were alone.

'If there was no woman, then I can live with it,' she said.

He nodded. He understood his daughter. He bent down and kissed her cheek. Now she would get better. He went out of the room to tell his wife.

'It's your brother,' Angela called out.

Steven was in the hall decorating the Christmas tree with his son. Hugh Drummond was fiddling with the string of coloured lights. Snow had fallen outside. It was going to be a proper Christmas. There were parcels in bright paper stacked under the tree. They'd only been back from France for ten days. Steven handed her the box of glittering glass balls.

'You take over, darling,' he told her. He went into the sitting room and closed the door. 'Piero?'

He listened for a few moments. His brother spoke in dialect. At the end he said in English, 'It was a laugh, I can tell you. The old bastard came to see Poppa and embraced him and said he shared his sorrow. Yeah, in those words. I could've kicked his balls in. Clara had to have the doctor. No, she's okay now. Grieving, he said. Like fuck, I said to Lucia. So no worries, Steven. You're

182

in the clear. And us too. How's everything going? You got the place in France tied up yet?'

'I signed the contract two weeks ago. Never tangle with a French lawyer; I nearly went crazy. But it's fixed and all I have to do is pay on completion. I wish you could see it, Piero. It's going to be one hell of a casino when I've finished.'

'I wish I could too. Maybe one day I'll bring Lucia and the kids on a trip to Europe . . . we might call in.'

'I'd like that,' Steven said. 'The family's well?'

'They're fine. Momma's got a cold. You know how she is in the winter. I told Poppa I'd be speaking to you. He sent messages.'

Steven didn't ask what they were. He knew his father wouldn't forgive his defection. Piero was trying to make it easy.

'You send love from me,' he said. 'You're staying home for Christmas?'

'No, we're going down to Florida. Momma needs some sun. What about you?'

'I'm in Angela's father's house. We're all together. She's well and the boy's great. He grows taller, Piero. I wish you could see him too.'

'Like I said, Brother. One day maybe,' Piero said. He felt choked with emotion. He wished he could say what he felt. But words were not easy for him.

Lucia had come in and, seeing his face, had slipped her arm round his waist. 'Send him love from us,' she said.

'A merry Christmas,' Steven wished him. 'And thanks for what you've done. If you hadn't stood alongside me, I couldn't have made the choice.'

'So long as it's what you want,' Piero answered.

'It's what I want,' Steven told him. 'I miss the family like hell. But I wouldn't change anything. I'll keep in touch.'

He rang off. It was settled. The Fabrizzis believed he was dead. There'd be no war between his father and them. Clara would find another man, get married. The book of his old life was closed for good.

It was a strange feeling of finality. He didn't go back to the hall and the Christmas tree. He threw some logs on the fire. It was a cold house by his standards. He'd no experience of an English Christmas. It would be very different from the noisy, crowded gathering which would be celebrating back home.

'Steven?'

He looked up and saw his son standing there.

'Aren't you coming back? We've nearly finished.'

'I'm coming,' he said. His heart lifted again. He put an arm round the boy's shoulders. 'When I'm married to your mother,' he said, 'I'd like you to do something.'

'What?' The young mirror image smiled up at him. He was tall, shorter than Steven by only a few inches.

'Call me Father.'

'Do I have to wait till you and Mum are married?'

'Not if you don't want,' Steven answered.

'All right then, Dad. Let's go and do the lights before Grandpa fuses them again!'

They were married in London. It was a registry office and Steven had filled it with flowers. The registrar was very nice and said he was sure other couples would enjoy them afterwards. Hugh Drummond and Charlie were there and so was David Wickham. Angela had insisted on inviting him. He'd been so understanding when she had to let him down. Steven didn't like pansies and he was cool when they were introduced. Wickham had given them an expensive wedding present, a decanter and six whisky glasses of cut crystal. Angela was delighted and Steven was annoyed. He didn't mind Angela inviting the doctor who'd been in love with her. He was the kind of rival Steven tolerated easily. Solid, older, as romantic as a brick wall.

She looked very beautiful and very happy. She'd chosen yellow, which was a bright spring colour for a

184

dismal January day. She carried a little posy of yellow and white flowers and wore a hat with a little silk veil. He suddenly remembered the hat with the feather she'd worn at that lunch in New York. The day that had changed his life. He held her hand and together they went through the ceremony and shook hands with the registrar afterwards.

David Wickham congratulated him and then kissed Angela lightly on the cheek. 'Lots of happiness, my dear,' he said. 'Such a jolly wedding service. I *hate* churches . . . so gloomy.'

Steven could have kicked him.

Then their son was embracing them and Angela's father was patting him on the back and they were out and on their way to a wedding lunch. They had chosen the Savoy again. Steven had booked a private room. It was, as Wickham kept on saying, a very jolly lunch, with lots of champagne and splendid food, even a wedding cake with two tiny figures on the top.

It was their son who surprised them all by getting up and proposing the toast. His face was rather flushed from champagne and excitement. 'Here's to Mum and my new father,' he said loudly.

'Long life and happiness,' Hugh Drummond prompted him.

Charlie repeated it, raising his glass to them both. 'Long life and happiness, Mum and Dad.'

Angela's eyes filled for a moment. She said, 'Thank you, darling,' and everyone else got to their feet and drank to her and Steven. She had never imagined she could be so happy.

Ralph Maxton had a merry Christmas. Falconi had finally agreed the price. He had to remind himself to think of him as Lawrence, but it wasn't easy. One million francs. Maxton had taken two per cent commission on the deposit. He decided to celebrate. He booked himself to the Hôtel de Paris – one of the cheaper rooms admittedly, but then the hotel was full. He was persona non grata at the casino, but he didn't care. He was glad to be back in his old haunt, and visibly prospering. He asked one of his women friends to join him. Not the one who had shown settling down symptoms when she lent him money. Madeleine was as footloose as he was; a lady who depended upon lovers and gambling and so far had done very well out of both. She claimed to be Lebanese and traded on her exotic looks. Ralph thought French with a dash of Moroccan was more likely. She had a delightful sense of fun and a flamboyant attitude he found amusing. Sometimes he imagined his father's reaction when she splashed champagne over herself and invited him to try the vintage, shrieking with laughter as they lay on the bed.

It was a gala Christmas and Ralph bought her an expensive Hermes bag as a present. She accepted it, pouted because it wasn't jewellery and then whispered mischievously that she had something for him too. They were sitting in the crowded cocktail bar and even Maxton was a little drunk.

'What?' he demanded. 'What's my present then?'

She slid her hand under the table. 'Me,' she giggled. 'And you know what that normally costs.' They both laughed immoderately at the joke. 'Thank God that old fart, Bernard, is back with his wife,' she went on. She took a cigarette out of a gold case and handed Ralph the matching lighter. He held it steady with some difficulty.

Bernard was old, and a fart. Maxton knew him and thought it a fair description. Madeleine fleeced him mercilessly when he came to Monte Carlo. He couldn't keep away from the baccarat table or from her. He said she made him feel a young man again. Ralph believed that too.

'Ah, Ralphie, my darling, what a pity you're not really rich. Then I could move in with you.'

'How do you know I'm not?' he asked her.

'Because you'd have a suite, my darling, not that little

186

fart-hole on the top floor! You know the only thing I can't stand about this hotel?' She didn't wait for him to answer. 'That!' She pointed to the woman with her back to them, sitting with a bottle of champagne on ice, playing patience on her own. 'Every time I see her, my stomach turns. Why does she show herself, Ralphie? Why doesn't she hide? I would, if I looked like that.'

'She lives here,' he told her. 'She's lived here for years. It's a strange story. She used to come here with her husband, years ago. He was very, very rich. Rumour said he'd played the black market for the Germans during the occupation. Anyway he died and she used to come here during the season alone. She was a damned good-looking woman. I often saw her about. She'd pick up the odd man now and then, but she didn't go in for waiters or bellboys. Her name's Madame Duvalier. She lived in a villa up by Beaulieu. She was attacked and robbed one day and beaten up till they nearly killed her. That's all they could do, apparently, to mend her face.'

'What a horror,' Madeleine exclaimed. 'I feel quite a *frisson*. Let's have some more champagne.'

Maxton said, 'She sold the villa and came here. She has a permanent suite and she never leaves the hotel. She's become a sort of landmark, one of the Monte Carlo legends.'

'If I owned this place I wouldn't keep her,' Madeleine declared. 'It must put people off. I'd tell her to go.'

Maxton allowed himself a cynical smile. For all her charm and gaiety, she was a heartless creature. He patted her hand and said, 'When God made you, darling, he missed out on only one ingredient.'

She demanded to know what she lacked. 'What? What's missing in me?'

'Nothing,' he retracted. He felt sober suddenly and he didn't want to. 'Here's our champagne. Drink up, darling, and then you can give me your present.'

It wasn't all pleasure and self-indulgence. He made contacts among the casino employees. Knowing that their movements and associates were checked by the casino detectives, he rang up his old boss Maurice and asked to meet him. On neutral ground, of course.

They had a drink together. The older man had heard Maxton was back and in funds. 'You seem to be doing well,' he remarked.

'I am. No thanks to you. I couldn't get a job anywhere along the coast.'

Maurice shrugged. 'Well, Ralph, you knew the rules. You can't blame us.'

'Oh, no hard feelings. I know you people play quite rough when anyone oversteps the mark. That's why I've asked you here. I want to put my cards on the table. If you'll pardon the metaphor.'

No smile. No lightness of touch. No education either. Stop treating these people as if they'd gone to Winchester like you, he chided himself. Little arrogant touches like that had made him secret enemies in the past.

'I'm here because I've been asked to open and manage a new casino.'

'The one in Antibes?' They had heard about it as soon as the first approach to the lawyers was made. They heard everything concerned with gambling on the coast.

'The one in Antibes,' he confirmed.

'And who's the buyer? We were told it was a consortium from West Germany.'

'I can't divulge that,' Maxton said. 'It's confidential. And for all my faults, Maurice, I never gave away anything to anyone. Which is probably why I've got the job. No, the reason I'm here is to try and recruit some staff.'

He saw the angry flash in the man's eyes.

'You've come poaching?'

'I've made inquiries, that's all. I wanted you to know. I don't like being underhand. You have the best men. If anyone wants a change, I'm prepared to see them.'

'You shouldn't do this,' Maurice said. He was pushing back his chair.

188

Maxton raised a hand to stop him. 'Be realistic. You're the best. There's nothing to touch Monte Carlo anywhere in the world. If anyone working in the casino wants to leave, then they're not good enough for you anyway. I'll only get what you'd have to sack in the end for one reason or another.'

After a pause, Maurice sat down again.

'You're a shrewd man, Ralph. You have brains. It's a pity. You could have risen high if you'd stayed with us.'

'Thanks. It's a nice compliment. But we both know I'd gone as high as I was ever going to get. I'd still be doing exactly the same if I was here today. No one who isn't Monégasque or French gets a look-in at the top. At least I've got a chance to manage something this time.'

'And you think it'll succeed? Against us, against Nice and Cannes?'

'I think so. Not that you need to worry. But the others might.'

Maurice stood up. He told the waiter to charge the casino for their drinks. He held out his hand, and Ralph Maxton shook it formally. There was no friendship, no human warmth, but a business understanding.

'It was good that we discussed this,' the older man said. 'I shall tell the directors they needn't worry about the staff. You're quite right. Only the second-rate would want to leave us to work for anyone else. I wish you luck.' He didn't, but Ralph thanked him.

By the middle of February he had lined up a small but competent staff, including one of the best croupiers. He didn't offer them bigger wages. As Steven had instructed, he offered them shares in their own enterprise. Each man would have a stake in the casino. And a personal stake in keeping out the con men and the professional cheats.

He cabled Steven in England, asking him to come down. He got an answer back the next day. 'Deal completed. Kindly arrange suitable rented accommodation for my wife and self. Arriving Saturday next week.'

Maxton wondered why they didn't go to a hotel, but he rang up all the best agents and got a list of flats and villas available. But first he telephoned his contact in Monaco to ask when his final commission would be paid on the sale of the Palais Poliakof. The postwar speculator was living in a house close to the Italian border. Maxton had a worry at the back of his mind that he might actually cross it without honouring his debt. The man had been short of money and living on credit, with few assets but the crumbling white elephant itself. Maxton needn't have concerned himself. The draft was paid promptly into his bank. When Maxton inquired after the owner, he was told that he had taken a long holiday.

'Someone suggested it was Cosa Nostra buying the property. He didn't wait around.'

So that was why he'd paid up so promptly, Maxton realized. A German consortium; the Mafia from Naples. Let them all speculate. What did it matter? All they'd ever find out was the name Stephen Lawrence. They could make what they liked of that.

'I hope you like the villa I've found for you,' Ralph Maxton said. He had met them at Nice airport. Steven had hurried down the steps and across the tarmac, Angela on his arm. They passed through customs very quickly in spite of the amount of luggage that came with them. Ralph was well known to the police, the immigration and the customs. He had smoothed many paths for clients in the old days. He gave Steven a brief report as they drove along the coast road.

'Buildings,' Steven remarked, looking at the construction going on in Nice. 'Nothing but new blocks going up. We're in for a boom.'

'It looks like it,' Maxton agreed. He glanced into his mirror. Angela was sitting in the back. She looked pale and hadn't said much.

'We had a bad flight,' Steven had explained at the

airport. 'My wife didn't like it, did you sweetheart? Quite a bumpy ride.'

'I've engaged a maid and a cook for you,' Ralph told her. 'The villa's ready. Shall we go there first?'

Steven answered. 'I'll stop off at the Poliakof. I want to see how they're getting on. You take Angela to the villa and come back for me. You could put your feet up, darling.'

'I'm all right now,' she insisted, and smiled at him. She didn't look it. 'It was really awful. I thought we were going to crash.'

They turned into the gates and Steven jumped out of the car. The palace was shrouded in tarpaulin across its roof and scaffolding was going up outside.

'Give me a couple of hours,' he called to Maxton. Then he took the steps two at a time and vanished into the house.

'It's chaos in there,' Ralph remarked. 'The villa's only about fifteen minutes away. I hope you like it,' he said again. 'I think you will. It was the best on offer.'

It wasn't big. He had Angela in mind more than her husband when he was viewing those on the list. She wouldn't want a vulgar, overpowering place. This was charming and intimate. It was comfortably furnished in Provençal style and had a beautiful garden. It belonged to a Parisian who wanted to let it for a year. It was up in the hills with plenty of shade against the scorching summer months.

He didn't know how long they intended to stay or how often they would come. But the Palais Poliakof would take months to repair and furnish. He could imagine Angela being happy at the villa. He rented it.

He brought her inside and the maid appeared. She was a thin-faced woman in a blue overall.

'I'm Janine,' she announced. 'Welcome, Madame. My mother is in the kitchen. Shall I tell her to prepare something for you?'

'Some coffee, please,' Angela said.

'I've ordered lunch,' he explained. 'They're a good couple and they won't fight, like two strangers might. Here.' He helped her off with her coat. 'Let me take that. Now, do you want to have a quick look round and then do as your husband suggested? Put your feet up, have your coffee.'

'I want to see over it,' Angela said. 'This is so pretty, Mr Maxton. I know I'm going to love it. You've been so kind, arranging everything.'

'It's what I'm paid for,' he remarked lightly. 'But it's been a pleasure. This is the drawing room. The dining room leads off. It's not too big, but you'll have plenty of space. Some of the places round here are so vast they can be rather gloomy.'

She looked less pale already. She exclaimed with enthusiasm over the reception rooms and said with her disarming candour, 'This is the prettiest bedroom I've ever seen. And look at the view over the garden!' There was a balcony and she opened the french windows and stood out on it.

'It'll be quite cool,' he explained. 'If you're here in the summer.'

'Oh, we will be,' she said. 'I don't think Steven wants to go back till he's seen things taking shape. Let's go down and find our coffee, shall we?'

The cook came in with a tray. She was plump and cheerful, as a cook should be.

Angela sat down and said, 'I feel at home already. Steven will love it here.'

'You're feeling better, aren't you, Mrs Lawrence?' he said. 'You looked rather pale when you arrived. It must have been very stormy.'

'It was terrifying,' she admitted. 'We were thrown all over the place. Steven didn't mind, he kept telling me not to be frightened, but I couldn't help it. I'm afraid I made rather a fuss. I'm not used to flying.'

'Personally,' Ralph Maxton admitted, 'I loathe it. I like trains and cars and ships. My mother used to say that if

192

God meant us to fly he'd have given us wings. It was one of the few things she said that I heartily agreed with!'

He laughed. It was high pitched and she thought suddenly: That's the only thing I don't like about you. That cold laugh.

'Does your mother come down here?'

'No, Mrs Lawrence. She's dead, I'm afraid. She wasn't the sort of person who came to the Riviera. She and my father liked to stay put.'

'Please,' she said. 'Call me Angela, won't you?'

'You're very kind. Are you sure Mr Lawrence won't mind?'

'Good Lord, no. He's the most informal person, surely you realize that by now?'

'Well, I hadn't actually. But if you say so, Angela it is.'

'More coffee?' she asked him. 'Do you go home often?'

'I never go home at all,' he said. 'The last time was for my mother's funeral.'

'Oh! Where is your home?'

'Derbyshire. In the bleakest, coldest corner of it, to be exact. And where do you come from?'

'Near Haywards Heath,' Angela said. 'My father is a doctor. He's retired now. We've always lived in the village. He still does. I do hope he'll come out and stay with us. He's rather a stick-in-the-mud too, like yours.'

Maxton smiled politely at the idea. He couldn't imagine any resemblance between a country GP and his awe-inspiring father.

'My son's coming out for Easter,' she said.

He was adept at hiding his surprise at most things. But he was taken unawares. 'I didn't know you had any children.'

'I was married before,' she said. 'During the war. He's fifteen now and he's enormous.'

'Oh, I see. You must have married very young.'

'I did.' Angela finished the coffee. 'You're not married, are you, Ralph?'

'No, no-no, not me. I'm a confirmed old bachelor.

Nobody'd put up with me on a permanent basis anyway. Good Lord, look at the time. I'd better go and pick up your husband.'

'And this time,' Angela insisted, 'you stay for lunch.'

When he had gone she went upstairs. The maid had unpacked most of her suitcases already. She wandered through the guest rooms, inspecting the place that would be her home for . . . how long? She didn't know. It had a restful atmosphere. For a moment she had imagined some awful gothic monstrosity with turrets and phoney battlements. She'd seen a number of them dotted along the coast behind their ornamental gates – many of them slightly rusting – relics of a vanished age. This was a charming house where she and Steven could be happy.

She went downstairs and, on impulse, asked if there was anything special in the cellar. She had been cowardly and silly on the flight and she wanted to make it up to Steven. Yes, she was told. Janine reeled off a list of spirits, wine and liqueurs. Champagne, of course. Would Madame like that before lunch? Mr Maxton had told her to put some on ice in case. Mr Maxton had thought of everything.

When Steven came in, he hurried to her and hugged her. 'Angelina, you must come down with me and see it. There's been so much done already.'

She saw Ralph Maxton in the background. He could blend into a setting so that you hardly noticed him. Or not, if he chose to make his presence felt. He wasn't looking at either of them, and yet she knew he was.

Lunch was relaxed; excellent food and some choice wines. Maxton set out to be amusing; he had a sharp tongue, but the joke was often at his own expense. Angela liked him for that. When he started telling anecdotes about the casino, they forgot the time. He was a gifted storyteller with a light touch. He had Steven's whole attention.

He's enjoying himself, Angela thought, play-acting, holding the stage. He's not really at ease with Steven and

194

this is his chance to get a little closer to him.

Like a true actor, Maxton knew when to bow out leaving his audience wanting more.

'I am sorry,' he said. 'I've bored the two of you to tears with all these old stories. I must be on my way.'

'I've enjoyed it,' Steven said. 'You must tell us some more.'

'Oh, I will, if you give me any encouragement. Some of the early stuff is fascinating. Before the Great War when the Russians used to come for the winter season.'

'Like Count Poliakof?' Angela asked him.

'Yes, there are some amazing stories about him. Anyway, thank you for lunch. I'll call in tomorrow morning, Steven, and we'll go through the estimates and progress reports if that suits you.'

'Nine o'clock,' Steven said.

'Nine o'clock it shall be.' And with a little bow to Angela, he left them.

'He's a strange man,' she said. 'I can't quite make him out.'

'Don't you like him, darling?' Steven frowned. 'I thought you got along well.'

'Oh, of course we do. He's very nice, very amusing too. It's just that he's different. He spoke about his home and his family in such an odd way. How much do you know about him?'

'Everything,' Steven said. They were sitting in front of the fire, holding hands. He was a very physical man, always touching her, claiming her. They hadn't gone back to the building. He said she looked tired and he'd been selfish to suggest it. Tomorrow they could spend a lot of time there. He said, 'I know everything about him. I had him checked out before I made any contact. You're right, sweetheart, he is an odd guy all right. His father's some English lord. Ralph started gambling in the clubs and private gaming parties in London. He got mixed up with some crooks who fleeced him over there, so he was sent to the States. They should have known better. He borrowed a lot of money and lost it. He was in hock so deep he took his mother's jewellery and tried to sell it. The family paid him off. I guess they wrote him off in the end. So he got a job with the casino and he stayed clear of the tables for ten years.'

'But why did they employ him? Why did you?'

'Because with his background he knew everybody. He knew how to handle his own kind. He puts on a very good front. You've seen it. People fall for that sort of thing. And being a cheat himself, he's good at spotting cheats. He did a wonderful PR job for them in Monte Carlo. He's sharp as a tack, darling, and that's what I need. He's got class. I like that. And he knows all the press. They'll write us up when the time comes. This Count Poliakof who built our place was some relation. He doesn't know I know that. I just wanted to make sure he hadn't got a stake in selling it. He hadn't. Just the commission.'

'I hope you can trust him,' she said. 'I feel rather uneasy about him now. Why shouldn't he try to cheat you in some way?'

Steven smiled down at her. 'Because he knows I'm not the kind to take it well,' he said gently. 'So don't worry about that. It'll work out fine for all of us. Now why don't we go up and try out our new bed?'

'Why don't we have another child?' he said to her.

'If we go on like this, we'll have a dozen,' she protested.

He stroked the full breasts, moulding them between his hands. 'A girl next time,' he said, and started kissing them.

The curtains were open and his body was silver in the light of a big cold moon. She drew him down and opened to him. 'You're the sort that only has boys . . .'

It was taking shape. Even Angela could see the skeleton

of the palace fleshing out. Every day she went with Steven, picking her way among the building materials, watching the plasterers and bricklayers moving from room to room, with carpenters repairing damaged panelling and doors. The marvellous ceilings were cleaned off and regilded and the scaffolding was coming down from the façade.

Time passed quickly because there was so much to do. Maxton was everywhere, directing the works, closeted for hours with Steven poring over plans and costings. Angela was planning colour schemes. She'd turned one of the guest rooms into an office, with wall charts and coordinates pinned up. She travelled to Lyons to look at specially woven silks and velvets, and together they scoured the antique shops along the coast. Steven didn't want too much modern reproduction furniture in the Grand Salon and it was Maxton who persuaded him to invest in eighteenth-century Aubusson tapestries instead of pictures. Bad pictures wouldn't do, and genuine period works of art would cost a fortune. Tapestries were not fashionable and therefore cheaper. Maxton had an eye for good pieces of furniture.

'How do you know so much about it?' Angela asked him once as he rejected a handsome black lacquer commode as a nineteenth-century copy of an early eighteenth-century Régence piece.

'Oh, we had a few nice things at home,' he said. 'I suppose you get an idea when something's right. My mother was always banging on about it. Bored me stiff.'

'You must tell me about her one day,' Angela suggested.

He looked at her and smiled. 'Not much to tell. She was quite sweet when you got to know her. Not that I and my brothers and sisters did, till we were nearly grown up. We had nannies all the time.'

'How many brothers and sisters?'

'Two brothers, three sisters. All well married and respectable. Not a bit like me. Come and look at this. It's rather nice.'

He wouldn't talk about himself. Every attempt to draw him out was waved aside with some flip remark or self-deprecating joke. He wouldn't let Angela come close and yet she knew he liked her, as much as he disliked her husband. She couldn't explain why she sensed this because outwardly they worked in harmony and were friendly on a superficial level.

Maxton was invited to dinner on a regular basis. It was always on a Friday at the end of a working week. And, as he once said of someone else, he sang for his supper. He fed them scandals, named names, conjured up the great courtesans of the past and their rich protectors. And he started introducing them to selected people during the spring, when the coast began to come to life.

He had an extraordinary memory for names and faces and could pinpoint the background and origin of anyone they met.

'You've got to start off on the right foot here,' he said. 'We must make a plan of campaign. It's called social climbing.' He laughed in his mirthless way. 'The French are terrible snobs. And one never really gets to know them, not that you care. You want a good, smart guest list to get our opening off the ground and some minor Royals and film stars, and I'll have a go at getting Nettie Orbach to grace us with her presence. She always draws the press.'

'Who's Nettie Orbach?' Steven asked.

'Wasn't she a child bride or something?' Angela said.

'Quite right. Married some Bolivian at sixteen and went off with a few million smackers after a couple of years and hooked some Kraut prince with more millions. There've been five husbands in all, and she's on the prowl for number six. She eats gossip columnists for breakfast. And they just can't get enough of her. I'll see what I can do. Nettie does owe me a favour. More than one.'

'What sort of favour?'

'Nothing to worry about,' he told Steven. 'She was in Monte a couple of years ago and one of the paparazzi got hold of some photographs she didn't want published. I bought the negatives for her.'

Angela went back to England to collect Charlie and her father. They were coming out to spend Easter at the villa.

Hugh Drummond was reluctant to come. He made excuses about leaving the house and the garden. Mrs P. thought she was keeping an eye on him but it was really the other way round. She was quite forgetful, he said, and might easily go out, leaving the gas on. Angela didn't take any notice. He wasn't a man you could bully, and she'd never known how to cajole him either. She relied on Charlie to do that. And of course, he came because his grandson urged him, and because they wouldn't meet otherwise during the holidays.

To Angela's surprise Ralph Maxton had offered to fly back to England to bring her family out.

'But you hate flying,' she protested. 'You said you did.'

'Not quite as much as you do,' he answered. 'I'd be only too happy if it would help.'

'Wasn't that kind of him?' she said to Steven afterwards. 'I said no, of course. I've got to get used to small planes if we're going to live here for long periods. But I was very touched.'

'Why shouldn't he offer?' Steven said. He saw nothing remarkable about it. Anyone of his own people would have done the same for the Don's wife and family.

'Well, it was thoughtful.'

'He's paid to be thoughtful,' was Steven's answer. 'He's paid to do whatever is needed. And very well paid, don't forget. So you don't have to be so grateful or I'll get jealous.'

She looked at him and laughed. 'Oh, I wouldn't worry about Ralph, if I were you.'

It was a glorious spring. The villa gardens bloomed luxuriously, and Angela watched her son and his father play tennis and go riding in the hills together as the sunny days ran on and the holiday was nearly over.

Her father was not his old active self. He preferred the garden and a book to the long walks she had associated with his spare time. He looked thinner, she thought, and asked if he were really as well as he maintained.

'Perfectly well.' He sounded irritable. 'Don't know what you're fussing about. When will they get back, do you know?'

He missed the boy and she could see he was a little bit put out by Charlie's infatuation with Steven.

'They've gone down to look at the palace again. You will come and look round before we go back, won't you? I know Steven would like it.'

'Yes, all right. Not that it's going to mean anything to me. Must be costing a mint by the way he was talking. Hope he knows what he's doing.'

'Oh, he knows,' she said. 'One thing I've learned about Steven. He's got a head for business.'

'And you're happy?' he surprised her by saying. 'You seem to be.'

'Daddy, you've no idea how happy I am with him. It just gets better and better. I wish you'd stay on here for a bit. Why don't you?'

He shook his head. 'I've got to get home. The place'd go to pot if I wasn't there. That lazy old bugger John doesn't even weed the border at the front if I'm not after him. It's lovely here, and it's been very nice. Very nice indeed. But I'll be glad to sleep in my own bed. Ah, isn't that the car? They must be back.' He heaved himself up and went in search of his grandson.

Angela picked up his book, marked the page and placed it on his chair. Not so long ago she would have been hurt. But not now. She could be tolerant of the selfishness and insensitivity of old age because Steven's love was proof of her own worth. He had given her confidence in herself. She knew that her father loved her in his own way and within his capacity. He didn't have to show it because Steven's love was enough. He's given me so much, she thought. Thank God I've given him Charlie. It helps to make it even. Then she got up and hurried out to find them.

'It's amazing, Mum,' her son said. 'It's huge, isn't it? And so swish. Will I be able to have my friends over and take them along?'

'As soon as it opens,' his father promised. 'You're coming to the opening, Charlie. You'll be there with your mother and me.'

'Have you fixed a date yet, Dad? When will it be ready?'

Steven had an arm round his son. He hugged him. 'August,' he said. 'At the height of the season. It'll be a gala evening and I'm going to show them that anything the other casinos do, I can do better!'

'I bet you will,' Charlie declared. 'I can't wait. Isn't it exciting, Grandpa? You haven't see it yet!'

'No. But you tell me when, Steven, and I'd like to, er, have a look at what's going on. Is that chap Maxton coming round this evening? He plays a damned good game of piquet.'

It was odd how well he got on with Ralph Maxton. They played old-fashioned games that Angela had barely heard of, and Ralph managed to let the doctor win. Steven thought it was amusing, and rather spoilt the picture by telling her that Ralph was a notorious card shark in his early years.

'When he wanted money he played bridge. If he wasn't winning, he palmed the cards. But he's being kind to your father and that's good.'

Hugh Drummond was impressed by him. 'He's a gentleman,' he said to Angela. 'It makes all the difference. I know that place in Derbyshire. I went there one year when your mother and I were on a walking tour. Magnificent house. They're the old aristocracy. He's a very charming chap. Very charming.'

It made her smile to realize that her father was a snob.

The time came for packing up and going home and Steven came with them. They spent a few days in the house at Haywards Heath. It was cool and it rained.

Steven said, 'Darling, I'm missing the sun. Let's go home.'

She realized that she was missing it too. Missing the villa which seemed less than ever like a rented house, missing the excitement of helping him create the new casino.

'I'll tell Daddy. He won't mind, now that Charlie's gone back to school.'

'It would make sense if he moved over with us,' Steven said. 'I think you worry about him, don't you?'

'A little bit. He's got very old, suddenly. But he wouldn't dream of it. He's a very self-contained man, very independent. He wouldn't be happy out of his own environment. But thank you for offering.' She reached up and gave him a kiss. 'I do love you,' she said and then hurried out to find her father.

The maid, Maria, watched Clara. She was frightened of her mistress. She had such bad moods when she shouted and lost her temper for no reason. She was always finding fault. She prowled round the house like a caged tigress – restless, bored and unhappy. No husband and no children, Maria thought sourly. All the beauty treatments couldn't soften that face. And she couldn't find herself another man yet. It wouldn't be proper. Maria missed Steven Falconi. He was a real Don, like his father. A good man, kind to his own people. A man you respected. She wondered if she could go and see Don Luca and ask if she could get a job with someone else.

Clara was restless. She wasn't sleeping well either, but she wouldn't take pills. She knew too many women who'd started on that path and slipped into tranquillizers and dependence. She would cope on her own. The maid got on her nerves. She was always shuffling about, pretending to work. She was a sly old bitch and Clara didn't trust her. She was one of Luca Falconi's people. Clara toyed with the idea of sacking her. It gave her pleasure to imagine it. But she did nothing.

It was getting hot and humid in New York. Her parents were moving to Santa Fe for the summer. She didn't want to go with them. She didn't know what she wanted to do or how to occupy herself. Her father had already mentioned the need to marry again.

'I don't want another man,' she declared and, for the moment, he accepted that. But only for the moment. In a few months when there wasn't a pretence of mourning, he'd start pressing her. She felt dead sexually. Cold in body and in spirit, as if she, not Steven, had died. He'd paid the price of his betrayal. They'd killed him as she'd warned him they would. She wished in her desolation that she had been with him in that car.

She had a hair appointment and lunch afterwards at the Plaza with two women friends. They weren't Italians. They didn't belong to her world and she had nothing in common with them except money and a liking for clothes and plush restaurants. She didn't feel like going. The day stretched ahead in emptiness. Dinner with the parents, TV and please to stay the night and not go back to that lonely house . . . Why didn't she sell the place and move closer to them? Reading her mother's sideways looks at Aldo, sitting over the pasta and the wine. She needs a good husband to take care of her . . . maybe some children this time.

It made Clara want to scream. She had been looking at a fashion magazine without taking any of it in, flipping the pages impatiently. She threw it aside and got up. She was thinner than ever, taut inside her black dress. No appetite still, living on her nerves. Maybe she couldn't face dinner at home that night . . . Maybe she'd go to a movie instead. They'd be hurt. She couldn't cancel them. She went into the bedroom to get ready. The hairdresser and the lunch would kill her enemy, time, for a few hours.

203

She retouched her make-up, drawing darker lines round her eyes to stress their size. They were huge and black as sloes in the thin face. She painted her mouth scarlet and opened the dressing table drawer to choose some earrings. There was a smart new fashion jeweller whose costume pieces were as pricy as the real thing. Ken Lane earrings and a matching brooch. They looked good. But the earrings pinched and she swore and pulled them off.

There was the little box. She'd put it in the drawer, right at the back where she couldn't see it, but it had worked its way forward and was under her eye. Her fingers touched it. A small square leather box with gold tooling round the edges. She'd made her father give her Steven's ring. Open it, temptation urged her. Touch it, indulge your pain. She took it out. The proof of his death. The pledge given by the Falconis that the debt to her was paid in full. It lay cold in her palm. She remembered the wedding service, when she had ex-changed it for the one still on her finger. The fierce joy and expectation welling up in her as she circled in his arms in the wedding waltz. She shut her eyes because it was an agony she couldn't resist. He had such beautiful hands. Sensitive, erotic. They had always roused her when she looked at them, imagining their touch. They'd struck her too, and even that became a memory she savoured. Once she'd slipped the ring off his finger and locked it over the one he'd given her. It was a symbol of her passion, her need to possess him completely and be herself possessed.

She did the same thing then. She slid the ring on to her finger. It hung loose. So loose that if she bent her hand it fell off, clattering on to the dressing table top. She stared at it. She tried again. It was too big for any of her fingers; even the thumb.

Clara held it in one hand, turning it to see the inscription. It was visible, a little worn, but still quite clear. S. & C. and the date in figures, 5.18.50. It was the same ring she had given Steven. The ring he had been wearing on the day he walked out of that bedroom and left her. But it was three sizes bigger. She went through the ritual again. Her right hand this time. The right hand was always bigger and the fingers thicker than the left.

It fell off. She held it up and stared at it again. No man with hands like Steven's could have worn it. She clutched it tightly and the reflection in the mirror contorted suddenly until the face was hardly recognizable. She stood up, knocking the stool over. She kicked it aside. She shouted a terrible blasphemous Sicilian oath.

'*Porca Madonna*!'

Maria heard it and cowered. She hid herself in the kitchen. She heard the bedroom door slam on its hinges and then the front door, till her ears hurt. An hour later she answered the telephone. The hairdresser was calling to ask if Mrs Falconi had forgotten her appointment.

The ladies at the Plaza waited half an hour, then decided she wasn't coming and started lunch.

'Clara, Clara, it's business. You can't disturb your Poppa.'

Her mother pleaded, wringing her hands. She had never seen her daughter like this. She was used to temper and outbursts, but not this deadly rage.

'This is business, believe me. Now do you call him, or do I?'

Clara swung away from her. She was trembling. She couldn't unclench her hands round the handbag. The box with the gold ring was inside it.

Her mother was arguing again. She was such a fool, such a stupid fat doormat of a woman. Savage thoughts chased through Clara's brain; cruel, unthinkable criticisms that she would have suppressed with shame before. No wonder Poppa goes for big tits and blondes.

She shouted suddenly, 'Shut up! Shut up and listen to me! Give me the number.'

'He'll be angry,' her mother said. 'He's with Gino over at the warehouse. There's a meeting today.'

Clara didn't listen. She knew the number of the warehouse where her father summoned his henchmen. She knew the big upstairs room above the containers and storage where they sat round a table. It would be smoky, with a smell of wine and garlic and human sweat. She knew, because she'd been there once. Aldo had given her the choice of a fur coat for her eighteenth birthday. He'd laid the minks and silver foxes out on the table and told her to pick what she wanted. She chose the most expensive and he had laughed and put it on her himself. She had it in a cupboard somewhere. A pastel-blue mink, which was not fashionable anymore.

She dialled the number and a man answered.

'I want to speak with Don Aldo.'

'He's busy.' The tone was rude.

Clara spat back. 'It's his daughter. You tell him it's urgent.'

'Okay.'

It seemed a long time while she waited. Then her father, not sounding pleased at the disturbance. 'Clara? What the hell do you want?'

She said in a calm voice. 'If there's any of Luca Falconi's people with you, don't say anything. They've cheated us, Poppa. Steven's alive.' Then she hung up. She spoke to her mother.

'That'll bring him home,' she said.

'Yes, yes, it's been altered all right.'

The jeweller put down his magnifying eyeglass. He had been an associate of the Fabrizzis over many years. Second-generation Russian Jews who ran a pawnbroking business on the West Side and fenced stolen goods for a few big clients. Aldo trusted him.

'Made bigger?' Clara demanded.

He nodded. 'By two sizes at least. It's well done. They haven't spoiled the inscription.' He checked again with the glass to his eye. 'You wouldn't see it without this, Don Aldo. It's a good job,' he said again. He handed it back.

Aldo weighed it in his hand for a moment. 'Thanks, Leo. I just wanted to be sure, that's all.'

'They used eighteen-carat even, to keep the colour of the gold the same,' Leo added. 'I guess it was altered for someone else to wear.'

'I guess it was,' Aldo said. 'Thanks. The family well?'

He never neglected the formula. It was expected of him to inquire about the Rabinovitchs' welfare and to spend a minute or two while Leo answered.

The woman was fuming with impatience. The old Jew was surprised to see the Don with a brunette, however striking. He brought his blondes along to buy them jewellery. Not too expensive, but nice pieces. Leo always gave him a special price.

He said, 'Julia's had some troubles. She has pain in the hip, but as I tell her, we're not so young anymore. But the boys are well and the grandchildren. They make life good for us.'

'Give Julia best from me,' Aldo said formally. 'And keep well.'

They got into the big limousine, Aldo's bodyguard protecting them, and sat in silence as the car speeded home. He took his daughter's hand and held it. They gripped fiercely for a moment. It was a pact between them, that gripping of the hands.

'They gave us a dummy,' he said. 'They set us up, Clara. They cut the finger off some guy and changed the ring to fit. They won't get away with it. I promise you.'

'I know they won't,' she answered. 'I want him found, Poppa.'

He turned and looked at her. She was all he cared about, his only child. He'd watched her suffer, tear herself to pieces over Steven Falconi. He thought suddenly: She's clever, my girl. She's got a brain. She saw through it. He was proud of her in a different way.

'We'll find him,' he said. 'But we settle with all the bastards now. We wipe them out.'

'Yes,' Clara said. 'And we take over everything that's theirs.'

He noticed that she had said 'we'. It didn't sound as presumptuous as it might have done. As they drew up before the entrance to his house he said gently, 'You were tough on Momma. I don't blame you, but you will make it right.'

'I'll make it right,' she promised. As soon as her mother came out to the hallway to meet them, Clara put her arms round her and said, 'Forgive me, Momma. I didn't mean it. You're the best mother in the world.'

She looked at Aldo, who nodded in satisfaction. He liked peace in the family. He sat down and let his women wait upon him. He took wine, a man at ease in his own home. And he planned the systematic murder of the Falconis down to the last male.

Tino Spoletto hadn't wanted to leave his home in Florida and come to New York. His wife had complained bitterly about uprooting the children from their schools and selling their nice house. They had a good business. They owned a chain of restaurants and bars with illegal betting on the side. Tino didn't need to employ accountants. He was too good with figures himself. He carried so much in his head and he was never out by a cent.

He'd never been in trouble, not even as a boy. He was the quiet one in the Spoletto family, always doing well at school. He had missed out on the Falconi blood. His wife, Nina, was happy with him, contented with their life and devoted to her three children. They were part of the Family, but on the fringe. Little was asked of them except a favour now and again which paid for the protection in their businesses. No one reneged on a debt to the Spolettos. No one in the local police department raided the back rooms where the bets were taken.

But when the call came, Tino knew he must obey. It

was an honour to be asked by Don Luca himself to fill a place left vacant by his eldest son. An opportunity not to be refused. They'd sold their house, found a good convent for the girls and a high school for their boy. Nina wanted a house in a neighbourhood where she'd make friends. They bought one in Little Italy. Her mother lived with them. She'd never learned to speak English and at least she could go to the shops and find a few old women to gossip with.

And after all the months of settling in they were happy. The Don and his family had taken them to their hearts. They were invited for the family Sundays and the children played with Piero's children. Nina and Lucia Falconi went shopping and talked women's talk together. Tino hadn't moved into Steven's office. That was taken by Piero, now designated the Don's successor. Nobody mentioned Steven. Tino didn't ask questions. There was disgrace and dishonour involved. It wasn't his business as a distant relative to inquire about details.

He was doing a very good job. Don Luca was pleased with him and Piero slapped him on the back and invited him out to Minoletti's Trattoria for a good dinner and to talk business. He had respect for Piero, who would be the top man one day. He wanted to please him and he was devoted now to the old Don himself. He had been good to them, generous over the new house, fond with their children. He was a family man inside the Family. Now when they came to the house on Sundays, Luca greeted Tino with a kiss.

It was a nice summer day and they were in the walled garden. A big table with a white cloth was set out under the trees and the women were busy in the kitchen while the men sat around in their shirtsleeves and talked over the chianti.

Tino said, 'I got a letter from a cousin yesterday, Don Luca. She mentioned the Fabrizzis are having a big get-together in Santa Fe.'

Piero said sharply. 'How the fuck does she know?'

They hadn't heard anything about it. Courtesy between them indicated at least a mention, if not an invitation.

'She's in the catering business. Her husband and his brother specialize in wedding parties, anniversaries, that kind of stuff. They didn't get the Fabrizzis' order but they knew someone in the business who did. Eighty people, she said, and all the families too.'

Don Luca said slowly, 'What sort of party?'

'She didn't say.'

'I'd like to know who's invited,' Luca Falconi said. 'And the reason.' He didn't show his anger. They were partners and tied by marriage. Clara was a Falconi by name at least. Aldo Fabrizzi had said nothing about a big party.

'Why Sante Fe?' Piero demanded. 'It's a hell of a long way for people to go without some special reason.'

'They have a place there,' his father said.

Piero looked at his Cousin Tino. He was sharp-eyed and long-eared. He'd picked up that item on the Fabrizzis and their 'party'. Piero could smell disloyalty in a man. And loyalty too. Tino was playing watchdog in his quiet way. Piero liked him for that. From the first day he had made his feelings about the Fabrizzis clear to his cousin.

'I don't trust that old bastard, Aldo. I don't trust any of them. So keep your eyes open, Tino. We won't always be partners with that load of shit.'

'Maybe it's because it *is* a long way,' Tino suggested. 'Maybe they thought we wouldn't get to know about it.' He picked up the bottle and refilled the Don's glass.

Piero banged the table. 'You think it's a Family council?' he demanded. 'You think they're getting the heads of their people together to agree something and not telling us?'

'It could be,' Tino said.

Luca Falconi leaned towards them. 'This cousin of yours, can she get someone into the caterers? Someone who can use their eyes and ears and let us know what they pick up?'

Tino looked abashed. 'I did that already, Don Luca. I hoped you'd think it's okay. I just had a hunch something was up.'

'You're a good boy,' Luca said quietly. 'You use your head. I like that. Good. You've done well.'

He saw his wife and daughter-in-law and Tino's wife come out carrying dishes of salad and cheeses, and said, 'We say nothing about this to the women. My wife's not been too well; she mustn't worry, the doctor said. It's been a hard year for her. A hard year for us all.'

'Leave it with me,' Tino Spoletto said. 'I'll find out what's going on. My cousin knows she'll be rewarded.'

It was a noisy lunch with everyone talking, the children of Piero and Lucia demanding their grandparents' attention and Tino's older family well behaved. The women were smiling and contented and the Don presided over them all, blessed with three generations round his table. And the cousin who was becoming more and more like a son to him. If there was danger, he would be forewarned.

It was a matter of honour, the old men said. The greyheads spoke in solemn language, using the distinctive phraseology of the ancient culture. The younger men responded with the language of the ghetto and the back alley. 'We blow their asses off!'

The party was on the beach. There was a big buffet that went on all day; the children and their mothers, the girlfriends and sisters were sunbathing or fooling around. Their laughing and calling drifted into the room with the shutters drawn against the bright summer sunshine.

Aldo Fabrizzi had spoken and they had sat there in a heavy silence until he finished. Not even the young men snapped a lighter while he talked. He called on them one by one, the heads of the eight affiliated groups within the

211

Fabrizzi Family. Eight powerful men, controlling little empires and armies of other men. They all owed their loyalty to Aldo Fabrizzi. He was their Don. In the old country their grandfathers had paid tribute to such men. Gifts of the best wine, cheese, livestock – the proceeds of robberies and extortion. And their lives and the lives of their sons, when he asked it.

But with the asking, there was always a promise. A rich reward for loyalty. He had spoken about the reward and seen their gleam of excitement flash like the summer lightning.

'I estimate their businesses are worth fifty million dollars, maybe more,' he said. 'The garment trade pays dues to them; they've got a stake in the construction companies that operate in downtown New York. They own casinos in Nevada and hotels along the coast; besides the cat houses and the dope. There's good money in them. If we get rid of Luca Falconi we move in and take over.'

'We get rid of them all,' someone said. 'That punk, Piero, and the little arse-creeper, Spoletto.'

'Piero's no punk,' someone pointed out. 'He's rough, don't underestimate him.'

'Yeah,' the other man boasted. 'So are we.'

'There are cousins and relatives spread all over,' an older man remarked. 'What about them, Don Aldo? We can't leave them to give trouble later.'

'The blood relatives all go,' he said. 'The small people – the little soldiers . . .' He shrugged. 'They follow a new Capo, that's all. It always happens. They have to live; their families have to eat.'

He paused; they were watching him, faces upturned as he stood at the top of the long table.

'I ask for your loyalty,' he said.

There was no dissenting voice. 'It's given, Don Aldo.'

And then the questions. How's it to be done? How long before we make our move? Do you plan to hit them all the same time?

212

A prudent voice, counselling caution: It won't be easy to get them to expose themselves. Falconi's played this trick himself. Remember how he took care of the Ryans? The Ryans were twenty-five years ago. Irish interlopers, hustling on Falconi territory. But Luca was an old man now. He wouldn't smell danger. He'd got away with cheating Aldo and hiding his renegade son from justice.

'They'll come,' Aldo promised. 'The three of them. Falconi, his son and the blood cousin, Spoletto. They'll come to a wedding.'

There was a murmur. He looked round and smiled. It was brief and frightening, like a wicked grimace.

'It's time my daughter, Clara, got married again,' he said. 'They'll come to the wedding. And we will all be there, with alibis. I think my Clara will like that.'

Clara was bored by the party. She had nothing in common with the other women and they didn't feel comfortable with her. They gossiped about the domestic details of their lives, their children, the schools, the trivia of married life that Clara couldn't share. She was alien to them in her status of a childless widow whose man had died dishonourably. She was aloof. She dressed too smartly, held herself proudly, showed a disdain for men that shocked them.

She had drifted away to a table by the beach and ordered champagne. She wore a dead white dress, with a daring side slit that showed her long legs. They were bare and brown, with gold sandals on her feet. Her dark hair was pulled back and dressed high, showing a graceful neck set off by big gold earrings. It was a simple provocative look, achieved at great expense. The man watching her thought she looked like a swan.

He was lounging up against the outdoor buffet table, sampling the food, joking with some young cronies. He watched the beautiful, sleek woman drinking champagne on her own, chainsmoking cigarettes. He was intrigued. She was Don Fabrizzi's daughter. The widow,

213

whose Falconi husband had disappeared. When he stared at a woman she felt it and always looked back at him. This one didn't. That intrigued him too, and challenged him. He paid less and less attention to the talk going on round him. They were all younger men, boasting of prowess on the streets, prowess with girls.

The men of importance were in the house with Don Aldo. He was related to one of the Fabrizzi capos' wives. He visited with them regularly, although he didn't work for them. He had grown up in a separate district, far over on the Lower West Side where the Giambino brothers ran the area and he joined up with them when he left school. He flexed his broad shoulders and ran a hand over his thick curly hair. He slung his jacket casually around him and moved off towards the woman seated at the table.

Clara saw him coming. She had seen him watching her and taken pleasure in ignoring him. He was big and handsome and common-looking; very sure of himself. The sniggering clique of young men were elbowing each other and waiting to see what happened. He came up to the table. She might be the Don's daughter, but so what? His technique always worked.

'Hi there, baby. Mind if I join you? You're too beautiful to be sittin' there all alone.'

Clara looked him up and down. She was bored and she had drunk a lot more champagne than she meant to.

'The bottle's empty,' she said. 'Get me a fresh one.' She opened her bag and studied herself in a gold compact.

He smiled down at her. 'I'll get it, if you offer me a drink, baby.'

She said, 'Why don't you go get it and see what happens?'

'Sure.' He turned and clicked his fingers. 'Tony!' he called out, and one of the youths started forward obediently. 'Get a bottle for the lady. And bring a glass for me.'

He pulled a chair out and sat opposite her. She snapped

her bag shut and glared at him. He smiled. He had magnificent white teeth.

'Who the hell do you think you are? When I want company I'll say so!'

'You look great when you're mad,' he remarked. 'I'll bet you scare the shit out of every guy who comes along. Only I don't scare easy. Not when it comes to a beautiful baby like you.' He leaned a little towards her. She smelt a strong aftershave or hair tonic. Musky, vulgar. Like the man himself.

'Don't call me baby,' she said. 'Keep that crap for the waitresses. Why don't you go and pester them?'

'Here's the champagne,' he said. 'Thanks, Tony.' He opened it with a flourish, poured her a full glass and helped himself. 'This is good stuff. But then the Don does everything in style.'

'Watch your mouth,' Clara warned him. 'He's my father.'

He opened his eyes wide, mocking her. 'You don't say? That makes you someone special, eh?'

Clara drank the champagne, emptying the glass.

'You'll get fried,' he said. 'Go easy on that stuff. Aren't you having fun? I'm Bruno Salviatti, I always have fun.'

She jeered, 'It must be wonderful to be you.'

He didn't take offence. It seemed nothing offended him. He sat there looking good-humoured and self-confident and she didn't know whether to get up and get rid of him, or go on sitting there, letting him play his cheap little game till she got tired of it.

'You're a beautiful dame,' he said. 'Why don't you try smiling?'

Clara did. She smiled at him and said, 'Why don't you fuck off?'

He laughed. He reached over and grasped her bare arm. He had big, strong hands with fine hair on the backs of them.

'Why don't I fuck you?'

They went walking, leaving the party in the distance.

215

She was a little unsteady, a little light-headed. I'm not dead, just because he's left me. I can still feel, still want a man. I've been a corpse for so long, waiting for a husband who didn't want me, lying in bed as if it was my coffin. If this big bull wants to hump me, why the hell don't I let him?

'Loosen up,' he kept saying to her, stroking her bottom, pinching the spare flesh of her buttocks between thumb and finger. He held her steady as they made their way towards the back of the big house; there was a grove of palm trees with a summer house. It was Clara directing him; Clara taking the decision to lie down for him. She liked the feeling of being in command. The champagne had made everything easy suddenly. She felt like it; she was going to have it.

She knew where they could go. The summer house was empty. It had been occupied – there were dirty glasses and an empty wine bottle inside it.

She said to him, 'Salviatti, lock the door,' and pulled the dress over her head. She stood naked except for flimsy G-string panties. He hooked his fingers in each lace strap and ripped them off her.

'Okay,' she said. 'You say you're good. Now prove it!'

'It was their wedding anniversary.' Piero scowled at Tino, who went on, 'They had a big cake and the old people led the dancing. Thirty-eight years married. That was the reason for the party.'

Piero said, 'You checked this?'

Tino nodded. 'I made some inquiries, I got a copy of the marriage certificate. It all checked out.'

'So it was on the level?'

'Maybe, maybe not. Why Santa Fe instead of some accessible place on the coast?'

'Didn't you hear my father?' Piero demanded. 'They got a fucking house down there, that's why.' He was angry with Tino Spoletto's persistance that something was wrong. 'They had a wedding anniversary with a cake and dancing and the rest of the shit – so what are you eating your arse about?'

'It's a small house for so many people,' Tino said. 'They had to use the hotel and some guest houses. I'm just mentioning it, that's all.'

Piero lost his temper. He didn't want Tino to be right. He didn't want trouble from the Fabrizzis. He was consolidating his position, feeling his way without the shrewd guidance of Steven. He wanted a couple of years before he had to move against Aldo. He liked Tino and he trusted him. But he was angry at him for stirring it up.

He shouted, 'For Christ's sake, you got nothing to go on! Okay so they celebrated their fucking wedding and they didn't say anything to us about it. They haven't asked us other years, so what the hell does that prove?'

Tino shrugged. He knew his cousin in that mood. He was uneasy, that was the reason for his outburst of temper. Unlikely to listen to anything till he calmed down. But he had one more try.

'Thirty-eight years isn't special,' he said quietly. 'It's no big deal. Forty years is ruby. That's special; that everyone celebrates. I think we should be careful, that's all I'm saying.'

'Okay, okay, okay.' Piero's voice was loud. 'Okay, we'll be careful. Now I've got fucking work to do.'

At noon he pushed his chair back, slung his jacket over his shoulder and went down one floor to Tino's office. He'd been rough on his cousin. He was sorry. And there was a creeping doubt in his mind that wouldn't be sworn and blustered away. He opened the door and called out.

'Hey, Tino? I'm going for some lunch. You want to come?'

They went down in the elevator together. Piero flung an arm round him.

'For Christ's sake. I shot off my mouth, forget it will you? You're right. We'll watch it. No chances.'

★

'You leave this to Gina and me,' Luisa Fabrizzi said. 'Go and sit with your Poppa. He wants to talk to you.'

'If you don't mind,' Clara said.

She hated helping to clear the dishes. Her mother always did it and the girls in the family were expected to help her. Clara was not domesticated and resented being relegated to the kitchen. A young cousin was staying with them. She was a nice, simple Italian girl who'd be in her element at the sink.

Clara went back to join her father. She wondered what he wanted to talk about; not marriage again. Not after she'd told him plainly that she would never tie herself to another man. Her mother had been in tears. He had been angry. She had stormed out and gone home, only to call them within the hour and apologize. She never let a quarrel last. She needed them too much, especially her father. Luisa spoiled her and fussed over her. It was nice to be pampered, having special food cooked for her, a bed always ready in case she felt like staying.

But her relationship with Aldo had changed and deepened. She was more than just his little girl, to be petted and protected. Subtly she felt he had accorded her a status unusual between father and daughter. He asked her opinion about people in his business. He talked things over with her, which was extraordinary. He explained some of their investments, coaching her on the financial side of their interests in the garment trade.

'You should learn to read a ledger,' he said one day. 'You should understand money and how to make it work for you.'

Clara had never bothered with such things. Her father managed whatever money he had settled on her and then it was Steven's responsibility. She had spent it, she didn't concern herself with managing her own investments. She wouldn't have known how. But now she would. Aldo had taught her a lot and she was a quick and intuitive pupil.

He was sitting in his usual chair, coat off, collar

unbuttoned, soft slippers on his feet. He looked up and said, 'Come and sit down, Clara.'

She lit a cigarette; she had started smoking heavily. 'What is it? Momma said you wanted to talk to me. Is something wrong?'

'No, no. Nothing wrong, Clara. Give me the ashtray.' He had a thin black cigar, which was his indulgence after a good meal. He drew on it and tapped off the ash. He said, 'You know how old I am?'

'Seventy-three. That's not old.'

'It's old enough,' he countered. 'I've been thinking. What happens to everything when I go? I've no son, no close relation of my own blood to take over from me. Only you, Clara. Only you.'

'It's not my fault. I know you wanted a boy.'

'It wasn't God's will,' he answered. 'When you married, I thought that was the answer. I thought you'd have children, there'd be a grandson.'

Tears came into her eyes. She said bitterly, 'Don't reproach me. I tried, and you know it. If it wasn't God's will for you, it wasn't for me either.'

'It doesn't matter,' Aldo said. 'I could have had a stupid son. Instead I have a clever daughter. Very clever. I've been watching you, Clara, seeing how you learned things, how you think. You know something? You think like a man when it comes to business.'

'I think like you've taught me,' she retorted. The tears had gone. There was a little colour in her pale face. He smiled at her.

'You're second guessing me, aren't you?'

'I don't know. Am I?'

'I want you to run the business when the time comes,' he said. 'You can do it. You can look after what I've made and maybe make it bigger.'

She got up and came to him. She knelt by his chair and lifted his hand and kissed it. She held it against her cheek.

'Oh, Poppa. Do you really mean it? How could I do it? There's never been a woman at the head of a Family.'

219

'That's not the question,' he said. 'Look at me, Clara. Tell me the truth. Can you do it? Can you be a son to me as well as my daughter?'

'I can,' she answered. 'I know I can.'

He nodded. He stroked her sleek black hair for a moment.

'I think so too. But there's one problem. You've just said it yourself. The only way the Family and the other Families will accept a woman is if she has a husband. You've got to marry, Clara. A man will save their faces. They'll take orders from him even though they know the orders come from you. There's no way round that.'

She got up slowly. He looked up at her. She knew that expression only too well. No argument, no backtracking. He had made a condition that must be accepted unconditionally.

'A man will take over from me,' she said after the pause. 'He'll want to be the Boss.'

Aldo grunted, puffing on the cigar. 'Not if we choose the right one.'

She turned quickly. 'You've chosen somebody for me?'

'It must be your choice,' he said. 'It must be a man that pleases you.'

'You think you've seen one?' She was sarcastic.

'How about Bruno Salviatti?' he said. 'I heard the two of you paired off at our party. In fact,' he added, seeing a blush creeping into her face, 'you went off alone for quite a while.'

Clara stood her ground. 'He made a play for me. He had his hand up my skirt and I let him. I didn't think anyone would notice. It meant nothing to me. He's pretty-looking and I'd had too much champagne. There are hundreds like him, hanging round the trattorias waiting for La Bella Fortuna to smile on them.'

Aldo was amused by his daughter's embarrassment. She'd picked up Salviatti and used him as he himself used his big-breasted blondes. She'd been alone for a long time. He knew her blood was as hot as his; she wasn't a virgin. She didn't have to be chaste, only discreet.

He said, 'If he pleased you, he'd be a good choice. He'd count his blessings and do what he was told. And he's fine-looking. A lot of women would envy you.'

She didn't answer for a moment. Bruno Salviatti: broad chest, small waist, thick curly black hair and big dark eyes. He'd count his blessings just as Aldo said. Good clothes, money, a chance to swagger as the macho man married to the Don's daughter. He'd brought her to a rapid and violent sexual climax and been ready for more. She'd pushed him off and dismissed him.

She thought for those few moments, and Aldo didn't interrupt. She would never love a man like Bruno. She would never suffer on his account, because she would always despise him. The roles would be reversed. She would be the dominant partner. If it wasn't Bruno Salviatti, it would have to be someone like him. And she would end up as the power behind the Fabrizzi Family.

Aldo was offering her everything he would have offered a son. There were millions of dollars in security abroad, property investments, and the huge income from the rackets. And her father was right. She would need someone like Bruno to front for her. The Families would never accept a woman. No man could take orders from her without losing face. Otherwise when Aldo died, the Fabrizzi empire would be divided piecemeal between the other Families. She had come to know and admire the subtlety of her father, the ruthlessness of his dealings. He had shown her a new and exciting world. A man's world, closed to women. If she did what he asked, it would be her world. The nursery and the kitchen were not for her. They never had been, once her marriage to Steven failed. Bruno Salviatti. It wasn't much to ask in exchange for what was on offer. He'd warm her bed and do what he was told.

'I'll see him again, Poppa,' she said. 'If I like him, then why not?'

He got up and came over to her. He placed both hands on her shoulders. She was still far too thin.

'I want you to be happy,' he said. 'You're all I have in the world.'

'You're all I have,' she said. 'You and Momma. I want to work with you now. I won't think about afterwards. That's going to break my heart. We'll be together. We'll do it together.'

He embraced her. It was a moment of deep emotion for both of them.

He spoke very quietly to her. 'I didn't invite the Falconis to our anniversary. I must make it up to them, *cara mia*. I must invite them to your wedding. I'll make you a present of them. Luca, Piero and the cousin Spoletto. How would you like that?'

They gazed into each other's eyes.

'I'd like it,' she said. 'But I want *him*. I want to see him dead.'

'You will,' he promised. 'Only have patience. Wherever he's hiding, when he hears what's happened to his family, he'll come back.'

She shook her head. 'So we can kill him? Not Steven. He'll come to strike back and we won't even know till it happens.'

Aldo said gently, 'I said you were clever, Clara, but you've still a few things to learn from your old father. It won't be *us* he'll come looking for.'

'Then who?' she asked him.

He gave his brief, cruel smile. 'Trust me,' was all he said. 'Now, go and call your mother and Gina. It's that quiz show she likes on TV.'

A month later Luca Falconi got a call from Aldo Fabrizzi. They exchanged inquiries about each other's health and the well-being of their families, and referred in passing to the state of their business.

'I want to have a meeting with you,' Aldo said. 'Just

222

you and me. It's a matter for the old men.' He gave his throaty laugh.

'You want to come here?' Luca suggested. 'You'd be very welcome.'

'No, no. Let's make it a dinner. How about La Scala?'

Luca sounded pleased. 'The food's good. Not as good as Minoletti's, but good.'

Minoletti's was the Falconis' favourite restaurant. They owned part of it and it was run by a family with close connections. For years, whenever Luca wanted to eat out or take the Family, he went there. It was like a fortress for the Falconis, especially during the war with Musso.

'You prefer Minoletti's we can go there,' Aldo said. He sounded disappointed. It was his invitation, after all.

'We eat in La Scala,' Luca answered. 'I look forward to it. And this is business between us, or family?'

'It's family,' Aldo said. 'But what's to stop us talking business too? We meet at around seven thirty, Tuesday?'

'I look forward to it,' Luca said. He put the phone down. 'What the hell,' he muttered. 'What the hell does that bastard want?'

La Scala was a big, fashionable Italian restaurant famous for its Neapolitan cooking. It was very pricy. Certainly Fabrizzi wanted something if he was prepared to spend that kind of money on a meal.

Luca took two bodyguards with him. Aldo had two of his men. They sat at a table chosen because it faced into the middle of the main restaurant. The adjoining tables were allotted to the men protecting them. It was a natural precaution that they took for granted. Both had enemies among the non-Mafia gangster groups. The Irish in particular had never made formal peace with Luca Falconi after the massacre of five Ryans. Nothing was proved and no charges could be brought for lack of evidence, but everybody knew.

Each thought the other had got older, as they embraced and kissed each other on both cheeks. Their henchmen watched, pretending to be friendly. The manager came to take their order. There was a lot of snapping fingers and hurrying waiters round them. They were important men. Respected members of the Italian American community. Businessmen, from the button-holes they wore – a carnation for Aldo, a rose for Falconi – to the well-cut suits and custom-made shirts and shoes. Big contributors to charity. Men with many favours in their gift.

'My friend,' Aldo said. 'I'm not here to talk about the past. The past is the past, eh? It only brings you pain, and pain to all of us. I want to talk about the future.'

'When you're our age,' Luca agreed, 'there's not too much future left. So we make the most of it. I believe in that. So what kind of future are we going to talk about? Yours or mine?'

'Clara's,' he answered.

'Ah.' Luca nodded. 'I know how she grieved. I was so sorry she had been sick. But you say she's better now?'

'She's better. She's a strong girl. But there were times when her mother and me were worried. Very worried.'

'I can believe that,' Luca said. 'So what about Clara's future?' Money? he wondered. Is that what he's after? She's not getting any more.

'She's been a widow for nearly a year,' Aldo went on. 'It's time she had a husband. I think I've found the right man for her. And she likes him. You know Clara, she wouldn't take anyone she didn't like.'

'No,' Luca agreed. 'She wouldn't. As you said, my friend, she's a strong girl. A girl with a mind of her own. Who is this man?'

Aldo pulled his napkin out of his neck. He turned aside politely and belched. 'One of the Giambinos' young men.'

Luca removed his napkin. The waiters were bringing them coffee. He asked for strega. Aldo refused anything more to drink.

'The Giambinos are not friends to any of us,' he said.

'No, but why not make them friends? When your son married my daughter there were advantages for both of us. Clara needed new blood. She met this man at Santa Fe. We had some people down and he was brought along. She liked him. They got along well. It's the first time I saw my daughter smile in months. It brought tears to my eyes.'

'I have no daughters,' Luca said. 'But I know how a father feels.'

'We talked it over, Clara and me and her mother. I said, "You like him, go ahead. See more of each other. Make up your mind and I'll make up my mind." I checked on him. He's a good boy. His name's Bruno Salviatti. He worked his way up from soldier to capo in Giambino's organization. He's a proper man. You'll like him, Luca. And that's important to Clara. She said to me, "Poppa, I want Luca's blessing." She said those words. She feels like a daughter to you, you know that?'

'And I love her like a father,' Luca said solemnly. 'She's suffered. We've suffered, you and I, Aldo. But we don't talk about the past. Tell Clara I wish her happiness. Her happiness makes me happy. Tell her that.'

'I will,' Aldo Fabrizzi said. 'You'll come to the wedding? We're fixing it for January. Here in New York. They're young, and you know what hot blood is. They don't want to wait very long.' He grinned.

Luca chuckled. He raised his glass of strega. 'Here's health and happiness and sons to them,' he said.

Aldo called for the bill, and side by side, surrounded by their bodyguards, they made a slow progress through the restaurant, stopping once or twice to accept greetings from other diners. Outside, the big sleek cars, armoured-plated under gleaming paintwork, glided up to receive them. They drove off together, and then at the first intersection swung apart and went their ways.

6

The casino was finished. The last decorator had left, the last curtain maker had settled the drapes and swags of silk and velvet, the last piece of furniture was in place. They were a month late. The opening was now scheduled for September. Steven and Angela toured the rooms. He didn't want anyone else to share his triumph. He brought her there at night to see it illuminated in its glory, as the rich and famous would see it.

The baccarat tables were in place in the Salon Privé, where only the richest were admitted. There were roulette wheels and tables for blackjack in the outer rooms, where the stakes were more modest. He held Angela's hand as they went round, and at one of the roulette tables Steven paused and spun the wheel, throwing the little ball. It rattled into a red socket.

'Seven,' he said. 'My lucky number, darling. And so much of it is due to you. You've made it beautiful for me.' He took her in his arms. 'I want you to be part of this. I want you to be excited by what we've done together. You are, aren't you?'

'You know I am,' Angela told him. 'It's wonderful, Steven. I'm very proud of you.'

'We'll have a good life,' he said. 'We'll make lots of money and we'll have a fine business to hand on to our boy. I'm not going to stop at this, darling. This is just the beginning. I'm going to build a hotel next. I'm going to invest in property down here. There's so much scope on the coast. So I won't be just a gambler. You'd like that too, wouldn't you?'

'Yes,' she admitted. 'I would. One thing worries me.'

'Tell me,' he said gently. 'Tell me what it is?'

'Ralph's stories about people killing themselves because they'd gambled everything away. You won't let that happen, will you?'

'I don't believe half what he tells us,' he said. 'He likes to make an impression. It's part of his job. What about the people who've made fortunes and walked off?'

'That doesn't seem to happen very often,' she answered.

'Thank God for that,' he teased her. Then seriously, 'But if it would make you happy, we'll have a policy. If it's known someone's getting in too deep, we'll close down the game. How would that be?'

'Oh, darling, will you really do that? I would be so much happier. And so would you.'

He said softly, 'I guess I would. I'll set it up.'

It was a perfect night for a gala opening. The weather was hot, with a light sea breeze, the sky a backdrop of black velvet, diamond-studded with stars. The casino was bathed in floodlight, the gardens illuminated.

Steven was there early, supervising the last details. Maxton had spent the day there. He changed into evening dress upstairs in the suite of offices. He was excited, and amused by the excitement. For years he had felt immune to strong emotions. Only the visceral thrill of gambling could affect him, sending adrenalin pumping, making the hands tremble. But tonight was an excitement.

It had come together very quickly, as such projects tend to do, after delays and frustrations that made the opening date recede into improbability. Then it was ready! Everything was done, down to the last flower arrangement, the emergency changing of bulbs that blew, a tray of glasses dropped, the line-up of the staff for

227

inspection, the croupiers and dealers in their places, immaculate in evening dress.

He had ordered champagne to be brought up; he had a handsome private office, with a nice desk and some comfortable leather chairs and a cocktail cabinet for entertaining. He opened the bottle and poured a full glass. He raised it and drank a private toast.

'To you, Uncle Oleg. Wherever you are, you old devil. You'd have enjoyed tonight.'

He had persuaded Falconi not to change the name. And Angela had been his ally. The Casino de Poliakof had a dignified, romantic sound. And it was good publicity. To whet public curiosity, Maxton had circulated enough stories, true and invented, about the origins of the splendid house built by a crazy Czarist aristocrat for his French mistress. As a final touch, he had suggested a portrait of the Count be placed in the entrance hall.

'But there isn't one,' Steven objected.

'I think . . . I think I can get hold of a photograph. Then all we have to do is get someone to paint a copy,' he explained.

And to Angela he said later, 'I didn't say anything to Steven, but the old boy was a sort of ancestor. His sister married my grandfather.'

'He knows,' she said. 'Have you got a photograph?'

'Yes,' he said. 'I have. I actually brought an old album back with me last time I went to England. It had pictures of my mother I rather liked and it seemed a pity to take them out, so I made off with the whole thing. There's a splendid snap of Oleg in uniform. I think we could commission a rather handsome portrait from it. I didn't know Steven knew there was a connection.' He'd said that at the end deliberately, as if it wasn't important.

Angela said, 'Steven knows everything about you, Ralph. Don't ever try to hide anything from him, will you? He wouldn't like it.'

'I wouldn't be able to, it seems. Fair enough.'

He hadn't been pleased, she could see that. He left her

rather quickly. When she saw him two days later he was his charming, easygoing self.

They'd brought the boy over to attend the opening. Ralph thought it a ridiculous thing to do. Charlie was a nice fellow, in Ralph's view, but in danger of being ruined by his parents. Steven was the most indulgent stepfather, worse than Angela who at least tried to insist that he didn't skip school and took his exams seriously. Steven's obsession with another man's son was very odd. He didn't seem the type to lavish paternal love on a stepson. Maxton resented the relationship. It upset his theories on fathers' attitudes to their sons. But he was intelligent enough to suspect that his own bleak family background was the reason.

It was laughable, but whenever he saw Falconi and Charlie going off together, he felt a jealous pang. Steven was teaching the boy to play golf. Steven was not a man interested in sports, but he had taken up tennis and riding and now golf, so as to be a companion to Charlie when he stayed with them. And then there were Charlie's friends. They flew in at Steven's expense and were put up at the villa. A boat and a skipper were chartered to take them sailing, every facility from water skiing to scuba diving was paid for and organized. Again, Maxton recognized that he was jealous. He envied Charlie Lawrence his good looks, his self-confidence. He envied him the kind of love and attention that had never come his own way. He was a changeling in his family. A clever, ugly child with a wild streak in him. A natural penchant for trouble, and no interest in the solid pursuits of horse, gun and rod. He hated hunting, which was a crime in his father's view. But he loved racing and even as a schoolboy had been caught out making a book on the Derby and threatened with expulsion. He had made them all ashamed, never proud. He'd heard someone say once when he was still in his teens and in disgrace for some misdeed he'd since forgotten, 'It's the Russian blood, I suppose – totally unreliable.'

He thought it was an aunt, talking to his father, but he couldn't be sure.

Steven was displaying a degree of nervousness about the opening that surprised Maxton. He was even more surprised at the new house rule which Steven had introduced. Clients were not allowed to gamble in excess of their known means. Experienced staff could quickly tell when a man or woman had begun to gamble out of desperation. They were instructed, on pain of dismissal, to close the game. Maxton had mentioned that such a ruling was unheard of in any gambling establishment.

Steven had dismissed the objection. 'That's the way Angela wants it. She got upset by all the suicide stories you told her. I promised, and that's the way it's going to be.'

He hadn't struck Maxton as a man likely to be swayed by his wife's moral scruples, but he was wrong about that too. She had changed him from the man who came to the casino at Monte Carlo all those years ago with that other wife; the man who stood coldly watching the German princess gambling and winning a fortune. She was dead now. Pills and drink, and debts which her husband wouldn't meet any longer, had killed her.

The Steven Falconi of those days wouldn't have given it a thought. The love of a good women, Ralph Maxton mocked to himself, but it was in self-mockery. And envy was deep there too. Falconi didn't deserve her. He couldn't think of anyone who did. 'I warm my cold heart at your hearth.' He enjoyed poetry and that line from a Renaissance verse often came to mind when he was with Angela. He was not in love with her. He had never been in love with any woman. Madeleine, the avaricious little *poule de luxe* who'd shared his Christmas bounty at the Hôtel de Paris, would have laughed him to scorn if he'd even used the word. Perversely, he had included her in the guest list for the gala opening. No, he was not in love with Angela Falconi.

'Perish the thought,' he said aloud, and finished a second glass of champagne before going down to join Steven. There was another rule, less surprising but more difficult to implement than the 'save the soul' dictum issued to the croupiers and dealers. No photographs were to be taken of the proprietor and his family. That was Ralph's responsibility. The press was excluded from the gala itself. That had been unpopular in view of the coverage they had already given the new casino. A house photographer would issue pictures of the celebrities among the guests and there would be no charge. Maxton implied that a sensitive situation involving a member of the Monégasque royal family was the reason. He muttered hints about a romantic liaison and hoped they believed him. If Steven had an aversion to being photographed, Maxton, well-trained in the hard school of Monte Carlo, would make sure his employer's wish was respected. He had a strong feeling that if anything went wrong, his well-paid job would be the first casualty.

Steven was waiting in the main hall. He looked at his watch. Charlie was escorting his mother. Steven saw Maxton and said, 'They're late. Five minutes late.'

'The traffic's heavy,' Maxton reassured him. He gave a quick glance at his own watch. A handsome gold Rolex. A present from himself. His old one had been pawned during the lean years.

'I see headlights.' He came away from the glass doors opening out to the portico entrance. 'They're here,' he said. 'No worry, Steven.'

The doors were swung open by two liveried doormen and Angela walked through them with her son.

'You look beautiful,' Steven said. He took both her hands. 'Doesn't your mother look beautiful?' he asked of Charlie, and then without waiting for an answer, 'And you look great, son. A white tuxedo – very smart.'

'Mum chose it,' Charlie explained. 'Gosh, doesn't everything look terrific! Look at the flowers and all the lights.'

231

Steven ushered them to the stairs. 'We have fifteen minutes before the first guests arrive. Champagne's on ice upstairs. Come on. Let's drink to success tonight!'

Maxton watched them go. It was a very wide stair, so Falconi was able to put an arm round his wife and the boy and walk up between them. He turned away.

Maxton had engaged a fashionable quartet to play during the reception. They were placed discreetly in the hall with orders to provide light, popular music for the first hour and a half. He checked his watch again. Gendarmes were on duty to direct the traffic and a crowd of sightseers was in place on either side of the entrance. Red carpet ran across the courtyard and up the flight of marble steps, protected by a long red awning in case it rained. He had dressed the doormen and waiters in red and gold livery, with powdered wigs. Yes, he had agreed when Angela had protested, very vulgar. But the clients would love it. He wondered how much his efforts had been appreciated by that smug bastard . . . then shrugged the silly self-pity aside. Just because he hadn't been invited to join the family gathering upstairs.

He sent a flunkey out to see if the cars were approaching. The big fish would arrive late. Only the arrivistes would be on time. He smiled at his own witticism. It made him feel better. He could tell Madeleine. She would appreciate it. He hoped she would bring her rich, ridiculous lover early rather than be fashionable. He wanted someone to share the evening with him. The flunkey reappeared.

'There are cars approaching, Monsieur Maxton.'

'Right, Go upstairs and tell Monsieur Lawrence.'

It was Charlie who proposed the toast. Angela remembered he had done the same on their wedding day. She was so proud of him and he was so proud of Steven.

'Here's good luck tonight, Dad. Good luck, good fortune and lots of lovely money!' They all laughed and drank with him.

Steven said, 'Thanks, Charlie. To La Bella Fortuna –

and to you, my darling, who've done so much to make it come together.' He took Angela's hand and kissed it.

Charlie grinned at them. 'Mum's blushing,' he said. Then, glancing out of the window, 'Gosh, I can see masses of cars.'

The flunkey knocked and Steven said, 'It's time we went downstairs. You ready, Angelina? And you too, Charlie. I want you with us.'

The main hall was soon full, the buffet and champagne bars set up in the ground-floor reception rooms crowded with people. The music was drowned out by a sustained chattering as four hundred people circulated round the food and drink, greeting each other, vying for the house photographers to take their pictures. Steven had given up shaking hands, trying to hear names; Maxton presented the important guests as they arrived and he was close at hand when the prize guest arrived on the arm of a big, handsome man.

Maxton moved forward, taking a hand that glittered with diamond rings and kissing it.

'Nettie, my sweet. How absolutely fabulous you look! Come and let me introduce you.'

Angela saw the woman approaching. She was more than beautiful. There were so many beautiful women, exquisitely dressed and bejewelled, that she had lost count. But this one was exceptional. She was tiny and yet she created space around her. She was always centre stage. Dark hair with a single streak of blonde from her left temple, a perfect face with huge blue eyes and a pink, pouting mouth that opened in a charming smile as she came up to Steven.

'May I present Monsieur Lawrence? And Madame Lawrence? Her Highness, Princess Orbach.'

She lingered for a moment, letting her hand stay in Steven's. Her neck and bosom were festooned with sapphires and diamonds, and huge earrings danced and flashed as she moved her head. Then she paused by Angela. 'Madame.' She inclined her head and kept the

233

charming smile, but the blue eyes were filmed with indifference. She passed on, and her escort, who had an unpronounceable name, kissed Angela's hand, muttered, '*Enchanté*,' and hurried after his princess. After that it was an anticlimax.

'Well,' Maxton murmured. 'At least she turned up. That's something.'

'But she accepted,' Angela said. 'I saw her name on the list.'

'That doesn't mean a thing,' he corrected. 'She says yes to anything that looks amusing, but she's quite likely not to come at the last minute. Now, let's see how long she stays. That's going to be important. What did you think of the Hungarian hunk?'

She hated his laugh. It cackled without a note of kindly humour in the high pitch. It was cruel, she thought suddenly, as if he only laughed at misfortune or the ridicule of someone else.

'I don't know,' she said. 'He didn't exactly stop to make conversation.'

'He daren't,' Maxton said. 'She calls the tune. She has the money. He thinks she's going to marry him, poor sod, but she won't. She'll suck him dry and then suddenly tell her friends he's "such a bore, darling, I simply couldn't stand another *moment* . . .".' He mimicked mercilessly. 'And that's the sentence of death among the so-called smart set down here.'

Angela didn't smile. She said, 'What an awful woman she must be. I'm going to find Charlie.'

'He's through there.' Maxton indicated the supper room. 'Let me get you something to eat,' he said quietly. 'You're quite right. She is absolutely ghastly, but I've lived among those sort of people so long I've got used to them. Thank God you haven't.'

'I hope I never will,' Angela said.

At eleven thirty the gaming rooms were opened. Maxton

had left her in Charlie's care after supper and hurried after a very pretty girl who signalled him from the doorway.

'I can't eat another thing, Mum,' her son said. 'Can I get something else for you? There's a super pudding called a Bombe Surprise. Have a bit of that?'

'No thank you, darling. Are you enjoying yourself?'

'Yes, I'm having a super time. Who's Ralph gone off with? Jolly pretty, isn't she?' He watched Madeleine admiringly. She had an old, overweight man in tow and she was introducing him to Maxton.

'Let's go and find Steven,' Angela said. 'I haven't seen him for ages.'

It was silly to feel ill at ease. Silly to be lonely among such a throng of people, some of whom she knew and who'd come up to her, all smiles and congratulations. Ralph had taken care of her. Charlie was solicitous in his concern that she shared his enjoyment of the 'super' food and drink, but she realized that he too was out of his element.

'Come on,' she said.

He caught her arm. 'Look, he's over there. I'll get him.'

'No, don't. He's talking to people; we'll go and join them.'

Madeleine was laughing. She pinched her protector's plump cheek and made a charming little grimace at him.

'Now Bernard, my sweet, you know you're dying to go upstairs and win some money for me. You go on and I'll come and bring you luck. One glass of champagne and then I'll join you, eh?'

Her fingers had left a little red mark on his sallow skin. He glanced at the ugly man, with his hooked nose and narrow features, and decided he could safely leave Madeleine with him for a little while. He was itching to play and she was encouraging him. She always encouraged him to do what he liked, whatever form it took. And she had such an adorable laugh, like a naughty girl. A vicious child, he called her, vicious and wicked and irresistible, like the gambling demon who devoured him equally. He left her with the ugly Englishman.

'Oh, *Dieu merci*,' she breathed when he had gone. 'He's so *boring*, Ralphie . . . and such a dirty old devil. You know what he wanted me to do to him before we came here?'

'No,' Maxton said firmly. 'And you're not going to tell me. To me you're just a sweet little innocent. Now let's sink some champagne, shall we?'

She hooked her arm through his and pressed against him. 'Okay,' she said. 'Then we go up and I get some chips from him and we have a bit of fun, eh?'

They settled into a sofa upholstered into an alcove. Madeleine made him laugh; she cheered his spirits and encouraged him to show the snide and cynical side which had upset Angela. He felt at home with Madeleine. They were part of the same worthless, superficial world. He poured and drank, never becoming drunk, just blurring the edges of sensitivity.

'Is that your boss?' Madeleine's strong little fingers gripped his wrist. 'I saw him shaking hands with people in the hall.'

'Yes, didn't you meet him?'

'No.' She lifted one silky shoulder in disgust. 'My old fart wouldn't queue up – you know what he's like. My God, Ralphie, isn't he attractive?'

'If you say so,' Maxton answered.

Steven was talking to a couple whom Maxton had invited to the villa. He had made a lot of money out of property on the coast. Angela was busy with the wife; she'd feel more comfortable with the pleasant French matron than with the glittering Nettie Orbach and her kind. He realized he was being nasty about Angela because she had rebuked him. He had never been able to accept criticism; a major failing, his father used to thunder at him. 'Never in the wrong, are you, my boy? Well, God help you, you'll find out one day.'

Madeleine was staring at Steven. He knew that look,

the narrowed eyes, the full, greedy mouth parting to show the tip of a libidinous tongue.

'You can forget him,' he mocked her. 'That's his wife, the blonde in the white dress.'

'So what?' she demanded. 'She's not anything special. His son's so good-looking too. Why don't I meet him then?'

'He's sixteen, darling,' Maxton jeered. 'And it's his stepson, anyway.' He tipped the last of the champagne into his glass.

Madeleine turned to him, her eyes wide open now. 'Don't be silly! Stepson my foot! They're the image of each other. They *must* be father and son.'

He'd never noticed it before. He took a long look at them, a proper look for the first time. She was right. Absolutely right. The same hair, eyes, very similar features, gestures and expressions that mirrored each other. You say stepson and nobody bothers to take a second look.

'You're bloody clever, aren't you?' he murmured. 'Sharp eyes, haven't we, sweetheart? You're bloody right. The boy must be his.'

She smiled and squeezed his wrist again. 'Have they been telling Ralphie lies? And Ralphie swallowed them? Ooh, that's not like you, darling. You can spot a lie coming before it gets round the corner.'

'That's because it's usually my lie,' he countered. 'I tell lies to people and they tell them back to me. Let's go and see what your fat friend is up to, shall we? Maybe he'll give you a few francs to play with.'

She got up, linking arms with him, and walked with the provocative hip swing that made men stare at her. He was cross, she realized. Poor Ralphie, the con man had actually been conned. She giggled. How very funny. He really was cross, she could tell by the set of his ugly mouth.

They went upstairs to the Salon Privé. They found Bernard at the baccarat table. He had been losing and he looked up, scowling, when she touched him.

'Where have you been? You said one drink,' he complained.

'I'm so sorry, my sweet, but I'm here now. And don't you worry, I'll change your luck.'

She did and Maxton stood beside her as the cards came out of the shoe and Bernard began to bet and to win. An hour later she demanded, and was given, ten thousand francs. She went off with Ralph to play roulette. She was lucky that night. Her excitement grew as her chips piled up.

He wondered whether she banked her money. The looks and the body wouldn't last for ever, if he was right about Moroccan blood.

'I'd stop now, if I were you,' he said.

She looked up at him. There was a bright flush on her cheeks. 'Why?' She lowered her voice to a whisper. 'You mean the wheel's fixed?'

'Nothing like that,' he answered. 'We play on the law of averages here. We don't run any crooked games. The law of averages says you're going to start losing. But it's up to you, darling.'

'I always do what you tell me,' she declared. 'I always think a man knows best.' She gave him a huge wink, gathered her winnings and left the table. 'I'd better go back to Bernard,' she said. 'I shan't tell him I won. Then if he's lucky he'll give me a present. When will I see you, Ralphie?'

'When's he going home?'

She changed the chips for cash, folding the notes into a tight little wad that fitted into her evening bag. It was a large bag, not a smart little pochette. I bet she banks every penny, he thought. Good for her.

'I'll let you know,' she promised. She reached up and kissed him lightly on the cheek. 'You're such fun, darling,' she said. 'I love our afternoons together. I'll telephone you.' Then she slipped away, the bag with the money pressed close under her arm.

*

'My darling,' Steven said. 'If you're tired, why not go home? It's been a long evening. I'll call the car and Charlie can go with you. Has he enjoyed himself?'

'Yes, he's loved every minute. But he's a bit young for it. I wouldn't let him gamble. He was very disappointed.'

'I'll talk to him,' Steven said. 'You wait here and I'll send him along to you. You were right. I'm going to tell him so.'

He had to look for Charlie. He wasn't in the supper room, where breakfast was being served. He'd slipped away, sulking perhaps, and left his mother. No excuses, Steven thought. He must learn. He must learn to take care of her and to respect me. I love him enough to be angry, even tonight.

Charles was upstairs in the smaller salon, watching the roulette. He started when Steven came up behind him.

'Oh, hello, Dad. Dad, I wanted to cash some money and have a try on the wheel, but they won't give me any chips. Can't you say something? It's pretty stupid.'

'The cashiers are doing what I told them,' Steven said quietly. 'You are not to gamble. Come with me, Charlie.' They went to Steven's office, where he unlocked the door, switched on a battery of lights and said, 'Close the door. I want to show you something.'

Charlie followed him. He felt embarrassed, even uneasy. Steven had never been angry with him before. He slouched, wondering whether he dared put up an argument. He shouldn't have left his mother. He was sorry he'd done that, but she'd made him feel a child when he wanted to feel grown up.

Steven pressed a wall switch. The panelling slid back. 'Come here, Charlie,' he said. 'Look at this.' It was a closed-circuit television screen. It showed the Salon Privé. Steven pressed another switch and the camera moved into close-up on one of the tables. There was no sound, just a picture. He changed it, from one salon to another, the roulette wheels, the card tables, zooming into focus, the faces enlarged until they filled the screen.

Charlie said, 'Gosh, I've never seen anything like it. It's fantastic. You can watch everything that's going on.'

'Yes. I can watch the games and the players and my own staff. I can see if anyone cheats, or looks like cheating. I can sit here and see people losing fortunes, making fools of themselves, getting drunk. I can see greed and cunning and people risking money because they want people to look at them.'

Charlie said, 'You make it sound awful. I thought it looked like good fun.'

Steven said quietly, 'That' – and he pointed to the overall view on the screen of the big gambling room beneath them – 'that isn't fun. That is business. My business, and one day maybe yours, too. I don't gamble and you *never* gamble, you hear me? You leave that to the suckers. Business isn't fun, Charlie. That's something I've got to teach you. It's not like anything else. It has different rules. You want to succeed, you want respect, you have to play by those rules. You run a casino, you don't play around with the profits. That's number one. If anybody had given you chips or let you play at a table tonight, they'd have been fired. And number two, when I say take care of your mother, I mean it. You understand me?'

'Yes. I'm sorry.'

'You do it again,' Steven said, 'and you will be. Now she's waiting downstairs. The car's on its way and you take her home. And you apologize to her.'

'I will,' Charlie said. He had blushed red at Steven's tone. 'I only went for a few minutes,' he said. 'I only wanted to join in like everybody else.'

'You're not everybody else,' was the answer. 'That's something else you'll have to learn. Now go on down and find your mother.'

He switched off the screen. The panel slid into place. He sat down at his desk, searching for a cigarette. He had been hard on the boy. But it had to be done. He could have the world, but he must play by the rules. He was a kid still, Steven admitted. His life had been turned upside down by Steven's advent – money, travel, glamour and anything he wanted. It hadn't turned his head, but it might in the end. Charlie's pride was hurt. His feelings too because of the way he had been judged and admonished.

Steven stubbed out the cigarette. He'd been sitting here longer than he realized. He was unhappy that he wouldn't see his son before the morning. He locked up and went downstairs. The supper room was nearly empty, the bars not quite, but most of the crush at midnight had disappeared. It was four in the morning.

He went upstairs on a tour of the rooms. Maxton was watching a game at the baccarat table. The hard core were still there. They'd be there till the casino closed. Steven went up to him.

'How's it going?'

'Fine. There's two of the high rollers fighting it out over there.'

Steven was surprised to hear him use a crap-game term. 'How high?'

'Half a million francs. Don't you want to watch? They hate each other's guts when they play, but outside they're the best of friends.'

'Who are they?' Steven could see two men, competing in cold fury with the banque.

'French. Stinking rich. One's electronics, the other one's got steel and shipping interests. This is their idea of relaxation. It's a good omen they've stayed on. And so did Nettie Orbach. She didn't leave till after two. That means we've arrived!'

He looked tired, his thin face sunken round the eyes and mouth. A very little drunk, Steven decided. Just a touch over the edge.

Ralph smiled and said, 'Congratulations. I think you've made the grade tonight, Steven.'

'If it's true, then we've all made it. You most of anybody. Thanks.'

241

Maxton made him a little, ironic bow. More than a touch over the edge. 'Thank *you*! This time last year I had paper in my shoes.'

Steven said, 'Close down in twenty minutes. I'm going home.'

Angela didn't wake him. He slept late the next morning and when he woke she had been up and dressed for several hours. He stood on the balcony in his dressing gown and stretched in the warm sunshine. Rich garden scents drifted up to him and he saw her moving among the shrubbery. She loved gardening. She would grow things in the desert if she were set down there. Steven smiled, watching her. He loved her more than he'd thought possible. He loved the directness, the honesty she had brought into his life and the odd streak of obstinacy that nothing could move. He loved her for her gentleness of heart and kindness.

Standing with the sun on his face he thought of Sicily and suddenly he longed for the red earth and rugged hillsides of his country, for the hot skies and sun-bleached buildings. It was his homeland, the place of his birth. He wanted to go back to the spot where he and Angela had poured wine into the dust and made love for the first time. And he wanted to take his son and show him where the other half of him belonged.

He called down to her. 'Angelina!'

She looked up and waved. 'Morning, darling. Do you want breakfast?'

'I'm coming down. Order some coffee for me.'

'I let you sleep on,' she said as they sat together on the terrace. 'It was such a long day. I woke up very early, I was still so excited about it all. It did go well, didn't it, darling?'

'According to Ralph, it was a great success. And he would know. I thought so too. You get a feel for atmosphere. You'll get a crowd wherever there's free food and drink and people to stare at. It's the electricity in

242

the air that tells you. And the big gamblers came and stayed till the end.' He smiled, holding her hand. 'I want to go down and check the figures. I want to see what our profit's likely to be.'

'When do you think we'll break even?' Angela asked.

'We won't begin to break even for a year,' he said. 'The winter is a slack time, so we'll close up then. But I can calculate pretty accurately what the revenue's likely to be. When we've recovered our expenses for the gala, we begin to recoup the initial outlay. Before you know it, we'll be rich!'

She said, 'Charlie's gone out for a walk. He was awfully sorry he annoyed you. Don't be cross with him today, will you, darling?'

'Don't be silly. Last night was last night. Let's take a walk through the garden, shall we?'

'Why can't we talk here? I'll only bore you to death showing you the plants. You don't know a weed from a wisteria!'

'And I don't want to know,' he agreed. 'The garden's yours. I leave it all to you. I want to walk with you because I can't even kiss my own wife without that old bat Janine spying on me. Come on.'

'You know she's a treasure,' Angela teased him.

'She's a snooper,' he retorted, pulling her to her feet. 'She needs to get a man of her own.'

The maid, Janine, was a domestic marvel. She cleaned and scrubbed and kept everything in spotless order. But she was incurably nosy. There were times when it got on Steven's nerves.

Out of sight of the house, shielded by trees and a great bank of flowering crimson oleanders, Steven took her in his arms. 'I missed you when I woke up this morning,' he said.

'I missed you,' Angela answered and drew his head down to kiss him on the mouth. It was a long kiss and they stood pressed close together afterwards.

'I was thinking how much I loved you,' he said. 'I saw

243

you down in the garden and I thought: I love her more and more every day.'

'I love you like that too,' she said. 'In the beginning I used to worry. I used to think what I'd made you give up.'

'Like what?' He stroked her hair.

'Your family. Your whole way of life. I don't mean the bad parts, but your home and your friends. I was so frightened you'd regret it. I didn't see how I could make up for all that, even with Charlie.'

'Then will you believe me if I tell you something? And never speak like that again? You promise me?' He was serious. The warm desire had gone out of him.

'All right, tell me,' Angela said.

'I am happier than I've been in my whole life. I miss my family, yes. I love them. I love my father and my mother and Piero and my nephews and nieces. I'm a Sicilian. We have very deep family ties, you know that. I'd give anything to bring you and Charlie and them all together. But, for the rest of it, you listen to me. Listen good, as we say. I don't miss the States. I lived there, I grew up there, but it's not my home. I didn't have any friends outside of the business. And I don't miss that. I don't miss travelling with bodyguards, riding in a bulletproof car, looking up and down the street every time I came out of the door. I don't miss living off crime, Angela. I have a hunch I'll die in my bed as an old man, and I like the idea. I have a home, a wife and son, and I love my life. And I have a business that doesn't have blood on the balance sheet. So will you look at me and promise to put all that stuff out of your head?'

'Oh, darling,' she said. 'I really will, from now on. So let's go for our walk, shall we?'

'I was thinking,' he said. 'Why don't we have a holiday? I want to take Charlie to Sicily. We could fly out, stay at Taormina if you like. It's very beautiful. Just spend a few days touring around.' He slipped his arm round her waist. 'Maybe go back up the hillside where we went the first day?'

'He's due back at school,' Angela said. 'We promised he'd go back at the end of the week. Couldn't we go in the Christmas holidays?'

'Don't you know how cold it gets in the winter? No, darling. I meant now, while the weather's good. It's the best time of year. Just a few days won't hurt. I'll show you Etna at night. That's really something to see. Say yes, sweetheart.'

'If you want to that much, then we'll go,' she said.

'No wonder I'm so crazy about you,' Steven murmured. 'And I'll call the school and make it right with them. They want a contribution to the new swimming pool, don't they? I'll get us booked out on the weekend.'

As they walked back to the villa Angela said, 'What are we going to tell Charlie? Why Sicily?'

'Because I was born there. It's my home. One day, when he knows I'm his father, he'll have something to remember. Let's see if he's back from that walk.'

It began as a whisper, passed behind the hand in bars and trattorias, in the kitchen and living rooms in Little Italy. A whisper among the small people, the common soldiers in the mighty Mafia command. Don Fabrizzi talks about business with his daughter. It started with the cousin Gina, who told her father that the Don shut himself up with Clara and discussed topics forbidden to women, while her mother and Gina worked in the kitchen. She hated Clara, who was cold and superior towards her. She liked Luisa Fabrizzi.

Her father sucked his teeth and didn't believe her. But he spoke about it and like a tiny ripple on still water the rumours began to swell into a tide. Roy Giambino and his brother, Victor, came to hear of it. They were incredulous. But they were curious too. They sent for the bridegroom-to-be and over a hearty dinner with lots of wine, they congratulated him on his good fortune and asked about the bride. A clever girl, they'd heard. Her poppa's favourite. He'd got himself a good thing going.

Bruno was flattered and expansive. He boasted to the men who had been his bosses since he was a runner on the streets.

He laid her good and often and she ate out of his hand. Sure, she had the Don's ear over most things. Which was good, he said defensively. Good for him, when he was the husband. Then he'd be the one to see the books.

She sees the books, the accounts, the *figures*? Victor asked him.

Wine made Bruno truculent. He'd resented being shut out, or sent away because Clara had to talk to her father. When he was married to her, he assured them, she'd learn a woman's place. They all laughed and made coarse jokes and he staggered home feeling good about himself.

The Giambinos were independent operatives, chiefs of a small but effective Family on the West Side. They ran the brothels and exacted protection money from every small business in their district. They had strong affiliations with the Lucianos in Chicago.

Roy said to Victor after Bruno had left, 'It looks like it's true. Holy shit! She goes through the books!'

Victor didn't answer in a hurry. He was a big, slow-moving man, but not slow-witted. 'It figures,' he said at last. 'After a guy like Falconi, why pick an arsehole for a son-in-law? You think Fabrizzi's going to put Bruno in Falconi's place when he dies? Nah! He's got other ideas, Roy. Bruno's the front man.'

'It can't happen,' Roy declared. 'It's crazy. Fabrizzi's nuts if he thinks he can put a woman in a man's place.'

Victor said, 'It could break up the Families. We have it fixed right for all of us. For Christ's sake, mobs from Chicago, Detroit, you name it! They get word of this and they'll come up here moving in. We'll have a war for the Fabrizzi territory – Irish, the Kikes, the Krauts – the whole fucking lot will be grabbing a piece for themselves. We got to stop it.'

His brother nodded. He paid the bill. 'We'll need help. Fabrizzi's too big for us. But I'll lay you a straight two to

246

one, his people don't know what he's doing. Not the top men.'

'Then maybe somebody should tell them,' Victor suggested.

The meetings were very discreet. Oaths of silence were taken at each one. Only five of the eight heads of the Fabrizzi Family were willing to talk to Roy and Victor, but those five were important men, powerful and respected second only to Don Aldo himself. They listened to the Giambinos and said nothing of the plan to wipe out Luca Falconi and his people. That oath of silence was as sacred as the one they had taken when they agreed to meet with Roy and Victor. It was agreed in principle that something had to be done, if the implications were true. Those who knew Bruno Salviatti were easier to convince. He might be a stud for the daughter, but he was no heir to Aldo.

It was suggested, and agreed, that a spy should be introduced into the Don's household. Someone who could check on the stories about weekly conferences between Clara and her father. One of Aldo's most trusted friends and henchmen from the early days offered to handle it. He was anxious to prove to them, he said, that the rumours were no more than silly gossip. He would ask Don Aldo to house a young relative for a few weeks. As head of the Family, the Don would not refuse a plea for help.

'How much longer is she going to stay here?' Clara demanded.

Her mother was placatory. 'Only a week or so. She's a good girl, she helps me. She doesn't get in your way.'

Luisa eyed Clara apprehensively. She was more difficult than ever these days. She had a handsome man, a wedding to look forward to, a new life; but she didn't seem to care.

She and Aldo talked privately together and even at the family table they were apart from the other women. She

247

watched her daughter and wondered at the change in her. She showed little respect or regard for Bruno. His swaggering didn't deceive the older woman. She might not have Clara's sophistication, but she knew men and she could tell he was ill at ease. And resentful. It wouldn't be a happy marriage unless Clara changed her attitude.

But she didn't dare say anything. She was glad to have someone like Nicole to stay with them. Of course, Aldo agreed to give her a home until the family problems had died down. He was a good man and he knew his duty to his people. The girl's father was in prison. She had run away from her mother's boyfriend to save her virtue. If she were living under Don Aldo's protection, the mother and her man wouldn't dare try to force her back home. And by the time she did leave, her father's relatives would have sorted out the problem.

Nicole was quiet and shy. Luisa was kind-hearted and maternal by nature. She couldn't mother Clara and there were no small children to occupy her. She was happy to take care of someone in trouble. She was happy to be needed. Clara didn't think of anyone but herself anymore.

Clara lit a cigarette. She resented having another girl living in her parents' house. She had accepted the hard-luck story with little sympathy. If her father had to offer protection, she couldn't argue. But she didn't share her mother's opinion of the girl. Clara thought she was sly and far less the wronged innocent than she pretended. Clara positively disliked her and made it plain. Why couldn't some other relative have taken her in, she demanded when the two weeks stretched out to a month with no sign of Nicole leaving.

'Only your father is powerful enough to keep her safe,' Luisa explained. 'The mother is living with a bad man, very bad. A man of violence. He tried to seduce the poor child. He beats the mother.'

Clara didn't care what he did to either of them. She didn't feel easy with Nicole on the other side of the door, but she couldn't explain that feeling to her father.

She had Bruno stay in her house when she wanted him. She took a cruel pleasure in their sexual relationship. He tried so hard to dominate her in the only way he knew, and she was able to resist him so easily. The convulsions of the body never inspired a spark of tender feeling in her. Lust, but not passion. She indulged her lust, but passion was what she had felt for Steven. To Clara passion meant love, with its vulnerability and pain. She never thought of Bruno Salviatti in any context except bed. He was coarse and ill educated, vain and stupid. She disregarded his good qualities because she wasn't interested enough to notice them. He was loyal, generous in his way, sentimental about children. He was brave. Roy and Victor Giambino weren't too worried about brains, but they could vouch for Salviatti's courage. Clara didn't think of him at all and if she gave him expensive clothes, it was because his lack of style annoyed her.

Aldo was content. Bruno was full of respect for him. He seemed to treat Clara well. Luisa approved of him. She had never felt comfortable with Steven Falconi. And father and daughter were deeply involved in a business scheme which had been Clara's inspiration.

She had drawn on her own experience in employing private detectives to spy upon Steven. Why not start their own agency and enlarge it to a chain across the States? It could provide the material and the front for a black-mailing operation that could be limitless. Politicians, public figures, movie stars – she listed the money-making potential. It was a long-term project, possibly five years, and the parent agency had to be arm's-length controlled. The higher the fees, she insisted, remembering how she herself had been fleeced, the richer, the more vulnerable, the clients. Aldo was gratified, and intrigued. She was a smart girl, with smart ideas. He saw even further than she did in terms of the power such an organization would give the man who actually controlled it. He told Clara to find a suitable office and then they would start by registering the agency.

Clara was engrossed in business. He had come to depend upon her as a sounding board for his own ideas. He consulted her on everything, from some small discrepancy in the quarterly take to the character and abilities of anyone he thought of promoting.

She had become his closest confidante and advisor. And inevitably they grew a little careless. The door wasn't always closed, the telephone conversations unguarded, and once Nicole came into the living room while they were both double-checking some accounts.

Nicole's relative called to collect her. Aldo welcomed his old friend, and the old friend kissed him on both cheeks and presented him with a case of fine cognac and a humidor of Havana cigars. A piece of elaborate Victorian glassware was their gift to Luisa Fabrizzi. Nicole could go home. Her mother had repented, the man would not trouble either of them again. They were for ever in Don Aldo's debt.

Aldo felt gratified. He liked to confer favours, to be admired as a patriarch.

Clara said acidly, 'They should have given *me* something. She's been getting on my nerves long enough.' Then she forgot about Nicole.

She had found a small detective agency in Newport, New Jersey, that seemed suitable. Two partners, both retired from the New York Police Department – one invalided out after a shooting, one voluntarily retired because of a growing family. Both were men of reputation with clean licences. And not much money. The business had only been established two years, and Clara had discovered that the family man had a mortgage on his house which was causing problems.

She drove down to Newport. It was a long day, but interesting. Posing as a prospective client, she managed to see and judge both partners in the firm. The Ace Detective Agency – how corny can you get? – she wondered as she shook hands with the ex cop who'd stopped three bullets in his stomach during a hold-up. He

250

had a lean, wary look about him which she didn't like. He was still very much a cop, still missing life in the precinct. The man with the kids and the wife and the mortgage was older. He was more what Clara had in mind. He was fit-looking, sharp-eyed. He was there with the lighter and the ashtray before she'd finished taking out a cigarette. He stared at the case a little too long. It was gold and expensive. He smelt a rich client. His partner smelt a case.

She talked about her husband, reeling off the standard tale of suspected adultery, and noticed which one of them was bored and which was trying to seem interested. She wasn't disappointed. She left without making a firm commitment, but promised to telephone when she'd decided to do something about it.

The married man was called O'Halloran. The other had an Italian name, Pacellino, and that had alerted her from the start. When Italians became cops they pushed harder against their own than the Irish or the Jews. He'd have to go. If it worked as she planned, he'd be bought out. And O'Halloran would find himself with a new partner. A lady, whose only requirement would be access to his files and whose contribution would be unlimited supplies of money and a brand-new office in uptown New York City.

She drove home to the house. Bruno was coming round. Clara never cooked, and eating at home with him bored her. She'd fixed dinner at a new Chinese restaurant on 43rd Street. She showered and changed, her mind busy with the details of her day. The weather was turning bitterly cold. She chose a top and skirt of dark red velvet that clung to her like a skin.

She poured a bourbon and settled down to wait for Bruno. He was never late. He came at eight o'clock exactly, sleek and trim as a boxer in a new pinstripe she'd bought him, with a heavy camelhair coat draped across his shoulders. He was strikingly handsome, she thought calmly, and she let him fondle her and kiss her mouth open. When he started easing her skirt up she pushed his hand away.

'Ah, baby,' he protested. 'What's the hurry?'

'I'm hungry. And this outfit cost three hundred dollars,' she snapped at him. 'Stop pawing me. Come on, let's go.'

He moved to the tray of bottles. She didn't see the look on his face and she wouldn't have cared anyway. 'I'd like a scotch,' he said.

'You can have one at Chow's. We'll miss the table.'

She went into her room and swept back, wrapped in a long hooded wild mink coat. He was drinking from a full glass. Clara glared at him.

'I said we'll be late,' she said, her voice raised.

Bruno didn't move. 'When we're married, I like to eat at home. I like to have my scotch and my food on the table when I want it.'

It wasn't much of a challenge to her. He often made gestures of independence and she knew exactly how to cope with them. She drew the coat back, rested one hand on the jutting hip and said, 'When we're married, big man, I'll be your little homebody wife. But right now, I'm going to dinner. You want to stay here – feel free!'

He caught her up outside the front door.

That night, when Clara was asleep beside him, Bruno Salviatti lay wide awake. He didn't like Chinese food. It left him feeling empty. He had been bored and sleepy through the evening because inside he was very angry and he couldn't let it show. He'd made love because she wanted it and she knew how to rouse him till he forgot about everthing else. But afterwards it tasted sour in his mouth. He felt like a performing animal, being asked for new tricks every time. He had been fascinated, challenged by her, lured by the prospects of the marriage, but as he lay naked, hip to thigh with Clara, he thought of how much he hated her already. She had bitten deep into his self-esteem. He found that hardest to bear. She

252

diminished him as a man. Other women had bought him clothes, and presents, but he'd accepted them as his due. He liked women to look up to him and in return he could be generous, he could be good to women. This woman used him and despised him.

He was ready to marry even before he met her, ready to raise a family. He was doing well, he had a reputation. Roy Giambino had given him a district. Then he saw her at the anniversary party and set out to make her. He wanted to show off before the young *ragazzi*.

It had looked such a great chance to rise in the world, to marry the daughter of a Don without sons or grandsons to follow him. It didn't seem so now.

When he woke in the morning Clara was still asleep. He didn't wake her. The maid was in the kitchen. She made him coffee and eggs. He thought, looking at her shuffling round him: This will be my life. My life at home. He banged out of the house without finishing his breakfast or looking in on Clara to say goodbye.

Ex Detective Sergeant Mike O'Halloran was coming up to forty. He'd put his savings into the agency with his friend Pacellino, and for the first year his wife had been happy. Happy that he was not in danger, that he was home at regular hours and able to spend time with his children. She looked ten years younger and their marriage picked up. It picked up so well that before they realized it she was pregnant.

That made four children on top of the mortgage on the new house. After that it started to go downhill. Small debts became bigger; the agency had some lean months in the first year and the doctor's bills for his wife and the baby were a worry. He was sorry she'd persuaded him to leave the Force. She nagged and he started losing his temper.

They got some good jobs, but the work wasn't consistent. A lot of it was small stuff, short on expenses. Routine surveillance for divorce, court attendances which took time.

Pacellino was a bachelor. He had a small rented apartment and a girlfriend who worked in real estate. O'Halloran bore the real burden. When two days went by and the rich bitch from New York didn't phone in, he became depressed. She'd looked like real money. When she called him personally and invited him to lunch, O'Halloran couldn't believe his luck. He even agreed to her request to keep the meeting private. Just between themselves. She had a proposition to put to him.

He didn't say anything to Pacellino. He just took off for the lunch hour and went to the motel she'd suggested. She was in the cafeteria when he got there, a glass of bourbon on the table. He apologized if he'd kept her waiting. She had a cool look about her. She pulled her sleeve back to show her watch for a brief check and then she smiled at him and asked him to sit down. He had a gut feeling as he did so that this was not going to be anything to do with a cheating husband.

His mind was a long way off his investigation that afternoon. He sat outside an apartment building watching a client's wife go in to spend time with her boyfriend and thought about the offer the woman had made to him. She wanted a detective agency all of her own, but she didn't want the connection made public. She had emphasized the necessity of complete secrecy and there was just a hint of threat in the way she repeated it. She was a beautiful, sexy dame, O'Halloran admitted, but he'd as soon put his hand into the tigers' cage at the city zoo, as try and touch her up. When she mentioned the investment, he managed to keep his face straight. If the business prospered, she added, there was plenty more for expansion into other major cities.

'I can see quite a network in a few years, if things work out,' she had said, and he'd nodded eagerly.

It was all wrong and he knew it, his instincts were flashing warnings like neon lights, but he went on sitting there; she made it sound so reasonable. The agency would move to New York, where she had an appropriate office in mind. He would recruit a reliable staff. His police connections would surely help there. He agreed that they would. The agency must have a broad prospectus, offering a comprehensive service to clients and prepared to accept business from corporations.

At one point O'Halloran had been constrained to interrupt. 'Lady, I did twenty years on the beat and made Detective Sergeant, but what I don't know about corporations you could put in a book!'

'You don't have to know about them,' was the answer. 'That'll be my responsibility. You'll just do what's needed, when it's needed. Okay?'

'Okay,' he said, and from that moment he shut down the switch on the warning lights. He needed money; he was being offered the chance to be rich for doing the same sort of thing he was doing at the moment for peanuts. He could afford good schools for the kids, nice clothes for his wife, a new car. He leaned towards her and said, 'So long as it's legal, it sounds like one hell of a good deal to me.'

He remembered her smile as he sat slumped down in the car seat, listlessly watching yet another marital two-timer sneaking out after an afternoon in the sack. It was a strange sort of smile, almost friendly for a moment. He had given her something she wanted and she was pleased with him. He had laid the foundation for their partnership with a lie and she answered it with a lie of her own.

'It will always be legal,' she said. 'I promise you that. Do we have a deal, Mr O'Halloran?'

'We have a deal,' he said.

She had got up and solemnly shaken hands with him. He insisted on paying for their drinks. She thanked him. She had magnificent black eyes. He was a bought man and he knew it by the way she looked at him. He had a twinge about his old partner, Pacellino, with the holes torn through his guts.

'You're sure you wouldn't want Tony in on this?'

'I'm sure,' she had answered. 'I'll get the new office set

255

up and you get out from under him. Call me when you're ready to move. And make it soon.'

He had the card in his pocket. Mrs Clara Falconi and a ritzy-sounding address on the East Side.

He noted the time the errant wife emerged and drove back to the office to check in. His partner was out. He looked around him. It was small, untidy, run on a shoestring. He paused for a moment, tempted to call someone in New York and ask them to run a check on the lady. He even reached for the telephone. But he never picked it up. He didn't want an answer. He didn't want to know for sure what he suspected.

He typed his report for the afternoon's work and went home. He made a big fuss of his wife and kids and told them he'd had an offer to run a new agency in New York.

Steven was right about Sicily in the month of September. It was perfect. The fierce August heat had become a lovely constant temperature with a light breeze that came up in the evenings.

They started in Messina and they drove up the winding mountain roads and through on to the coast. Steven showed them Greek ruins and Roman amphitheatres, abandoned for two thousand years to the ravages of sun and weather. They wandered through hillside villages where the streets were too narrow even to admit the painted carts that trundled behind the sad donkeys. They saw the grand fortress houses of the ancient aristocracy, mostly abandoned for life in the agreeable confines of Palermo or the Italian mainland. Little by little, Steven taught his son about Sicily, and the word Mafia crept in unchallenged.

Charlie listened, infected by Steven's passionate interest in the strange, barren country with such a violent history. It helped a lot that Steven was such a good storyteller. He made boring ruins and crumbling buildings come to life and Charlie responded by asking questions and wanting to know more.

256

It was a pilgrimage full of memories for Angela. They crowded in upon her as they travelled towards Palermo. When they reached the city she took Charlie to Tremoli, to the site where the hospital had stood. There was a four-storey hotel built on it.

'I nursed here,' she said. 'My best friend, Christine, was killed when the hospital was bombed. There's nothing left of anything now.'

Charlie linked his arm through hers. 'Don't be upset, Mum. It was a long time ago. Why don't we go and see the place where you married my father? You told me it was up in the hills near here?'

He didn't see the quick glance she exchanged with Steven or his nod in agreement.

She smiled at him. 'Why not? It was in a little village called Altofonte. Do you think you could find it, darling?'

'I'm sure I could,' Steven said. 'I'd like to see it too.'

Little had changed. True to his promise to the priest, Steven had arranged immunity for the village and its people. They paid no Mafia dues and suffered no Mafia murders. It was sleepy and sunlit. The paint on the houses was faded and peeling, the geraniums still bloomed in fierce profusion, the washing fluttered like flags of poverty in between the houses above the dark little streets. The church was smaller than Angela remembered it; the inside even darker.

Her son said, 'It must have been a funny wedding, Mum. It's jolly gloomy in here.'

They walked up the aisle towards the gilded, painted altar with the saints dressed in real clothes, faded flower offerings withering at their feet. The red eye of the sacristy lamp burned above them.

'It was a wonderful wedding,' Angela said, and reached for Steven's hand.

The door of the sacristy opened. It was a young priest and he came hurrying towards them, buttoning his cassock.

Steven spoke to him in the dialect. The priest smiled at them all in turn. Angela and Charlie shook hands, not understanding what was said.

'We were married here during the war, Father,' Steven explained. 'This is my wife and son. Are you the new parish priest?'

'I'm Father Alberto. The old priest died three years ago. You come from here?'

'Yes,' Steven said. 'Stefano Falconi.'

They shook hands again and the priest said in a low voice, 'We know that name. We've cause to bless it. You gave us protection. We have our crops and our wine and we're at peace. Thanks to you, Don Stefano. God's blessing on you and your family.'

He bowed to Angela and the boy.

Steven took some notes out of his wallet. He handed them to the priest. 'Give this to the families that need it most,' he said. 'And the rest, keep for your church and yourself, Father.'

'Dad must have given him a big present,' Charlie whispered as they came out. 'Did you see his face, Mum? He couldn't believe it.'

'It's a custom,' she explained. 'And you know how generous he is.' And then because she knew how much it meant to Steven she said, 'Now we'll go and see where his family used to live before they went to the States.'

Charlie stared at her. 'You mean they were here too? The same place where you and my father got married?'

'Yes, isn't it a coincidence, Steven? I was just telling Charlie about your grandfather living in the village. Would you know where the house was? It would be nice to see it, wouldn't it, Charlie?'

'It's not much,' Steven said. He put his arm round Angela, pressed her close in silent thanks. 'We were poor people, poor peasants.'

Charlie asked him, 'Will it still be there?'

'Nothing changes in Sicily,' Steven answered. 'It'll be there.'

258

And it was, just as Angela remembered it so many years ago. The door and shutters were freshly painted a bright green, and a young woman nursing a baby sat on the doorstep, her bare feet in the dust. She looked up at them suspiciously as they briefly passed. The baby sucked greedily and she gave it her attention when the strangers moved on.

Steven said to his son, 'Not what you expected? I told you, we were dirt poor. That's why they emigrated to America.'

Charlie said, 'Don't blame them. Still, they must have done jolly well over there. Look at you, Dad!'

'Yes,' Steven said. 'They did well, Charlie. All they needed was the opportunity. But I'm proud of my grandfather. He was poor, but he was a man of respect in this village. Now, let's see if there's anywhere we can get something to drink and eat. You hungry, sweetheart?'

'Yes, and thirsty,' Angela said. 'It was good of you to help the priest, darling.'

'It was expected,' Steven said.

They had the best suite in the Palazzo Palermo Hotel. Charlie had gone to his room to read after a rich Sicilian dinner and a lot of the heavy local wine.

Angela had laughed when she saw the bed in their room. It was an antique and quite narrow by the current standards, but it made up in splendour for the lack of mattress space. It was dressed in crimson silk with gold cherubs supporting the drapery from the ceiling. More gold cherubs disported at the foot of the bed and a red and gold confection topped with a ducal crown and coat of arms towered above their pillows. It was the bridal suite, the manager informed them. Furnished from the sale of the last Duchess of Finchula's estate. The dressing table was a crimson and gilt extravagance, miniature cherubs supporting an elaborate mirror above the silk flounces, and the chairs were carved and gilded thrones with matching footstools.

'It's unbelievable,' Angela exclaimed. 'It's amazing! Did people really live in rooms like this?'

'The Finchulas were poor,' Steven told her. 'They had big estates, but no money. This stuff was sold for pennies, I expect. I can't wait to see you sitting up in that bed!' And they both laughed at the idea.

It was indeed a narrow bed and their bodies were confined so close that it was well into the night before their lovemaking was over and they drifted to sleep. In the morning, with the sun streaming through the drawn curtains and the shutters fastened back, Angela and Steven talked about their son.

'I know it's bothering you,' Angela insisted. 'I know how much you wanted to tell him when we were at Altofonte.'

'I hoped there might be an opportunity, he might ask something, but he didn't. So it's not the time to tell him yet. When it is, it'll happen.' He held her close to him; her head leaned against his shoulder.

'Perhaps I ought to tell him,' she said. 'I know it frustrates you, Steven, when you love him so much. And I love you so much too.' She twisted round to kiss him, holding him close to her. 'Last night was the best ever,' she whispered.

'It was the bed,' he teased her. 'All the dried-up old dukes and duchesses must have been sick with envy watching us.'

'What are you talking about? You talk such nonsense, darling.' She drew back, teasing him, holding him at bay as he strained to kiss her.

'It's not nonsense. If you make love in someone else's bed, they come back from the dead to watch you. All Sicilians know that. That's why they only put foreigners in here.' He pulled her down on top of him. 'And there's another superstition. When you do it like this, you make daughters. I want a daughter.'

Charlie flew back to England direct from Italy.

'It's been a wonderful trip,' he told Steven. 'Really super. I'd love to come back again.'

Steven embraced him. Angela could see the pleasure in his face.

'You will. We'll have a proper holiday on the island. Now work hard or I'll get in trouble with your mother for keeping you out of school.'

Arm in arm they watched the aircraft take off.

'He did enjoy it, didn't he? Maybe he felt some tie with the place.'

Angela hadn't noticed anything beyond a schoolboy's enthusiasm, but she knew how much Steven wanted to think it was more.

'I wouldn't be surprised. You have such strong roots; but you brought it all to life for him, darling. You made it real. He got quite upset about the way the landlords treated their tenants. He actually said to me the Mafia were the only protection those poor people had. He'd always thought they were a lot of gangsters in America.'

'And what did you say to that?' he questioned.

'I said what you said. It started out well and went wrong.'

'It surely did,' he said. 'My grandfather killed tax collectors. Now we *are* the tax collectors. Come on, darling. I'm looking forward to going home. I must call Maxton and tell him to have a car at Nice to meet us. I want to plan something special for the end of our first season.'

'Why don't you spend Christmas here?' Ralph Maxton asked.

Angela shook her head. 'My father's not well enough to fly out. He's insisting on staying at home so we've got to go over and be with him.'

It was a slight deterioration of his heart condition, nothing serious, Jim Hulbert had reassured her. But long journeys and upheavals were not sensible at his age. Especially during bad weather. Steven had agreed to a second Christmas spent at Haywards Heath, when she knew he wanted to stay in France.

The villa belonged to them now. He had persuaded the owner to sell it by an offer of twice the market value. So it was truly their home and Angela could change the furniture and redecorate. She found little to alter. She liked the previous owner's taste and it seemed as if the task of transforming the casino had exhausted her inventive powers. She bought some pictures from a gallery in Cannes that specialized in good French contemporary art, changed the curtains in the dining room and decided to leave anything else till the spring.

There was a gala evening planned for the middle of October. After that Maxton recommended they close down till spring. When the casino was in profit, they could afford to stay open during the quiet winter months, but not yet. He and Steven had decided on a charity performance as their curtain-closer for the casino.

It was Maxton's idea to contact Renata Soldi's agent. She was the most promising young opera singer since Maria Callas.

'She'll come because she's poaching on Callas's territory. And the glitterati'll come to give Callas a poke in the eye. She's made a lot of enemies. Renata Soldi can't hold a candle to La Callas, but that's not the point. She'll pull the crowds. We'll sell out for the charity and pick up some of the big gamblers who can't afford not to be seen at this sort of thing. And we'll shut up shop with a bang!'

As always, Angela wished he could have toned down the ruthless cynicism. It spoiled the excitement of the evening. She was looking forward to hearing Soldi sing. She didn't want to connect a great artist with malice and infighting towards another great artist or see her audience as little more than spectators at a social blood sport.

Ralph Maxton saw her reaction and tried to put it right by changing the subject and talking about something agreeable. Like Christmas.

'It'll be fun having Christmas in England,' he said. 'You had snow last year, didn't you? It was just cold and rather wet here.'

They were having their weekly dinner together and Steven had left them at the table to finish their coffee while he made some calls. Angela knew he always telephoned New York around this time, so she kept Maxton on in the dining room.

'Where will you go?' she asked him.

He shrugged. 'It depends. I was hoping to spend it with a friend, but she's got elderly relative trouble at the moment, so I don't suppose it'll come off. Is there more coffee there, Angela? . . . Thanks.'

Madeleine was doubtful about sneaking off with him for Christmas. Her lover was demanding that she stay near him in Lyons so he could escape his family's clutches and visit her. As Madeleine explained, she was squeezing him for a really big present this year and she didn't think she'd get it if she didn't stay close. She told Ralph how annoyed she was and pulled pretty faces, calling the old man a string of dirty names, but Ralph understood. She couldn't pass up a valuable piece of jewellery, or a block of shares, just to screw and laugh with him over the holiday.

He'd planned to spend Christmas in a new hotel at Val d'Isère. He was a good skier and Madeleine was more athletic than she looked. They'd have had fun. He hated Christmas, it was so depressing, with its insistence upon family gatherings and children. He'd have to go up there alone. He was sure to find someone congenial. He had a lot of money to throw around on a pretty girl.

He heard Angela say, 'What will you do, Ralph, if your plans have fallen through?'

He smiled in his twisted way, mocking himself. 'Make new ones. I'm very adaptable. And be a dear and don't suggest I go home, because I want to see the family about as much as they want to see me.'

'I wasn't going to suggest it,' she said. 'I was going to

263

ask you if you'd like to come over and have Christmas with all of us.'

To her surprise he turned slightly red. 'How very kind. Were you really?'

'Why not? If you can't or won't go to your own home, why not come to mine? Charlie'd love it, so would my father, and Steven and I would be delighted. Just so long as you don't expect this sort of standard. It's a very modest village house, but we'll have a happy Christmas, I can promise you. I love all the trimmings, the tree and the presents and going to Midnight Service. You said it was wet and miserable here last year.'

'I said it was wet and it was miserable because I was extremely hard up, if you remember.

'Don't dodge the issue,' Angela challenged him. 'Why don't you say yes? If your friend solves her problem with the relative, then we won't mind a bit if you cancel. How's that?'

'That's the nicest bit of blackmail I can think of,' he said. 'Hadn't you better mention it to Steven? He may not want the hired help eating his Christmas turkey.'

'Shut up and don't be silly. He's very fond of you. We both are.'

He was so adept at hiding his feelings that she noticed nothing except that hint of colour. It was funny, she couldn't imagine Maxton being embarrassed by anything.

He leaned a little towards her across the table. She looked very pretty and soft in the subdued light and, however hard he'd tried, he couldn't find anything but gentleness in her eyes. He reached out and took her hand. He did it in an exaggerated way, robbing the gesture of serious intent. He raised her hand to his lips and, for the merest second, touched it.

'My fair benefactress,' he declaimed. 'Thanks to you, I shan't spend a lonely Christmas, sobbing into my pillow! Tell me, why are you such a very nice person?'

'Why do you make a joke of everything?' she

264

countered. 'I'm not particularly nice. I can be very nasty when I like, so just be careful!'

'That, I doubt,' he said. 'Hadn't we better join Steven? Otherwise he'll come storming in and fire me for kissing your hand!'

'You're an idiot,' she laughed at him. 'Come on. Let Janine clear the table. Steven says she gets on his nerves, she's always hovering round us. He even suggested I get rid of her.'

'You'd lose the mother and she's a marvellous cook, as we've just proved. And the next one could be a thief as well as a spy. All French servants spy on their employers; the Italians steal from them. I could have a word with her if you like?'

'No, don't bother. I'll probably lose my temper if I catch her outside the door and do it myself. As you say, Ralph, I don't want to lose both of them. That fish soufflé was delicious, wasn't it?'

'Exquisite,' he said. He opened the door and stood aside to let her pass. 'But I bet your Christmas turkey will be better.'

'Darling, you don't mind, do you. It seemed awful for him to spend Christmas all alone.'

'I don't think it means the same to him as it does to you,' Steven said. 'He'd have found some company. But if it makes you happy to have him come over, that's fine by me.'

'Thank you, darling. I think it's a kindness. He's so bitter about life, but deep down there's a lot of niceness in him. He's so lonely, it's sad.'

Steven smiled. 'You find good points in everyone, sweetheart, that's your trouble. The hell of it is, you seem to bring them out! But don't be too sorry for him or I'll get jealous.'

'I can imagine,' Angela teased him back. 'He's quite a charmer, so you better watch out.'

They ended by hugging each other and laughing.

★

The gala was a sell-out. Angela sat entranced by the strength and purity of the young opera star's voice. She had never heard Maria Callas sing in the flesh; she had to take Maxton's word for it that Renata Soldi was not in the same class.

It was a glittering evening with the women dressed and jewelled like peacocks, and afterwards when the concert was over and the supper room cleared away, she went upstairs and watched the closed-circuit TV with Steven. He was in a buoyant mood, pointing out the big gamblers on the screen. A number of them were women, including a famous Hollywood star.

Angela was tired after the long evening and the singing had been a powerful experience that left her feeling drained. The next morning they would close down the casino for the winter. The staff went on to half pay, except for the croupiers and dealers who kept their full salaries, but were free to seek employment elsewhere till the spring reopening. And the move to England for the Christmas holidays was drawing near. Charlie had phoned and written. He was in good spirits and assured them that he had been working hard.

She was sitting with Steven one chilly November evening, a wood fire burning in the grate and a sense of utter peace and happiness in her heart, when the telephone rang. It was New York.

Steven said, 'It's my brother. I'll take it in the study, darling.'

It was a long call. Angela almost fell asleep in the warm room.

'Angela.' She roused with a start. She often drifted into a doze in the evenings these days.

'Steven? What's the matter? Is something wrong?' She was instantly alert at the sight of him.

He dropped down beside her. 'Clara's getting married again,' he said.

'But isn't that good news?' she questioned.

'My family thinks so,' he said. 'But I'm not sure. I'm not sure at all.'

'Why, why not? That's the proof they think you're dead.'

'That's what my brother said. The heat's off. She's found herself a man and they're getting married after Christmas. He works for two brothers on the West Side. The way Piero spoke he sounds like some cheap punk who's good with the girls.'

'Perhaps that's what she wants,' Angela suggested. 'Someone the opposite of you.'

Steven was frowning, hardly hearing what she said. Clara, intelligent, educated, with a taste for music and the arts – he remembered her saying when they were in Paris on their honeymoon that she'd wanted to be a painter. Clara, marrying a good-looking, low-class muscle man from the Giambino mob?

Perhaps Angela was right. Perhaps the only way Clara could come to terms with her jealous sexuality was to go slumming. But he didn't believe it. She would eat a man like that alive and then spit out the remains.

He said, 'Why don't you go up to bed, darling. I won't be long. I just want to think it through.'

'All right. I nearly dropped off while you were on the phone. Don't worry, it must be a good thing. She'll make a new life for herself. Wake me if you're worried. Promise?'

'I promise,' he said and kissed her.

It wasn't right. The more he considered it, the less the pieces came together to make Piero's complacent scenario. The only way Clara Fabrizzi would marry a small-time Mafia hood was because she was pregnant. The time scale of the wedding ruled that out. So there was another motive.

A motive in her father letting her make such a marriage. A big wedding in New York, Piero said. Everyone invited. Steven was pouring himself a whisky when he repeated that out loud. Everyone from the Falconi Family. All gathered together in one place.

267

Steven slammed the glass down so hard that the bottom cracked. He didn't notice. He was reaching for the phone to break all the rules and call his father. Piero wouldn't see it. Only Luca, subtle as a snake himself, would listen to his son's instinct and accept his warning.

His mother was crying down the telephone. 'Oh, my son, my boy. It's so good to hear your voice. How are you?'

'I'm fine, Momma. Just fine. So good to hear you too. You've had my messages from Piero?' He found himself swallowing hard at the sound of his mother choking back the tears.

'Yes, yes. He tells me when you call. I think of you all the time. I pray for you.'

'I know you do, Momma, and I think of you and Poppa and the family. I miss you all so much.' Piero had told him she'd been unwell with a chest cold again. 'How are you feeling, Momma? You taking care of yourself? You catch too many colds.'

'I'm better, don't worry about me. Piero makes too much of everything. Lucia moved in to look after me and took care of your father.'

'I have to talk with him,' Steven said. 'Get him to come to the phone; tell him it's important. I *must* talk with him.'

'I'll try, Stefano, I'll try. Hold on.'

It seemed a long wait to Steven. He knew his father's pride.

Luca Falconi looked up at his wife. He had no pity for her tears. 'No,' he said. 'I have no son to talk with. There's nothing he has to say I want to hear. You want to talk with him, you talk.'

He raised the sound level of the television. For a moment his wife hesitated, nerving herself for one more try. Without looking at her he said loudly, 'Shut the door, Anna.'

She banged it in her despair. 'He won't speak to you,' she said. 'I can't persuade him. I'm so sorry, Stefano.'

Steven swore in helpless anger. Then he said gently, 'Momma, Momma, don't upset yourself. Don't cry. I understand how he feels. Listen to me. Just tell him this. Make sure he listens. Tell him not to go to Clara's wedding. Tell Piero not to go. It's a trap they've set for all of you. Tell him, Momma. Make him hear you.'

She promised and he hung up. He balled his fist and rammed it into his palm in frustration. He'd call Piero back right away, deliver the same message, hope he'd take it seriously. But Piero was an optimist. He didn't see round corners. He'd talked so jauntily about finally getting Clara off their backs, making a crude joke in illustration. He wouldn't want to hear that it was a ruse to get the Falconis off their guard.

But Steven had to try. He caught Piero half asleep after a heavy lunch. And not receptive, as he'd feared. Steven had been absent from the scene too long. Piero's awe of him was tempered with a growing confidence in his own abilities. Spoletto was the watchdog and he hadn't come up with anything suspicious. And, Piero insisted, he was always looking under the bed, for Christ's sake.

'You're getting jumpy down there. Back home we just get on with business and lead a quiet life. Clara's got herself a big hunk, that's all there is to it. Relax, Brother, relax.' He ended the conversation with a cheerful laugh.

In the morning Steven told Angela. He was restless, unable to stay in bed beside her. He paced up and down while he talked.

'I know it,' he insisted. 'I know it in here!' He struck his chest. 'It's phoney – the whole thing's a set-up. Clara wouldn't marry a slob and Aldo wouldn't let her. All that crap about wanting my father's blessing. Didn't I tell you about that? She hated Poppa's guts and at the end he hated hers. So they tell a pack of lies, they set a wedding date and my family starts to sit back and look the other way. If only I could see Piero, talk to him face to face. He laughed at me last night, Angela. Can you believe that? What the hell am I to do?'

269

She got up and came to him. 'Calm down,' she said quietly. 'That's the first thing. This wedding is weeks away. You don't have to do anything on the spur of the moment. You've got time, Steven. Your family's got time.'

He pulled away from her. 'No, they haven't,' he said harshly. 'I know the Fabrizzis. They'll fix alibis and get agreement among some of the other Families for what they're going to do. They'll make it a matter of honour, that's how it's done. My father and brother won't stand a snowball's chance in hell. And there's always a back-up plan to an operation like this. If the target gets suspicious, or shows signs they've figured out what's going on, you hit them ahead of the date. I shouldn't have talked to Piero. I should have got on the plane and gone back when my father wouldn't talk to me.'

Angela's colour drained. 'Steven, you can't! You can't go back. You'd be killed!'

'I swore an oath to my father, I swore it to my brother too. If there was trouble, I'd come back. Nothing can make me break that promise. Not even you, Angela.'

She said, 'What about your son? What about Charlie? What do you think it'll mean to him if something happens to you? And it's not just Charlie either, now.' She went back and sat on the bed.

He wasn't listening to her. He had become a stranger, a man caught up in a frightening, alien world.

'You go home to your father,' he said. 'Get ready for Christmas. Maxton can close up the villa. I'll join you there as soon as I can.'

'No, Steven!'

He turned at the tone of her voice. 'Angela, don't try to stop me. Please don't try to stop me. I have to do this.'

'You have to stay with me,' she said. 'You can't go back and risk your life on account of your family because you've got another family to think about. I'm having a baby. I was keeping it as a surprise for Christmas.'

She broke down and began to weep. He came and sat

with her, taking her in his arms. She turned and clung to him.

'If you go you won't come back. You'll get drawn in. It'll be the end of everything for us.'

'Angelina.' His tone was pleading now. 'I have a duty. I swore an oath.'

She drew away from him. 'You swore one to me when you married me, in that church we went back to in September! You swore to keep me and cherish me, to put me and our children first. That's the oath that matters, Steven!'

'You should have told me,' he said slowly. 'You should have told me you were pregnant.'

'I had it all planned. My Christmas present to you, Steven. You've said you wanted another child and I wanted one too, to make you happy. Try to make your father see sense. Try once more, before you do something that could destroy everything for us. You gave up the old life. You had no right to promise anything that meant getting involved in it again.'

He asked her, 'What are you saying to me, Angela?'

She took a deep breath, 'I'm saying this. I love you with all my heart, Steven. But you've got to find another way. If you leave me to go to the States, I don't want you back.'

She went out of the bedroom and closed the door.

In the last days of November Ralph Maxton noticed the strain between Angela and Steven. Steven was grim and short tempered, tense as wire. There was no concealing their unhappiness. Maxton hated seeing Angela pale and withdrawn. But he hated Steven Falconi more for being the cause of it. He was travelling with her for Christmas. Steven mentioned abruptly that he had to make a business trip and would be joining them in England later. He didn't say where he was going or why. Maxton didn't ask.

He went shopping for presents. A present for the old

271

father; he found a nice antique backgammon set. He
could teach the doctor to play. He'd cut his gambling
teeth on that particular game when he was in his teens. A
tennis racquet for Charlie from a smart sports shop in
Monte Carlo. He'd actually bought it for himself in the
summer and never used it. For Angela, what? What
could he give that was personal enough and yet not too
personal? The *bibelots* from Hermes – scarves, expensive
gold-plated key rings and costly knick-knacks – were not
Angela's style. In the end he found a silkwork picture of
flowers in an oval frame. She would appreciate that. He
wrapped it carefully. It was just possible that Steven
might not be there when she opened it. His absence at
Christmas was hinted at, but not confirmed.

She had been crying on the morning they drove to the
airport at Nice. She had a lot of luggage, he noticed.
Steven drove them. He looked grim. Angela sat beside
Steven in the front seat, and once when he put out his
hand to touch her, Maxton saw her move away. In the
departure lounge Maxton pretended not to watch them
say goodbye. It was painful and not just the pain of a brief
parting.

For a moment Angela looked up at Steven.

'You won't change you mind?'

'I can't,' he whispered. 'We've been over and over it.
Oh darling, I beg of you, try to understand.'

'I don't care about your promise to anyone else,' she
said. 'But you've broken your promise to me. I've got to
go now. They've called our flight.'

She literally pulled herself away from him and started
off towards the gate. Maxton called goodbye to Steven
Falconi. It wasn't acknowledged. Falconi stood looking
after his wife and then abruptly swung away and
disappeared. Maxton settled into the seat beside her. He
dug into his pocket.

'From one coward to another,' he murmured. 'Have a
drop of this before we take off.' He offered a little silver
flask of brandy. 'It'll make you feel better.'

272

Angela took it from him. He had unscrewed a tiny cup from the top. 'I don't think anything will do that,' she said, and drank it down.

The plane was taxiing on to the runway, the engines gathering power for the take-off. She closed her eyes and then opened them, watching the ground speeding away from them.

'If you feel like clutching something . . .' Maxton said, and she gripped his hand as they lifted off with a thrust of the engines, the plane climbing steeply. 'All over,' he said. 'Hang on if you want to, in case we get a few bumps through the clouds.'

Angela said, 'Thanks, Ralph. I'm all right now. It's just the take-off I don't like.'

'I don't like the bumps,' he admitted.

'I don't think you're frightened at all,' she said. 'You're just saying it to make me feel better.'

They weren't holding hands any more. The signs for no smoking and fasten seat belts were switched off above their heads. People round them were relaxing, opening newspapers. There was a rattle as the drinks trolley started on its journey.

'You know what you said when we took off,' Ralph Maxton reminded her. 'If there's anything wrong and you think I could help, you will ask me, won't you Angela?'

'Yes, Ralph, I will.'

He didn't press her further. He ordered a drink for them. There were English newspapers on board. She tried to read. She felt sick with the baby inside her and heartsick at what lay ahead. Thank God Ralph was going to be there with her. At least she could confide in him. Her father and Charlie had to be protected up to the last moment, the façade that Steven was on business kept going till the holiday was over. He hadn't changed his mind. She wouldn't change hers. She wouldn't be going back to France.

7

They met in the back of a trattoria on the corner of Mulberry and Grand in the area of New York where the first immigrants had settled.

They'd come from Sicily, from Naples, from Calabria, from the bitterly poor industrialized towns in the North, and made their home in the rat-ridden tenements and tumbledown shacks of a sprawling slum. It was known as Little Italy. The small food shops were still there, selling pasta and salami and wine from the old homeland. The cafés and restaurants, the tenement blocks, the Catholic-run schools and the big churches built with the poor people's money; the funeral parlours and the flower shops, the markets where the old women liked to congregate and bargain, talking their native dialect. It was the heartland of the Mafia and its Neapolitan offspring, Cosa Nostra. The trattoria was owned by one of the New York Families; they ran the gambling and the drug factories and the whorehouses in part of the neighbourhood. They were affiliated to the Fabrizzis, who were much bigger and more powerful. Their trattoria was chosen for the meeting, before Christmas. It was snowing, with temperatures of savage cold. The men came in their cars, wrapped to the ears in coats and scarves, hats pulled low against the wind that blasted round the corner. They went in one by one and were shown to the room at the back. They took their places at the table. When the door opened and closed and the last man was in place, the meeting was called to order by Joe Nimmi, the old friend and business associate of Aldo Fabrizzi.

The brothers Roy and Victor Giambino were among the group.

Joe Nimmi was a powerful man, a senior Capo di Mafioso, respected for his loyalty and wisdom. He spoke with due solemnity. Everyone stayed quiet.

'You all know why we've come together,' he said. 'It's a sad day for me; maybe the saddest of my life. For forty years I've been a friend of Aldo Fabrizzi. We worked the streets together, we were like brothers. We fought side by side in those early days when the Irish tried taking over our territories. I've got the scars right here to prove it.' He laid a hand on his chest. 'Aldo's become a big man. We respected him. We owed him loyalty. But I tell you, he's been cheating on us.' He looked around them.

'A few months ago he called us to a meeting. He says he wants to eliminate the Falconis to avenge his daughter's honour. But he lied. He had another reason. My niece Nicole stayed in Aldo's house. I tell you the truth, I sent her there. I'd been hearing things I couldn't believe. Nicole heard Aldo and his daughter talking business. Our business. She saw Clara reading the ledgers. Checking the figures. Aldo Fabrizzi wants the Falconis rubbed out. He wants the territories and their business to give to his daughter Clara. He wants us working for her.' He paused and there was an angry murmur. He said to Victor Giambino, 'Isn't this true?'

'It's true,' Victor agreed. 'They fixed the marriage so he could put the power in Clara's hands. Bruno's our boy, and he admitted what was going on. We made a few inquiries of our own. We found out she's running the protection for the garment business. There's a mouthpiece, but she's giving the orders.'

Joe Nimmi took it up. 'Men have ruled our Society as they rule their families at home. No woman has ever been admitted. We are the Men of Respect.' He gave the ancient Sicilian title in all its solemnity. 'What he has

275

done is a crime. A dishonour to us all. My friends, we swore an oath not long ago. It was a false oath. It doesn't bind me anymore. Are we to put a gun to Luca Falconi's head, so Clara can take us over?'

There was a shout of 'No' almost in one voice. He nodded.

'What Aldo was doing would have meant war on the streets. We've had peace for many years. I say his life is forfeit. I call on you to vote.'

He sat down. One by one the hands were raised. There were no abstentions. It was a solemn moment.

Victor Giambino asked the only question. 'What about Bruno Salviatti?'

Joe Nimmi shrugged. 'We'll think about Bruno,' he said. He cleared his throat. It had been a long, emotional speech. He asked for some water.

Gradually the mood lightened. People started talking about family plans for Christmas. The meeting broke up and they exchanged festive greetings.

They left as they had come, one by one at intervals, speeding away in their cars, back to their homes or their offices. Life went back to normal.

Joe Nimmi was the last to go. He stayed talking to the man and his wife who ran the trattoria; he shared a pot of coffee with them against going out into the cold. He gave them an envelope full of money and wished them a merry Christmas. He pinched the plump little boy's cheek as he sat on his mother's knee.

'What a fine-looking boy,' he said. He slipped a ten-dollar note into his mother's hand. 'Buy him something from me.'

He went outside into the street. It was nearly dark. Men in Santa Claus costume were ringing bells in the main shopping centres and collecting for the poor.

'What's the matter?'

Angela was on her way out and there was Charlie barring her way.

276

'Nothing, nothing's the matter.'

'You've been crying,' he said, 'I can tell. Why isn't Dad coming home? Come on, I'm not a baby. I want to know.'

'I told you, it's business,' Angela said.

He had grown up even since September. Grown and matured with the rapidity of his Sicilian blood. And he looked so like his father standing there. She had been a fool to think he wouldn't notice.

'I don't believe it's business,' Charlie announced. 'The casino's shut down for the winter, Ralph was telling me . . . You've had a row, haven't you? He hasn't even phoned to speak to me –'

'Yes,' she admitted. 'We have had a row, Charlie. I didn't want him to miss Christmas. He may still change his mind. So don't worry about it, will you? Please?'

'Of course I'm worrying,' he said angrily. 'It's just not like you two – you never row about anything. Mum –' He hesitated and went red. 'He hasn't met someone else, has he?'

'Oh darling, no. It's nothing like that! I can't really talk about it. And I'm going to be late, Grandpa's waiting in the car. I must go –' She pushed past him.

If they went on discussing it, she might break down in tears. She had kept up a facade of cheerfulness, hoping to deceive him. And hoping, in spite of everything, that Steven would call and say he'd changed his mind. She had noticed that Charlie was quite hostile to Ralph Maxton, and that disturbed her. Now she knew why. He resented any man in Steven's place.

'What kept you so long?' Hugh Drummond grumbled. 'I won't have any time to get anything, at this rate.'

She has found him very frail and inclined to be querulous. He wanted to get an extra present for his grandson and something for Maxton. He was always saying how much he liked Maxton, and that irritated Charlie too.

Maxton was very good with the old man; he listened patiently to Hugh's rambling stories of his early days in medicine, never once showing that he was bored.

And the preparations for Christmas went ahead, with the question mark hanging over her that was becoming less of a question with every day that passed. Steven wouldn't go back on his promise. His responsibility to his family came before his love for her, their son and the baby she was carrying. And she could never accept that and resume their life together. Beyond that, she was unable to think. There would be a hideous bloodletting in America, and inevitably he would become part of it.

She said, 'I'm sorry, Daddy. Don't worry, we've got plenty of time before the shops close.'

Charlie watched them drive away. He let the curtain fall back, and stood staring down at the fire. He loved his stepfather too. He wanted them to be together, to celebrate this Christmas as they had done the first one, after they were married. He didn't want that beak-nosed bugger Maxton hanging round his mother either, making himself useful. The way he pandered round the old boy turned Charlie's stomach. Charlie wasn't taken in, even if his grandfather thought his long stories about hospital life in the twenties interested anybody but himself. A row, his mother called it. A pretty serious row about business to set them apart like this.

'Business, my bloody foot,' Charlie announced out loud. His hero, Jordan, instigator of that trip to New York, had flunked out halfway through his end of term exams and been sent home. His parents were getting a divorce. The news had shattered him. Charlie was shattered too, when the story went through the school. If it happened to Jordan, then couldn't it happen to him too? Unless he did something about it. He had learned from Steven. You didn't sit on your hands and wait for fate to slap you down. You got up and threw the first punch . . . he remembered Steven saying those very words about some problem Charlie was having with one of the senior prefects.

'Well then,' Charlie said, nerving himself, 'I'll ring him. I'll tell him we'll have a rotten bloody Christmas if he doesn't come home.'

Steven was packed. He was booked on the plane to Paris and then on to New York. He had called Piero, and got Lucia instead, who panicked when he told her he was coming. He didn't argue.

'Just give Piero the message,' he told her. 'I'll contact him when I get there. And Poppa's not to know.' He'd hung up while she was still talking.

The villa was chill with impending desertion; the heat was turned low and the windows were shuttered. The cat-footed Janine had driven him crazy, padding after him with sly little questions about when he was going to join Madame. She'd probably seen his ticket lying on his desk. She was packed too, ready to move out with her mother till she was told they were returning. He looked round to see if he'd forgotten anything.

There was a sad sense of finality. Angela had been gone for nearly a week and he'd got as far as dialling the English number several times, before he put the phone down. There was nothing to say that hadn't already been said. He didn't want to lie to his son; he didn't want to think about what Angela had said before she left. She couldn't carry out her threat. She'd take him back, forgive him . . . she'd have to, with a new child coming. But there was a terrible doubt that wouldn't leave him. He had his sense of honour. But she had hers. For all her softness, her kindness of heart, she had proved before that she had a steely courage to do what she felt was right. She had left him once, facing a far worse future . . .

He was at the door, his coat already buttoned against the cold outside, when the telephone rang. He hesitated. Hope surged for a moment. She had relented. She was ringing him. He went back and picked up the receiver.

'Look, Dad, whatever it is you've got to do, couldn't it wait? Poor Mum's miserable. We'll all miss you, it'll be awful . . . What sort of business is it?'

'Family business,' Steven said. If only he'd gone a minute or two earlier – if only he hadn't stopped and answered. Charlie was turning a knife in his heart with every word. 'My father has a problem. He needs me, Charlie.'

'I didn't know you had a father,' his son said. He sounded bewildered. 'You've never mentioned him before. Dad, please, I know there's something wrong with you and Mum. She won't tell me, but I don't believe all this stuff about business. It's just an excuse! Jordan's parents are getting divorced. He's so upset he had to go home early . . . Dad, there's nothing like that with you and Mum, is there? Dad? Are you there?'

After a pause Steven answered, 'Yes, son, I'm here. Is your mother there? – let me speak to her –'

'She's taken Grandpa to the town. Why haven't you rung us up?'

'Charlie, I tried but I couldn't get through –' He let the excuse die away. He put one hand over the mouthpiece and swore in anguish.

There was a clock on his desk; if he didn't leave immediately he might miss his flight. He could still make it if he drove like fury and the traffic lights were on his side. He could still catch the plane from Nice, change at Paris and be on his way to New York. His son was still on the line; he could tell him not to worry, not to think about Jordan and his parents and imagine that anything like that could happen to them.

He heard Charlie say, 'Please come home for Christmas. Make it up with Mum.'

Steven looked at the clock once more. Then he said, 'I guess it can wait. Don't tell your mother we've talked. I'm coming home and don't you worry about a thing. I'm sorry to hear about Jordan.'

'I didn't really think anything like that,' his son protested.

'Sure you didn't,' Steven said gently. 'You keep this under your hat and we'll make it a surprise, okay?'

'Okay, Dad, super. See you!'

There was no doubt about the relief in Charlie's voice. Steven hung up. He opened the buttons on his overcoat one by one and sat down behind his desk. He picked up the desk clock and watched the hands move very slowly, till the last possible chance had gone. Then he reached for the phone and called through to the airport to change his tickets and get a reservation for the next direct flight to London. As he was speaking, the door opened and Janine looked round it.

'Monsieur – I thought you'd gone.'

He said, 'Not for another two hours. You take your mother and be on your way. I'll lock the doors when I leave.' He turned his back, dismissing her. Reluctantly she closed the door.

He sat on, waiting. The airline phoned back to confirm his change of travel plans. He had a seat on the seven o'clock plane.

'I didn't know you had a father. You've never mentioned him before.' He covered his face with his hands. A life built on lies, on deceiving his own flesh and blood. A life where his oath to one family loyalty was in conflict with the greater love he owed his son and his wife.

Pride and guilt had made him risk everything that really mattered to him. He had stood against Angela because it was a reaction bred into him, absorbed with the air he breathed since he was a child. When the call came, the men went, leaving their women and children to weep.

But not now. He hadn't been proof against his son. He remembered her fierce reproaches through the unhappy days of argument and counter argument. They had wounded him, made him very angry.

281

'You think it's right to risk your life for your father and brother? They've chosen to live with violence and death! You owe them more than you owe that boy who thinks the world of you? Then you're not fit to be his father –'

Bitter quarrels, tears, pleas on both sides. Pride and old traditions building up between them like an unbreachable wall.

He would have gone to New York if he hadn't heard the dread in Charlie's voice. 'Jordan's parents are getting divorced . . . he's terribly upset . . .' The boy had sensed danger in a gut reaction.

He thought suddenly: That kind of instinct is a gift from God . . . It'll protect him always. And then realized he was thinking in the past. His own past, learning to watch out for strangers, to sit with his back to a wall in public places. To see a car pulling up beside him at traffic lights as a possible assassination threat. The bullet fired at him in just that situation, deflected by toughened window glass. The car screeching off from a standstill. Not for his son. Not for Charles Steven Falconi the life led by his father as a young man. He wouldn't need that sixth sense of danger.

He said out loud, 'Holy Jesus, what am I going to do if Piero still won't listen and I haven't gone?' and the phone rang again as if the oath had been a prayer and God had answered.

'Stefano?' It wasn't his brother. It was his distant cousin Tino Spoletto.

'Piero's out of town for the rest of the week,' he explained. 'Lucia didn't get a chance to tell you. She came to me, she was so worried. Can we talk for a while?' The voice sounded thin and the line crackled.

Steven said, 'Yes, we can talk. She told you my reason for making the trip?' There was a burst of double echo; the words 'making the trip' were bouncing back. Then it cleared.

'She told me. Your mother was worried. I was worried too, but now I don't need to worry anymore.'

'Why not? You mean my brother Piero's listened? Not two nights ago I spoke to him again and he said it was all crap. Those were his words to me. I knew I had to see him; there was no other way he'd open his eyes.'

'They're open now,' was the answer.

Steven said slowly, 'What's happened? What's wrong, Tino?'

'Nothing, nothing. Piero went down to see to some business in Vegas. Your father and me went to a meeting last night. There were a lot of big men there. Men from the Families. You were right – Aldo has a contract out on us. At the wedding, just like you said. But that was cancelled at the meeting. I can't say too much, you understand. But the Families have decided against Aldo. Your father gave his consent. There's nothing to worry about now. Me and my wife Nina and the kids all send our best to you. Have a nice Christmas over there. And watch the papers. Round about January twelfth. It'll be one helluva wedding party.'

The echo returned. Steven hung up. His instinct was right. Clara's father had set up the Falconis with the wedding as a front. Now, the same sentence had been passed on him. He stood up slowly. He couldn't help imagining the scene. The marriage, the nuptial Mass in St Mary and the Angels, the cortège of cars on their way to the reception. How would it be done? An ambush, a hidden sniper –

There was no bloody surge of vengeance in his heart. He felt sickened.

Angela and the family were watching a programme on television when the sitting room door opened and Steven walked in.

He heard his son's cry of welcome, but it was Angela who sprang to her feet and ran to him. Hugh Drummond struggled to get up, smiling with pleasure, and Ralph Maxton kept still in the background. He had no place in this family reunion.

283

Alone in their room, Steven told her what had happened. 'Charlie called me. You mustn't mind, Angela. He did it for the best.'

'Mind? Thank God he did – oh darling, when you opened that door and walked in, I couldn't believe it! And he was so happy tonight. So am I–' They held each other close.

'I'd decided,' he went on, 'I knew I couldn't do this to him and to you. I was coming home, and then I got this call from a cousin in New York. There's no danger to them now. I didn't need to go. But I'd made up my mind and told our boy before I knew that. I want you to understand that, sweetheart. You believe me?'

'You know I do,' she answered. Then: 'You weren't right about this wedding?'

'I was right,' he said slowly. 'My father-in-law had it all figured. The Falconi Family were going to be wiped out.'

'Oh Steven, don't. It's like a nightmare.'

'It'll be his nightmare, not ours,' he said. 'And that's all we need to know. Forget it, my darling. It came near to us, but it won't ever touch us again. Forgive me, will you?'

She kissed him. 'You came home to us,' she said. 'That's all I care about. We'll have a wonderful Christmas and pretend this never happened. The three of us.' And she placed his hand on her stomach.

She slept deeply and peacefully in his arms that night.

They had a truly merry Christmas. The tree sparkled in the hallway, snow didn't fall that year but the weather was cold and bright with sunshine – perfect for walking. Steven and Angela kept very close, drawing Charlie with them, in recognition of the danger that had threatened.

Maxton accepted the role of companion to the old doctor. He liked Drummond, and in spite of Charlie's jealous judgement, he didn't find him a bore. He was solid and familiar, a father figure in place of the remote reality who would sit down with his big family in the Great Hall in Derbyshire on Christmas Day. Maxton imagined it sometimes, indulging in a little self-inflicted pain, then turning it to mockery. He had hated the formal gathering at Christmas. The relatives summoned out of the woodwork, the ritual present–opening which was at three thirty precisely after they had all been forced to listen to the King's speech.

The forced gaiety that never included him because he was inevitably in disgrace about something. He'd given a vulgar comic book to an elderly aunt one year, or forgotten to give someone else anything at all, or made an ill-timed request for money to cover his overdraft. He never got it right from the time he was a little boy and he'd helped himself to too much champagne and been sick in the middle of the Christmas lunch. He settled for old Doctor Drummond and his stories, and was grateful.

Angela was happy now, he admitted, happy that Steven was back and their rift, whatever it was, had healed. She was happy, and she spent so much effort spreading it around. He remembered how his parents had despised the middle classes. The backbone of England, no doubt, but terribly dull and easily ridiculed. His family had a lot to learn from people like the Drummonds. He was glad to be with them, and yet he felt lonelier than he had done for many years. He missed Madeleine; he missed the decadence that made him feel at home and safe from sentiment. He had turned his face from a Christmas that began in the village church. He wondered which felt the more incongruous, himself, or the reformed Mafioso, kneeling beside his wife and son.

His real son, as Madeleine had pointed out. One day, Maxton thought, leafing through the hymn book without joining in, one day I'll find out what really happened. What happened to the first wife I saw him with, the new bride on her honeymoon . . . He'd seduced Angela and left her with a bastard child. Married one of his own kind. And then came back and claimed

Angela. How many men could get away with that? He would find out one day. The idea cheered him all through the service.

On Christmas morning, amid the debris of present-opening, Steven appeared with a bottle of champagne, and with his arm round Angela announced that she was going to have a baby. The cork popped, glasses were filled up and they drank to the happy news.

'How splendid,' the doctor kept saying. 'What good news – nice for you, Charlie, to have a brother or sister.' He went round beaming, the champagne tipping over the edge of his glass.

Maxton watched the boy go up and embrace his mother and Steven. His nose might just be put out of joint when he wasn't the sole object of their attention. Maxton hoped so. He didn't like Charlie. He saw more of his father than Angela in him. One day, that English public-school veneer would rub off . . . He came and congratulated them.

Angela said sweetly, 'Thank you, Ralph dear. I'm so glad you're with us today. It's a real family celebration, isn't it, darling?'

And Steven looked down at her fondly and said yes, it was.

They had plans for New Year's Eve, and they were insisting that Maxton stayed on. He couldn't come up with an excuse immediately, but risked a telephone call to Madeleine, asking her to send a phoney message. The last thing he wanted was to stay and celebrate with the inhabitants of those neat little houses round the village green. Nice, proper people, neighbours of the doctor and his late wife, people who'd known Angela all her life. He scorned them in his mind; he'd had enough of clean living. He needed some decent debauchery to wash the taste of turkey and plum pudding out of his mouth. He didn't want second best; the role of good old pal was not for him. He'd played enough chess with the doctor, he wanted to play a different kind of game.

286

Madeleine obliged. It was an ill-phrased telegram about a sick aunt who needed him, and he turned it very skilfully into a joke, reading it out to them.

'My friend thinks I need an alibi,' he said. 'Just because she has to have one herself. You will forgive me, won't you, if I slip back ahead of the party? She is rather special and it's been difficult for her to get away.'

'Of course we don't mind,' Angela said. 'Are you going somewhere nice?'

'Our original plan,' he said. 'A little skiing and a lot of après!' His harsh tuneless laugh rang out.

He went to pack, to get his goodbyes said and put space between him and all of them. When you're going, for God's sake hurry up and go. That was an old saying in his family. The departing guest was speeded off; the ones that lingered were not popular. Steven offered to drive him to Gatwick airport, but he refused firmly.

'Jolly kind, but no thanks. I'm not tearing you from the bosom of your family. I'll be back in Antibes in two weeks; I'll keep an eye on the villa and see what needs to be refurbished at the Poliakof – you mentioned something about the cloakroom facilities.' Back to business, back to the safe relationship.

'Okay, you do that. Sorry you have to leave us.'

'Where will I contact you when I get back? Will you still be here?'

'No,' Steven answered. 'I'm taking Angela and the boy away in the New Year. Somewhere in the sun. I'll let you know.'

The doctor was sorry to see him go; he cleared his throat and fiddled furiously with his pipe, and Maxton understood that he couldn't say how much he'd miss his company. He shook hands and patted the old man on the shoulder. He had never dared such intimacy with his own father.

And then Angela came and kissed him on the cheek, and he could feel the colour sweeping up, betraying him.

'Thank you for being so sweet to Daddy and to all of us,' she said. 'Happy New Year, Ralph.'

'Thank you,' he said. 'It's been the best Christmas I've spent in a very long time. Happy New Year, Angela, take care of yourself.'

He sprang into the local taxi, waved to them and settled back. For such a long time, hope had been on offer, now it was dashed for ever. From the moment Steven Falconi walked back into that house.

Back to the old life.

He hummed a little tune. As a very small boy, he used to hum when he was unhappy. It gave him comfort.

The party was a success. Angela said so. Steven found it very dull. They were so low key, these English people. They enjoyed themselves in whispers. He was charming and friendly to all of them, and endured the inquisitive looks with patience. This was Angela's background; Charlie's too. He saw his son fitting in happily with boys and girls of his own age, finding them fun. Steven thought them boring and stiff. He remembered the uninhibited, noisy parties back home, where the New Year was toasted in with shouts and music, everyone embracing and kissing, the children of all ages romping round as midnight struck. He didn't say anything, but he couldn't wait to get to the sunshine of Morocco. And he had timed it deliberately. The 12th of January, his cousin Spoletto had said.

On that day, he and Angela and their son would be thousands of miles away from newspapers and television. The Falconis were safe. That was all he needed to know. He wouldn't think about Clara and her father.

It was no concern of his.

Clara hated Christmas that year. She hated it, because custom forced her family, and the widowed mother and relatives of Bruno her bridegroom, to spend part of it together. They gathered in Aldo's house for a big

288

traditional dinner, they all exchanged gifts and drank toasts to the couple who were soon to be married. Mrs Salviatti was a fat, nervous woman, a gasbag who chattered on and on out of nerves till Clara could have screamed. She kept glancing at her son, saying to Clara, to Luisa, 'Isn't he a handsome boy? Just like his father – And such a good son he's been –' They were peasants, all of them; uncomfortable in tight suits, strangled in neckties, their women badly dressed; the children irritated her, running up and down without hindrance, indulged by doting parents, shrieking and getting in everyone's way. Clara hated them, and barely held on to her temper. Bruno was proprietorial with her, forever pawing at her, until she snapped at him under her breath to leave her alone. Her father was the perfect host, the Don entertaining his underling relatives-to-be. He condescended to Bruno, who flattered and fawned on him, and then preened in front of her. He'd given her a good ring; someone with an eye to the future had lent him the money. They all ate too much, and some of them drank too much, too. One of the old Salviatti uncles fell asleep at the table. Aldo saw him and his eye was cold. Someone got him up and took him to lie down. Several children cried from tiredness and over-excitement. There was much cooing and comforting. Clara felt as if she were living a nightmare wide awake.

The wedding presents had come flooding in. And a flood it was, from the humblest to the most important in the invited families. A lot of silver and crystal, for a second marriage. Wines by the case, linen and exquisitely embroidered cloths, ornaments, some of them in terrible garish taste, others fine antiques. Pictures, with views of the Old Country. Clara couldn't stand nineteenth-century sentimentality, and Bruno liked the pictures and engravings best of all. She told him, very early on, that rubbish like that wasn't hanging in her house.

Her wedding outfit had been ordered from Bergdorf Goodman. She chose it carefully, determined to look her best on the great day. And what a day it was going to be. What a contrast to that other wedding, when she had gone to the altar in her virgin white, consumed with a young girl's passion for her bridegroom. She dwelt on her memories of that day. The marvellous singing in the church, the first sign of Steven waiting for her by the altar. The joy of their reception, everyone congratulating them, saying how beautiful she looked, how radiant with happiness. Dancing the wedding waltz in his arms. There was no pain left in the memories now, or if there was, her hatred used it as a goad, urging her to the second marriage with a man she saw only as a means to an end. A life of power and independence, cleansed beforehand of all taint of feeling by an act of bloody retribution on her enemies.

And running through the fabric of that future life there was a single scarlet thread. The agency she had created and controlled would find Steven Falconi. They had already begun the search.

O'Halloran was a happy man. He liked his smart new office in uptown New York. He liked having two assistants to do the routine work, the boring grind that had been his lot for so long. He liked the batteries of copiers and typewriters and recording machines; they signified money and success, like the gold-painted name on the frosted outer door. Ace Detective Agency. She had kept the corny title. He liked the young secretary in the outer office; she called him Mr O'Halloran and made him cups of coffee. Most of all he liked the money. His wife and his children had made the move and settled in; as why shouldn't they, he would demand to himself, with a decent house and garden in the suburbs and a new car in the garage? He was a happy man, and he worked as hard as he did because he was also frightened.

His employer frightened him. Whenever she called him to see her, he could feel the presence of her father, as if he were the other side of the door.

He had made a few discreet inquiries, asking around his old contacts in the Force. It was too late to turn back, so he felt free to find out a little more of where his backers came into the scheme. All they had needed was the name Falconi. From there they linked it with another, equally infamous. Fabrizzi. Aldo Fabrizzi had a daughter who'd married a Falconi. Someone had fried him in a car down on the south-eastern seaboard. Nobody in the New York Police Department sent any wreaths to the funeral. Nor in Florida or Las Vegas. They were shit, those two Families. O'Halloran had agreed. He was asking on account of a case he had on hand.

Then just you watch your step, his contacts warned him. If it's tied in with the Mob, don't touch it. The last private eye who went sniffing around them ended six floors down from his apartment window. They didn't leave much of his agency in one piece either.

O'Halloran promised to drop the case and tell his client to go look elsewhere. He went home to his new house and convinced himself that he was being too well paid to mind being scared. So long as he gave that black-eyed bitch what she wanted. And what she wanted was dirt. Dirt of any kind. She'd put the first clients in his way herself. Divorce investigations; lousy stuff as usual, but this time the quarries were rich, and their wives were out to screw them till the naughts ran off the page. He'd done a very good job and they were satisfied. The fees were settled promptly. In his old business he and Pacellino had threatened to sue the clients who were suing, it was so hard getting the money. Word crept round the money circles that this was a very reliable agency. Other clients showed themselves, different clients from the women or their husbands, or the small-time businessman trying to trace a bad debt. There were corporations who wanted a check run on prospective employees in responsible positions. On their rivals' employees, searching for scandal of a personal nature if they couldn't pin anything else on them. O'Halloran had spent his life among the poor and the petty criminals; when he left the Force and set up with his old partner, he found the sins of suburbia no less unsavoury. But the rich were something else. They really knew how to root in the garbage and still come up smelling sweet.

And then, just before Christmas, she had sent for him unexpectedly. He went to the brownstone house and was kept waiting. He didn't like to smoke. It was all set out like one of those homes they featured in his wife's magazines. When she came in, he got to his feet. She didn't apologize for keeping him so long. She didn't even ask him to sit down. She just walked up to him and held out an envelope.

'This is your Christmas present, Mike. I haven't time to gift wrap. And there's a personal favour I want you to do for me. You personally. The details are in that envelope. I'm getting married in January, so I won't be around till mid-February. But I want you to start in on this right away. And have a merry Christmas, won't you?'

'Thanks, Mrs Falconi. And the same to you. Congratulations on the wedding. He's a lucky guy.'

'I'll tell him,' she said. 'In case he doesn't know. See yourself out, will you?' Then she walked out of the room, leaving him with the envelope.

He opened it in the car. There were ten thousand dollars and details of the favour she'd mentioned. She wanted him to find her husband Steven Falconi, who she believed was still alive. She believed he had faked his death and run off with another woman.

She emphasized a visit to one of the city's best-known restaurants, Les Ambassadeurs, giving a date more than a year ago. She suggested – he noted the tactful way of putting it – that he start with a list of all the diners in that evening and go on from there. A previous investigation had come to nothing because the operative had inquired directly about Steven Falconi. He sure had; O'Halloran grimaced. And someone had made scrambled egg out of him. He was going to step very carefully around this one. If the lady asked a personal favour, you didn't say sorry, but no. He had a feeling you would end up by being very sorry. No assistant could be trusted with this one. He sighed. When she said 'personal' that's what she meant. He would have to take the case himself.

He sat thinking about it when he got back to his office. So Falconi wasn't dead. The burned-out corpse belonged to someone else. Or so she thought. First thing was to check the details and the death certificate. He decided he'd better get on it right away before she took time off from getting married and asked him what the hell he was doing about it.

He banked the ten thousand in his personal account, and the next morning left New York for the nearest town to the site of the accident. It was a real hick place, with a few scattered houses, a supermarket and a repair garage. The local police patrolled a wide area. He started with the back files of the country newspapers before he went anywhere near the police.

He noted that the dead man's brother had identified his remains. So if the lady was right, her in-laws were part of the cover-up. If she was right. He wasn't sure about that yet. Women could get obsessed about husbands, even a dame with ice in her veins like the lady.

He called her that to himself and his wife. His wife had been curious at first. He'd quieted the questions with some glib lies, putting twenty years on Clara Falconi. She wanted an investment and some fun poking into other people's business. It might be kinky, but it sure as hell paid plenty. His wife didn't bother after that.

The local papers had made a big story out of the dead man in the burned-out car. A cigarette and a petrol leak were blamed. It was all good clean provincial stuff. But to an experienced nose like Mike O'Halloran, something about it stank. The low-key funeral, a cremation for Christ's sake, he said to himself. Any Mafioso worthy of the name was planted with full Catholic rites. Falconi's own brother had identified him and made the arrangements.

To them, it was the way you buried a dog. Unless you wanted to make sure nobody exhumed the corpse. He wasn't surprised to find that the ashes had been scattered, and the grieving brother hadn't even waited for the funeral service. They killed each other like other people swatted flies, but they had this ritual about death. When a big man died, his assassins sent flowers and often wept at the graveside. It was part of the tradition of respect. Whoever got barbecued in that car, it wasn't the son and heir of Luca Falconi.

Mike didn't ask around anymore. Whoever did it must have had contacts in the area. They might still be there. O'Halloran went back to New York and took his employer's advice.

He started his investigation with the dinner reservations on the date Clara had given him at Les Ambassadeurs.

He didn't try and bribe the maître d'. He didn't show a wad of dollar bills to the barman or the girl on the reservation desk. He went to see the manager and told him what he wanted. He had a story already, and it sounded plausible. He gave the manager his card, and the manager was impressed by the office address. And by O'Halloran. He was well dressed, quiet-spoken. He had shed the provincial gumshoe image under Clara's brutal tutelage. She ordered his suits, she told him how to present himself to people like the suave and clever man who ran the smartest restaurant in New York.

'My clients,' O'Halloran said, 'want to stay anonymous. Until they can be sure of their case.'

The manager understood that. He knew about clients and their need for anonymity. He said, 'But surely the police are the right people to track them down?'

O'Halloran agreed. 'Sure they are. But my clients don't want the publicity. They feel, and I have guaranteed it to them, that when the fraud is uncovered, the couple concerned will make a full restitution rather than face a criminal prosecution.' The manager thought that was a sensible solution.

'And they operate in hotels as well as restaurants?'

'They specialize in hotels,' O'Halloran said. 'They have worked their way through my client's chain of hotels and associated restaurants for the last three years. The sums of money have amounted to a big total. The last bill left unpaid was' – he consulted a nonexistent note in his briefcase – 'the bill came to three thousand eight hundred dollars. For a four-night stay.' He cleared his throat. 'They also filled a suitcase with ornaments including some prints off the wall of the suite. It's become part of their trademark.'

'And the restaurants? They leave a signature there too?' The manager was personally interested now.

O'Halloran said, 'The best vintage champagne, always a magnum. The guy always says they're celebrating. Then comes the caviar, the top of the à la carte list, and they disappear before you can put the check on the table.'

'Well.' The other man couldn't help looking satisfied. 'We've had no such instance here, I assure you. So you're wasting your time coming to me.'

'They came here to dinner,' O'Halloran said. 'They were here on eleventh August two years ago. We know because they left a receipted bill from your restaurant in the wastebasket the last time they booked into one of our hotels. It's our only chance to identify them. If you will let me have the names and what you know about them. I understand that you keep records up to three years.'

The manager nodded. 'We do. We have a regular client list with credit ratings, and a list of casuals. I'll get it for you.'

An hour later O'Halloran left the office. He had a number of names and a lot of information, all of it irrelevant except for half a dozen couples. Steven Falconi had dined there with a congressman and his wife. O'Halloran started checking on the six couples via the maître d', Luis. Luis was instructed to give him what help he needed, and Luis didn't disobey the manager. And the guy asking the questions never mentioned Steven Falconi. He didn't know two of the customers except slightly; both were businessmen and they came in from out of town with a client now and then. O'Halloran said not to bother.

Out of the remaining four one was a regular client. Mr Forrest, who ran a big leather goods manufacturing business. He'd brought a lady guest that night. The other couples were unknowns, come in for dinner and not seen since.

O'Halloran said thanks, he'd been a great help, and drove himself back to the office. It was easy to find Forrest, there'd been something shifty about Luis when he talked about him. Forrest Leather Goods, Park Avenue.

Mike O'Halloran decided to pay him a call.

Clara was trying on her wedding dress. It was simple cream silk, pencil skirt and fitted jacket with a ranch mink collar and cuffs. They'd made a hat to match, a plain pillbox in the same material.

Her mother was sitting in the bedroom of the brownstone house, looking distressed. 'You shouldn't do this,' she repeated. 'It's unlucky – you know it's unlucky to wear it the night before!'

'Balls,' Clara said briskly. 'I've never believed in all that stuff.' She took off the neat little hat and put it in its bed of tissue in the hatbox.

Behind her, Luisa made the forked finger sign against the evil eye. Clara never listened to her even when she was young. Now, she wouldn't listen to anyone, except her father. Luisa was a simple woman, but she understood basic things like jealousy. Bruno was jealous and so was she. Father and daughter shut them both out, and didn't bother to be tactful about it. They paraded their intimacy, Clara especially, as if she gloried in her status of substitute son. She was hard and cold-hearted, Luisa thought, and felt bitter. Less of a woman because she was being given the respect from Aldo that belonged to a man.

It would end badly, Luisa insisted to herself. The marriage would fail like the first marriage. And Clara was defying every rooted superstition by parading herself in her wedding gown the night before she married.

There was a knock on the bedroom door. There was a new maid in the house now. Maria had been pensioned off somewhere else; she couldn't stand up to Clara's tempers and moods, and her health began to suffer.

The new girl was made of stronger stuff. 'Telephone, Madame,' she said, and closed the door.

'Who is it?' Clara shouted after her.

'She's such a dummy,' she snapped to her mother. 'I've told her and told her to take a name.' She lifted the extension by her bed. It was O'Halloran. She said to her mother, 'Momma, this is business. Go find a magazine or something, will you? I won't be long.'

She sat on the edge of the bed in her wedding suit and listened. She had a habit, lately developed, of tapping her fingers while she talked to someone on the phone. The long fingers beat a silent tattoo on her knee and then suddenly were still.

'I think I've found something,' O'Halloran was saying. 'Like I said, everyone checked out except the guy Forrest and the dame who was with him. I went to see him; he was ready to talk about it, he was still sore at the way she'd behaved. She ran out on him in the middle of dinner, sent a message by the hat-check girl that her son was sick, and never came back. She called him later to apologize but he wasn't buying. I got a lot of details about her out of him. She was English, representing some advertising firm he used in London. So I figured I'd better talk to the hat-check girl. She wasn't working for Les A anymore but I found her. Now hang on to your hat, Mrs Falconi. It took a little sweet talking and a few dollars on the table, but she told me the woman left with your husband. She also said she looked like she didn't want to go, but he had a hold of her. The hat–check girl was scared. She knew your husband and she did what she was told. I asked if they said anything, and she said your husband sent a message to some congressman he was with, and the dame said about her boy being sick. The girl said she acted frightened. She said your husband would have scared anybody the way he looked. He called her Angelina, she remembered that. Hallo – Mrs Falconi?'

'I'm here,' Clara said. 'Angelina? Did you say that's what he called her?'

'That's her name,' O'Halloran said. 'Angela Lawrence; Forrest told me. He gave the address of the apartment she was staying at, so I went along. There were two fags living there. I gave them a spiel about trying to trace a Mrs Lawrence for a relative in the States, and they bought it. They liked to gab, you know the type. They'd lent the apartment to a Mrs Lawrence and her son as a favour to the guy she worked for back in London. They spilled everything you could think of – Look, why don't I come over and see you? I've got a hell of a lot of stuff on this.'

She didn't answer.

He backtracked in case he had gone too far. 'Listen, it can wait if tonight's not convenient.'

'It can't wait.' She was breathing hard, with something choking in her voice. 'You come on over,' she said. 'Give it half an hour. I'll see you then. And bring everything you've got with you.' She put the receiver back on its cradle. She opened her free hand. The long painted nails had scored her palm, breaking the skin.

Angela. She said it out loud. 'Angela. Angelina.' The name he cried out as he made love to her on the first night of their honeymoon.

Her mother came back into the bedroom. She had one

298

of Clara's fashion magazines rolled up under her arm. They weren't her kind of reading. 'Clara? Clara, you all right?'

To her surprise her daughter answered quietly, almost kindly. 'Yes, Momma. I'm all right.'

'You don't look it.' Luisa's motherly instincts took over. She hurried to her daughter. 'You look sick,' she said anxiously.

She sat beside Clara and slipped an arm round her. She was ashamed of her harsh judgement of the past few months. The girl was the colour of a winding sheet. And in the deep black eyes there was a sheen of tears.

'Tell me,' Luisa said. 'What is it? You nervous about tomorrow? Don't you want to marry Bruno? He's a good man and he loves you, Clara. He'll make you happy.' And she said something she had never dared mention for such a long time. 'He'll be better for you than the other one. He didn't make you happy. You take care of Bruno. Be kind to him. He'll be good to you. I know it.'

Slowly, Clara turned to her. She reached up and wiped a single drop of water from the corner of her eye. She said, 'Don't worry about me, Momma. I know how to manage Bruno. Tomorrow's my big day, isn't it? It'll be a bigger wedding than the first one. People will talk about it for long after. Now I'll call the car and you run back home. Tell Poppa I'll be waiting for him right on eleven o'clock. I won't be late.' She squeezed her mother round the waist, and suddenly kissed her on the cheek.

Luisa flushed. It was like Clara used to be, wilful and spoilt, but she'd turn loving suddenly and that made it all right. She said, 'You sure you won't come home to us and spend the night? You want to be all alone here this evening?'

'I won't be alone, Momma.' Clara stood up. She began unfastening the little buttons of the jacket. 'There's a man coming round on business. We have a lot to talk about. And don't worry. I won't be late tomorrow.'

299

Mike O'Halloran stared up at her. 'Mrs Falconi,' he said. 'She's dead. She's been dead for seventeen years –'

She had been walking up and down, up and down, pacing the floor like a prisoner in a cell.

'It's the same one,' she said. 'Angela. Angelina. The same name. And she left New York on the same day my husband walked out on me!'

'There are thousands of Angelas,' he said. 'It's a common name. Why don't I get you a drink? I could sure use one,' he added.

She made an impatient gesture. 'She was at Les A that night. I'd had a row with Steven and I didn't go. They met there, that's what happened. That's when it started.'

O'Halloran poured himself a stiff scotch.

'She had a son,' Clara went on. 'A boy of fifteen, sixteen, isn't that what the owner of the apartment told you? Well, that figures too. The woman was pregnant when my husband married her . . .'

'Listen, Mrs Falconi,' he protested, 'This dame was killed. Your husband told you – how could she be alive and in New York? It's all on account of the name.' He swallowed hard on the scotch. He couldn't stop her; she wouldn't listen to anything he said. She had made up her mind.

'Everything fits!' Clara rounded on him. 'How did he know she was dead? He never saw a body. He saw some goddamned watch he'd given her – it could have dropped off. She didn't die, Mike. She wasn't killed. She had the child and she met up with my husband that night at Les A. God knows what she told him. But he left me for her. He walked out on his family, they faked a death in that car to cover for him, and he's gone to be with her.' She went and poured herself a drink. Her hands were shaking, she couldn't hold the glass steady and it rattled against the bottle.

She came and sat down facing him. She said in a low voice, 'He wanted children. When I called her a whore, he hit me. We never had any kids.' She clutched the drink in both hands, and suddenly it flew across the room, scattering the whisky, crashing against the wall and splintering all over the carpet. O'Halloran had good nerves, but it made him jump.

He thought suddenly: She's crazy. What the hell have you got yourself into –? He tried again: 'You're speculating. You're crucifying yourself on a hunch, that's all it is. Okay, your husband ran out on you, and he's alive someplace. But you've no proof the first wife wasn't killed in that hospital. You've no proof that woman in the restaurant had anything to do with her.'

She said, 'I nearly had it. I set a detective on him; not for the first time. But this was different. He was so happy. He was singing. I knew this wasn't some hooker like the others he screwed with. But the detective never got further than that night at Les A. My husband took care of that. He had something to hide. And you've found it. Clever Mike.' She scared him by bursting out laughing, and stopping as abruptly. 'He married her,' she said. Her eyes were black slits.

He said, 'You told me. In Sicily.'

'I want you to go there.'

He swallowed scotch the wrong way. 'You what?'

'I want you to go there. I want you to check up on the marriage, the bombing of the hospital. Then I want you to follow it up. Go to England. You know where this woman worked in London, didn't they tell you? Yes, they told you. Find her, Mike, and tell me when you do. Tell me if my husband Steven Falconi is living with her.' She didn't laugh this time. She smiled, and it was as if she were in dreadful pain.

'You said I hadn't any proof it was the same woman. I don't need it. I know it here.' She pressed one long hand against her heart. 'I'm right. You'll find I'm right and you'll come and tell me so.'

'What about the agency?' He knew it was a hopeless try but he took a chance.

'Fuck the agency,' she said. 'It can tick over. You've got enough people for that. This is the assignment I want

301

you to work on. And don't worry, Mike. I know you. You like money, and there's plenty of it if you do this right. You can write your own expense account and I won't even check it.'

She watched him silently. He hesitated, argued with himself and made his choice. 'Okay, if that's what you want.'

'It's what I want,' she said.

Mike O'Halloran got up. 'And if this whole crazy business comes out that you're right – what happens next?'

Clara stood up. She smoothed her hands down over her skirt in search of creases that weren't there. 'Sometimes when we weren't getting along,' she said quietly, 'some years ago now, I put a scare into him. I had someone fire a shot at his car. I didn't mean to hit him, you understand. It was bullet-proof, armour-plated. I just wanted to scare him into being nice to me. Next time, it'll be for real. You'd better go now. I have to get some sleep tonight. Tomorrow I'm getting married. See yourself out.'

'Goodnight, Mrs Falconi.'

'Goodnight. And you get started right away.'

He said, 'Right away.' He glanced at her as he left the room. She hadn't moved. Her hands were still smoothing her skirt. He closed the front door behind him. Sicily. England. He could write his own expense account, she said.

On the way home he stopped off at a florist's shop and bought his wife fifty dollars' worth of flowers. He hoped that would make it easier to tell her that he'd be away on a job for quite a while.

Steven had planned to fly to Paris and then on to Morocco. But Angela wanted to spend a few days in Paris and show some of the sights to Charlie.

Charlie was less than enthusiastic, and so was Steven. Charlie didn't want to miss part of their precious holiday in the sun by going to museums and art galleries with his mother, and Steven didn't want to stay there because it reminded him of Clara. He was thinking about Clara these days, and she haunted his mind by day as well as by night.

Clara wouldn't be hurt; women weren't targets for high-level contracts on a Mafia boss. Aldo would die, and Clara's new husband, Bruno Salviatti, and some of the senior Fabrizzi lieutenants who couldn't be trusted to betray him. Clara would see them slaughtered. She would be spared to live with the horror for the rest of her life. She plagued him, and it was worst of all in those few days they spent in Paris. It seemed to Steven that they were following exactly in her footsteps, going to the Louvre, the Tuileries, the tomb of Napoleon at Les Invalides. Charlie was impressed by that in spite of himself. He lingered by the great black marble mausoleum sunk deep in the heart of the monumental building, and stared down. The solemn splendour of it caught his imagination.

'I must say, Dad,' he remarked at last, 'it beats anything we've got in Westminster Abbey.'

'Let's go,' Angela urged. 'It's overpowering. It's so dark.'

'Death is dark,' Steven said. 'It's such a huge tomb for such a small man.'

'He was a great man,' Charlie protested. 'Even though we beat him in the end. All right, Mum, you're looking a bit green. We'll go. But this is the best thing I've seen so far.'

As they walked across the road Steven looked up and almost halted in the path of the traffic. It was the Rue Constantine, and there on the opposite side was the classical façade of the beautiful apartment Clara had wanted to buy. The windows were shuttered. 'A place we can come back to, just to remember how happy we've been.' He could hear her saying it, feel the tug of her hand on his arm.

'Steven,' Angela said that evening, 'aren't you feeling well? You seem so off colour.'

'I didn't want to stay here,' he said. 'I told you, I wanted to go on to Morocco. Clara and me spent part of our honeymoon in Paris. We've been to the same places, done the same things. It makes me think of her.'

'I'm so sorry,' Angela said. 'You should have told me. I really wanted to let Charlie see it. All he really enjoyed was that awful tomb!'

She came and slipped her arm around his waist. 'Why are you thinking about the past now? Your family's safe, you told me. She'll be married soon. Why now, darling?'

He drew her close to him. 'You've made me soft, you know that? I don't feel like I used to anymore.' Aldo had planned to murder his father and his brother Piero; he deserved no pity. It never occurred to Angela that the executioners would be executed.

He reached up and kissed her. 'Why don't we cut it short and go tomorrow? I'll telephone the Mamoulian and change our reservations. Charlie's had a bellyful of culture and I've had a bellyful of Paris.'

'I happen to have a bellyful too,' she reminded him. 'I felt some movement today. You were in such a funny mood I didn't tell you. Why don't you ring up now?'

He turned her round to face him and pressed his face close up against her. 'If it's a girl,' he said, 'what are we going to call it?'

'If you go on doing that,' Angela murmured, 'it'll be a sex maniac, whatever it is. Aren't you going to phone the hotel?'

'In a while,' he said. 'We can call from the bedroom.'

On the way to the airport next day, he stopped off at a bookstore and bought his son an English translation of the *Life of Napoleon*.

'You look feverish,' Aldo said. He touched Clara's forehead with the palm of his hand. There were two bright scarlet patches on her cheeks, but her skin was cold.

'I'm fine,' she said. 'Shouldn't we be going?'

'There's time,' Aldo assured her. 'And remember, when it happens you've got to be surprised, eh? – you think you could faint?'

'No,' Clara answered. 'But I'll try not to clap and cheer. I just hope you've got the best man.'

'The best money can buy,' Aldo said. 'Two top piece men from the West Coast. They'll get them coming out of the church. And we'll be right there, with all our people. Clean-handed for all the world to see.' He laughed. He was excited by his imagination. Hate had festered in him for a long time, and vengeance was only a matter of an hour or so away.

They'd betrayed his daughter; they'd humiliated and rejected his blood and tried to make a fool of him. The Falconis would pay for that in the only coinage acceptable. His hired assassins would gun them down as they left the wedding ceremony. Two superb marksmen, ex army snipers who had gone into the contract business. They cost a fortune, but you paid for results. And the results were very final. He had enjoyed the planning of it. He had personally handed them photographs of Luca and Piero, and a street snap taken of Tino Spoletto without his knowledge. They had studied them, and nodded. They were men who didn't talk much. One of them said he wanted a closer look so they were sure. Aldo gave them addresses and asked no more questions. He looked at his watch. Eleven ten exactly. The wedding car was waiting outside, festooned with bunches of white ribbons.

Bruno Salviatti would be in place in the church, waiting for his bride. Aldo had gone the night before with Luisa to check that everything was right. The church was like a florist's, with big arrangements of hothouse flowers, garlands stretching the length of the nave from pew to pew and the altar itself massed with

305

lilies and mimosa, the flower of Italy. Specially flown in.

Luisa knew nothing of his plan. Women were never told about such things. She was delighted with the church, worried because Clara had defied superstition by trying on her wedding outfit on the very night before . . . Aldo had let her chatter on, and smiled in secret to himself. Clara had the nerve; he was proud of her coolness, the steel of her resolve. She had the heart of a man, he exulted. And maybe Salviatti would give her children. Then Aldo's cup would overrun with happiness.

'Let's go,' he said. 'Here, take your flowers, Clara. Are you happy? Are you happy with what your old Poppa's fixed for you?'

She turned to him. 'I'll be happy when I see those bastards dead at our feet,' she said. 'When it's all over, Poppa, I've got something else to tell you.'

He opened the front door and they went down to the car, shadowed by bodyguards as always. 'Tell me now,' he said.

'Not now,' Clara answered. 'Later. After the wedding.'

'I know what you're thinking,' her father said. The doors were closed and the car moved away towards the Church of St Mary and the Angels. 'You're thinking of Steven. Don't worry; he'll show up and we'll be waiting.'

Clara glanced out of the window for a moment. The winter sun was shining. 'I'm not waiting,' she said.

Bruno was nervous. His wedding suit was tight, or so it seemed, and he was sweating in the warm church. The smell of flowers was overpowering. His cousin had the ring in his pocket. Clara for some mean motive had refused to give him a ring in exchange. Later, he'd have one. All married men had a proper gold wedding ring. She was just being a bitch when she said no.

306

Once they were married, he promised himself, he'd make her behave herself. If she gave him the kind of lip she'd been handing out before the wedding, he'd take his belt and lather the skin off her. He rather liked the prospect. It made his sense of humiliation easier to bear. The organ played, and the congregation waited; people turned in their seats, watching as the pews filled up. He saw the old Don Luca Falconi with his son and his sidekick Spoletto take their places high up in the church. Places of honour, as in-laws of the bride. Luca bowed to Clara's mother who smiled and waved her hand to him. Bruno knew all about the first husband. He'd ratted on the family and on Clara, and they'd knocked him off . . . He didn't think about it much.

It was a hell of a marriage. Everybody said so. His friends and his family were all so impressed. He was going to be a big man. Groomed for stardom, someone said. He liked the sound of that. Then the music changed to a triumphant peal and they all stood. Clara and her father were walking towards them down the aisle.

'It's such a lovely place,' Angela said. 'And the weather is perfect.' She reached out for his hand. They were sitting in the Hotel Mamoulian gardens in the warm sunshine. She felt relaxed and deeply content. This pregnancy was easy; very little sickness in the early weeks and nothing now but a sense of expectation for the new birth. Steven said she looked beautiful, and teased her about a string of babies in the future.

Charlie was playing tennis with a girl he'd met. The family was American. She was two years younger than he was, flirtatious and pretty. He had already confided to Steven that he usually let her win.

The hotel was luxurious, the food exotic, and the service better than the best in Europe. Above all the sun shone, though it grew cold in the evening. There was nothing to do but wander through the lovely grounds or laze on the terrace.

'I'm so glad we left Paris and came early,' she said. 'You were quite right.'

'I hate Paris,' he said. 'I never want to go there again. I'm glad you like it here, darling. I'm glad you're happy.'

He held her hand tightly. The date on his watch was 12 January. 'It makes everything right.'

Angela said, 'Why do you say that? Everything's perfect for us. I can't believe it sometimes. You and me and Charlie and a new baby coming. And just when it seemed as if our luck was running out, your family was safe after all. I prayed every night you'd come back to us. And you did.'

He didn't answer. He went on holding her hand, seeing her smile at him. Let her believe in her prayers. Let her go on being happy and seeing the world through her own prism of honesty and innocence.

As they sat there in the Moroccan sunshine, Aldo Fabrizzi was still alive. Clara had not woken to go to her wedding. He didn't want to work out the time difference. He didn't want to look down at his watch and say to himself: Now. It must be happening now. He had put an ocean between himself and his family, and the act of cold-blooded murder. By the time they went back to France, and Charlie flew home to school, it would be stale news. Angela need never know.

'Why don't we go and watch the tennis match?' Angela suggested. 'Charlie's got a real crush on her; it's so funny.'

'He's growing up,' Steven said. 'At his age I'd had a lot of girls. He'll be a man soon. Let's go and see how they're making out.'

He helped her out of the chair. She didn't need help, but it was an excuse to touch her, hold her close to him for a moment.

'Come on, darling.' She led him by the hand towards the sound of balls thudding and shrill cries of excitement with laughter from Charlie in the background.

The American couple were on a tour of Europe with

their daughter. They lived in Westchester County, and they were eager for companionship. Their name was Thorpe, and the daughter was their only child and the centre of their world. He was a senior executive with an oil company; he found Angela charming, but reserved judgement on the husband. Steven was less than out-going, he confided to his wife. And owning a casino was not his idea of a respectable business. Still, the son was a good kid. Nice manners, and Shirley liked him. It was so important that Shirley had a good time on this trip. She'd taken a lot of persuading to come with them. But she was an easy teenager. No problems. They encouraged Charlie, but gave up on Steven and Angela after one dinner date.

Thorpe said to his wife, 'Let the kids get together, we don't have to spend time with them.' He couldn't have explained why a fellow American should make him feel uneasy.

Steven was on his way down to the cocktail bar before dinner when he met his son rushing up to change. Angela was taking her time and would follow him down.

'Dad?' They paused on the stairs. 'You going to the bar?'

'I feel like a drink. Hurry up and join me. Your mother's coming later. Had a good day?'

'Great,' Charlie said. 'Mr Thorpe's got the most fantastic radio. He tunes into the States every day for the news broadcasts – I listened too. And you know what, Dad – there's been some massacre at a wedding party. He said they were gangsters. It sounded terrible!'

Steven stood very still. His son looked excited. 'Mr Thorpe said it was like St Valentine's day. I didn't know what he meant.'

'Never mind,' Steven said. 'It happened a long time ago. I don't want you talking about this in front of your mother. She hates that kind of thing. It makes her feel bad. So you forget it.'

'Yes, yes, I won't say anything.' Charlie looked

bewildered. 'I'll go up and change and come down. Shall I see if Mum's ready?'

'You do that,' Steven answered. He still hadn't moved to go downstairs. 'And remember what I've told you. It's bad for a pregnant woman to hear about people getting killed.'

He saw his son sprint up to the landing, and then he walked down to the cocktail bar. The Thorpes were sitting there. He went over. He didn't smile at them. He said, 'Charlie tells me he's been listening to the news from the States on your radio. My wife'll be joining me in a minute. I'd be glad if you don't tell her any horror stories.'

He went and sat at a table and left them looking at each other. After a few minutes, Thorpe whispered to his wife and they both got up and left.

By the time Angela came down, Steven had put down two large bourbons on the rocks and there was a bottle of champagne on ice waiting for her and for Charlie.

Clara made her wedding vows. She heard Bruno saying his, and felt him slip the ring on her finger. She did everything she had done before, when she married Steven, but it was as if she moved in some kind of dream. She had been cool, pitiless in anticipation of the bloody revenge exacted by her father. Now as she stood at the altar with Bruno beside her she began to tremble at the approach of violent death. She had never seen death at close quarters. It had been so easy to contemplate because it wasn't real. Superstition flickered like a warning light inside her as she faced the altar. She had been brought up by Luisa to say her prayers, educated by nuns, gone through the whole Catholic ritual of the Sacraments. To her, as to Aldo, it had been a matter of form once she grew up. Now, in the presence of God himself, she panicked. It shouldn't be done here. It belonged in the dark, down some alleyway . . . not in the shadow of the church. Fear rushed over her and she turned, searching for her father. He was back in his pew, his part in the ritual completed.

She heard Bruno whisper, 'What's the matter –' Then her eye met Aldo's gaze. He stared at her and the look was fierce and without mercy. She turned back to her bridegroom. It was too late.

Too late to have scruples. She conquered the fear, the impulse to turn and run all the way down the aisle and out into the street so she wouldn't see it happen. She had been abandoned, betrayed. The man she had loved had left her for his first love. For a woman who had given him a child . . . And the Falconis had known it, connived at his desertion, put his ring on another dead finger and then cut it off to prove their good faith. When the anthem pealed from the organ, Clara took her new husband's arm, and with a nod to her father, she walked firmly past the congregation to the open doorway.

Photographers were waiting. Bruno held her there, posing for them, resisting her efforts to hurry him to the waiting car. He was smiling, enjoying it. He kissed her for the cameras. She saw Aldo come out on to the steps behind them.

'Bruno,' she insisted, 'Bruno, that's enough. Let's go!'

'What's the hurry?' he demanded. He was smiling, looking ahead of him. She didn't hear the shots. The cameras were snapping and suddenly there was a great splash of blood all over her jacket, and he was falling backwards, dragging her down with him. She heard screams, and more screams. She was on the ground, entangled with him. Blood was pouring through the back of his head. Someone was trying to help her. Then she screamed and screamed and fought them off because she had seen her father lying sprawled halfway down the steps with a small round hole in the middle of his forehead, and a long scarlet trickle creeping towards her. In the confusion, two of the photographers disappeared. They weren't interested in taking pictures anymore.

311

8

Ralph Maxton liked reading newspapers in bed. Madeleine was lying beside him, running her fingers down his thigh to attract his attention. Newspapers bored her except for the gossip columns.

'Stop it, darling,' he said absently. 'You can't bring the pitcher to the well again –'

'Oh yes I can,' she giggled.

He was about to prove her point. Or his point, he thought, and smiled at his own wit.

Then he saw the news item and the photographs. MAFIA MURDERS AT WEDDING. The name Falconi shouted at him in black type. He threw Madeleine off him and grabbed the paper. He didn't even hear her angry protest.

'Shut up, shut up for Christ's sake –'

She sat up sulkily. 'What's the matter? Oh, all right. I'm going to take a bath. You can stuff your silly paper!' She banged the door.

He didn't notice. He read and read again the account of the shooting of gang boss Aldo Fabrizzi and the man just married to his daughter, Clara, widow of top Mafioso Steven Falconi. Police investigating talked of a gangland revenge, and predicted a war for the Fabrizzi succession between rival Families.

Maxton got up. He phoned down for any other American papers. He and Madeleine were due to go to the ski lift in an hour. They'd had a very successful short holiday at Val d'Isère on and off the piste, and until that moment he had been convinced that he was happy, that life was good. Cosy Christmases in England were, as Madeleine liked saying, strictly for the pigeons. He never told her why that made him laugh, in case she changed it.

He looked at the photograph; mercifully it wasn't very clear. Someone had thrown a coat over the corpse in the foreground; only a pair of feet protruded. Blood stained the area black. A second body was lying halfway down the church steps, partly obscured by people crouching over it.

Maxton sat down with the newspaper on his knee. The shower was switched off in the background and Madeleine appeared, partly wrapped in a towel.

She said, '*Chéri*, what's wrong? You look dreadful.'

Maxton looked up at her. 'The bastard,' he said slowly.

'Who? What?' She came and sat with him. She took the paper up. 'It's this murder in America? Why do you care about it? Who are you calling a bastard?'

He took the newspaper away from her and said half to himself, 'She's not even married to him – it's bigamy. He fooled the other poor bitch and he's fooled her too –'

'I'm getting dressed,' Madeleine announced. 'We'll be late.'

He didn't say anything more. He bathed and changed into ski clothes and they weren't late after all. But she knew the holiday would be cut short. Women who made their living out of men had an instinct for shifts in mood. And Maxton didn't even try to pretend. He was very nice about it; he softened the blow by taking her on a shopping trip. She punished him a little for changing their plans by spending more than he expected, but he didn't seem to care. They went their ways, and at the airport she kissed him.

'I'm fond of you,' she said. 'And we've had fun, haven't we?'

'A lot of fun,' Maxton assured her. She looked very appealing in a fox coat with a big hood tied under her chin. She'd find men to look after her so long as that

313

special talent for pleasing them and squeezing them lasted. And she'd say she was fond of them, as she was fond of him.

He could have put his fist in the emptiness where the heart should be. He kissed her, and waved her off to her Paris-bound plane. He was on board the flight to Nice that evening.

The full story was carried in all the American papers, and if he needed confirmation, there was a picture of Clara Falconi in the *New York Times*. He recognized her easily. An older, cooler version of the dark Italian beauty he had met at the casino on her honeymoon. So Falconi had faked death to get away. He'd married Angela while he still had a wife. The baby would be a bastard like the boy Charlie.

No wonder he'd taken the name Lawrence. No wonder he wouldn't be photographed at the casino. He'd lied to Angela; Maxton didn't doubt that. The sudden trip to Morocco had been lucky, just when this blood-stained bombshell was about to burst over the media. He must have known . . . his father was mentioned among the guests who had seen nothing and recognized no assassin.

Omertà. The silence enjoined upon them all to deny justice under the law. One report said briefly that the bride had collapsed by her dead husband and been taken to hospital.

Maxton went to the casino. Work was under way. He checked everything; he supervised the rebuilding of a grander suite of cloakrooms. Nothing suggested the turmoil inside him.

Now he could admit the truth to himself. He was liberated from his own lie. He hated Steven Falconi, not because he was a gangster, perhaps with murder in his past, but because he had possession of the only woman Maxton had ever loved in his whole life. And done it by deceit and false pretences. She didn't belong to him morally, Maxton had always felt that. She wasn't his

314

legally either, now. He couldn't do anything or plan anything until her child was born. But he had hope, and hope bred a fierce determination. He did his duty by his employer. He earned his big salary and justified Steven's reliance upon him. But he waited. He knew all about patience and nerve. It had made him one of the best poker players of his generation.

'You're looking better,' Joe Nimmi said. 'We're all glad to see that.'

'It's been a long time,' Victor Giambino said. 'We were sorry to hear about your Momma. But maybe it was better for her than living that way.'

They were gathered in Aldo's front room. They had come to pay their respects to his daughter. She had been doubly bereaved by her mother's death. And only out of hospital a month herself.

She didn't look well, but what else could I say? Joe Nimmi asked himself. She was white like paper, and thin so you could see through her. But better. Out of hospital and back in her parents' house. She was sitting in her father's chair. Everything about her was black, except for that white face and a garish slash of scarlet lipstick. It looked as if she'd been sucking blood. He didn't think she should have worn make-up on such an occasion. He'd led the deputation to see her and offer help if she needed it. And to give advice. Sound, sensible advice to a woman without a man to guide her. The kind of advice she had to take, because they didn't want trouble. The goddamned newspapers had got sick of writing about the gang war going to break out on the streets. There hadn't been a war. It was all settled peacefully. Fabrizzi territories had been parcelled out while Clara was in hospital. Everything was running smoothly. Her mother had had a stroke; they were all sorry about that. Paralysed and dumb. She'd been visited in the hospital, they'd all sent flowers.

They'd given Aldo a proper funeral, and the relatives

of Salviatti had buried their son along with him. The traffic came to a stop for the processions, and a few Fabrizzi cousins had been found in the Old Country to sit in the chief mourners' car, since the wife and the daughter were too sick to go. The flowers had been magnificent. They had all gathered in the church and at the graveside, the heads of the Families, many representatives from Florida, Chicago, Detroit, and all the New York bosses. They'd wiped the tears from their eyes as the coffins were lowered, and scattered the Holy Water into the graves. It was done well, with the respect and solemnity a man of Aldo's standing deserved. It was a pity he had to be gotten rid of, but he'd only himself to blame. No personal feelings involved, no sense of satisfaction, no score paid off. It was a business necessity, and they all recognized the priority for that.

Clara sat with her hands folded. She looked at them, one by one. Joe Nimmi, her father's old friend from the early street days. His niece had been given refuge in that very house. The Giambinos, Bruno's bosses; the heads of the smaller Families. Luca Falconi hadn't come. He was sick, they told her. The brother hadn't come, he was out of town on business. Only the cousin, Spoletto.

She said, 'It's good of you all to come. My mother's better off. It was quick and she didn't suffer. For myself, I've come to terms. I've lost a father and a husband. Two husbands. I've had my share of grief.'

There was a genuine noise of sympathy. 'You have, Clara,' Joe Nimmi said. 'God knows, you've had it hard. We all feel it. And that,' he said, raising his tone a little, 'is why we're here. We're all your friends. We want to help.'

She waited; she looked expectant. They'd all been party to it. They knew that when she talked of Steven Falconi's death, she was lying; that the bullets had been meant for Luca, Piero and Spoletto. They knew and so did she, that this was a charade, but it had a purpose. The purpose was the reality. She was now going to be told what it was.

316

She said, 'I'll be glad of help, Joe. I'll be grateful for it.'

'That's what we all hoped,' he said. He smiled warmly at her. 'We want you to be happy, Clara. To make a new life for yourself. Without your Momma to take care of, you have that opportunity. Your Poppa's business is in safe hands. There's been no trouble; and we've allocated a proportion to you. You'll see it's very generous.'

'Thank you,' Clara said. They'd split up Aldo's interests like carrion crows picking over a corpse. 'Thank you, I know you've all done the best for me, and I know you won't rest till you find out who killed my father and my husband.'

They were expecting her to say that. Giambino said, 'We'll get them; we'll get them for Bruno too. He was a good guy. We'd known him since he was a kid.' There was another mutter of agreement.

'But for now,' Joe Nimmo took it up. He leaned a little towards her, hands clasped in front of him. He spoke gently, like an uncle.

'For now, you best leave everything to us. It's our business, Clara. Don't you think about it anymore. If my old friend was here this day, I know what he would want you to do. I knew him like my brother.'

'You tell me,' Clara asked him, 'what would my father want I should do?'

The scarlet mouth disturbed him; he kept looking at it. In the Old Country when a man was killed, his women kissed the wounds, before they cried out for vendetta.

'He'd want you should go away,' he said. 'Right away some place different. Leave the house, forget the grief. You've been a sick girl. You need a nice long vacation. Six months, a year maybe.' He smiled persuasively at her, his head a little on one side. 'Believe me, Clara. It'll be best for you.'

She smiled back at him. The red lips parted a little and then closed over. She said very quietly, 'You give good advice, Joe. My poppa always said so. You're right; he knew you like a brother too.'

317

Someone offered a place they owned in the Bahamas. 'One helluva nice villa, Clara. All the help you want, for as long as you want. It's yours.'

She said thank you for the offer. 'You're good to me,' she said. 'I appreciate the offer. I appreciate everything my poppa's old friends have done for him and for me.'

Victor nudged his brother in the ribs. He whispered, 'She getting at something, or what?'

Roy nudged him into silence. He said, 'Anything we can do, Clara. We don't own properties outside of the city, but anything else –' He let the sentence die away.

She looked round at them and quietly moved out of Aldo's chair on to her feet. The black mourning dress hung loose on her. 'I have a place I can stay. I guess it's far enough away.'

They came up and embraced her, these old friends of her father's; others, who weren't on such close terms, shook hands. They all promised anything she needed.

Tino Spoletto came. He made a little bow. 'Don Luca says anything you want – just say the word.' He was thin and pale, with spectacles and a wide forehead that would soon be part of premature baldness. He stared for a moment into Clara's eyes, his own distorted by strong lenses. He had never been afraid of a woman in his life, and of few men, in spite of his lack of weight and inches. She filled him with fear.

'My thanks to Don Luca,' she said. 'Tell him to get well soon.' She turned away.

She didn't come to the door; she said goodbye and one by one they filed out and got into their fleet of cars, ready with engines running. She stood behind the shelter of the curtains until the last of them had gone. The street was empty. She was alone in the house. She had offered wine, and the traditional olives. Some of them had smoked, and the haze was visible in the artificial light. It was a wet, overcast day in March, and the heavy curtains were not fully pulled back. It was a house of mourning, of darkness. Clara found a cigarette and lit it; she opened a

318

cupboard and poured herself a straight scotch with ice. 'Clara, Clara,' her poor dead mother had protested, 'you drink like a man . . .'

They agreed the murders. They had gone back on their oath to Aldo, and reprieved the Falconis. The men he had hired had been contacted and given different targets. So simply done. And they'd come with their sympathy and their offers of support, to tell her to get out and stay out and not try to cause trouble. She sat down, not in her father's chair – that had been a gesture – but on the sofa, where they usually sat together. She drank the whisky, and finished her cigarette. She was off the dope now. No more tranquillizers. The rest and sedation had let her heal. She had played the part expected of her, because she knew, as they knew, that she was helpless. She couldn't strike back. They were men of power. She was just a woman, and no one would go against them for her sake. Not even for all the money she could offer. There was nothing left for her but exile and obscurity. The villa in the Bahamas – she laughed aloud at that. Somewhere she could be watched, where the Mafia had influence and friends.

Paris. She'd thought of it in the hospital, as she came out of the haze of shock and medication. Paris, where the apartment she'd bought in secret lay empty and dust-sheeted. Unused for all these years. The apartment she'd planned as a retreat for Steven and herself, a place to recapture their honeymoon happiness. She'd go to Paris. She'd throw off the black drapery of mourning.

She'd let them all think they were safe, that the terrible cry for vengeance wouldn't be uttered. She had painted her mouth in symbolism, daring them to read the sign. They would pay for Aldo. For her mother, struck down through grief. For Bruno, falling backwards with half his brain shot out. But Steven Falconi would pay first.

She had Mike O'Halloran's file on his investigation locked in her father's desk drawer.

*

Joe Nimmi was going to the opera that night; he was anxious to get home in time to change his shirt. He loved opera; Verdi was his favourite. He had a fine collection of records; he thought Tito Gobbi was the greatest tenor in the world.

Victor and Roy were going home. They lived in the same street in houses two doors down from each other. Their children played together, went to the same school. Their wives were related. Every two years they took their families on holiday to Naples, where the Giambinos had come from two generations back.

Victor said to his brother, 'I still feel lousy about Bruno.'

'Yeah, me too. But it had to be. Bruno would've made trouble; she'd have seen to it. He was her husband. He had honour. He wasn't just a punk.'

'He was a good guy. Roy, I guess she knows. The way she said that, I appreciate all you've done for Poppa and me.'

'Sure she knows,' Roy said. 'But what the fuck can she do? She brought the whole goddamned mess on herself. Her and Aldo. She knows what's expected. She'll take her ass off someplace. Forget about her. Why don't we all go to Gino's for dinner tonight? We'll bring the kids, make it a party?'

Victor brightened. 'Why not? I got an idea for setting up Bruno's old lady. There's a nice little grocery business over on Seventy-first. The guy's a real schmuck – we could move Bruno's momma and the kid brother into the business. It'd give them a good living.'

'Why not?' Roy agreed. 'We owe them. Okay, we go to Gino's and then maybe take in a movie. See what the kids want to see –'

Clara had packed up her parents' house. She let the maid stay on to caretake; she had two sons and a layabout husband who pretended to have a weak heart if anyone suggested work. Clara would have thrown him out years ago, but her father had a soft spot for him. He'd been a good man once, he used to say, and wouldn't hear any complaint against him. Clara left the family there out of respect for Aldo.

She hadn't been back to her own brownstone house since she left to go to her wedding. That was going to be a real test of nerve. What if she went home and found Aldo there, waiting for her as he had done on the last morning of his life? Waiting to take her down the steps to the car dressed in silk ribbons. She was fierce with herself; contemptuous of her superstitions. It was nerves, that was all; a brief death rattle from the old nightmares that had had her screaming in the hospital.

She swallowed a very strong scotch and drove herself uptown. She opened the front door. It was very quiet inside; the blinds had been left drawn. There was no maid to come out and make a cheerful human sound. She'd left after the tragedy. She didn't feel she owed Clara anything. It was quiet, Clara thought. But no Aldo. No shade in the corner. The scotch had chased him away. She laughed, and heard a funny echo that scared her.

'You go on like this,' she said out loud, 'And you'll be back in the Portchester instead of Paris . . . for Christ's sake take a hold of yourself . . . and don't go looking for a drink. They warned you about that, didn't they?'

She let the blinds up; immediately the sunshine flooded in. She drew a finger over the table top; the magazines were two months out of date. The tip of her finger was smeared with dust. She took in a deep breath. No ghosts. Only memories, and all of them bitter as gall.

Her life there with Steven in the early years. Her disappointed hopes of children. Month after month ending in tears. The loveless coupling in the end, when she was desperate for him and he only performed as a duty. The rows, the walk-outs when he left her and she knew he had gone to some woman.

Her self-inflicted torture of jealousy. The last insane act of spite when she refused to go to dinner with him,

321

and he went alone and found the woman whose name he'd gasped out on their wedding night as he climaxed inside her. 'Angelina.' She put a hand to her cheek as if she'd been struck a blow. He had struck her, she remembered. As she told O'Halloran. He'd slapped her when she called the woman a whore.

She opened the report and read it. That woman was the cause of what had happened. Like some malignant figure in a Greek tragedy, she had drifted on to the stage of Steven's life and out again, and blighted Clara's happiness from the wings. Only to return from the dead and claim him. The bloody cycle of betrayal, vengeance, and finally death began with her. It would end with her. And Clara would be there to see it. Not like the woman who'd taken Steven from her for a night in Monte Carlo. She hadn't thought about that since it happened. The memory made her smile. Clara felt suffused with cruelty, with a sense of power. That Frenchwoman had paid a price for having Steven Falconi in her bed.

Poppa had seen to that. All it needed was a telephone call and a sob in her voice to ensure disfigurement and near death.

But she had only a scrap of newspaper cutting to soothe her pride. Now that Aldo was dead, she had to deal with such problems herself.

She had money. She was so rich she could pay any price to get what she wanted. And the agency revenues were flooding in. O'Halloran had been a good choice. She thought about him. He was as rotten as she had suspected he might be. As corrupt as she had made him. A cop gone bad was the worst. Thank God. He was efficient; he'd recruited people outside the Families. The agency was her operation, staffed by people who owed no one any favours except the front man who paid them. She reached over and picked up the phone. She hadn't spoken to him since he got back to New York. He'd sent flowers to the hospital. She didn't know about it, but someone told her. She'd been too sick to cope. Until now. After she'd read his report. She had begun to make her plans. His assistant answered.

Clara said, 'Mr O'Halloran. Never mind who's calling. Put him on!'

'Mike? Yes, it's me. I'm fine now. Yes, I've seen it. You did a good job. How's the blackmailing business?' She laughed, hearing him swear in surprise. 'Are we doing all right? I'm sure. You must bring me up to date. I'm flying out tomorrow. Paris. Yes, Paris. I'm going to live there for a while. And I want you to come out. I'll be staying at the Crillon. Get there by Thursday, will you? We've got a lot to talk over.'

She hung up. The silence came down on her like a shroud. She sat up, grabbed her shoes. I'll sell this place, she decided. I'll get good money for it. When I come back, I'll live in Poppa's house. I can do it over. She had deliberately thought 'when', not 'if'. They had written her off, Nimmi and the rest of the old friends who'd sentenced her father to death. Let them. All she needed was time. And to settle the first of her debts of honour.

'Darling,' Angela asked anxiously, 'are you sure it's safe?'

Steven put his arm round her. 'I'm sure,' he said.

They were preparing for a gala night early in the new season at the casino. And he was allowing press photographers free access. It worried her and she said so.

'If your picture got back to America somehow – why shouldn't you care now when it was dangerous all last year?'

He made her sit on his knee. 'You're getting to be quite a weight,' he said. 'You know, I'm really excited already.'

'Don't change the subject,' Angela said. 'Why are you taking a chance, Steven? It isn't worth it.'

She's got to know some time, he decided. It's old news now. I can soften it, make it less shocking.

He said gently, 'Clara can't hurt us now. Her father's

dead. The family's business has been divided up. I've talked to my brother, and we don't have to worry anymore.'

'Why didn't you tell me?' she asked.

'Because it all happened while we were in Morocco. Her father got it wrong. People didn't like what he was planning to do to us. So – it's all over.'

She said, 'He's dead?'

He nodded. 'Don't think about it. It's nothing to do with us.'

Angela said, 'What's happened to her?'

'Nothing. She's gone on a long vacation. It was made clear to her. No trouble. She understood.' He held her close to him. 'I didn't tell you,' he said, 'I knew you wouldn't like it. You were just on four months with the baby. I'm not glad about it, I promise you. It's not part of me anymore. I made my choice at Christmas, and I'm never going back, not even in my mind. We have our lives here, our son, and the new little one. And let me tell you something, my darling. I'm going to make up to you for having the boy all on your own last time. You're going to be a princess with this baby.'

Angela let him hold her. No danger, no need to hide any more. But at a price. I can't think about it, she said to herself. I don't know and I don't want to know any more than he's told me. So easy to say, while we're like this, and I feel how much he needs me. It's when I'm alone, or wake at night, it's going to be different then . . .

She said, 'I wish I could have it at home.'

'No way.' He was adamant. 'You go to the clinic, you have the best doctors, the best attention. We're not taking any chances. Now you should go and take your rest. And don't worry about a thing. Promise me?'

'I promise,' Angela told him.

He held on to her for a moment longer. 'I love you very much,' he said. 'Now go on, put your feet up. I'll wake you when I get back.'

She slept in spite of herself, longer than she meant to.

Nature was making it easy to keep her promise to him. Not to worry, not to think.

When she woke it was late in the afternoon, and the telephone beside her bed was ringing. She answered it sleepily. It was a call from England.

It was Jim Hulbert calling. He told her, as gently as he could, that Hugh Drummond had died of a heart attack. Mrs P. found him in his chair after lunch and thought he was asleep. It had been peaceful and painless.

'I should have gone to the funeral, Ralph!'

'No you shouldn't,' Maxton said. 'You nearly lost that baby. Steven was quite right. Angela, your father wouldn't want you taking any risk. The only reason I'm not there is to make sure you stay in bed and do what you're told.'

The pains had begun within hours of that telephone call. She had become so upset at the suggestion of being moved into the clinic that the doctor left her at home overnight in the hope that the spasms would stop with medication. Any sign of bleeding, he told Steven, and she was to be rushed in immediately.

He had sat up with her while she slept under sedation, watching over her till she woke in the morning.

'It's all right,' she murmured to him. 'The pains have stopped . . . Oh, poor Daddy . . .' And she cried out her grief in Steven's arms.

No question of travelling, the doctor insisted. No emotional upset. At less than seven months, she'd lose the child. Maxton had volunteered to stay with her. Steven had agreed provided he moved into the villa.

'I don't trust her not to get up, or do something crazy like trying to fly out at the last minute,' he told Maxton. 'Janine couldn't stop her; you could. It's just because he died so suddenly, sitting up in a chair . . . if she'd had warning, she wouldn't be taking it so hard.'

'She won't risk the baby,' Maxton reassured him. 'She's not irresponsible, to do something like that.' He hated Steven so much, he wondered how he managed to conceal it. He couldn't see the exaggerated anxiety as anything but a slur on Angela. He didn't understand the fear for her, for the child, that made Steven sound harsh. Maxton hadn't sat with her through the night, waiting for signs of a premature birth that might end in losing them both.

'You watch over her,' Steven told Maxton. 'The doctor's visiting every day. I'll be bringing Charlie back with me. I'll get everything settled over there. She's not to be worried with goddamned wills, or what happens to the house or Mrs P. I've told her. She's got to leave it to me and just take care of herself and the baby.'

He'd driven to the airport and Maxton had seen him off.

Maxton went upstairs to Angela's room. He'd brought flowers, and a translation of a new French novel from the English bookshop in Cannes.

She looked white and wan sitting up in bed. He had never been demonstrative; displays of affection weren't encouraged by his parents or the nannies who substituted for them. And he'd been an unattractive-looking child. He had never before wanted to put his arms round a woman and just cradle her for comfort. He sat on the edge of the bed and allowed himself to hold her hand.

'You've got to be good,' he told her. 'Otherwise I'll ring up old Martineau and tell him you're doing the Twist round the bedroom, and he'll whip you off to his clinic in no time!'

She smiled at that. 'I can't even do that when I'm not pregnant,' she said.

'Nor can I,' he admitted. It was the latest dance craze sweeping Europe from America. 'The osteopaths are making a fortune out of slipped discs.'

'Thanks for the flowers.' Angela picked up the novel. 'And for this. I ought to be able to read it in French by now. It's said to be a very good book.' She wiped away a tear with her free hand. 'I can't stop doing this,' she said.

326

'I feel so awful not being there . . . And I've stopped you from going too. He was so fond of you, Ralph.'

'I was very fond of him. You wouldn't try not to cry, would you, Angela? Just for me?'

'All right. I don't want to upset you too. You know, it's funny, I wasn't all that close to him. Or to my mother. But when she died I missed her dreadfully.'

'I'm not surprised,' he said. 'Being left with a child and having to cope on your own. It must have been bloody for you.' He's making a fuss about this one, he thought, but he left you to sink or swim with Master Charlie . . .

'It wasn't easy,' Angela admitted. 'They took it well, considering.'

'Considering you weren't married?' he said it very gently, and with a little pressure on her hand. A step forward in intimacy. A risk taken, but then he'd always taken risks. Never for something he wanted as much as this.

She didn't say anything for a moment. She let him go on holding her hand; she thought: He's so kind. He's like my brother Jack would have been to me if he hadn't been killed . . . 'How did you know?' she said.

'I guessed,' Maxton answered. 'I knew Charlie was Steven's son as soon as I saw them together.' That wasn't true, but the lie came more easily than the truth. 'And of course I'd met his first wife in Monte Carlo. It wasn't too difficult to figure out what had happened.'

She said, 'We married in a little church in Sicily. My parents said it wasn't valid. He never told me you'd met her.'

'No reason why he should,' Maxton dismissed it. 'She wasn't very nice. Now why don't I get Janine to put the old bouquet in water and see about some tea for you? And I've brought some cards. We could play gin rummy if you like? I could do with winning a few quid.' He used to let Hugh Drummond win when they played cards.

She said, 'I don't really feel like playing anything. Let's have tea together instead.'

He had a charming smile; it quite transformed his ugly, aquiline-nosed face. 'Let's,' he agreed. 'That would be very nice.'

O'Halloran had never been to Paris. He hadn't been to Europe till he took the first trip out to Sicily. The flight had been via Naples. He had heard that old adage about seeing Naples and dying. It didn't make any sense to him. He thought it was sprawling and dirty; he got sick to his stomach eating some dish with shellfish in it. Sicily was cold and dry like a desert, with powerful colours that appealed to him and a sparse landscape dominated by mountains. He had to take an interpreter to the village where the Falconis had originated.

The interpreter talked to the young priest for him. How strange he should be asking about Signor Falconi. He was the village benefactor. Their protector. Yes, he had been married there during the war, and only a few months back, he'd returned with his wife and a fine big son. He was a generous man, much honoured in the village.

O'Halloran copied down the entry in the church register for 1943. He wrote it in English with the interpreter's help. Steven Antonio Falconi. Angela Frances Drummond. The date and their signatures. The priest saw them out, smiling. He didn't even ask why the American wanted to see the evidence of the marriage. He was a simple man, and a stranger to mistrust.

From Sicily, with the proof and the unexpected corroboration of that visit by the far from dead Steven Falconi last September, Mike O'Halloran flew to England. He thought that was the worst part of the trip. The weather was vile; raining, dull and cold.

He stayed in a comfortable little hotel, made his contact with David Wickham over the telephone and worked out a careful cover story. It was one thing to fool a peasant priest in a hill village. Less easy to get information out of a smart businessman. Wickham's advertising agency was very smart, he'd found out. One of the best in London. Wickham was cagey, but polite.

O'Halloran was amazed how polite the English were, with their thanks and pleases. He didn't like them any better. His old man had been an Irish Republican nut. He'd brought up all his children on the iniquities of English rule in Ireland over seven hundred years. Wickham made Mike feel clumsy and out of place in the elegant office, as if he'd left his flies undone. But he took the bait about the relative in Ohio who'd left money to a cousin called Angela Drummond, last heard of taking a vacation to New York. He had no more to go on than that till a series of adverts in the *Herald Trib* and the *New York Times* brought a response from someone who'd lent her an apartment.

When he mentioned the name, Wickham opened up. Yes, he knew Angela Drummond; she'd been engaged to work as his assistant. It was his bad luck that she went on her New York vacation; he'd even got her the loan of the apartment. The bad luck, he explained to O'Halloran, was her meeting a man and getting married, without taking up her job. Dislike of the bridegroom had loosened his tongue. O'Halloran was getting the picture. The picture of the man honoured as its protector by a Sicilian village, and the sinister Italian American that Wickham was sticking his knife into.

He could have painted Falconi's portrait from these two descriptions. He'd seen a number of such men during his years in the police. Older men by that time. Men with expensive suits and gold watches, who'd earned their place in the hierarchy the hard way. With guns and knives, and ice picks. They had brains, and they went on to sit behind the desks and let others bloody their hands. He could sure imagine Steven Falconi.

And then it went out of focus. It went out of focus in a two-bit English village, so different to the hilltop cluster of houses in Sicily. Just outside of Haywards Heath, with a sodden area of grass surrounding a stone cross on a plinth commemorating their war dead; old houses, picturesque for sure, standing behind little walls and railings and front gardens, all bare and dripping in the godforsaken winter weather. He'd found the house with the brass plate, and they told him in the pub, forcing down tepid beer, that the old doctor didn't practise any more.

He had the same story for Hugh Drummond as he'd told Wickham, but a different ending. He was ninety per cent certain that the Angela Drummond he was looking for was not Doctor Drummond's daughter, but he was just drawing a line under all the old leads. He expected to find the young lady in Scotland. He said Scotland because he knew Drummond was a Scottish name.

The old man was not over friendly at first. But Mike had a way with him. He wasn't Irish for nothing, as his father used to say about himself. He could be good company, and the old doctor offered him a cup of tea and started talking. A lot about his grandson. Mike had to prise him off the subject of how well the boy played cricket and rugger, and how he was passing everything at school. He was nice about the daughter in a noncommital way. He was far more enthusiastic about his son-in-law.

'I wasn't too keen at first; I would've preferred an Englishman, no offence meant by that, you understand . . . but naturally I hoped she'd settle down with someone here. But I must say, she's lucky. Very lucky. He's a damned good chap. Loves her, marvellous with the boy too. Always makes me feel welcome. Even wanted me to live with them in France. Not that I would, mind you. Too hot for me. Can't stand that sort of heat . . .' He'd come out to the front door with O'Halloran, shaken hands and apologized for keeping him jabbering, as he put it. 'Old man's disease, talking too much. Not the one people think you mean, though,' and he'd chuckled at his own joke.

And then Mike O'Halloran knew where to find them. Falconi had started a casino. The doctor seemed rather proud of it. He'd filled in a lot of details, seeing that his listener was interested.

It was time to go home. Time to write up his report, and pick up a fat cheque. He bought English cashmere for his wife and a lot of souvenirs for his children. When he got home, he heard about the mob killings.

That had been the day after he'd been to see Clara Falconi at her house. By the time it happened he'd been airborne on his way to Italy. His wife had raised hell at him taking off at such short notice. The flowers hadn't won her over. He had called on the telephone, but the lines were poor, and by the time he was in London she was missing him and asking when he'd be home. He hoped she'd like the cashmere sweaters. He'd bought her three in different colours. He'd been busy, but he was anxious, calling the hospital to find out how Clara was getting on. 'Severe shock' was all he could get out of them. Not surprising. Back numbers of the papers showed the carnage on the church steps, reporters dwelt on the bride in her blood-drenched clothes, being taken by ambulance away from the scene.

If she didn't get over it, what the hell would happen to his agency? Then he quietened down. Clients were coming in all the time; money was coming in with them. If she ended up in a funny farm, he could just keep on going till someone came along and asked about her share. But she was tough. He had to admit that. She was out of the hospital and asking for his report. In a way he felt relieved. He couldn't have felt sorry for her – he shrugged off that idea. She wasn't the type to be pitied. Maybe admired a little, for the sheer guts of her.

He told his wife he'd be flying to Paris, but this time it would be a short trip. And he'd bring her back something really special.

Clara met him in the bar at the Crillon. He thought: My Christ! when he saw her first. She was so thin, so gaunt in the face that all you could see were big black eyes like burnished jet. So thin and so eye-catching in a scarlet suit. He came and they shook hands.

He said, 'It's good to see you, Mrs Falconi. And you look great.' He meant it.

She said, 'Sit down, Mike. Let's have a drink. And it's Mrs Salviatti, not Falconi. I did get married to him. Just.'

'Sorry,' he said. 'I wasn't thinking. I'll try and remember the new name. What can I get you?'

'Scotch,' Clara said. He didn't look out of place, though she'd expected he would. But then she chose his suits for business. She'd picked Bruno's clothes for him too. Made him look less like a street-corner Romeo . . . She put the memory of him away. It was odd the way he crept into her mind when she wasn't looking. She'd wake at night these times, thinking he was touching her. Unlike Aldo's, his spirit hadn't settled.

O'Halloran came back. 'They're bringing the drinks.'

Clara said, 'Before we get down to my business, how's our business?'

She had a cool way with her; she could be rude one minute and then relaxed, almost pleasant. You never knew which way she was going to jump. She didn't play round with the scotch. She finished ahead of him, and signalled the waiter. 'Another,' she said. 'Mike? I'm getting this.'

'Another the same would be nice,' he said. 'I brought these to show you.' He unlocked his briefcase and handed her a folder. 'Just a few figures on our take since you've been sick. And some names. One or two are pretty interesting.'

She read very quickly; and she took everything in. Her questions were always to the point. She repeated one of the names and cocked her sleek black head on one side. Her hair was like polished silk. A thick knot of it was twisted up at the back. It must hang down a long way without any pins in it. She was smiling over the prominent US senator with presidential ambitions who was among the clients of a prostitute with very special sado-masochistic talents.

'Some pillar of the Church,' O'Halloran agreed. 'I never trusted the son of a bitch with all that holy yap.'

Clara closed the folder. 'I guess his family will want to keep his name off that lady's list. Have we done anything about it yet?'

'I've put out a few feelers. But we've got to go easy. They play rough, and they've got friends who play rougher.'

'I know they have,' Clara said. 'But not when they know there's a copy waiting to be mailed to every major newspaper. They'd be able to stop one or two but not half a dozen. In different States. We'll get to work on this. The last count, his father was worth around eighty million dollars.'

The drinks had come and gone, and he said, 'Do you want to talk about the other business now, Mrs Falconi?'

'Salviatti,' she reminded him. 'If you can't remember my goddamned name, why don't you just call me Clara?'

'Okay.' He was taken by surprise. 'Okay. Clara. Thanks.'

'We've got a lot to talk about,' she said. 'I guess you'd better stay to dinner. I don't want to rush this. And I'm going to need you, Mike. I hope you're not planning to go back home for a while?'

After a pause he shook his head. 'I've left it open,' he said. 'Till I knew what you wanted.'

He'd seen it coming; the same old warning system went into action just like the time she asked him to work for her. And he switched it off.

'It beats me,' he said, 'how any guy could want to leave you.' The black hair was as long as he'd imagined. He draped it over her, covering each breast, and traced the outline of her navel with a forefinger.

She was too thin, but the body was lean like whipcord. She lay back on the pillows with her arms above her head. He leaned over her, stroking downwards. She sighed and raised her pelvis to meet his questing hand.

She was the most exciting woman he had ever met, and he'd been a keen sack man from his early teens. Animal images flitted through the pace and intensity of making love. Something strong and supple was suddenly, amazingly under his control. It made him feel a giant, just to satisfy her.

She pulled him down and closed her eyes. He wasn't Bruno. He wasn't Steven. But he was good; he seemed to know what she wanted without being told. He had a male identity of his own, and she was surprised how much she liked it. And needed it. She didn't want to be alone. Too many things waiting for her in the silence; she submerged herself in the renewed pleasure he gave her, drowning in the sensation, willing it to go on and on . . . No Bruno in her dreams tonight, no nightmare about a creeping snake of blood inching down the steps from her father's dead body, threatening to stain her.

He was a sentimental man; he wanted to hold her afterwards, to tell her she was wonderful. I bought him with money first, Clara thought. Now he really belongs to me. And in the sleepy interlude she asked him, 'You'll help me, Mike? I need you. I hate to say it, but it's true . . .'

He promised, not thinking or caring what she would ask of him.

She said, 'We make a good partnership. I want you out of that crappy hotel and right here with me.'

He didn't argue. He liked the idea.

He moved into the Crillon the next day. When Clara told him to fly down to the South and positively mark where Steven Falconi and his family were living, he went without remembering to send his wife a cable. She was expecting him home; it was Clara who reminded him.

O'Halloran and Clara talked on the phone. He'd scouted out the casino. He'd driven up in the area where he thought the Falconis' villa was, but he didn't want to

334

make a positive inquiry. When did she want him back in Paris? She noted he hadn't mentioned going home to the States.

'Not yet,' she said. 'Stay down there, see what you can pick up. I've got things to do here. When you get back, Mike, we'll go out on the town.'

'You know where I want to go,' he said. 'I get hard just talking to you.'

She had a low, suggestive laugh. 'Just you keep it for me. I'll be moving out of here soon. I'll call you.'

When she hung up, she put him out of her mind. She was going to see the apartment on the Rue Constantine that morning. It would be a test of nerve and resolution to go there and relive the barren hopes of the early days with Steven.

'She's going to be all right, isn't she, Dad?'

Steven had waited for Charlie to come down from his mother's room. He had left them alone to mourn. 'She's going to be fine. I've just spoken to Doctor Martineau; he was with her this morning and he's not worried anymore. So you mustn't worry either.' He put an arm round Charlie's shoulders.

'You were awfully good, Dad, you got everything organized so quickly. But I do wish Grandpa hadn't left everything to me, though Mum doesn't seem to mind.'

'I'm sure she doesn't. Your grandfather knew she didn't need anything. He did the right thing; he wanted you to have whatever there was. I'd like to talk to you about that a bit later. Whether you want to sell the house, what you want done with the furniture. But there's no hurry. When you finish your exams and leave school, we can have a talk about the future. Now, I'll go up and see your mother. Martineau says she can get up at the end of the week.'

'Dad?' Steven paused at the foot of the stairs. 'Dad, when is Ralph moving out?'

'I haven't thought – why?' He frowned. 'Charlie, what are you getting at?'

Charlie said, 'I don't like him much.'

Steven came back into the hall. 'You don't have to like him,' he said. 'What's this all about? He's here because I asked him to look after your mother while I went to the funeral. He's been very helpful; she told me so.'

'He's a bit too helpful if you ask me,' his son said quietly. 'I shouldn't say this, but I don't like the way he hangs round Mum all the time. And I know he doesn't like you.'

It was the last thing Steven wanted to hear. He said roughly, 'Don't talk balls, Charlie.' But to his surprise his son didn't back down. He stood his ground.

'It's not balls. I was there at Christmas when things weren't too good with you and Mum. You should've seen his face when you walked through that door! Anyway, I've said it.'

'Yes,' Steven admitted. 'You sure have.'

'I'm not a fool, Dad,' Charlie said. 'I know you're pissed off with me about it, but I don't like him and I don't trust him either.' He walked away before his father could say anything.

Steven went upstairs to see Angela. Outside the room he paused. He could hear voices. Maxton was in there with her. He hadn't waited long after Charlie came down.

He opened the door quickly and went in. It was foolish of him to expect anything but what he saw. Angela sitting up in bed, holding her arms out to him, Ralph Maxton the other side of the room.

'I don't like him and I don't trust him,' Charlie had said.

Stephen sat on the bed and took his wife's hand. He said, 'When Angela's able to come down, you must come over for dinner, Ralph.'

He wondered whether it was his imagination, but he thought Maxton looked angry. It was such a fleeting impression that he dismissed it. Instantly Maxton was all charm, making light of the dismissal. He even pre-

336

empted Steven by saying that he really had a lot of details to work out for the spring gala and he hoped they wouldn't mind if he slipped away immediately and got on with them. Angela thanked him warmly; he made light of that too, mocking himself.

'My dear lady, all I did was sit around having tea with you and enjoying myself. Now you're back, Steven, it'll be plain sailing!'

When he had gone, she said, 'Darling, weren't you a bit abrupt? You didn't have to get rid of him so quickly. I thought he looked rather hurt.'

'He'll get over it,' he said. 'I just wanted you to myself.'

The shutters were open, the concierge had dusted and swept the parquet floors. Clara stood in the middle of the long drawing room. The Beauvais tapestry had been covered. The concierge had excused herself for not removing the dustsheets. 'It was difficult for me, Madame, I didn't know what might happen if I pulled them.'

It was smaller than Clara had remembered; there was a musty smell in spite of the windows flung wide to let in fresh air. What plans she'd made, walking through it all those years ago with Steven. What parties she'd imagined giving when they came over for a visit. They'd been happy in Paris; she'd told him about her ambition to become an artist. He'd taken her seriously by the end, but not too seriously. She was a girl of twenty-one, newly fledged into womanhood and marriage. Her hope of early pregnancy was disappointed and she'd fastened on the apartment as a compensation. There was plenty of time, she had insisted; they were going off to Monte Carlo to end their honeymoon. Prophetically, she hadn't wanted to go. She thought of the apartment as a kind of talisman, and bought it out of her settlement without letting Steven know. He had never known. By the time they arrived in the States, their marriage was already on course for disaster.

337

The secret love nest. She laughed aloud in bitterness. No cooing doves had settled there; it was as empty and barren as her life. She lit a cigarette. It needed furnishing; the decorations could wait. She had to move out of the Crillon, leave no trace of herself. She walked across the floor, her steps echoing on the bare parquet, and on an impulse took a corner of the sheeting that covered the tapestry. It had brilliant colours, if she remembered, a typical eighteenth-century pastoral scene with lovers dressed up as shepherdess and gallant. She pulled at it and the covering came away. It fell to the floor, revealing the glowing colours, fresh and beautiful. The lovers dallied and the whiff of subtle eroticism was in their woven faces and sly eyes. She stood and stared at it. Not love as she understood it, no visceral torment of desire and jealousy; no passion. They fondled each other in a bower of flowers, with cupids spying on them from the clouds. A bloodless sensuality, a concept of love that was no more than scented dalliance. Clara reached up and caught the tapestry by the corner. She wrenched with all her strength; the backing tore a little, but the tapestry resisted her. She couldn't pull it down. The lovers went on simpering and eyeing each other, watched by the lascivious siblings of the god of love. She turned and hurried out of the room.

Clara didn't waste time. She toured the shops in the Faubourg St Honoré. She ordered Savonnerie carpets, sets of comfortable chairs and sofas, a modern bed dressed in the most expensive and elaborate style, and some fine pieces of early French furniture. She sold the tapestry, and the price gave her a morbid satisfaction. It paid for most of what she bought for the apartment.

The concierge, smelling a very wealthy patroness, found her a suitable maid and the services of an Algerian cook. The activity kept Clara going; she gave herself no rest until the miracle was accomplished and the apartment ready to walk into. She told herself she had killed the memories of Steven when that hated tapestry was taken down. The gilded mirrors and a fine flower painting made the whole room look different. She could be happy in it. She might even settle in Paris permanently.

But the fantasy didn't last long. The reality was O'Halloran phoning from Valbonne to say that there was a gala evening planned for Steven's casino in May. And he'd found out quite a lot about the man in charge of running it. A man it might be possible to approach. Clara told him to come back to Paris. She had cancelled the room at the Crillon when she moved out. But she wouldn't ask him to stay at the Rue Constantine. He'd come by appointment, and stay the night by invitation. She wanted no misunderstanding. She might delude him with pleas for help when they were between the sheets, but outside the bedroom, she paid the bills and called the shots. That way she kept control.

She wondered what he had found out, what kind of man Steven had trusted, that Mike thought might not be trustworthy. Not like Steven to make a mistake, she thought. Always so shrewd, so ruthless in detecting a phoney. She smiled in hatred. Maybe he had slipped just once. And once might be enough.

It was the boy, Ralph Maxton agreed. Not so much of a boy, at six feet two and growing into a man, the mirror image of his father. He'd come out of the lanky stage. He was a very mature seventeen. It was the Italian blood, Maxton realized. Like the women, they grew up fast and faded early. He had never liked Charlie; had been jealous at first, because his parents doted on him, but increasingly Maxton found the teenager grating on him. He wasn't the nice middle-class English lad, about to leave public school and begin life in the adult world; he looked like it and talked like it, but Maxton wondered how deep you'd have to scratch to find a very different animal. Now he knew. Charlie hated him.

Charlie, with an intuition sharper than his years, knew

that Maxton was in love with his mother. And he didn't try to hide his hatred. He wasn't rude; he knew that wouldn't have been tolerated. But he conveyed his feelings to Maxton very clearly. And he had said something that had affected Steven's attitude. They might be subtle and deceptive, but the Falconis and their kind couldn't hide their feelings for long. Poker wasn't their game.

The change was almost imperceptible, but not to Maxton. A coolness in Steven's eye, a reserve when they were all together. And a watchfulness that warned Maxton to be very careful when he was with Angela. Careful to hide the little intimacies that had grown between them when they had spent time alone. She didn't see it, of course. She was too open, too straight in her attitude to people. She was generous with her affections, loyal and trusting to the people she loved. And he believed that he was included in that love. As a friend, as a confidant. She didn't see him as he hoped one day she might. She wasn't ready for that yet. Maxton didn't know when it would happen, but he was certain that it would. Falconi would shipwreck himself. He'd almost done so last Christmas. There would be another time.

Ralph worked prodigiously, and waited for his young enemy to go back to England. And he kept a little distance between Angela and himself. The need to do so made him hate father and son even more.

They had planned a spectacular firework display for the gala. Steven costed it carefully, but refused to cheese-pare. Their second season was going to be the one that established them on a firm basis on the coast. They wanted to lure the clients back and get them to become regulars; above all, the heavy gamblers were Steven's quarry.

He spent a lot of money on advance publicity and harassed Maxton about a new batch of celebrities. 'We need some big-name movie stars –'

It gave Maxton pleasure to debunk that suggestion. 'The big movie stars wouldn't be seen dead at a casino gala these days – you're thinking of Monte Carlo in the fifties – the Brandos and that lot are into meditation. But I'll see what I can come up with.'

He consulted Madeleine. They met at the Hôtel de Paris in Monte Carlo.

She was in high spirits, bubbling with them, in fact. The faithful Bernard had been replaced by a younger, richer man.

'He's fabulous,' she confided to Maxton, who wasn't in the least bit jealous of this paragon, the more she talked about him. 'Persians are so generous – look what he gave me last time.' She held out a smooth arm encircled by a Bulgari bracelet set with emeralds and rubies. He'd given her some bruises too, she admitted, but then he liked that kind of thing. She was quite philosophical about a few punches as part of foreplay. Provided that the rewards were big enough.

'I was so bored with that old fart Bernard,' she said, pouting. 'He was talking about losing money too; that really bothered me. So when Mahmoud came along, I thought: Adieu, Bernard.' She giggled delightedly and showed off her newest piece of jewellery.

And she gave Maxton a celebrity for the gala opening that would raise eyebrows all along the coast.

'I'd like to help you, Ralphie darling. My friend is very close to the Shah – he's got signed photographs and personal presents all over his apartment. I was telling him about the gala, because I want him to take me. He said it was a bad date for the Shah. But the Shah's sister's on a visit here. She said she wanted to go to Monte Carlo, and guess what I said?'

Maxton didn't spoil it for her. It wasn't often she did anyone a favour. 'No idea,' he said. 'Tell me.'

'I suggested she should come to your casino instead. And he said "Yes!" Isn't that wonderful? She gambles like a lunatic. And she's so rich, you can't even imagine it –'

'You're a clever girl, darling,' Maxton told her. 'This is going to please my charming boss. He's been climbing on my back about getting new names to come along.'

'You mean that handsome man I saw? Falconi? Don't you like him anymore?'

'I never did like him much,' Maxton said lightly. 'Gangsters don't exactly grow on one. On the strength of this, I'm going to order some champagne for us. And what time do you have to be available for your rich Iranian friend?'

'When does your boss Mr Falconi expect to see you?' she retorted. Her voice had risen; it always did when she was excited. He leaned over and stroked her knee.

'Some time tomorrow morning. I've booked us in on the chance you'd be free.'

She smiled at him, pinching the loose skin on the back of his straying hand. 'Not that nasty little attic room again?'

'No. A nice double on the second floor.'

'It's my favourite hotel,' she declared.

'Mine too,' Maxton agreed. 'Why don't we have them send the bottle up to our room?'

'Why not?' They got up and left the bar arm in arm.

She looked over her shoulder and whispered to him, 'My God, there's that freak! Sitting in the corner there —'

'What freak?' he asked.

'That woman with the dreadful face . . . you know the one. She lives here. Ugh – she ought to wear a yashmak.'

'Now I know you're sleeping with a Persian,' he said and their laughter drifted back behind them into the bar.

Pauline Duvalier didn't move. She had her pack of playing cards set out for patience, and the daily bottle of champagne leaning in its ice bucket. She kept herself in shadow; the corner table was reserved for her. She spent most of her day there, drinking and playing patience. She ate upstairs in her suite. She watched television there. At night she dressed for her solitary dinner and festooned herself with jewels. Nobody saw her but the floor waiters.

The niche in the dimly lit bar was her foray into the outside world. If she wanted to buy anything, the goods were sent to her in the hotel.

Sometimes she listened to other people's conversation, but not often. She'd seen the Englishman and his French whore on several occasions. She hadn't forgotten the girl's reaction the first time she came into clear view. The intake of breath, the grimace of revulsion. It had happened often enough over the years. She'd had a lot of plastic surgery, and they'd repaired what was left with great skill. Her eye was gone, but the little silk patch covered that. There was no pain anymore; they'd rebuilt her shattered jaw and done what they could to reshape her nose. The result was hideous but she had grown used to it. Champagne sustained her. When her doctor warned her of the effect on her liver and kidneys, she dismissed him.

When they gave out, it would be time to stop. Robbery, they'd said. A petty thief surprised in her bedroom. But Pauline Duvalier knew better. She suspected that the police knew better too, but there was nothing they could do about it. She hadn't been robbed, she'd been punished. She hadn't surprised the thief, he had surprised her. It was odd to her, how her memory was still clear right up to the moment when she went into her bedroom to change for lunch, and then there was a blow and total blackness. He had watched her, crept after her when she went inside the house. And then systematically beaten her. In all the years she had never understood why. And then she read about the murders at a Mafia wedding. Sitting up in bed with her breakfast tray, and the array of newspapers spread out. There was the name. Falconi. Steven Falconi's widow. She had read the details, studied the gory photographs. Falconi. That was the name of the last man she had slept with. The handsome American on his honeymoon in that same hotel.

Widow. He was dead then. She hadn't known he was a

big name in the Mafia. It might have made her think before she picked him up in the same bar. Or it might have intrigued her, added an extra spice to the affair. She hadn't been afraid in those days. He had been a very satisfactory lover. An angry man making love to a stranger while his bride slept alone that night.

She never saw him again. And a week later she was attacked and maimed for life. Almost killed.

Her friends had been very loyal, people who'd known her late husband offered help and hospitality when she came out of hospital. But when she looked in the mirror she knew what the answer must be. Flowers from the manager and staff at the Hôtel de Paris gave her the solution. She could never live in a house alone, or be left alone again. She went from the hospital to a permanent suite at the hotel and she had been there ever since. It was her home, and she was free to live there until she drank herself to death. It was taking a very long time.

Falconi. She mouthed the word. What had she just heard, the brittle voices only a few feet away, discussing a gala at some casino . . . and then the shrill young woman . . . 'Falconi? Don't you like him anymore?'

And the nasal English answer: 'I never did like him much . . . gangsters don't exactly grow on one . . .'

She had listened then, not touching the cards, leaning towards them. Her heart had begun beating too fast. They'd warned her about that too. Falconi owned a casino. The Englishman worked for him; she knew him vaguely by sight. He was one of the publicity people at the Monte Carlo casino. That was a long time ago; he'd been there when her husband used to gamble. She'd never wanted to play the wheel or the cards; after he died she didn't go to the casino anymore. She didn't know the Englishman's name, or whether he still worked there. They left, arm in arm, to keep their tryst in the nice double on the second floor. Pauline's body was a shell; the man who destroyed her face had killed all instincts for men at the same time.

She could remember him vividly. Their cool formality: Madame Duvalier; Monsieur Falconi. Never Steven or Pauline, even in the lazy aftermath of making love. Falconi. The Mafia. Gangsters don't grow on one.

She called the barman over. He'd been there for three years. He looked after her. Nobody ever got her seat in the corner, even on the days when she didn't feel like leaving her suite. He was almost a friend because he looked at her so kindly.

'Madame?'

She said, 'Who were those people – the couple that just left?'

He leaned towards her. 'Monsieur Maxton and the lady? I'm not sure of her name, I think it's Madeleine. He brings her here sometimes. Why – did they disturb you?'

'No, no. But they talked so loudly. He works for the casino, doesn't he?'

'Not for some time now, Madame. He runs the new one down at Antibes. It's a big success, I believe.'

'Ah,' she said. 'And who owns that? I heard him talk about someone called Falconi?'

'Not Falconi.' The barman shook his head. 'It's an American, Steven Lawrence, who's the front man. Nobody knows for certain who's behind it. There've been a lot of rumours that it was the Mafia.' He spoke very quietly. 'This is the only place they can't get a foothold. Maxton couldn't ever come back here if he's mixed up with them.' Then he said, 'You're not worried are you, Madame?' He was genuinely sorry for her. She had her odd ways, and she could be irritable and demanding. But she was generous, and she never carried a complaint to the management.

'No, I'm not worried. Why should I be? I was just interested, that's all. Eugene, I want you to do something for me . . .' She opened her handbag and began taking out notes. 'Find out about this casino . . . they talked about a gala evening.' She pushed the money towards him.

He shook his head. 'That's not necessary. I can ask for you.' He lifted the champagne out of its nest and checked the level.

Pauline Duvalier thrust the notes into his pocket. 'Don't be stupid, take it. And pour me the rest of that. Let me know about this gala . . .'

'Yes, Madame. Thank you very much.'

She hadn't left the hotel for nearly ten years. He went back to the bar. It was very strange. Maybe she was going off her head. But the tip was a big one. The questions were easy to answer. At lunchtime, he came across and helped her to leave the table. She was always steady on her feet. She gave him the pack of playing cards.

'Keep them for me for this evening,' she said. 'And one more favour. Find out what this Steven Lawrence looks like.'

'This is one helluva place,' Mike O'Halloran said. 'And you've fixed it all in six weeks!'

Clara shrugged. 'It's all right. It needs doing over properly, but that can wait.'

'You're going to stay here alone?' he asked her.

She'd met him at Charles de Gaulle off the internal flight from Nice. He wasn't expecting that and it pleased him. She had moods. Moods when she felt sexy, moods when she behaved like a bully, and other, softer moods that made him feel he was important.

'I've got a maid,' Clara answered. 'She sleeps down the hall. I've got you a room in the Place de L'Opéra.'

'Thanks,' he said. No invitation to move in. But hopefully an invitation to stay the night; he badly wanted that. She seemed on edge; smoking too much, moving about with restless energy. He said, 'Clara, why don't you relax? Stop burning yourself out.'

'Why don't you get us both a drink and then get down to business? I want the details, everything.'

'Okay, okay. Scotch coming up, followed by progress

report. Just try and sit still, for Christ's sake. You'll wear out the floor –'

She bit back an angry retort. She'd taken him into bed; he'd naturally presume on that. She needed him too much to slap him down. She threw herself into the deep sofa, watching him move round the room, getting the drinks. He moved well; he was fit and light on his feet. He was a crack shot with a revolver. He told her he had trophies for marksmanship at home.

'He's using the name Lawrence. Her name. He bought this place a year or so ago. Spent like it was going out of fashion and turned it into the smartest casino outside of Monte Carlo. He employed this guy Maxton to negotiate and set it up for him. They rented a villa and bought it outright last year. Her old man died recently in England. The son is around seventeen years old and in school over there. You want to see pictures?'

'How did you find out all this – where did you get the pictures?'

'From the maid. It's pretty much a village up there. I took a room and hung around. I said I was an artist. Set up with an easel and painted by numbers. So long as I spent money and bought the wine, nobody gave a damn what I was doing. And she came in to buy groceries and the old dame behind the counter couldn't wait to tell me what a good job the maid and her mother had, working for the rich American who owned the casino at Antibes. So I picked her up in the café, and we went on from there.'

Clara was not really listening. He had an envelope and the photographs were sticking out of the open flap. Pictures of Steven, of the woman, of the son, now turned seventeen. She reached forward and took them. Mike went on talking.

'It wasn't too difficult to get her to open up about them. She was full of yap. I got the feeling she didn't like him much. I had to pay for those; they sure know the value of money.'

Steven smiling up at her, with his arm round a tall, dark boy. She felt as if she were being knifed. His son; no possible doubt about that. Another photograph, a woman with blonde hair, laughing at the camera, wearing a sun dress that showed her to be full-breasted, smooth-skinned.

'That's her.' O'Halloran leaned over. 'Jesus, you really had it figured. I didn't believe it right up until I went to Sicily . . .'

'She's nothing,' Clara said slowly. 'She looks like nothing.'

He could see she was going to tear the picture to pieces. He took it away from her, put them all back in the envelope and slipped it into his pocket. 'Like I said,' he reminded her, 'how could any guy want to leave you? She's nothing, you're right. Just another blonde.'

'He threw everything away for her,' Clara said slowly. 'He could have ended up the head of all the Families. My father'd be alive today if he hadn't run out on us. It must have been for the son. That's what got to him. That's what I couldn't give him. And there was no reason. No goddamned, fucking reason why he never got me pregnant.'

She was on her feet by then. He didn't try to stop her. He had never imagined she could cry.

'I went everywhere. Every specialist, every quack practitioner promising miracles. I made him take a test; I thought it was him. I though she must have cheated on him and I said so. He hated me for that. He hated me for being jealous – he hated me, period! His test was okay. He had his pride in his dead wife and baby, and I had nothing! You know what happened on my wedding night? He was screwing me, Mike, and he yelled out her name. Angelina!'

O'Halloran said, 'Jesus,' under his breath.

She stopped in front of him. 'I was crazy about him. He went with a woman on our honeymoon. I wanted to kill him, kill myself –'

There was a moment, as he watched her and listened, when he recoiled. He had his soft side; he was a fond father and he loved his wife, even if he'd got between the sheets with other women now and then. It didn't mean anything serious. But this was different. He didn't like this kind of savage self-exposure. He felt as if she might tear at her clothes, rip her own skin open. It wasn't love as he understood love. The word evil scared him. He came very close to getting up and getting out while the going was good.

'I'll pay a half million dollars,' she said.

He stayed where he was.

'What are you buying with it, Clara?' he said after a pause.

She had calmed suddenly. She sat down beside him; she reached for her drink and sipped it. She was so cool. 'My peace of mind,' she said. 'My family's honour. I want them dead, Mike. All of them. I'll pay half a million dollars to the man who fixes it. Or does it.'

He reached for his own glass. His hand wasn't quite steady. 'You could get the President of the United States knocked off for that.'

'For less,' she corrected him.

He still didn't get up and leave. 'With your contacts that shouldn't be too much of a problem,' he said.

'I can't use them,' she said. 'No one from back home would touch a contract for me. The word's gone out. No trouble. That's why I'm here. That's why I need you, Mike. I need you to find a killer for me. But we won't talk about it now. Tell me about the man my husband hired. What was his name?'

'Maxton,' he said. 'Ralph Maxton.' He was finding it hard to concentrate. It wasn't the scotch. He had a head like a rock.

'Tell me about him,' Clara insisted. Her voice was soft. She laid a hand on his knee. She had long nails and very white skin. A half a million dollars. And she meant it. She had the money.

He said, 'He's English. His old man's some kind of lord, who kicked him out for stealing and gambling. He was into every kind of shit before he came out here. He worked in Monaco; they caught him with his hand on the roulette wheel and he was out. Then your husband picked him up. He sounds the kind who'd do anything for money.'

'And where did you get all this?'

'From his old bosses at the Monte Carlo casino. They're not too pleased with him there. He's done too good a job pulling some of their customers into the new place. They don't like him for it. They hoped they were getting him in some kind of trouble.'

'He'd need money,' she said thoughtfully. 'If he gambles he'd always need money.'

'That's what I figured,' O'Halloran said. 'But we can't rush it. We've got to get an angle on this guy first. He doesn't fit into the picture they gave me up in Monaco.'

'Why not?'

'Because the maid, Janine, talked about him too. He's some kind of family friend from what she said. Stays at the villa to take care of the wife, goes to England with them at Christmas. He's gotten himself stuck in there.'

Clara snapped impatiently, 'Then why waste time on him? Why the hell think he'll be any use?

'Because from what the maid said, he's got the hots for the wife.'

Clara stared at him. She said, 'And my husband doesn't know? They're cheating on him?'

'No. That dame'd bad-mouth anyone, but she didn't even try that on. She said Maxton was crazy about her. "Madame doesn't see it," she told me. She was thinking all over her face. "And Monsieur Lawrence must be blind . . ." She's the kind that gets a kick out of that kind of situation. I guess she'd look through the keyhole when they were in bed.'

Clara was silent. He waited. He hadn't told her the

woman was pregnant. He didn't think she was ready to hear about that yet.

He said, 'If the target was only your husband, this could be the guy. He could have two motives. The money and the widow. But we're speculating, Clara. Nothing adds up till I've made contact with him.'

'And you think you'd be able to judge?' she demanded.

'I spent the best part of twenty years with crooks and I always reckoned I could smell the ones who'd murder. Why don't I go to this gala and take a look at him?'

'Why don't you?' Clara said quietly. 'And if you like what you see, Mike, then maybe I should meet with him. I went to the casino at Monte Carlo on my honeymoon with Steven. Maybe he was there. When is this gala?'

'Middle of May,' he told her. 'I'd have to get an invitation. They're pretty choosy who gets in.'

She smiled at him. 'You'll fix it,' she said. 'Show someone a wad and turn on the charm. Now why don't we eat? You like Algerian food?'

He stroked the back of her neck, feeling the small nape and the silky hair under his fingers. 'I've never eaten any,' he said.

'It's spicy. I like it. And you'll stay, won't you?'

'I'll stay,' he said. He leaned over and kissed her. A half million dollars. He could really get out from under if he had that kind of money.

Meantime she was writhing under him like a beautiful snake. They didn't eat till very late.

9

'It's a girl,' Steven said. 'She's beautiful!'

'That's great,' Piero said, 'just great! The mother's okay?' He covered the telephone mouthpiece and shouted to Lucia. 'Steven's had a girl – yeah, yeah I'm here. So what's she weigh?' He was an expert on babies. Lucia was expecting their fourth child.

'Just on six pounds,' Steven said. 'She came a little early, but it was easy and Angela's fine. Tell Momma, won't you? And Poppa –'

'I'll tell them,' Piero promised. 'Momma will be happy. You know how she is about babies. Listen Steven, maybe we could come out and visit and bring her. How would that be?'

'You think Poppa would let her go?'

'Well, no, I guess he wouldn't. But it was a nice idea. Lucia and me and the kids would love to see you. When the new one's arrived, we could talk about it. We miss you, Steven.'

'I miss you too,' was the reply.

'How's everything? No troubles?'

'No troubles,' Piero assured him. 'No Fabrizzis, no troubles,' he laughed. 'And Clara's gone off on her broomstick! If Poppa'd see sense, you could come home and bring the family with you!'

Steven didn't answer. He would never go back, and never bring his wife and family. Whether his father forgave him or not, that would never happen now. He said, 'It's good to talk to you, Piero. Give everyone my

352

love and I'll send you pictures of the baby. She's beautiful. She's like Angela. I'll call again soon.'

For a moment the old nostalgia clouded his happiness. He missed them. He missed the warmth that was so much a part of his old life in his family. The birth of a new baby was such a celebration. Everyone participated. Cousins and uncles and relatives stretching way back. They were all involved in the event. But the feeling didn't last; by the time he'd left the booth in the clinic and gone back to Angela, he'd forgotten his regret. The baby had come early; there'd been a late-night dash to the clinic with Angela, and the little girl was born within two hours. He'd held her in his arms and loved her instantly. As he loved her mother.

He'd missed the birth of his son; he wept at the thought of that lonely birth in England without a father to comfort and rejoice with her.

And she smiled with the baby in her arms and told him not to be so silly. She loved him more for those tears of emotion than for the pride and happiness that followed on. 'You said we'd have a girl,' she reminded him. 'In that crazy old bed in the hotel at Palermo.'

In the end the nurse insisted he went home and let them sleep in peace. Three days later Angela and the baby were driven back to the villa. He'd filled the house with flowers; in spite of Angela's protests he'd engaged a nurse to look after the child so she wouldn't be tired.

She telephoned Charlie at school. Steven had already given him the news as soon as his sister was born.

'I wish I could get over,' Charlie said. 'I'd love to see you, Mum. But it's right in the middle of the exams. They'd have a fit if I suggested it. But I wish I could. You sure you're okay? Dad said it was very easy.'

'I'm fine darling,' she told him. 'And don't you think of anything but passing and getting the best marks. You'll love the baby, she's sweet. Looks a bit like a little monkey; Steven goes mad when I say that! No, she's quite fair. She may be dark later, But I don't think so. Yes, I will. You too.'

At the other end Charlie rang off. Steven had been so excited. He'd said, 'Charlie, you've got a little sister –' and run on about how long she took to be born and how much she weighed.

It was great news; he only wished he could be there to see her and share in it all. He met his housemaster on the way back from taking the call. He had only been at the school for two terms; he was young and Charlie liked him. He had a nice wife who asked some of the sixth formers round for tea or supper.

'I've got a sister,' Charlie greeted him, 'born this morning!'

'Congratulations.' The housemaster seemed very pleased. 'What splendid news. Your parents must be delighted.'

'Yes, they are,' Charlie said happily. 'My stepfather's over the moon.'

'I thought he was your father,' the young man said. 'You're so much alike. So it's a half-sister then? Jolly good! Come round this evening and we'll have a drink to celebrate.'

'Thank you sir, I'd love to.'

There was no class that period. Charlie went back to his room to study. He was sitting his first exam at nine o'clock the next morning. A half-sister. He hadn't thought of it like that. He hadn't thought about Steven as a stepfather either. Not for a long time.

The baby was christened Anna Joy after her grand-mothers. They delayed the ceremony until Charlie came home after the exams were over. To Angela's surprise, Steven refused to have Ralph Maxton as a godfather. Two of their French acquaintances stood for the child. They weren't even close friends. But they were Catholics. Steven wanted his daughter baptized, and Angela didn't object. To her, all religions were much the same. She preferred the less flamboyant Anglican

354

services but that was only because she had been brought up with them. It was a happy day, and they gave a party at the villa afterwards. She went round the guests carrying her little daughter in her arms. Toasts were drunk and a handsome cake cut to applause from the guests.

Maxton had been very generous. Too generous, she felt, since he must have hoped to be a godfather. His gift stood on the table with all the other presents, the mounds of sugared almonds exquisitely tied in blue and silver ribbon, the boxes of baby clothes and the silver dishes and spoons given by the French couple they had invited instead of Maxton. He had given a silver rattle with a coral handle, festooned with little silver bells. Angela thanked him; the tiny child was wrapped in lace and silk and fast asleep in her arms.

'What a lovely present,' she said. 'It looks very old.'

'It is quite old,' he said. 'I got a chum in England to get it for me.' The chum was his younger brother, and the rattle was a Maxton heirloom. It had been passed on by tradition to Ralph at his own christening.

'I'm glad you like it,' he said to her. 'I hope she'll play with it one day.' He touched the tiny closed fist with the tip of his finger. 'She's a pretty little thing. Very like you.'

'Darling.' Steven was beside her. 'Why don't we give her to the nurse and let you mix around and have some fun?'

'I am having fun,' Angela answered. 'Isn't Ralph's present beautiful? What date is it?'

He said, 'About seventeen twenty; there's the nurse hovering over there – shall I call her for you?'

'Thanks,' Steven said. He was pleasant, but there was a note of firm dismissal in the word.

Maxton gave his crooked smile. 'At your service – as always,' and moved rapidly away through the crowd.

'You should have thanked him for the lovely rattle,' Angela said.

'I thought I did,' Steven answered. 'Here, give her to me for a minute. *Bellissima*,' he murmured to his tiny daughter, and kissed her gently on the downy head. 'Here, go to Natalie,' He handed her over to the nurse and took Angela by the arm. 'Stop looking reproachful at me,' he said quietly. 'You make too much of a fuss of him. He might misunderstand it. And it annoys Charlie. It's even starting to annoy me.'

'Then you're both being very silly,' she said.

'Maybe, but we love you too much to share you,' he whispered.

She was angry and he didn't want the day to be spoiled for her. He regretted saying that about Maxton. He shouldn't have brought Charlie into it. For all her gentleness Angela could be surprisingly firm with their son. Much firmer than he was, he thought. But then why not spoil him? He was a son to be proud of – the way he looked, the way he handled himself. And he was sure to have good results in his exams. He was talking about university.

That was something, Steven exulted. Oxford, or Cambridge. They were envied even in the States. The best there was. He talked about the prospect with enthusiasm, refusing to listen when Angela suggested that perhaps Charlie wasn't exceptional. There were other universities, prestigious enough for most young men.

'Not for my boy,' was all he said, and that was that.

'What a charming party – what a beautiful baby –' The compliments flowed like the champagne.

So different, this time, Angela thought, so different from that other christening in the village church at home. Her parents there, the few friends gathered at the house for tea. And dear Jim Hulbert, the good man they hoped would marry her one day. He'd since married a widow. She could hardly remember what he looked like.

'Are you happy?' Steven asked her. 'It's been such a good day, hasn't it? She never even cried when the priest baptized her.'

'I'm very happy,' Angela answered. 'I just wish my mother and father had been here with us.'

'I was thinking the same thing,' he said. 'How my parents would love to see her. My mother was crazy about my brother's kids. But I'll send pictures.'

Later when everybody had gone, and the debris of the party was cleared away, they walked through the garden together.

'I've been thinking about Charlie,' he said.

'What about him? Not Oxford and Cambridge again? Next thing you'll be expecting him to get a scholarship.' She smiled, teasing him.

'I was wondering when we were going to tell him the truth,' he said. 'Don't you think it's time? I heard him say to someone, "She's my half-sister." I didn't like it, Angela. He should know he has a real family.'

'Oh darling, I'm sure he didn't mean anything by that. Of course he's got a real family! He adores you, he's thrilled with Anna Joy, and he seems to be pretty fond of me too. Don't let a slip of the tongue upset you.'

He looked down at her. 'You don't want me to tell him, do you?'

'No,' she admitted. 'Not quite yet.'

'Not quite ever, isn't that it? What are you scared of, Angela?'

'I don't know,' she admitted. 'He's a Falconi; there's not much of me in him that I can see. I don't know what it might do to him if he starts probing. Won't you wait at least till he's left school and set on some career? University – that's what you want for him, isn't it?'

They had reached the villa. Angela sat down on the terrace.

'Steven darling, give it a little more time. Please? And when it is time, I'd like to be the one to do it. I want to tell him about us; how we met, how much we loved each other. I don't want anything to seem cheap or sordid to him. I want him to know how it really was between us. The only different thing about the father I told him of when he was a little boy, is that he didn't get killed after all. That way it'll be easier for him. Sit down with me.'

'You're right,' he said at last. 'We'll do it your way.'

The barman at the Hôtel de Paris couldn't believe it. The manager couldn't believe it either. Madame Duvalier was going to the gala at the Casino de Poliakof. Going out for the first time in all these years. He was so concerned he went to see her.

'Madame,' he said gently, 'do you think it's wise? It's a big occasion, crowds of people – won't it be too much for you?'

'Don't worry,' she said. 'I'll hide my face. Oh, don't be embarrassed – I know that's not what you meant. You're a good friend. You've taken good care of me. I shall need a car and a driver.'

'That'll be arranged. I was thinking, wouldn't you like someone to escort you? Someone to look after you for the evening?'

She laughed. 'You're not suggesting some boy? I pick my own men. Maybe I wouldn't be like this if I hadn't.'

He didn't know what she meant by that. She could be very eccentric at times. He ignored the reference to the hotel's list of gigolos. 'One of the staff would be glad to go with you,' he said.

'No thank you. I can order my own drinks and take myself home when I get bored. It's good of you to think of it. It should be an interesting evening. Won't you join me in a glass of champagne?'

He excused himself. He thought she was insane to contemplate such an excursion after ten years of seclusion. Cover her face. How?

When he had gone Pauline Duvalier picked up her glass. He was a good friend; not just because she was a permanent source of income. The hotel didn't need her that much. He was kind, protective. She appreciated that. He'd be surprised how much, when she died and he learned what she had left him and the staff who looked after her.

Steven Lawrence. She said the name aloud. It didn't sound very Italian. But then Eugene said he certainly had Latin blood. He was very tall and very dark; he could have been French from the South, or Monégasque by the look of him. Nobody knew much about him, except that he had an English wife, and a son. He wouldn't allow personal publicity or photographs to be taken. He'd employed Ralph Maxton when he was almost in the gutter after being dismissed and couldn't get another job along the coast. He seemed very rich, judging by the way he'd restored the old Poliakof Palace.

Eugene had been able to find out so much because his sister's niece worked at the casino as a waitress. Pauline knew the web of relationships that stretched throughout the families along that coastline. His description could be made to tally. Or could it prove false and misleading? Steven Falconi the gangster was dead. The newspapers said so. His widow had just remarried when the massacre began. Minutes after the ceremony, the report said. On the church steps.

There was no Falconi at the Poliakof; Eugene was definite. Maxton worked for Steven Lawrence. But she had heard them, those two in the bar, sniggering together: 'Falconi . . . don't you like him anymore? Gangsters don't grow on one . . .' She finished the champagne. She touched her face with her fingertips.

'I'm going,' she said aloud. She often talked to herself. 'I'm going and I shall know if it's the same one. Then I can ask him the question. I'll show him this and I'll say: "Tell me, was this done because of you?"'

She dressed for dinner as usual; she put on her fine rings and a ruby necklace. When the floor waiter arrived with the trolley, he couldn't believe what he saw. She was sitting on the sofa with a black veil over her head.

'Come in,' she called out to him. 'Come in. Set it up over there, please. Don't you think this suits me?'

He went out followed by her low, self-mocking

laughter. He confided to a fellow waiter that she had given him the fright of his life.

The date chosen for the gala was 28 May. It had been widely publicized, and to Steven's gratification there was a scramble for invitations. Maxton had carefully leaked the rumour about the Shah and the Empress Farah, and nobody discouraged it. They'd have to make do with Princess Ashraff. She was glamorous enough. They'd been open for business since April, and the casino was well attended, with some serious gamblers coming there regularly. The new cloakrooms were larger, more luxurious. Preparations went ahead for the gala and there was an air of excitement among the staff as the evening came near. Steven worked as long and as hard as anyone, supervising the smallest detail, poring over the menus, working out the firework displays and the timing. Flowers were Angela's province, and he told her to be as lavish as possible.

'This is going to make or break,' he insisted. 'We can't afford to do this every year, so we've got to make a big splash that will be remembered.'

Ralph Maxton called the staff together. The croupiers and dealers gathered in the Salon Privé for a final briefing. Everything was ready; the roulette wheels were polished, the green baize tables brushed to perfection. 'Gentlemen, tomorrow's the big night. We've got to make it a bigger success than our opening. I don't have to remind you that all our jobs depend upon it. You've had the list of names; you know who should get the star treatment, and one or two that shouldn't.'

A few people laughed. There were those who tried to pay with cheques that weren't guaranteed to be met. The dealers knew them and how to cope. They'd find it very difficult to get into the play.

Someone called out, 'What about the Save the Soul Rule? Do we still apply that?'

Maxton shrugged. 'Those are the orders. The boss

says no one's to be allowed to play beyond the limit.' He made a joke of it. 'The only thing we want hanging from the trees round here is fairy lights!'

They didn't understand this philanthropy. Suckers were suckers; the more compulsive, the better for the casino and the profits they all shared. But when Steven made a rule, nobody broke it and kept their job. They dispersed and Maxton went to his office to take a breather. He needed one. They'd all been flat out for days.

Angela was coming; he still dined there once a week, and she went out of her way to be friendly with him. She was trying to make up for Steven's reserve. It was even harder for Ralph not to respond. But that way lay dismissal. He knew Steven Falconi. He'd stopped thinking of him as Lawrence since that morning at Val d'Isère when he read about the Mafia killings at the New York wedding. He called him by the name that denoted what he really was. A hood, a fraud.

He couldn't chance being fired. He had to keep his feelings tied up tight, not to look at her too often, not to talk more to her than to Steven or anyone else who happened to join them. If he lost the job he'd lose the opportunity. And that would come. He knew it.

'Remember our first gala, when we opened?' Steven asked. 'This has something more – no rough edges this time!'

'There weren't any then,' Angela said. 'You're a perfectionist, that's the trouble. It looks marvellous and you're right, darling – there's a very special atmosphere tonight. It'll be a huge success.'

'It had better be,' he muttered, 'I've spent a fortune on the firework display alone. Did I tell you how beautiful you look?'

'You said the same last time,' she reminded him.

'You chose the dress to match the necklace,' he noted. 'Blue always looks good on you. Wait a minute, sweetheart. I just want to check something.'

361

Angela could see her reflection in the big gilt-framed mirror that hung in the entrance hall. He'd given her a sapphire and diamond necklace after Anna Joy's birth. It glittered as she turned. Too expensive, too generous, when he admitted he had stretched his resources for the gala. She had stopped him giving her jewellery, because she felt uncomfortable wearing it. This time he hadn't listened. He wanted to deck her out in a visible sign of his gratitude and love. She would sooner have had a single string of pearls. She had kept her slim figure; the dark-blue dress fitted closely and she looked very well in it. In spite of her dislike of show, the gleam and flash of the jewels round her neck was exciting. It was going to be a very special evening. A huge success.

Then he was hurrying towards her, and they were side by side as the first guests arrived, waiting to greet them. Photographers began snapping, flash bulbs popped. He wasn't hiding anymore. Steven Falconi was truly dead and gone. Steven Lawrence was in his place, alive and free of danger. It was nearly midnight when the Iranian Princess arrived. By that time the reception was long over; they came to the entrance and on to the steps to meet her.

Steven conducted her upstairs for a private supper party before the fireworks began. After that, she could play a little baccarat if she wished. And she did wish. After forty minutes of watching the multicoloured stars and rockets blaze into the sky, the set piece – the Iranian royal coat of arms – finally sputtered and died.

The Princess hurried to the Salon Privé with her escorts. When she was settled at the table, with cigarettes in case she wished to smoke, and a waiter ready with champagne in case she wished to drink, Steven was able to go up to his office with Angela and watch the TV screens. And Maxton decided he could slip away and join the friendly American, O'Halloran, for a drink at the bar.

'How does this compare with Monte Carlo?'

Maxton didn't see why he need be tactful. 'It doesn't.

362

It's well done, very spectacular, but it's all a bit new. The old Queen invented the gala night; here we're looking for gimmicks.'

'Who's the Queen? I thought Grace Kelly was a princess,' Mike said. He really disliked Maxton's laugh.

'Oh, how confusing for you – that's the name we all call the casino at Monte Carlo. The Queen. The Queen of the Coast. You better go up and see for yourself.'

'How come you're advertising the opposition?' O'Halloran finished his scotch. 'Let me buy you another, Mr Maxton. Waiter?'

Maxton accepted. He was adept at not drinking if he didn't want a drink. The trick was not to annoy a client by refusing.

'I'm only suggesting you take a look,' he said. 'I've got a soft spot for the place. I worked there for ten years.'

'Were you a manager there too?' Mike said. He sounded really interested. So many of the people Maxton entertained only talked about themselves. He mustn't keep him talking too long. He'd have to suggest a down without taking more than a sip. What the hell. O'Halloran wasn't a rich fish to hook. He'd got the invitation through the Carlton Hotel at Cannes. He'd booked in there specially to come to the new casino.

'I managed the PR,' Ralph said. 'The celebrities who got drunk, welshed on their bets, touched up ladies at the baccarat table. I told the press the right things about the wrong people, and I made sure nobody made any trouble. It was a fascinating job. Didn't do much for one's opinion of the human race, though.'

'I guess not,' O'Halloran agreed. 'So why did you leave? Or was that why?'

'I'm afraid not.' Maxton had his own brand of charm, and the self-deprecating smile was part of it. 'Nobody leaves a well-paid job in a paradise like Monaco just because they don't like people. I was offered something better here. Let's say I needed a challenge.'

'Starting up here from scratch must have taken a hell of

a lot of nerve. But your boss looks like he's got plenty. Quite impressive when you meet him. I only shook hands and got passed on, but all the same . . .' He left it open for Maxton.

'He's got plenty of nerve. He knows exactly what he wants and he goes out to get it. It helps to work for someone like that. You always know where you stand. You deliver the goods or you're out on your ear. Now, why don't I stop boring you, Mr O'Halloran. Let me take you over and see whether you can get back some of your ticket money. Do you play roulette?'

'I've always wanted to; my game is craps back home.'

'Then let me introduce you. It's very simple. You put your money down, and we win it off you!' He brayed with laughter, ushered Mike over to the roulette tables and presented him with a thousand francs of chips. 'No payment,' he insisted. 'On the house, Mr O'Halloran. Once you've lost that little lot, then you have to start writing cheques –'

O'Halloran grinned. 'Is this casino policy?'

'Not in this casino. Others, yes. In fishing terms it's called baiting the hook, but we don't do that here. These chips have absolutely no strings attached to them. I shan't encourage you to go on playing if you lose. That was only my little joke. We run a very straight ship. I am getting nautical, aren't I? It must be your whisky.'

'Must be,' Mike agreed. He had noticed Maxton avoided drinking it.

'There's a high moral tone you won't find in many casinos on the coast. Or anywhere else. Which has its funny side. Now, if you're a real beginner, why don't we start with a simple bet on *Rouge ou Noir*, and see how we get on?'

Angela had kicked off her shoes. It had been a very long evening and very few people had gone home. The rooms were full of gamblers and onlookers. Steven was watching the Iranian Princess playing at the top baccarat table.

364

He was concentrating, absorbed. Angela closed her eyes for a moment. It had been a triumph. Just that extra bit over their first effort. Crowned by the attendance of one of the biggest and richest gamblers in the world. Even Steven had to give Maxton credit for that particular coup.

She had drifted to sleep because she woke suddenly when there was a knock on the door. Steven switched off the screen.

'Come in?'

'Pardon, Monsieur Lawrence. There's a lady asking to see you.' It was François, one of the assistant managers. He saw Steven frown and said quickly, 'I couldn't see Monsieur Ralph anywhere and I was afraid she'd make a fuss. She's insisting. She's come up here with me, I couldn't stop her.' He lowered his voice.

Steven said, 'Did she give a name? What does she want?'

'I don't know. She just said she wanted to speak to you in private. Monsieur, she's wearing a veil so you can't see her face . . . I don't know how to get rid of her.' He glanced behind him at the closed door. 'She's been sitting in the bar all night. Alone.'

'All right.' Steven made up his mind. All casinos had their share of eccentrics. If she was veiled as François said, she might be connected with Princess Ashraff's visit. Gambling was forbidden to Moslems. The last thing he wanted was someone making a scene about that.

'Take her to Monsieur Ralph's office,' he said. 'I'll see her there. Tell Gerard to send up a woman from the cloakroom and one of his men from the door. Just in case she causes trouble. They can wait outside.'

'What is it?' Angela asked him.

'Just some nut, I expect. Don't worry, I won't be long.'

He opened the door of Maxton's office. A woman was sitting in one of the armchairs. François was quite right. She wore a veil that covered her face. A handsome diamond comb kept it in place.

'Good evening, Madame,' he said. 'You wanted to see me?'

She didn't speak; she sat there and stared at him from behind the tulle.

He came towards her. 'Madame. What can I do for you?'

It was a husky voice. 'Hello, Monsieur Falconi. It's been a very long time, but you've hardly changed at all.'

Steven said slowly, 'Who are you?'

She got up; she was not very tall.

'What do you want?' he said. Falconi. There was something, something familiar about that voice. Something from the past he had hoped to bury.

'I knew it was you,' she said. 'I saw you downstairs and I was sure. I knew you, even though we only spent one night together.'

He said, 'Take that thing off! I don't play games –'

'If you wish,' she said. 'but I don't think you'll recognize me.'

Slowly she lifted the tulle and looked up at him. He couldn't stop the shocked intake of breath.

'It isn't very pretty,' she remarked. 'I was a good-looking woman before it happened. I'm Pauline Duvalier. We slept together at the Hôtel de Paris. You were on your honeymoon at the time. Do you remember?'

'Yes. Yes,' Steven said. 'I remember. I remember you. I'm so sorry. Sit down, please.'

'Thank you. Do you have any champagne? I could do with a glass.'

'I'll get some,' he said. Pauline Duvalier. The night he'd slammed out of their suite leaving Clara alone. The elegant older woman who'd picked him up in the bar when he was getting drunk, trying to come to terms with himself and the nightmare of Clara's jealousy. They had gone up to her suite and he'd made love to her. For a few hours he'd forgotten his anger and despair. He remembered it all only too well.

Maxton kept a supply of drinks for hospitality. Steven opened a bottle of champagne. He poured a glass and gave it to her. Her hand trembled a little. She had lost an eye. She was a travesty. He sat beside her.

'What happened to you?'

She sipped the drink. 'A robbery,' she said. 'That's what they called it in the newspapers. But the police had a different idea. I never saw anyone. I was knocked out and beaten. Only my face, Monsieur Falconi. I think he took a gold watch and some trinkets. To make it look like theft. They even asked me if I'd had any dealings with the underworld. It happened exactly a week after I spent the night with you.'

'Oh Jesus,' he said slowly. 'Jesus.'

'It was because of that, wasn't it? Who could have done it, Monsieur Falconi? Who had me beaten almost to death?'

He covered his face with his hands. There was a long silence. Then he raised his head and looked at her. He reached out and took her hand and held it.

'I know who did it,' he said at last. 'God forgive me, I told her, and that's what she did.'

'Told who?' Pauline Duvalier asked. He was gripping her so hard it hurt.

'My wife, Clara. I told her I'd been with someone else. She'd been accusing me, driving me crazy. She must have found out who you were. Oh God, what can I say to you? What can I do?'

'Is she the woman whose husband was shot in New York at their wedding? It said she was your widow. Are you hiding from her, Monsieur Falconi?'

He said, 'Yes, Madame, I am. I have a wife and a family. You saw my wife with me tonight.'

'A blonde girl, very pretty,' Pauline Duvalier said. She held out the empty glass. 'I live on this,' she said. 'Do you know this is the first time I've left the Hôtel de Paris since I came out of hospital? I live there all the year round. Everyone knows me; they don't look at my face anymore. The surgeons did their best, but there wasn't much left for them to work on.'

Steven said, 'You were beautiful. I remember that well. Tell me, what can I do? Is there anything, anything at all I can do for you?'

She smiled; it was a painful sight. 'Nothing. You've been kind. I appreciate that. You have a manager here, I saw him. An Englishman?'

'Yes, Ralph Maxton. Do you know him?'

'By sight. He comes to the Hôtel de Paris; he has a woman he brings there. That's how I found you. He talked about you, Monsieur Falconi, and the woman said your name out loud. Perhaps you should speak to him about it?'

Steven said, 'Thank you. I will.'

'I must go now,' she said. She drew the tulle down over her face.

Steven helped her to her feet. 'I would like it very much if you'd come here again,' he said. 'As my special guest. I'd like you to meet my wife. We would look after you.'

'Thank you, but I don't think so. I'm happy enough. I just wanted to know why it happened, that's all.'

'I'll take you to your car,' he said.

People paused as they came down and through the entrance hall. The woman with the veil intrigued them. He waited with her till the car and driver came to the front steps.

'Goodnight, Monsieur Lawrence,' she said. She held out her hand and Steven brought it to his lips and kissed it.

'I want you to know one thing,' he said. 'If I'd found out, I'd have killed her.'

He closed the car door and stood on the steps watching till it had driven out of sight.

'Great you could spare the time to come,' Mike O'Halloran said.

'Nice of you to ask me,' Maxton answered.

O'Halloran clapped him on the back. 'Least I could do after the great time I had. And winning a few dollars too!'

His luck had certainly been in. He'd never touched roulette in his life but it hadn't taken him long to calculate the odds and by the end of the evening he'd come away twenty thousand francs in pocket. Maxton had accepted the invitation to drinks at the Carlton. He looked edgy, Mike decided. Nothing ruffled the exterior, but there was tension underneath. The laugh was an ugly cawing sound with nothing humorous about it.

'Well, you sure had a big success the other night! The newspapers here ran a lot of publicity about that Persian princess what'ser name –'

'Ashraff,' Ralph said. They were drinking bourbon. Champagne would have been sour in his stomach that evening. The American was right. The gala was a smash success.

His reward had been the summons to Steven's office and the bald statement that, after the summer, he wouldn't be working there anymore. He kept going over the conversation in his mind, absently saying inconsequential things while O'Halloran talked on about himself. 'I'm not firing you,' – Steven's words went round and round – 'because you've done good work. I'm telling you to look some place else. And I'll give you a reference that'll make it easy. But you're through here.'

He had been stood back on his heels, almost literally, by the shock. After a pause he'd said, 'Is there a reason, or aren't I to know?'

Steven looked at him. 'When I hired you I specified one thing. That you kept your mouth shut. You've opened it wide, and that's why you're going.' He'd turned away with a gesture of contempt.

'That's a pretty sweeping accusation,' Maxton said. 'I think you owe me more than that.'

'You're owed nothing. You were on the skids when I

369

employed you. I'm calling it quits.' Steven hadn't turned round.

Maxton had walked out of the office.

He had only just remembered he was meeting the American that evening. Nobody knew. He'd gone back to his job and carried on as if nothing had happened. He hadn't seen Falconi again. Work there for the next few months . . .

O'Halloran leaned forward and tapped him on the knee. He'd been so lost in his own predicament that he jumped.

'What's wrong? What's eating you? Come on – maybe I can help?'

'I've lost my job.' Maxton said it before he could stop and consider. What did it matter if this outsider knew? He was a fly-by-night friend, gone in a few days. He had to tell someone.

O'Halloran looked surprised. He was surprised. 'Jesus,' he said. 'I guess you weren't expecting it. Any reason? If you don't mind me asking –'

'No reason I know of; certainly not the one I was given.' There were two red spots on his cheeks, like dabs of paint. He was naturally pale and sallow; it made him look ill.

'I'm sorry,' O'Halloran said. 'It sounds like you've been given a real bum deal.'

'Oh, I think that's fair comment,' Maxton said. 'You were rather impressed by my boss, weren't you? But you only shook hands, of course.'

'I'm not so impressed now,' was the answer. 'What kind of a shit is he, to treat you like that?'

'A very special kind,' Maxton said slowly, 'I built that place up singlehanded. He knew nothing about running a casino. He didn't know anyone on the coast, who to employ, how to get the press interested – nothing! All he had was money. I did the donkey work, Mike. And now he thinks he's got it in the bag, he kicks me out. With a good reference, of course.' His eyes were bright with rage.

O'Halloran watched him closely. He could be nasty, he decided. Very nasty, if you crossed him. He decided to press a little further. 'Listen, Ralph – don't take this wrong . . . I made a bit of money thanks to you . . . If you're needing anything, I'd be only too happy . . .'

'Thanks,' Maxton said.

He wasn't grateful, Mike realized that. There wasn't room for anything like gratitude, he was brimming over with rage.

'I don't need money; he always paid well.'

Nothing substantial stacked away then, O'Halloran decided. He made sure. 'You'll get another job?'

'Oh yes, I'll have to. I have expensive tastes. I don't have the piggy-bank mentality. I'll go to another place. I could try Italy . . .'

Mike didn't go any further. He let a silence grow between them. Money wasn't an immediate problem. Immediate meaning a few months till he got another job. Finally, he said. 'What a bastard. Listen, why don't we have some dinner? I'm doing nothing tonight. You know, I just might be able to think of something for you. I've got a few contacts. Unless you've got some girl waiting –'

Maxton shook his head. 'My girl's busy tonight,' he said. My whore is being kicked around by her rich boyfriend. And the woman I love is sitting down to dinner with him . . . 'I'm free,' he said. 'And just because I've been so boring, dinner's on me.'

Clara sounded impatient. 'What the hell have you been doing? It's a week since you called!'

'If you want me to foul it up, then I'll rush –' Mike said. He was bolder over the telephone than face to face. 'I've made contact with this guy Maxton, and I think luck's running our way.'

'Why? What's changed?'

'He's just been fired and he's sore as hell about it. I spent this evening telling him what a crap deal he's been handed.'

371

'Will he do it?' Clara demanded. 'Where's your goddamned instinct you gabbed on about? I'm not interested in grievances, I want someone who'll take on the contract!' The week had made her edgy. She was sleeping badly, mentally abusing O'Halloran for wasting time, for not getting any action.

'You've got someone,' she heard him say. 'Wait, before you start bawling me out. Just get ready with the half million dollars.'

She swore in Italian down the telephone. 'Maxton? You don't even know –'

'Not Maxton,' he interrupted. 'Me, Clara. I've got it all figured out. Just trust me.' He hung up.

He waited for the phone to ring back. It didn't. She wouldn't like that. He could imagine that bloodthirsty temper erupting, but he wasn't to be shot at. He grinned to himself. She'd rage at him, but there wasn't much else she could do. No one else she could trust to commit three cold-blooded murders for her. She'd taken him on and they'd ended up as partners.

And she'd pay. He sat back, sipping scotch, thinking how he could jack in the agency, take his wife and his kids and buy a place in Mexico. Live in comfort for the rest of their lives. They'd taken a cheap holiday down there some years ago and loved the place. The sun, the easygoing tempo. It was cheap too. They could live it up, have anything they wanted. He could work when he felt like it. Half a million dollars.

He'd thought about it carefully, testing his nerve. He'd shot men, and on two occasions women, during his time in the police. He knew what it felt like to pull a trigger, see them arch up on themselves and then fall. He'd smelt blood and the death stink of human excrement. This could be a lot easier, less close quarters. He was a very good shot. He'd taken a sight on Falconi that night at the gala. A matter of psychology, they were taught during their training. You look at the target without seeing them. They could be cardboard cut-outs. Dummies set up in the range. You dehumanize them and then it's easy. Because you've dehumanized yourself. Falconi wouldn't keep him awake at night. The blonde wife was a target, not a breathing woman. He couldn't have described her face, but the part of him that needed to identify her could have picked her out of any crowd. He could smell the ones who'd kill, because he recognized them. It was a brotherhood that went deeper than any uniform or any oath sworn to uphold the law. Sometimes the law was a good excuse. Half a million dollars.

Maxton had gone home. He'd felt worse after Mike had finished being sympathetic. And Mike had made a judgement. He'd have knocked off Steven Falconi for nothing. That was the irony of it all.

Steven was in his office. He spent every night at the casino, greeting guests, walking round watching the service, the play. He had seen Maxton briefly, and had spoken equally briefly about something concerned with the casino. He wasn't expecting him to come to the office late at night.

'Can I see you for a moment?'

'Sure. Come on in. Anything wrong downstairs?'

'Nothing. You're making a lot of money as usual.'

Steven didn't rise. He knew that mocking tone, and the supercilious twist of the thin mouth. 'So what brings you up here?' he asked.

Maxton had a habit of standing with both hands in his pockets. He said, 'I've been thinking about our conversation the other day. I don't want to hang on here till the end of the summer. Wouldn't it save a lot of trouble if I just resigned?'

Steven hesitated. It sounded like a dignified way out for them both. No explanations to Angela. That was something he'd dreaded. And put off. The act of a gentleman. He didn't know why he thought of it like that. He saw the cold and bitter hatred lurking in Ralph

Maxton's pale eyes. He said, 'Who are you letting off the hook, Ralph? Me or yourself?'

'Me,' was the answer. 'One should never remind someone of what they've said in anger. Some pompous ass said that to me one day. I thought it was rubbish at the time. You told me you didn't owe me anything. Not even a proper explanation for throwing me out. So don't fool yourself I'm thinking of you. It suits me to go early. Then I don't owe you anything either. And it makes it easier to say goodbye to your wife. Unless you've told her what you wouldn't tell me. Why I'm being fired?'

Steven had been tempted to face him with what Pauline Duvalier had overheard. Tempted, and then rejected the idea immediately. He couldn't involve her. He couldn't risk Maxton seeking her out. She'd suffered too much already.

He said, 'I told you all I'm going to tell you. I trusted you, I treated you like one of my own family. When I don't trust a man, he doesn't work for me. Okay, you want to leave early, you leave. Anything else?'

'No,' Maxton said evenly. He turned. It was a nonchalant walk, hands thrust into his pockets, insolence in every line of the tall, angular body.

He opened the door and looked back. 'You know, Steven, you remind me of those gentlemen in Las Vegas who let my poor friend drown himself for a couple of thousand dollars. What a bloody fool I was to think you were any different.' He closed the door quietly behind him.

He was lying on his bed, his shoes kicked off, his shirtsleeves rolled up. He'd made the gesture, salvaged something of his self-respect. Falconi had winced at that parting shot. It helped, but very little. He'd forced himself to be practical, reminding himself of those hungry days after he'd left Monte Carlo. The dwindling money, the borrowing, the move to cheaper hotels that ended in a single room in a mean boarding house. He got out his bank statements and calculated. He had enough to keep him comfortably on the coast for at least six months while he looked for a job. Thanks to a large salary and a generous bonus which he knew came out of Falconi's own pocket, since the casino hadn't broken even.

But six months could pass very quickly; inertia was always at his elbow, urging him to wait in times of trouble for something to turn up. He wasn't going to risk it again. Italy, he'd said to Mike O'Halloran. There were rich resorts on the Italian Riviera, fine casinos. But Italy meant losing touch with Angela. Out of sight, out of mind. He'd been so sure that he would be in place, ready to step forward when the inevitable happened, when there was a second crisis between her and Falconi. A repeat of the near miss at Christmas. But the cards had run against him. Falconi had found an opportunity to get rid of him. In Maxton's view he'd been waiting for an excuse ever since that little bastard Charlie had put in a bad word after Hugh Drummond died. He owed him one for that. He didn't even think of him as Angela's son. To Maxton he was an enemy, a clone of his father.

He was sunk in bitter thoughts when his telephone rang. It was the ubiquitous American. The friendly American. He just stopped himself from cutting off with a curt excuse.

'Come on over, Ralph,' he heard O'Halloran say. 'I think I've got a proposition for you. Can you make it right away?'

He didn't sound so friendly, so hail fellow well met this time. He sounded cool and businesslike. Maxton considered for a moment. Why not? What had he got to lose but an evening spent alone in fruitless longing for someone who was even further out of reach?

He said, 'No harm in having a drink and a chat. I'll be along in half an hour.' He tried to probe in case it was a wasted journey. 'What kind of proposition is it?'

O'Halloran answered, 'See you in half an hour,' and hung up.

*

In spite of the air conditioning the room was hot and smoky. As soon as he opened the door and saw O' Halloran sitting there with his feet on the coffee table, everything looked different to Maxton. The American was different too. No tie, crumpled shirt, cigarette butts and a half-empty bottle of scotch, a glass on the floor beside him. At first he thought: He's drunk, and kicked himself for bothering to come. But he wasn't. He had simply shed a skin.

'Come on in, pal, take a glass and help yourself. Found another job yet?'

'No.' Maxton was cautious. He didn't take a drink. 'I haven't looked. It's early days, I'm not rushing anything.'

'You see much of that bastard, Falconi?' It was delivered straight, like a blow.

Maxton prided himself on taking the unexpected in his stride. He managed very well, considering. 'Sorry,' he said, 'who did you say?'

Mike shook his head at him. He had the shrewdest eyes and a mouth that could set like a trap. Not the same man at all: friendly, likable in small doses. He'd put on a very convincing act, Mr Mike O'Halloran.

'Cut the crap, Ralph,' O'Halloran said. 'I know who he is, the same as you. As a matter of fact, that's why I'm here. You're not the only one he's screwed up. And you're not the only one who hates his guts. It's my guess you've got the balls to do something about it. How would you like to earn yourself a half a million dollars?'

'I'm sorry I was asleep when you got home,' Angela said. 'How did the evening go?'

They were taking breakfast out on the terrace. Charlie was going back next morning to finish the term at school. They were waiting for him to join them.

'It was great,' Steven told her. 'Full house, some big spenders. We're home, sweetheart, home and dry! As your father used to say –'

376

'He did, didn't he – it sounds so funny when you pick up his expressions. I often think how kind you were to him. He was really fond of you.'

'I liked him a lot,' Steven said gently. 'Is Anna coming down?'

'It's too early.' Angela smiled at him. 'The doting father will have to wait till she's had her bath and is ready to go out in the pram. I'd better go and call Charlie; he's overslept again. Won't we miss him when he goes?'

'We will,' he agreed. 'But he's back with us for good in a few weeks. I'll have to talk with him about his future. Angela – before you go –'

'Yes?' She was on her feet, ready to run up and wake their son.

Steven said, 'Ralph's given notice. He's leaving.'

She came and sat down again. 'Oh no – why? When did this happen?'

He didn't lie to her. 'I've known he was going for a while. He told me last night he didn't want to see the season out.'

'But didn't you try and persuade him?' she asked.

He hesitated for a moment. Then he looked up at her. 'No, I didn't. I think it's best he goes.'

'Steven, its not because of all that nonsense Charlie started? Don't tell me you really took any notice –' She looked so distressed.

He said quickly, 'No, darling. Maybe he was a bit soft on you – so what? It was nothing like that, I promise. He'd started talking. Using the name Falconi.' He heard her draw a breath.

'Oh no – he didn't –'

'Somebody tipped me off. I guess, for some reason he'd gone sour on me. He's got a woman he shacks up with; he even told her my real name. So you see, it's better this way.'

'Yes,' Angela said firmly, 'it is. Just think what might have happened a few months ago if the wrong sort of person was listening, if the newspapers got to hear of it –'

'Right,' Steven said. 'I'll give François a trial; he knows the running side of the business. I'll find myself someone else to do the PR by the end of the year. We've had so much coverage we don't need anyone for a while.'

'I expect he'll come and say goodbye,' Angela said. 'I'm so sorry it had to end badly. There was something pathetic about him; I always felt it.'

'Who's pathetic, Mum?' Charlie stood there, smiling and looking cheerful. A good-looking young man, brimming with confidence in himself and his world.

'I was talking about Ralph,' she said. 'He's leaving.'

'I know. Dad told me last night.'

Steven explained, 'Charlie was up when I got home. We had a drink together and I told him.'

'He's not pathetic, Mum. He just put that on to get round you. I'm starving – any coffee left?' Charlie sat down and started eating breakfast.

'I'll go see how Anna's getting on.' Steven got up. 'Darling, why don't you drive down and I'll take you out to lunch today?'

She smiled up at him. 'I'd love to – where shall we go?'

'Leave it to me.' He bent and kissed her. 'I'll surprise you.'

Angela looked at her son. She said, 'Why do you hate Ralph?'

Charlie set down his cup of coffee. 'Because he hates my father,' he said calmly. 'That's why. I didn't like him smarming round you either, playing up to poor old Grandpa – it was all part of the process. But it was the way he used to look at Dad. He didn't think I noticed. I didn't like him, or trust him. I'm glad he's going. I said so last night. Don't be too sorry for him, Mum. He's a nasty piece of work. Can I have another croissant?'

'I didn't realize you were so implacable,' his mother said. 'You're very young still, Charlie. Don't judge too harshly.'

She got up and left him. He finished his breakfast. She was too soft-hearted for her own good. If you have an

378

enemy, why treat them like a friend? It didn't make sense. He went off to pick up a friend and spend the morning playing tennis.

A half a million dollars. Maxton didn't try to sleep that night. He took his car and drove along the coast road, all the way past Juan Les Pins, past the casino at Antibes where his great-uncle had dallied in the palmy days before the Russian Revolution; on through Nice itself, still pulsing with life in the restaurants and bars. He drove through Beaulieu and the little fishing village of Ville-franche and up on to the Moyenne Corniche above Monte Carlo. When he stopped the car there was a magical view of Monaco itself, the yachts in the harbour lit up at night, the glitter of the pleasure palaces of the rich, greatest of all the casino complex in all its extravagant glory. The sea was like black satin, streaked by moonlight. A light breeze fanned his face as he stood by the side of the car, looking at the mirage which had been his life. A half a million. Five hundred thousand dollars. For the life of Steven Falconi.

He lit a cigarette. He'd tried to take it as a joke at first. But the American wasn't amused. He'd gone on talking, overriding Maxton when he protested. There'd been an option, of course. All he had to do was turn around and walk out. He didn't have to listen to the proposition when it came down to murder. He didn't have to pour himself a drink and stay. But he had. And O'Halloran had known he would. He could see that. He could see that the man had judged him and come up with an answer he wouldn't have thought possible. He was prepared to listen.

He remembered saying it. 'Why so much money? It's a fortune. You could hire someone in Marseilles for a few thousand francs who'd do it.'

And then O'Halloran had known he was talking business. No criminal connection. Nothing that could lead back to his client. A clean killing, the pay-off and a ticket on the next plane leaving Nice. The gangsters in Marseilles, the Mafia in Nice would be the obvious suspects in any crime connected with gambling. That's why he'd been picked. And then the next questions, drawing him further in.

'Who's paying for this?'

'A client,' O'Halloran had said, 'who is none of your business. You want time to think about it?'

Maxton had tested him. Or perhaps himself. 'How do you know I won't tell the police?'

The American had grinned. It was a sneer he didn't try to hide. 'You won't. You won't even think about it, you've made your mind up already, pal. I'll call you at home tomorrow. Don't try contacting me, I'm checking out right now.'

Maxton had one last try. 'If I say no?'

'No sweat,' O'Halloran said. 'Someone else'll do the job and collect the dough.' He'd got up and opened the door for Maxton to go.

A fortune. Enough money to start all over again. To change his way of life. A house in England, a stable future. Angela would need him. She would turn to him, as she had done before. He was in the best of all positions. The faithful friend, ready to comfort and protect after a tragedy. All he had to do was nerve himself to just one desperate act, and he would scoop the pool. He would be truly happy. Conscience wouldn't be a problem. He had never had one. He prided himself on regretting nothing except when it turned out badly for himself. If he did what was needed, it wouldn't haunt him. He didn't suffer guilt. He'd break the bank and walk away for the only time in his life, and without a backward glance. He threw the cigarette over the side of the road, into the abyss. He got back and started the engine and drove quite carefully back down the steep road to the safety of the coast.

He wasn't tempting fate at this stage by careless driving.

*

380

Steven had found a charming little restaurant in the hills above Mougin. It was an old farmhouse, imaginatively converted, with tables set out on a terrace with a commanding view of the valley. The food was simple but excellent; it was remote enough not to attract tourists. He was in a happy mood, holding her hand as they drove up through the lovely countryside. They sat shaded by olive trees, and ordered lunch. He looked at her and his heart was full of contentment.

Life had been good to him, he thought. His wife, his son and his little daughter. The child was growing visibly, smiling, developing into a person in her own right. He had everything he could desire, and he owed it all to Angela.

'You know something,' he said suddenly. 'You're as good as you're pretty, And I mean good.'

She was embarrassed. 'Don't be silly, darling. I'm not good at all.'

'I think so,' he said. 'You've made sense of so many things for me. You've brought up a fine son too. I was just thinking about it; I've never heard you do or say a rotten thing to anyone. I wonder what I've done to deserve you?'

'I wonder.' She made light of it. 'You're in a funny mood today.'

'Happy,' he corrected. 'It's all come right for us, hasn't it?'

'It certainly has.'

'Maybe I shouldn't say that. In Sicily you don't boast about good fortune. It makes the gods jealous.'

'We're not in Sicily,' she reminded him gently. 'So we don't have to worry.'

He stroked her arm, catching her fingers, playing with the wedding ring. The same ring he'd been given by a frightened jeweller in Palermo all those years ago. 'You're right,' he said. 'We don't. Here comes our lunch. Maybe we might slip home for an hour or so afterwards?'

'Why not? The afternoons were our best times.'

*

The villa was very quiet; it was the siesta hour. Charlie had gone off with his friends for the day. Janine and her mother were resting, like the nurse and baby Anna. It was the hottest part of the day, even in the cool hills. The sun throbbed in the brazen sky. The air was still and heavy with heat.

As they walked through the gardens he said to her, 'Remember the first time? When I took you into the hills? It was hot like this.'

'You talked about the gods,' she reminded him. 'I poured some wine on the ground.'

'And we made love out there. Why don't we just walk and find a place . . .'

There was shade beneath the olive trees, the earth was cushioned in soft grass.

Afterwards it was Steven who put it into words. 'It wasn't the same, my darling – it was something new – different to any other time. Or any place.'

She reached out and kissed him. 'When will I ever get tired of making love to you? It's always different. It's always the best –'

They swam naked in the warm water of the pool, and dried each other lazily in the hot sun. He liked to look after her, to touch the firm breasts and feel the texture of her skin. He told her how beautiful she was and how she made him feel. She had learned a little Italian and now when he spoke in his native language she understood more than the music and rhythm of the words. The time passed, the siesta was over. The household would soon come back to life. They covered each other, tied on their robes and walked back into the villa. He caught her from behind and lifted her against him.

'Upstairs,' he whispered. At that moment the telephone began to shrill. He let her go.

'Nemesis,' she laughed and went to answer it. It was Ralph Maxton asking if he might come and see her to say goodbye.

*

382

'You fixed it?' Clara asked.

'He said yes, about an hour ago. I even gave him time to call back if he wanted to rat, but he didn't.'

At the other end he heard Clara's excited laugh. 'Clever Mike,' she exulted. 'Clever Mike – when? When's it going to be?'

'Sooner the better, I guess,' O'Halloran answered. 'I don't want the bastard going cold. And I don't want to hang around here. He wants to know about payment. What do I tell him?'

She thought quickly. 'Is he going to be around to cash it?'

'He thinks he is,' was the reply. 'He wants a banker's draft.'

'He can have one on my bank in Paris,' Clara said. 'So long as you get it back. I want to be there, Mike.'

He was thrown by that. 'Don't be crazy,' he protested. 'You stay right where you are – you'll hear about it as soon as I can call you –'

"I'm not sitting here waiting,' she said. 'Don't argue with me. I'm flying down there.'

He almost shouted in exasperation. 'For Christ's sake, Clara! You want to stand and watch?'

'That,' she said, 'would make it perfect. I said, don't argue. I've waited a long time for this. I want to be close by when they all get it!' The line went clear while he was still trying to talk to her.

She packed; she threw clothes into the case. Her hands were trembling. She called for the maid and told her in her peremptory way that she was taking a trip and wouldn't be back for some days. No, she snapped back, she didn't know how long . . . As long as it took, she said to herself. Steven first. Then that whey-faced blonde and the boy.

'Oh Poppa,' she said out loud, 'Poppa, you'll rest easy when I've finished. They'll pay for what they did to me. And then I'll go home and I'll get Nimmi and the rest of them for what they did to you. It'll take a little time, but I swear it, I swear I'll get them all . . .' She smiled as an idea came to mind. Where should she stay? O'Halloran had left the Carlton. He was holed up in a small pension inland in case Maxton tried to trace him for the wrong reasons – he took precautions, her clever Mike. Good, cops' precautions learned from criminals. He'd get his money. When he'd done what she wanted. You never welsh on a contract, Aldo had impressed that on her. They deliver, you pay up.

He could go back to New York, back to his wife and his children and his agency work. She didn't much care what he did once it was over.

Where should she stay? The only place she knew. The honeymoon hotel. Romantic Monte Carlo, where her husband had betrayed her with a woman for the first time. The first of so many times, just as he had promised while she wept and pleaded, and the smell of that woman's scent, Joy, was choking her. The Hôtel de Paris. She got the number and made an open-ended reservation. Then she called Orly airport and booked herself on to the afternoon flight to Nice.

'You know how to use a gun?' O'Halloran demanded.

'I know how to use a shotgun. For pheasants, not people.'

O'Halloran gave Maxton a glare. 'Cut the crap,' he snapped. He took out his own automatic, laid it on the table. He unloaded it, loaded it, gave it to Ralph. 'You do it,' he said.

He was surprised how nimbly Maxton handled the weapon. Then Mike pulled a pillow from the bed, up-ended it on a chair. 'Now aim at that, and pull the goddamned trigger.'

Maxton had a trained eye, trained in the great country sport in spite of his resistance to it. Not because he objected to the annual grouse and pheasant slaughter at home, but because it bored him. He levelled the gun, aimed at the centre of the pillow and fired. It made an alarmingly loud noise. The hole was straight in the middle. A few feathers fluttered in the air and then drifted to the carpet. 'Aren't you worried someone might hear?' he remarked.

'No. They're in the kitchens. If you hit a man with that calibre bullet at that range, you'll blow a hole big enough to put your fist in. You want to try again?'

'How do I know it'll be that close?' Maxton demanded. 'Make it a smaller target. If you're sure no one's going to come rushing in with the noise.' He examined the automatic. The standard Smith and Wesson. Big-calibre bullets indeed. He watched O'Halloran.

It was a room rented in a small hotel. An empty room, not where the American was staying. Maxton didn't know that address. He marked the man's caution. His lack of trust.

'Try this,' O'Halloran suggested. He marked the same pillow with a ballpoint pen. A circle, the size of a man's head. He set it up again. 'Okay,' he said.

Maxton hit within the circle.

Mike took the pillow and stuffed it under the bed-cover. More feathers were floating about. He said, 'You don't need to worry. I'd say you were a natural. Now, let's get down to the details.'

Ralph handed him back the gun. 'Let's get down to the money and how it's going to be paid,' he said.

An hour later they separated. They didn't leave the hotel together. Ralph Maxton left first. He had the Smith and Wesson in a carrier bag, imprinted with the name of a local supermarket. It was arranged that he should murder Steven Falconi in the evening, two days away. Mike would give him the draft when the job was done, and he could cash it as soon as he arrived in Paris. The name on it would be a nominee's, a front for whoever O'Halloran's client was, Maxton guessed.

O'Halloran went and paid the rent of the room. They didn't ask questions. He'd only used it for the afternoon.

Another man had gone up there to meet him. They assumed it was the usual reason. The room was not booked till the next casual visitor arrived. They didn't bother to check the bed until then.

Pauline Duvalier had not been feeling well. She'd spent a lot of time in her room resting after the gala night at Antibes. Nothing wrong, she assured the manager when he called to inquire. Just tired. The excursion had been too much of an excitement. She didn't plan to sally into the outside world again. Eugene the barman came up to see her. He brought the patience cards. She thanked him, but she didn't feel like playing.

The next day she was sure she'd feel up to going to her old corner in the bar and watching the world go by. She was late going downstairs. It had been an effort to get up, to let the chambermaid help her dress. She had fought off the lethargy that only wanted to stay in bed and let the hours drift by. Her champagne was on ice; her cards ready for her to play.

But someone was trying to sit at her special table. She saw the woman's back, and the stubborn stance of Eugene, telling her he was so sorry, Madame, but that place was always reserved. The woman's voice was American and loud.

'It doesn't say so. There's no notice on it. If it's reserved why doesn't it have a notice? I'm sitting here anyway. Bring me a scotch and water and plenty of ice.'

Eugene didn't move. Pauline had stayed back, just outside the entrance to the bar. She felt weak, and trembling suddenly.

Her place, her safe corner in life was being taken from her. She had to hold on to the door frame. She heard Eugene's voice. It wasn't discreet anymore. It was raised and it was angry.

'I'm sorry, Madame, but that table is always reserved for one of the hotel guests. She lives here, and that is her place in the bar. If you will kindly move somewhere else, I'll bring your order.'

The woman said in a furious tone, 'Goddamn you, you'll bring me the manager!'

Eugene had been hoping for that. 'I was going to call him anyway. And don't swear at me, Madame!'

He was muttering with rage as he hurried towards reception to take the woman at her word and bring Monsieur Jacques himself to deal with her.

He was shocked to find Pauline at the door to the bar. He led her away, taking her arm. 'Don't worry, I'll get rid of her. I'll see you to the lift, and when Monsieur Jacques has told that one where she gets off, I'll ring you and you come right down, eh? Here, let me get someone to go up with you. Take Madame up to her suite —' He surrendered her to a young waiter and hurried off to the manager's office.

She went into her room and sank down on the bed. She meant to take off her shoes, then she forgot and kept feeling her face with her hands instead.

She wouldn't go down. She'd never risk that again. If she had only been a few seconds earlier the woman would have seen her, seen the special guest Eugene was protecting. She would go back to bed, stay there where she was safe. There was a knock at the door. It was the manager himself. He was shocked. She looked so old suddenly; the eye patch was awry, showing the corner of the empty socket.

'Madame Duvalier, I've come to apologize. That most unpleasant scene downstairs. The lady has left the bar. Your place is waiting for you. I've come to escort you myself.'

'No,' she said. 'Not today. I won't come down today.'

He was a kind man; he had admired her courage for many years. He came and sat beside her. 'Madame,' he said gently, 'you must come to the bar as usual. If you don't you may never leave this room again. Do you understand me? And all your brave efforts will be wasted. Now give me your arm, and we are going down in the lift together. I shall join you for a glass of champagne to celebrate, if I may. Allow me.' He reached out and moved the eye patch into place. 'Now,' he said, 'we are going.'

At the door of her bedroom she hesitated. 'You say she's left the bar?'

'She won't be going there again. She said so. I did suggest she might be happier in another hotel. When guests here aren't welcome, Madame, they don't stay long.'

She drank a lot of champagne that morning. The bar filled up, but the woman didn't return. Pauline had only seen her back and heard her voice, but felt she would have recognized her. She was feeling less tired; she'd got out three games in a row, smoked half a pack of cigarettes and got her confidence back. Someone had shielded her still further with a large vase of flowers strategically placed. Eugene most likely. He was kind, she thought, the champagne melting her perceptions into a benevolent blur. She had been weak-willed, foolish to behave as she did that morning, because an outsider had seemed to threaten her secure routine, her safe little world. She despised herself.

When the trade slackened at lunchtime she called the barman over. 'I've had a good morning,' she announced, 'three games in a row! Do you know how difficult that is? Three games. Who was that creature shouting at you this morning, Eugene? Monsieur Jacques said she was staying here.'

Eugene leaned towards her. 'You ought to have heard her, Madame. These rich Americans think they can buy their way in anywhere. "I came here in the old days," she says to him. "When you had staff that knew how to treat important guests and a manager that made sure of it! I wouldn't be seen dead in this lousy little bar." And she swept out. She's taken the best suite, that's the trouble. I asked about her afterwards. Her name's Salviatti. Mrs

Salviatti. When my father worked here, we never allowed rubbish like that into the hotel!'

Pauline stayed on till long after lunch. When she did go upstairs she was rock steady, no sign visible of the bottle of champagne she'd drunk, or its half-empty companion in the bucket of melting ice.

She slept that afternoon, waking in time to rise as usual and dress for dinner, choose her jewels for the solitary evening in her suite.

What had Eugene said – Salviatti – why did she think she knew that name? She hated her lapses of memory. It only happened when she was upset like this morning. The waiter came in to take her order and she put it out of her mind. If you didn't force it, memory readjusted itself. It would come back to her.

'It's such a lovely evening, why don't we have a drink outside?' Angela suggested. Ralph had brought her flowers. It was sad and touching to have to say good-bye.

'He hates my father,' Charlie had insisted. Did he, she wondered?

Ralph followed her out on to the terrace. It was a beautiful evening, the aftermath of another blistering day when it was almost too hot.

A pleasant breeze stirred the trees overhead; that was the joy of living in the hills. The coast was merciless in such weather.

'You're looking very well,' he said. 'I'm sorry I haven't been up before. I thought you might come down to the casino this evening.'

'I won't be coming this evening,' she said. 'I like to spend time with the baby, and Steven is always so busy. Ralph, it's so sad you're leaving.'

'Do you really mind? I rather hoped you would.' No mockery, no light touch this time. He had pale eyes, a watery colour that changed from green to grey blue. He was looking at her intently.

389

'You know I do,' she said. 'We've always been such friends. All of us. Steven'll miss you too.'

'I doubt that,' he remarked. 'We've come to the end of the road. He doesn't need me anymore.'

She rose quickly to defend him. 'You shouldn't say that, Ralph. It's not true.'

'No, I shouldn't say it,' he agreed. 'Certainly not to you. Forget it, don't let's spoil our time together.'

'What are you going to do now?' Angela asked. The exchange had made her feel uncomfortable.

'Take a short holiday, look around for another job. I thought I'd see what Italy has to offer. I need a break from the coast, I've been here a very long time.'

'You wouldn't go home?' she asked him.

'No.' He shook his head. He smiled at her and said, 'It's not home to me. Except when I stayed with you that Christmas. I'm going to miss you, Angela. You've been very special to me.' He was going further than he meant, urged by the gambler's need to try his luck. Flying a kite to see if the wind would lift it even for a moment. She didn't say anything in answer. She poured a glass of wine and sipped it. No wind, no flutter of the kite as yet.

'I hope I mean something to you,' he said.

She knew then that her son was right. Right about Ralph's feelings for her. She had blinded herself to what was happening, leaning on him, encouraging him to think he meant more to her than a friend. A brother almost, like the one killed in the war.

'Dear Ralph,' she said gently, 'of course you mean a lot to me. I had an older brother – I told you about him, didn't I? That's how I look on you. I often said to Steven, if only Ralph could meet a really nice girl and get married, settle down . . . I hope you haven't misunderstood –' She left the rest unsaid. The long, thin face was a mask when she looked at him. No reaction, no expression. 'I'm making such a mess of this,' she said desperately.

'Oh, I don't think so,' he said. 'I'm the one who's made

390

a mess of it. But you'll forgive me, won't you? We'll go on being friends?'

'You know we will. This isn't why you're leaving, is it? Please –'

'No. Nothing to do with it. Can I ask you just one question before I go?'

She nodded.

'Are you really happy? I've wondered sometimes.'

'I'm happy,' she said. 'He's the only man I've ever loved or ever will. From the moment I met him, Ralph. There'll never be anyone else for me but Steven.'

He got up and she rose with him. 'That's clear enough,' he said. 'I hope he knows just how lucky he is. Goodbye, Angela.'

She said, 'Goodbye, Ralph. Keep in touch, won't you? And look after yourself.' She reached up and kissed him on the cheek.

He didn't touch her; he didn't respond. His skin was quite cold. 'Throw the poor dog a bone,' he said and laughed his high-pitched, mirthless laugh as he turned and walked away.

'Ralphie.' Madeleine's voice was plaintive. 'I *can't* get away this evening.'

He said into the telephone, 'I've got to see you. Make an excuse – think of something. Just get down and meet me. No, darling, there won't be time for bed. This is money. Lots of money for both of us.'

There was a pause; he knew her so well. Death and disaster wouldn't motivate her; she'd only risk her rich protector if more money was in prospect.

'All right, I'll manage somehow. He's such a pig about letting me go out without him. Where shall I meet you?'

'The bar at Eden Roc,' he said.

She gave a delighted giggle. 'Ooh Ralphie – you must be feeling very rich –'

'Seven thirty,' he said, and rang off.

He had an hour to spare. He had already packed his

bags; the air ticket from Nice to Paris on the early morning plane was in his pocket. He had spent the afternoon saying goodbye to the staff at the casino before he travelled up to the villa to see Angela. He had gone out of his way to present a cheerful picture. He'd praised Steven, said how sorry he was to leave them and the old place, but he'd had such an outstanding offer . . . He managed to avoid saying where it came from. Poaching wasn't popular, so no one pressed him. He was especially friendly to his successor François, making jokes and offering tips on how to deal with certain clients. He had been waved goodbye in an atmosphere of good wishes and good will. The impression was important. A disgruntled ex-employee would certainly come under suspicion.

He looked round his apartment. He'd lived there on the Croisette since Steven put him in charge. He felt no twinge of nostalgia for the place. Just rented rooms like all the other rented rooms he'd lived in for so long. He sent his baggage down to his car. That could wait at the airport till he sent someone down to drive it up. He closed up the apartment and left the keys with the concierge. The rent was paid up till the end of the year. He said he was going away, but might be back from time to time. He paid her extra money to keep an eye on the place. He drove off through the heavy traffic through Cannes and up the coast road to the beautiful Eden Roc Hotel.

He had waited for Madeleine. He bought himself a glass of Pernod. It raised the barman's eyebrows. It wasn't a drink his customers usually ordered. The bitter, cloudy drink burned on his tongue.

'Oh, darling Ralphie, I'm so sorry . . .'

She came hurrying up to him, bestowing a light kiss on his cheek as he greeted her. She was looking very attractive. Beautifully, expensively dressed, with some new jewellery. People were admiring her. Wondering what she was doing with such an ugly man, he thought, savaging himself. For money, of course. What else had he got to offer?

'Now tell me, what's this about us being rich?' she questioned. She looked at the glass of Pernod and made a charming little grimace.

'What's that! That filthy stuff – only workmen drink that!'

'I've got very common taste,' he said. 'That's why I'm so fond of you. You want champagne of course?'

'Of course,' she said. 'Don't be nasty, Ralph.' She knew him in this mood. He could be cruel, insulting. Sometimes she put up with it, sometimes she didn't. She was used to being ill used by men. And he could be very generous and rather sweet at other times. 'Now tell me – what's happened? I'm so curious, I'm dying!'

He sipped his Pernod. He taunted her, keeping her waiting. So greedy. Licking her lips already at the idea of money. 'I've had a bit of luck,' he said at last.

She jumped in eagerly. 'Gambling? You've won a lot?'

'Not gambling. I never did win, actually. Not as often as I lost. No, my sweet, someone has died and left me a fortune. What do you think of that?'

'I think it's wonderful,' she said. She laid her hand on his upper thigh. 'How much?'

It amused him to watch her face. 'Half a million dollars,' he said. 'You're catching flies, sweetheart, you'd better close your mouth –' The hand on his leg began to grip. He pushed it aside. 'Not in full view,' he chided her. 'You're not in one of your old haunts now.' She'd started in the red-light district in Marseilles. A very superior type of brothel where the girls were able to come and go. Madeleine had formed an association with one of the clients and gone. Her career took off after that.

She ignored him. He was trying to hurt her, to goad her. Something had upset him. She smiled, showing her lovely white teeth, and wet her lips at the same time.

'I'm so happy for you,' she said. 'What are you going to do with it?'

He summoned the barman. 'Another of those. And champagne for Mademoiselle.

'I'm going to spend it. I'm going to book myself into a nice cruise, where I might play a little bridge or poker if I get bored. I shall spend the winter in the Caribbean. I've always wanted to go there. I may even buy myself a permanent house on the coast here when I've got sick of travelling. I just wondered whether you'd like to come along.'

'Ralph! Oh darling, you really mean it?'

'Why not? We've always got on. We have fun when we're together. And at least you won't have to be a punchbag if you're with me. Is the boyfriend still knocking you about?'

She looked down and then shrugged. 'Sometimes,' she admitted.

'What do you say, then?' he demanded.

She looked startled. 'You mean you want me to make up my mind now? This minute?'

'No. But in, say, the next ten, while we finish our drinks.'

'Why such a hurry?' she asked. Then eyes suddenly narrowing, 'You're telling me the truth – you haven't stolen it? Somebody died?'

'Somebody died,' he assured her. 'But I'm leaving for Paris tonight. Either you come with me, or you don't come at all.'

She hesitated. But not for long. He could be sweet. He was a very active lover. And straight. The Persian got too enthused by his fantasies. She was becoming scared that one day he would carry them too far.

'To hell with the pig,' she declared. 'I've decided. I'm coming with you, Ralphie. You know, I think I'm a bit in love with you?'

'Madeleine,' he mocked, 'you love me as much as I love you. For as long as the money lasts. Now you get your things together and meet me at the airport for the eleven o'clock flight. Au revoir, my sweet.'

She turned at the little flight of steps leading out of the bar and blew him a kiss. It was a charming gesture. He paid the bill and left. The waiter muttered under his breath. English pig. Hadn't even left a tip.

Clara was early. She'd arranged to meet O'Halloran at Beaulieu. There was an unobtrusive little fish restaurant with a bar. She ordered a drink. She felt conspicuous in her smart clothes. She was irritable at being kept waiting, and on edge. When he hurried through with an excuse about the traffic she snapped at him.

'Where the hell have you been? You're late!' Even though he'd slept with her, and felt a transitory dominance because of that relationship, she could still overawe him.

He said, 'I'm sorry –' and sat down.

She said, without preliminaries, 'Well?'

He looked at her. 'It's tonight,' he said.

She felt short of breath suddenly. After a moment she controlled the rush of excitement. It had left a deep flush on her pale face. 'Tell me,' she demanded. 'I want to know everything!'

He had made up his mind not to give too many details. She was quite capable of getting herself there to watch. 'Maxton gets him on his way to the casino,' he said, lowering his voice.

'And then you go to the villa,' she breathed. 'And you kill *her* and that son –'

He hadn't mentioned that there was a baby girl. He had a gut feeling that she might ask for that too . . .

'With the same gun that shot the husband,' he went on. 'The maid told me that the staff go off duty at nine. After dinner. There won't be any witnesses. Just the shots and the sound of a car driving off. I'll make it sound real panicky, squealing tyres, the works.'

She smiled slightly, savouring it. 'You're Maxton,' she said. 'You've just killed the husband. You have a fight with the wife, the son interferes and you go haywire and shoot them both.'

He nodded. 'So haywire I drive myself over that hundred-foot drop.'

They had talked it over and over, planning the details. The talkative Janine, with her compulsive curiosity, had given them the motive. The motive which would explain three murders and a suicide. Maxton's love for his employer's wife. Janine hadn't confined her spiteful gossip to the American who'd stayed in the village painting bad pictures. Everyone knew about it. The café owners, the couple who ran the patisserie, the old woman in the grocer's.

Maxton had been dismissed from his job, and the cycle of revenge and ultimate despair was set in motion. It would fit into the pattern of crime that the French had made their own. The crime of passion.

'All neat and tidy,' O'Halloran said.

'When will I know?' she demanded. He calculated quickly. 'Around eleven o'clock. I'll go back to my hotel and call you from there. Don't worry. It'll work out exactly like we planned it. You just relax.'

She gathered her bag, her cigarettes and lighter. 'You do it, Mike,' she said softly. 'You do it for me.'

And for the money, he said to himself, and for the chance to get out from under you, before it's too late . . . 'Consider it done,' he said.

Ralph Maxton drove up into the hills. He knew every twist and turn of the road. He'd driven it so often. Taking Angela there for the first time to see the villa he'd rented for them. She was shaken after a bad flight over from England. Dinner every Friday night. Thinking to himself: By God you've fallen on your feet at last. He needs you and she likes you. All you've got to do is be your witty self, my friend, give him what he wants with Uncle Oleg's great white elephant on the seafront and make up amusing stories for the dinner table. It hadn't stayed like that, unfortunately.

He'd gone there too often, allowed himself to get

involved. He even enjoyed playing picquet with her old father. 'The trickster tricked,' he murmured, watching the empty road ahead. But in the end it led to riches. Considerable riches. Enough to make a very different dream come true. Not the original, of course.

'There'll never be anyone for me but Steven.' The kind little kiss on the cheek. 'Keep in touch . . . look after yourself.' She wouldn't be sitting with him in the candlelight. Madeleine would. He deserved Madeleine. They deserved each other. He pulled the car into the side, off the road. He checked his watch. Steven always left home at the same time, arriving at the casino at nine thirty sharp. A very punctual man, our Mafioso. Never late for an appointment. He'd be on time for this one, though he didn't know of it. Unless he'd brought Angela with him. Maxton hadn't warned his American about that. He'd made sure that afternoon. 'I won't be coming down this evening, Ralph.' He didn't have to worry about stopping the car and finding her sitting next to Steven Falconi, saying, 'Oh, Ralph, have you had an accident?' He looked at his watch again. The hands had hardly moved.

He shook his wrist, thinking. It must have stopped. I've been here God knows how long . . . There was nothing wrong with the watch.

The Caribbean for the winter. He and Madeleine would have fun. She'd drive him wild with the tricks she'd learned since she was a little whore at sixteen years of age. They'd dine and they'd dance to steel bands in the lovely warm evenings. They'd have the best suites in the best hotels. He'd wear her like a lucky charm, showing the world what a delicious woman he could get for himself. But he'd forgotten about the cruise.

Where would they go to? The Far East? Hong Kong? He'd often thought of going there. The Chinese were mad gamblers. He might even make some money. It had a marvellous racetrack. Madeleine would love it. He would take her shopping. He'd heard that you could get a suit made up in a day. As good as Savile Row. Well not quite as good, perhaps. People exaggerated. His father had ordered him a suit from his own tailor when he was eighteen. His father had all his suits made there. His grandfather too. They said the suits lasted for thirty years if you kept the same shape. They wouldn't be able to guarantee that in Hong Kong. What a bloody idiot to think he could settle in some dreary English village, with a wife and possibly a child of his own. What a bloody silly idea. He must have been out of his tiny mind.

He could see headlights rounding a corner high above. Falconi, due in a few more minutes. He switched on the engine and eased the gear into place. He saw the big Peugeot glide past him, with only Steven in the front, behind the wheel.

He let it go and then pulled out. There was a little side road, not more than a track, that would bring him out on to the road ahead of Steven. With time to swing half round and block the way. The Smith and Wesson, fully loaded, was on the seat beside him. All he had to do was get out and fire through the window at close range. It was a thousand to one against another car following in that isolated place.

O'Halloran was to meet Maxton at the turn-off to the Autoroute to Nice at nine thirty. He'd driven very carefully on account of the big drop down on the bend of the road. He had the banker's draft in his pocket. A blackjack nestled in the other one. A cosh didn't break the surface of the scalp like a blow from something made of metal.

Nine thirty passed. He wasn't worried. A few minutes either side to allow for Maxton manoeuvring his car back on the road. Maybe Falconi had got out of the car when he was forced to stop . . . A few minutes was okay.

Nine thirty-five. 'Hell,' he muttered. Where was the son of a bitch? He heard the car before it came into view. A sports model as you'd expect with that type, the hood folded back, the driver easily recognizable as he slowed down and stopped. O'Halloran opened his car door and got out. He walked quite slowly towards Maxton. Not hurrying, not seeming edgy. Like a cop on his beat. His hand was locked around the cosh in his pocket.

He stopped by the side of the little car. He looked down at Maxton. Maybe it was the moonlight but he looked a ghastly colour.

'You got him?'

'Yes. Where's the money?'

'Right here,' Mike O'Halloran said. He had the draft in his left hand. He held it out to Ralph Maxton. 'No trouble?'

'No trouble at all.'

He saw the glint of the gun and opened his mouth to yell. The bullet knocked him backwards before he could made a sound. He spun and then collapsed face down.

Maxton got out. The American was right about the damage that calibre could do. There was a gaping hole in his back.

He looked at him for a moment. Nothing moved. A lot of blood was spreading over the road like spilled ink in the silver light.

'Sorry about that,' he said. 'But you'd only have found someone else.' He climbed into his car. The banker's draft was lying on the seat. 'Sorry about you too,' he told it, 'but I can't cash you. After all I have my standards.'

He tore it up and laughed as he threw the pieces into the air. The breeze caught them, whirling them down and out of sight into the valley.

He began to drive, taking the corners at his usual speed. He was a first-class driver, eyesight like an eagle, reflexes lightning fast. He reached the coast road in less than ten minutes. He stopped at a bistro on the outskirts of Juan Les Pins.

He bought himself a brandy. The proprietor said he could use the telephone at the back if it was urgent. For five francs.

'Monsieur Lawrence, please,' he said. He'd brought the brandy with him. He sipped most of it while he waited.

'Steven Lawrence.'

'Good evening,' Ralph Maxton said. 'It's me.'

'What do you want?' Steven's voice grated on him.

'Just to tell you there's a dead man lying in the road just on the intersection to the Autoroute. Our shortcut to the airport. He was offering half a million dollars to anyone who'd kill you. You'd be amazed how close I came to doing it. If it wasn't for your wife, I'd be a rich man by now. Give her my love.'

He put the receiver down, finished his drink and left a twenty-franc note on the corner as he went. The proprietor stared after him in amazement. But he didn't rush out to give him change.

It was a lovely evening. A perfect evening for a drive along the splendid road up to the Moyenne Corniche and then the great panoramic view from the Grande Corniche itself carved out of the topmost lip of the mountain. Bright moonlight, a little cold up there, a constant breeze that sang around him as he drove. He found a place to stop, reversing carefully back from the edge. It was eerily beautiful to be so high, with the pigmy towns below, their lights reduced to twinkling dots, the black sea with the silver path of moonlight that was supposed to beckon suicides. Like his old friend of all those years ago. Swimming out because the sharks on land had eaten his heart out.

What a waste his life had been. Worthless. So nearly doomed to years of yet more waste. He and his soul mate, Madeleine. No cruise to the delights of the Far East now. No steel bands and limbo dancers in Jamaica, with someone as rotten as himself to share it. And all because he knew what it would do to Angela. It wasn't scruples, or a sudden rush of morality to the head that stopped him. He'd never known the meaning of either. He was rather proud of that. He just couldn't make her so unhappy.

Love, not conscience, had made a coward of him. Poor Madeleine, waiting at the airport. She'd be so furious, so disappointed. Thank God he wasn't going with her. What an appalling prospect.

'You'll come to a bad end if you don't mend your ways.' He could hear his father, thundering away at him. Such a Victorian he was; never quite at home in the modern world. His mother, hoping against hope that it was just a phase and he'd grow out of it. He'd stolen the jewellery out of her bedroom. That was the reward of her faith. He hadn't mended his ways. But he hadn't come to as bad an end as he might have done.

He switched the engine on and put the car into first gear. The bonnet aimed at the black chasm in front of him. He didn't like the idea of that plunge downwards very much. He set his foot on the brake, holding the engine in thrall. Then he put the American's revolver into his mouth and pulled the trigger. A few seconds later there was a distant tinkling crash and a flare of flame that licked upwards as the car began to burn.

Steven came down the grand staircase at a run. He pushed past anyone in the way. Outside to where the car was parked. He heard his new manager François calling after him. He turned and shouted back through the car window.

'I'm going home – take over for me!'

He drove faster than he had ever driven in his life. Maxton's voice was ringing in his head. 'Half a million dollars to anyone who'd kill you . . . a dead man lying in the road . . .' Angela, Angela and his son and baby daughter, unprotected in the villa, unsuspecting of any danger.

Twice he almost hit another car; he didn't hear the furious hooting of horns and the shouts that followed him. Up into the hills, round the dark, twisting little roads, approaching the turn-off to the Autoroute. He saw lights flashing, police cars, an ambulance. Someone had found him, whoever he was . . .

He put his foot down and went faster. He saw the lights on in the villa, in the ground-floor drawing room, where his wife and son would be after Angela had given the little girl her late feed.

He raced inside, throwing the door open. They were sitting together; the TV was on, and Angela had been reading. He saw them safe, and forgot momentarily about everything else.

He heard her say, 'Darling, darling what's the matter? What is it?' He saw Charlie staring at him, both on their feet with alarm.

He said to Angela, 'Maxton called. He said there was a contract out on me. It's Clara – it has to be.'

She went white. 'Oh my God –'

Charlie interrupted. 'Contract? Dad, what are you talking about?'

'A contract to kill me,' Steven said quietly. 'It failed. But there could be another attempt – on you or your mother. It's a long story and this is one hell of a time to tell you.'

'Steven – no!' Angela cried out.

He held up his hand to silence her protest. 'It's no good, darling; he's got to know the truth.' He turned to his son. 'Charlie – I want you to listen to me. Don't ask questions, just listen. Your father wasn't killed in the war. I'm your real father.' He paused, seeing the pain and confusion on the boy's face. 'I loved your mother,' he continued, 'the first moment I saw her. I married her in Sicily but we got separated. I thought she'd been killed in that hospital bombing. Years later I married someone else. Then I found your mother again in New York. And I found you, my son.' There were tears in his eyes.

Angela came and stood with her arms round him, facing Charlie. 'I lied to you, Charlie,' she said. 'We both lied, but we did it for the best of reasons. Your father

402

gave up everything to be with us, to make a new life for all of us. He's been in terrible danger ever since. I hope you'll forgive me, but you mustn't ever blame him!'

'I'm not blaming anyone.' Charlie's voice wasn't quite steady. 'I don't know what to say . . . I can't believe it's happening.'

'I love you, Charlie,' Steven said. 'You're my son and I love you. That's the only important thing right now. And I want you to do what I tell you. I want you to take your mother and the baby and get the hell out of here. Just drive. Drive as far away as you can get.'

'Not without you!' Angela insisted. 'I'm not going without you!'

'Yes you are,' Steven said. 'So long as I know you and the kids are safe, I can take care of myself. It's between me and Clara now. Charlie?'

'Yes?'

'Come here, son.'

For a moment he hesitated. A long moment, an eternity to Steven and to Angela. Then he rushed forward to be clasped in his father's arms. They didn't speak; just held each other, and then the boy looked up at him and said, 'I'm glad. I love you too.' His cheeks were wet.

'We haven't time to talk now,' Steven said. 'But we will. I promise. No more secrets between us. Now you get the car, and I'll bring your mother and Anna.'

It took Charlie some seconds to fit the key into the lock, to start the ignition and reverse out into the drive. His hands were shaking. He saw the lights go on and off in the nursery, and then Steven and his mother were outside, the baby still asleep in her arms. He opened the door and helped them inside. Steven laid a hand on his shoulder.

'I'm relying on you, Charlie. Take good care of them. Call me tomorrow and let me know where you are. And stay put till I tell you.'

403

'I will. Don't worry. And Dad – you'll be careful, won't you . . .'

Charlie heard Angela's anguished whisper as she said goodbye, 'Oh Steven, darling.'

And Steven's reassurance. 'Don't worry; we'll be together soon.'

He looked back quickly as he drove away, and saw his father wave once from the doorway with the lights behind him. In the back seat, cradling the sleeping child, Angela was crying.

'You're sure?' Madeleine demanded. 'You're certain there's no message for me?'

The girl at the airport desk looked bored. This was the third time she'd been back to ask. 'No, Madame. No message.'

Madeleine turned away. She cursed under her breath. She'd phoned the apartment. No answer. She'd tried the concierge, who was sleepy and ill tempered. Monsieur Maxton had gone a long time ago. The flat was closed up.

There she was at the airport, all her luggage, her jewellery, the loot of five years on the coast waiting with her. The last flight had gone. Something must have happened. An accident? He always drove like a maniac. She wondered for a moment whether he hadn't played a vicious practical joke. He'd been in such a strange mood that evening.

She couldn't go back to her Persian friend. He would be very angry. Very angry indeed. She didn't want to risk it.

She went back to the information desk. To her relief it was a man on duty. He told her the next plane to Paris was at seven in the morning. Did she wish to go to a hotel? No, Madeleine decided. She wasn't risking her luggage, her clothes and precious jewellery in some strange place. He directed a porter to bring everything to the VIP lounge, which he unlocked specially for her. She was so attractive and charming, and he was aware of her distress.

She smiled at him, and thanked him. If something had happened to Ralphie what could she do about it? She'd stay there for the night. Only a few hours. They boarded at six fifteen for the early flight. She'd be quite comfortable. She settled herself on a sofa with her baggage piled up round her. Maybe it was fate. Time to leave the coast and start afresh. She had a big savings account. Paris was as good a place as any. There were lots of rich men to be picked up there. She slipped off her shoes, made herself comfortable, and dozed off.

Clara dressed for dinner. She chose carefully, for an occasion known only to herself. A long cream dinner dress, part of the trousseau for her honeymoon with Bruno Salviatti. The diamond earings Steven had given her for a wedding present. She'd worn them in this same hotel. She twisted and turned before the looking glass, assessing her appearance. This was her night, her moment of triumph. She would make an entrance into that restaurant, when she walked in to dine alone. People had stared at her then, seeing her as beautiful, desirable, with her handsome husband at her side. No husband this time. She looked at her watch. Eight thirty.

The hours had dragged since she'd come back from Beaulieu. The hairdresser, the beautician – that had been a long diversion. But not quite long enough. She adjusted her left earring. It had always pinched, in spite of a new fitting put in before she left Paris. Then she went downstairs in the lift, and into the restaurant. The head waiter showed her to her table; he hovered deferentially. She had the best suite in the hotel, with an open booking. She wasn't hungry, but she ordered just the same. Some champagne, she decided, and looking coolly at the *sommelier*, she mentioned that she was celebrating.

It was difficult to eat; she picked at the courses, smoking between them. She took her time drinking the champagne. She wanted to enjoy every moment, to let her imagination range to the isolated road where Steven

Falconi would meet his just end. How she had wor-
shipped him all those years ago, when they had come
here, dined in this same restaurant together.

And how she had suffered, impaled on the sharp stake
of her own jealousy, all through that miserable marriage.
Misery had made her barren. There was no other cause.
He had rejected everything she had to offer: her love, her
sexual passion, the family traditions that bound them
together.

For the woman she'd seen in that photograph. A pale,
bloodless image of a blonde like any other blonde. A
nothing, Clara had called her, and O'Halloran had echoed
it. How lucky she had been to find him. How wise to
approach him with her proposition for the agency instead
of the ex-policeman with the Italian name. She was a
shrewd judge like her father Aldo. She smelt corruption in
the dingy little office. The Ace Detective Agency. It made
her smile. Fate had directed her that day. The fate that had
overtaken Steven Falconi, even as she saw the time in the
glitter of diamonds on her wrist. He was dead. The woman
and the son she had borne him were dead too. She'd
lingered so long over her coffee, dreaming of vengeance. It
was a quarter to eleven. She thanked the head waiter for an
excellent dinner, and made her way back to her suite. A
good-looking man with a much younger girl gave her an
admiring look as she passed. She smiled provocatively at
him. She was free. Free at last. She went into her suite. The
bedroom door was open, her bed turned down, the satin
nightdress laid across it. She kicked off her shoes, and lit a
cigarette. Eleven o'clock. She curled up in an armchair by
the telephone to wait. The earring hurt a little. She
unfastened it, put it on the table. It rolled back and forth for
a moment, glittering under the light. She was reaching up
to undo the other one when there was a knock on the door.

'Mike –' She jumped up. He'd come, instead of ringing. She called out, 'Come in,' and hurried to meet him.

It was the worst day in the history of the hotel. Worse

406

than the fire of 1937, which had destroyed one third of the building. But without loss of life. It started at seven a.m. with a commotion on the first floor. The manager was roused out of sleep. He came hurrying up to the suite. He was a man used to dealing with crises.

The young floor waiter was shaking like a leaf. 'I stumbled over it,' he kept repeating. 'I opened the door and nearly fell on top of it.' He had dropped the breakfast tray. The manager crouched down beside the body of Mrs Clara Falconi Salviatti. She was lying on her back, and she had been stabbed to death with one of the hotel's own pointed steak knives. Right through the heart. The handle was sticking out of her chest. That was enough to shatter anyone's nerve. But the dead woman's face was twisted in a grimace of such naked horror, that he hurriedly covered it with his own handkerchief.

He stood up; he spoke kindly to the trembling boy and sent him downstairs. But on pain of instant dismissal, he was ordered to say nothing. Nothing at all until the police arrived. He sidestepped the body. Thank God he didn't have to look at her face. And only God knew what she had seen that terrified her so much at the moment of death. He went to the telephone and dialled the private number of the Superintendent of the Monaco Police. There was a lull while it rang. He was aware, just before the call was answered, of a strong smell in the room.

He recognized the distinctive scent of Joy.

Pauline Duvalier's funeral took place at the end of the week. She had died peacefully of a heart attack in her sleep, but the discovery of the dead woman in the suite on the same floor overshadowed her passing.

Her possessions were locked up. The old copies of the newspapers she'd hoarded were thrown away. Her will was found, addressed to the manager. She had repaid their kindness and care over the years by leaving everything divided between the staff. She was buried in Monaco, as she'd requested, and old friends like Eugene wept at the graveside. Among the mourners was the owner of the Casino de Poliakof. Rumours were circulating that he was putting it up for sale.

Epilogue

It was a long flight from Barbados. An interruption of two weeks of sun and sea and making love. Charlie had become engaged when he came down from Cambridge. Steven said they were too young, but Charlie expected that. His mother supported them; he expected that too, because she liked the girl, and she believed in romantic love. Not surprising, Charlie thought; his parents still held hands and gazed at each other as if they were the only people on the planet. He was proud of them. Proud of his father. He'd made such a success of changing businesses. He owned a big hotel and a chain of top-class restaurants.

Biarritz was nicer than the Côte d'Azur. Charlie loved the house they bought after they moved. It was bigger than the villa nestled up in the hills at Valbonne. The climate was cooler, with stiff sea breezes. He'd become a keen sailor. They were all very happy there; Anna was growing up, and there was a small boy who had come as a surprise two years ago. He was called Hugh, after his grandfather. Charlie thought he looked like his grandfather, and said so, which pleased his mother.

She was very special; Charlie was as proud of her as he was of Steven. She held them all together. She made them happy. And kept them straight. He and his father ganged up and pretended not to pay too much attention to her, but nobody was fooled. Steven gave the orders, but Angela made the rules. He hoped his marriage would turn out like theirs.

There was no real reason for him to do what he was

doing now. No logic. Only an instinct that had nagged at him for a long time. A question that formed when he looked in the mirror. Charles Lawrence, soon to be called to the English Bar. Soon to be married to a suitable English girl, and start his life in earnest. The holiday in Barbados had been at her parents' invitation. They rented a house there during the miserable winter months. Charlie hadn't wanted to go; he had a lot of work to do. But he went because the lure was more than a holiday in the Caribbean.

He'd made an excuse to get away for two days. To leave them all behind while he went off alone.

As the aircraft started coming down through heavy clouds, he remembered that other journey all those years ago, Angela sitting beside him as they prepared to land in New York. He'd been so excited; he could feel it still. The holiday that had changed his life.

If they hadn't made the trip, what would have happened? He'd have probably ended up a doctor, destined to take on his grandfather's practice. He'd thought of medicine as a choice; he still owned the house in Haywards Heath, rented out to Hugh Drummond's partner, Jim Hulbert.

He'd have grown up with a dead hero as a father, with a background of blurred lies. From the night he drove his mother and his baby sister through the darkness to escape the threat of murder, he had been trying to come to terms with who and what he really was. And he was sure that he had succeeded.

He'd taken a strong grip on himself and pulled the shutters down, exactly as his father had advised. It was the only way.

He'd lied to his parents. They didn't know why he'd broken off his studies and gone to Barbados. They didn't know he was on his way to New York. But it was something Charlie had to do. And he hoped they'd never find out.

There were plenty of cabs at Kennedy, and he didn't

410

have to wait long in the cold. The driver didn't speak English too well, but recognized the address when Charlie showed it to him written down.

It was a broad street, lined with trees. Old-fashioned houses with generous gardens behind. Some children were playing in the road: they scattered as the cab drew up. A woman leaned out of a window on the opposite side of the road and yelled something in Italian. Charlie paid off the driver.

It seemed a long time before the front door opened. A gangling teenager in a sweatshirt and jeans stared at him suspiciously.

Charlie said, 'Is your father in?'

'Who wants him?' the boy demanded.

A big man in shirtsleeves came out into the hall behind him. Charlie couldn't see in the dim light but he thought he had a gun in his hand. The man said, 'Someone asking for the Don?'

A smell of Italian cooking wafted towards the open door and the step where Charlie was standing. He only had to turn and walk away.

But he didn't. He spoke to the man in the dim hallway and said:

'I'm asking for him. I'm his nephew, Charles Falconi.'